HOW SWEET IT IS

What Reviewers Say About Melissa Brayden's Work

About *Waiting In the Wings*

"This was an engaging book with believable characters and story development. It's always a pleasure to read a book set in a world like theater/film that gets it right…a thoroughly enjoyable read."
—*Lez Books*

"This is Brayden's first novel, but we wouldn't notice if she hadn't told us. The book is well put together and more complex than most authors' second or third books. The characters have chemistry; you want them to get together in the end. The book is light, frothy, and fun to read. And the sex is hot without being too explicit—not an easy trick to pull off."—*Liberty Press*

About *Heart Block*

"The story is enchanting, with conflicts and issues to be overcome that will keep the reader turning pages. The relationship between Sarah and Emory is achingly beautiful and skillfully portrayed. As each woman goes through her own set of difficulties, the story advances to its final conclusion. This second offering by Melissa Brayden is a perfect package of love—and life to be lived to the fullest. So grab a beverage and snuggle up in a comfy throw to read this classic story of overcoming obstacles and finding enduring love."—*Lamda Literary Review*

"Although this book doesn't beat you over the head with wit, the interactions are almost always humorous, making both characters really quite loveable. Overall a very enjoyable read."—*C-Spot Reviews*

Visit us at www.boldstrokesbooks.com

By the Author

Waiting in the Wings

Heart Block

How Sweet It Is

HOW SWEET IT IS

by

Melissa Brayden

2013

HOW SWEET IT IS
© 2013 By Melissa Brayden. All Rights Reserved.

ISBN 10: 1-60282-958-6
ISBN 13: 978-1-60282-958-9

This Trade Paperback Original Is Published By
Bold Strokes Books, Inc.
P.O. Box 249
Valley Falls, NY 12185

First Edition: November 2013

This is a work of fiction. Names, characters, places, and incidents are the product of the author's imagination or are used fictitiously. Any resemblance to actual persons, living or dead, business establishments, events, or locales is entirely coincidental.

This book, or parts thereof, may not be reproduced in any form without permission.

Credits
Editor: Cindy Cresap
Production Design: Susan Ramundo
Cover Design By Sheri (graphicartist2020@hotmail.com)

Acknowledgments

I've never lived in a small town. Not one like this. But there's something about the concept that drew me in and made me want to write about it. Applewood, Illinois, is a fictional place, but it charmed me and made me want to stay awhile. I hope you'll feel the same way.

As with any creative project, there are a lot of working parts. There were so many people who had a hand in bringing this novel into existence, and as always, I'm in awe and I'm grateful. Here are some thoughts:

Family plays a big role in this story, and that's a reflection of how big of a role it plays in my life. I'm the youngest of three sisters and my parents have been married for forty-five years. No family is perfect, but mine is pretty close. I'd like to thank them for giving me the best foundation possible as well as tons of laughs along the way.

Sometimes when you're close to a story, it's hard to see the forest for the trees. Thereby, I was lucky to have my editor, Cindy Cresap, be my eyes on this one and offer perspective when I didn't have it. This book is stronger as a result.

Len Barot, Bold Strokes Books, and everyone associated with it have been nothing but friendly, warm, and encouraging to me since we first started working together. I feel at home here and that's everything.

People do judge books by their covers. It's just a fact of life. I'm lucky in that my cover artist, Sheri, is top-notch and can somehow mirror the stories as I see them. This cover is certainly no exception.

Inspiration is an important component when it comes to writing. In good news, Alan inspires me daily. Whether it comes from silly jokes, softball pep talks, or long discussions over a bottle of red, it's always there.

As much as I love to write, to create worlds in my head, it can feel a little bit scary to send those stories out into the great abyss when I'm done. However, the readers of lesbian fiction have made that part of the process so much easier for me with their e-mails, tweets, and Facebook messages. Thank you so much for reading, for spending a few hours of your life with me, but also for stepping out from behind the book and reaching back.

Dedication

For my sisters

CHAPTER ONE

There's just something about chocolate.

It's enough to cause a person to abandon the rest of the world in favor of complete immersion in the power of its taste. Few things in life compare. Molly O'Brien knew this as clearly as she knew the sun was going to rise the next day. It was an inarguable fact of life.

She concentrated, biting her bottom lip, as she folded the ribbons of dark chocolate in the pan once, twice, and a final time before sampling her work with her index finger. She closed her eyes in surrender. Perfection. Next, she checked the thermometer in the pan. An even ninety-one degrees.

Showtime.

One by one, she bathed each truffle in the dark chocolate coating before rolling it in the cocoa powder that would offer a nice contrast to the amaretto in the truffle. Finally, she placed the last truffle on the wire rack with a slight twist of her wrist. She set the timer and took her spot on top of the stepladder nestled in the kitchen's corner and waited in anticipation for the required twelve minutes to creep by.

She felt good about things this time. She'd used a tad too much heavy cream in the ganache on the last go-round, and the hint of coconut she'd added this time might be the missing link to bridge the flavors.

The kitchen was quiet while she waited, the morning just getting started. Distantly, she heard the bell in the front of the shop, but ignored it. She checked the clock again. It was time. Biting slowly into a truffle, she closed her eyes and allowed the flavors to play in her mouth as she assessed. It was closer this time. She was on to something, but the recipe wasn't quite there yet. Damn it. Just a hint too sweet. It lacked balance.

The bell. A second time.

Where was Louise? With an exaggerated sigh, she abandoned her project and made her way from the kitchen to the front of the bakeshop.

Mr. Jeffries, one of the regulars, scowled deeply at her. "Well, it sure took you long enough." It was nothing new. Sort of his thing. He harassed her daily and she smiled through it. The man was pushing eighty-five and pretended to hate the world. The problem was he didn't and everyone knew it.

"Good morning, Mr. Jeffries. Sorry about the wait. Just taking care of a few things in the back. Your usual?"

Mr. Jeffries eyed the display case suspiciously. "What are those?"

She followed his gaze. "Caramel apple cinnamon rolls. Made with cream cheese frosting. My father's recipe."

He studied her skeptically. It was rare for him to deviate from his standard blueberry muffin. He was a staunch creature of habit. "Are they fresh?"

"Made this very morning."

He rolled his eyes as if he couldn't stand another minute of her. It was part of his charm. "I'll take two and a cup of joe. Regular, *not decaf*." He scowled deeper. "Don't you think you should write it down, for heaven's sake?"

She grinned patiently. "Two cinnamon rolls and a cup of coffee. I think I got it."

"Good thing you can bake or you people would run this place into the ground. Your father never used to keep his customers waiting. Where's Louise?" He scanned the area behind the counter for any glimpse.

"Around here somewhere, I hope." Louise, her elderly employee, was MIA but happened to be the one person Mr. Jeffries seemed to tolerate. Which meant he was hot for her.

Molly prepared his order as she did every morning, and as he headed off to his regular table by the window, she turned to her next customers, a young couple smiling brightly, a toddler at their sides. In fact, one of the most adorable toddlers she'd ever seen. "Morning, guys. Welcome to Flour Child. What can I get for you?"

"Well, you've already sold us on the cinnamon rolls, I think," the man said. "And an orange raspberry muffin too. The lady at the inn said we have to try those."

Molly nodded knowingly as she rang them up. "That's Alice. She's a fan."

The wife smiled. "She insisted we stop by. Said you had pastries sent by God himself. The best in Illinois."

"Well, Alice leans toward hyperbole, but they are pretty good. You'll have to let me know what you think."

"Are you the owner?"

Molly nodded. "I am."

"It's such a cute little place. So much character."

Molly looked around, taking in the bakeshop through new eyes. Checkered tablecloths, lots of framed art, photos from over the years. "Thanks. My father opened the place not long after I was born." She pointed to Flour Child's logo on the wall affectionately, zeroing in on the little girl with the halo of flowers in her hair. "And that's me. My dad's retired now, but he's left us all his great recipes, and hopefully, I've added a few decent new ones." She handed them their plates. "Enjoy and come back and see us."

"We definitely will." The family picked out one of the five tables in the shop and sat down to enjoy their breakfast. As she wiped down the counters, Molly's gaze drifted back to the couple and she watched as they fed the toddler, encouraging her to taste the cinnamon roll and laughing when she grinned back at them in lip-smacking approval. She couldn't help but wonder if that's how she and Cassie would have laughed with their own child, if they'd had one. With so much warmth and adoration. She'd like to think so.

She shook herself out of it.

Cassie's commuter plane had gone down four years ago.

Actually, four years, two months, and a handful of days, but somehow it didn't seem that way. It felt like yesterday that Cassie was teasing her or whispering sweetly in her ear each morning.

It was easier now, thinking about Cassie. But it was moments like these that Molly wondered if she'd ever get a chance at a family of her own someday. She wanted that. Kids, someone to share it all with, the whole deal. And other than the debut of her first two gray hairs, the ones she'd hastily plucked from her head that morning, it seemed she was still capable of having them.

She sat on the stool.

Time was marching on, and sometimes she felt like it was marching on without her. Thirty-two years old was still young… kinda. She wandered back into the kitchen and did what she always did when something was on her mind. "What do you think, Cassandra? Is it time for me to get back on the horse?"

Silence. As there always was when she talked to Cassie.

But there *were* times when she felt Cassie's presence in her life; she was sure of it. The number eight had a way of showing up a lot, and she suspected strongly that Cassie had something to do with it. It had been her favorite number if for nothing else than the Magic Eight Ball she consulted for all important life decisions.

"Sorry I'm late." Eden Young rushed into the kitchen and began putting on her apron, pulling Molly abruptly from her thoughts. "Bless her heart; my next-door neighbor didn't know how to program her cable box. One sandwich short of a picnic, that one. I had to step in and help out and…" She paused and shot Molly a curious glance. "What is it, sugar? You look like you just solved the mystery of life for all of us."

"Eden." Molly turned to her best friend and employee thoughtfully. "I think I might be ready to start dating again."

Eden's eyes widened in supreme delight and she shook Molly's hands eagerly. "Well, hallelujah. It's like a hug from little baby Jesus in here." Eden's Southern sass was out in full force today. "What, may I ask, brought this on?"

"I don't know. There was the cutest little family in the shop earlier, and I watched them and thought, yeah, I want that. And I do. I think I'm ready to take that step."

Eden clapped her hands once. "Well, who's it going to be? Who's the lucky girl you've got your eye on?"

Molly was at a loss. She didn't have her eye on anybody. In all honesty, Cassie had been the only woman she'd ever been with, and they'd been a couple since high school. The concept of dating at all was a little foreign to her.

Then there was the little matter of living in a small town.

The lesbian-to-Molly-ratio was crazy small. There was Celia the librarian, but she was at least twenty years older. Savanna and Trish were both great, but, well, they were a couple already. That left Summer Siller, who she'd gone to high school with. Summer had never quite forgiven her for taking Cassie off the market and still seemed to have it out for Molly to this day. Summer was definitely not a prospect. In fact, Summer should be avoided at all costs. Summer was lesbian Satan. "I think I'm going to have to broaden my horizons. Maybe look beyond the borders of Applewood."

Eden did a little hop. "Sugar, I know just the person to call. My friend Paulene lives two towns over and knows absolutely anyone who is worth knowing. I'll put a call in to her, and we'll have more lesbians than you can shake a stick at lining up for you."

Molly's face went hot and she felt all sorts of reluctance. "You know what? This whole thing sounds a little too crazy. Bad idea. Are we sure I should be doing this? I think we should rewind."

"Don't you dare back out now. This is progress." Eden took a step forward, her eyes steely in almost scary determination. "Do you know how long I've been waiting for you to utter those adorably tentative words you said earlier? Since God was a baby, that's how long. Now stand up straight and be strong."

Molly stood tall for no other reason than because Eden said to and she was a little frightening in this moment. "Strong. Got it. Working on it. A little." Seriously, who was she kidding?

"Sorry I disappeared on you, Mollydolly." Louise puttered in carrying a brown paper sack. Saved by the bell! Or the little old lady who worked for her. "The used bookstore next door was having a sale, and I scurried in to pick up some of their old recipe books. I knew you wouldn't miss me."

"What, had to beat the crazy crowd?" Eden deadpanned because there wouldn't have been one.

"I had to beat old Mrs. Bleakerson is what I had to do. She's getting on in years, but she's aggressive when it comes to her marinades. I'm stronger though." Molly smiled because Mrs. Bleakerson was sixty-one and still nine years younger than Louise herself.

Switching gears, Molly turned to Eden. "Do you think you can close for me? It's Wednesday, so I need to stop by the cemetery and still have time to freshen up before my dinner at Gibson's tonight. You know, try to look presentable. Lose the flour glaze."

"I suppose you could twist my arm if you threw in a few of those truffles on the house."

Molly followed her gaze to the latest batch. "Help yourself. You always do anyway."

"This is a fact. So Gibson's, huh? What's the occasion?"

"Cassie's little sister, Jordan, is coming home for a bit. It's kind of a major deal. She hasn't been back since, well…the funeral."

"Wow."

"Yeah. It'll be nice for Amalia and Joseph to get to spend some time with her." In actuality, Molly knew it was that and more. Her mother- and father-in-law would pull out all the stops to celebrate Jordan's homecoming. They'd already closed down the clinic for the day, rented out Gibson's restaurant that night, and were hosting the immediate family—which still included her—for a celebratory dinner in Jordan's honor.

Jordan Tuscana.

While part of Molly wanted to smack Jordan on the back of the head for staying away for so long, the other part of her was genuinely excited to see her again.

"So what do we know about the mysterious younger Tuscana?" Eden nibbled on a truffle. "These are amazing, Mol."

"Thanks." She considered the question, reminding herself that Eden hadn't grown up in Applewood. "Jordan? Oh, she's—"

"As wild as they come. Or at least she used to be," Louise supplied dryly. "Gave her parents fits when she was in high school, dropped out of college with only one year left, and ran off to make movies, skittering about the country. It about broke both doctors' hearts. They wanted her to go into medicine like the rest of them. Friendly kid though. You couldn't help but forgive whatever trouble she got into because she was so darn sweet and charming. Could grin her way out of anything."

Molly tilted her head and tried to explain things another way. "She went through a rebellious patch in high school, that's all. But the Jordan I remember was good at heart, a rascally little kid that would follow Cassie and me around incessantly. I used to babysit her back when I was fifteen, sixteen. That would have made her ten, I guess. We'd read books together for hours until she fell asleep." Molly felt that wistful lump of nostalgia in her throat for a time when everything felt simpler, lighter. Like nothing bad could ever happen to any of them.

But Jordan's growing up years hadn't been so easy. It had been hard for her with Cassie as an older sister. Cassie got straight A's, broke school records on the soccer field, and followed all of her parents' rules to a tee. And with the bar set so high, Jordan simply didn't measure up. After a while, she purposefully stopped trying. She lived life on her own terms, and that often made waves in the Tuscana household.

"So she and Cassie were close?" Eden popped her fourth truffle.

"Um, mostly, yeah, especially in their younger years. But once Jordan went off to college, they drifted a bit. She took Cassie's death incredibly hard though and pretty much shut everyone out. We haven't seen her much since."

"I hope I get to meet this person. She sounds intriguing."

Molly picked up her messenger bag as she prepared to leave. "I'm sure you will, Eden." She paused for a moment. "You know what? I'm just glad she's coming home. It's time."

❖

Molly's house was pretty. That was a good word for it. But old and in desperate need of some repair. It was on her to-do list in addition, of course, to learning *how* to fix up a house. Maybe that would happen after she figured out a way to manufacture more time in the day and you know, learn to fly.

She fumbled in her bag for her keys and subsequently struggled with the front door that always managed to stick. A daily battle. At least her arms got a workout. She suppressed a cheer when the door finally gave in after she rammed it like a goat. In unfortunate news, the force of the impact caused one of the decorative shutters on the outside of the house to fall decidedly on one side. It clung to life, but seemed sad now, hanging there so crookedly. She felt sorry for it and herself, as it was yet another repair to deal with.

Molly had purchased the home three years prior, having gotten it for a steal when the elderly owner moved in with her son's family. It was the first major purchase she'd made on her own since Cassie, and it had been just what she was looking for. Tall, mature trees, friendly neighbors, and the perfect amount of space to cozy up in. She'd taken the modest two-story with the cute blue shutters and made it her own over time. It was comfortable, simple, home. She was rather proud of her little place, even if it was falling apart.

Once inside, she fed her beta fish, appropriately named Rover, and watched him celebrate with three laps around the tank. "Nice form, Rover. Seriously. Those Olympic scouts aren't gonna know what hit 'em." That's when her phone vibrated in voice mail notification. She studied the screen curiously. How had she missed the call? Because you were busy masquerading as one of the Billy Goats Gruff, she reminded herself.

The singular voice mail was from her father, who now lived at Applewood Manor, a retirement home a couple of miles up the road. She listened to his voice as she perused the contents of her closet for a passable outfit for the evening's festivities.

"Hey there, Mollydolly, I got your message about the dinner tonight. Don't worry about stopping by. I've had a great but very tiring day and will probably just turn in early anyway."

She paused and looked down at the phone. It wasn't often she went a whole twenty-four hours without stopping by to visit her dad. He'd been in better health lately, but the congestive heart failure he suffered from seemed to affect him more in spurts. She expected a rough few days ahead in exchange for the good ones he'd experienced so far this week.

While she wanted to call him back to make sure he'd eaten well and received his daily medication on time, the clock on the wall reminded her she was dangerously close to arriving late for dinner, a crime her time-conscious in-laws, the dueling Dr. Tuscanas, would frown upon despite their adoration for her. To make it up to her dad, she'd stop off and see him for lunch the next day, maybe bring him a snack or two from the bakeshop. That always seemed to perk him up.

Molly tackled her closet, spending the next ten minutes trying on upward of seven different outfits, all with the same devastating result. Too tight. Okay, how had this happened? She'd weighed an even hundred and twenty-two pounds since the age of fifteen when she'd first hit puberty. Blinking back a frustrated tear or two, she stepped onto the scale in her bathroom, her mouth falling open at the news.

Six pounds.

She'd gained six pounds in addition to the two gray hairs.

Wonderful.

Now on a fact-finding mission of horror, Molly turned next to the mirror. She studied the lines on her face up close, and what she found there made her want to just curl up into a little ball and abandon the evening altogether. Just as she suspected, the early signs of crow's feet. At least when she smiled just wide enough. She blew out a defeated breath. She was getting old and fat and there was nothing she could do about it. Okay, so maybe she was indulging her dramatic side a little. She was allowed in such a moment.

Gathering her courage, she swallowed solemnly and shook herself out of the downward spiral. No more time for this. Downward spiraling would have to take five.

Instead, plan B.

She shimmied into her loosest pair of dark blue jeans and capped it off with a white dress shirt, and simple heels. Less is more when the going's rough. Plus, she was going to see family, who loved you no matter what, right? There was no one there she needed to impress.

CHAPTER TWO

Jordan Tuscana felt strange as she drove through the streets of Applewood. Perhaps she should have prepared herself more. It was home, but it wasn't. So familiar, yet so much had changed at the same time. Her old high school had an electronic marquee now. The hardware store looked to have been remodeled, and then there were the sidewalks through the center of town. They'd been repaved and had kind of a winding quality to them now. A nice touch. She studied the faces of the people she passed, recognizing many and some not at all.

It looked great, she thought, the town. She'd known Applewood practically her entire life and though it felt different, it was still close to her heart. Still hers.

But this wasn't going to be easy, the whole being back thing. There had been a reason she'd stayed away for so long, and the weight of that sadness now sat heavily upon her heart. She'd avoided it for as long as she possibly could. Declining invitations, evading family gatherings, and ignoring phone messages. She'd exhausted every tactic in her arsenal, and it was time to face what lay ahead.

But this time when she pulled into the driveway, there would be no Cassie to hug her until they both fell to the ground outside of their parents' home. She wouldn't be there to tease her mercilessly or call her "kiddo." They wouldn't spend hours together on the old soccer field knocking the ball back and forth while they talked about every aspect of each other's life. Shooting the breeze, they'd called it, when those talks were actually so much more than that to Jordan.

Of course, there'd been no Cassie for years now, but Jordan had done everything she could to avoid the places she'd recognize her sister's absence the most.

And that meant Applewood.

Her phone buzzed and she clicked it to speakerphone just as she stopped at one of the town's two traffic lights. A line of elementary school kids was led across the crosswalk in front of her car by, wouldn't you know it, Mrs. Altschull, her teacher from back in the day. This was seriously the twilight zone.

"You still alive?" Her best friend George's voice filled the car. He was in LA for another week or so at the premiere of a film they'd worked on together.

Jordan sighed. "Thus far. But the day is young."

"Don't be dramatic. That's my job. Just wanted to check in on you, stroke your head from afar if that's what you need."

"I'll be fine. I'll call you when I'm settled and you can tell me about all the fashion catastrophes at the premiere."

"Will do. Wish you were here."

"Yeah, well, I don't think the studio shares that sentiment. Plus, I need some time away."

"I know, sweets. I love you more than Prada. We'll talk soon."

"We better. Bye, Georgie."

It was five minutes later when she took a deep breath and eased her car into the driveway of the Tuscana home. As she looked up at the house she'd spent most of her childhood nestled inside, her heart thrummed nervously in her chest.

Yeah, this was gonna be rough.

Rallying, she reminded herself of all the reasons she'd come. The biggest of which was easy. She missed her family. It was her father's sixtieth birthday in a few weeks, and her mother had begged her to not let it go by without a visit. Then there was the fact that her own life was radically off-kilter. She'd spent much of the year on location shoots from LA to Austin and hadn't seen her apartment in Chicago in months. Her love life was a joke. And then there was the fact that the studio had her banned from her own movie set when she'd shown her highly inappropriate lead actor she wasn't his personal blow up doll.

So here she was, needing to take a few steps back, assess her life, and find a way to put it all back together again. And that meant going back to basics. She had to remind herself of who she was before she could figure out where she was going. Deep down, she knew her family, her old friends, and this town would do that for her…if she could just let them.

"Jordana Avery Tuscana," her mother practically shouted from the front porch. "You come here this minute!" She held her arms open and smiled widely as Jordan approached. Once her mother's arms enveloped her, she instantly sank into that feeling of comfort they always provided. It felt good, and in response, her eyes welled up at the long forgotten feeling. She pulled back enough to meet her mom's sentimental gaze. She wiped away a tear from Jordan's cheek and Jordan laughed at herself and the unexpected emotion.

"Hiya, Momma. I missed you."

"Hi, sweetheart. It's been too long since I've seen this face; you know this, don't you?" She shook Jordan's chin slightly.

"I know."

"And you should be ashamed of yourself for not coming home in so long. Now that you're here, I'm not letting you get away again so quickly. You're staying for a while. Understood?"

"Feisty. But yeah, that's the plan. If that's okay with you and Dad."

"We insist. Daddy's taking care of some of the details for dinner at Gibson's. Your brother will be there, and Teresa and the kids along with the rest of the family." She paused, studying Jordan a moment. "How are you? And don't kid a kidder."

Amalia Tuscana had aged since Jordan saw her last. Not a great deal but enough that it caught her attention. Small lines had sprung up around her eyes. She was thinner than ever before, and most of her hair was now white, not just the subtle streaks she remembered. She decided to answer honestly. "I've had better months. I think I just need a little break from everything. The studio thinks so too. Actually, they've insisted on it, which is kind of the problem. I was pulled from the movie. They've brought in another producer to fill my slot."

As her mother opened her mouth, probably in question, Jordan held up a hand. "Can we maybe talk about it later? I don't think I have it in me right now."

"Of course. I'm here if you want to...talk." Jordan nodded. She'd not had many heart-to-hearts with her mother over the years. It had always been Cassie she'd turned to for advice or to confide in. And more recently, George. He was pretty much her go-to. Her parents, though always well intended, had never understood what motivated her and disapproved of many of her choices. Okay, all of them. They disagreed with all of her choices. But then she hadn't been exactly helpful in that department either. Not the easiest kid to raise.

"Thanks. Maybe."

Her mother's eyes dimmed in defeat. "Well, your room is waiting for you if you'd like to take an hour or so before dinner to rest or freshen up."

Jordan leaned in and kissed her mother's cheek. "It's good to be home."

❖

Gibson's Steak House was the most expensive restaurant in town, and it was bustling with Tuscanas and their closest friends by the time Molly arrived. She was pulled immediately into one big bear hug after another, an Italian family imperative.

Cassie's older brother, Michael, swooped in, took her coat, and placed a big, sloppy kiss on her cheek. "Molly's here; the party can begin," he called over his shoulder to the room at large.

She smiled happily at her brother-in-law and held up the brown paper sack. "Chocolate chip cookies for the kiddos. I promised and I always make good."

"Nicely done." He dipped his face deep into the bag and inhaled. "Wow. Are you sure we have to let the kids in on this little deal?"

She popped him playfully on the shoulder. "Mikey, don't you dare play cookie monster. Come by the shop tomorrow and I'll hook you up. Those are for the munchkins, who I have to kiss at least a million times right this very minute. Directions, please?"

"About fifty feet in. Kids' table is on the left."

"On it."

Molly said a few passing hellos as she made her way to the kids' table where she found her six-year-old nephew, Zachary, and her four-year-old niece, Risa, coloring before dinner was served. "There are my two favorite small people." She ruffled Zach's hair and received an adorable smile in response. Risa, however, bounded from her seat and leapt easily into Molly's arms. She had a special bond with the little girl, who now clung to her gleefully. "What's up, little Risa? How was your week? You married yet?"

Risa giggled. "No, silly. Zach and me got to help Grandpa at the clinic and he let us pretend to be the doctor. I was the best one. Oh, and Aunt Jordan is here."

"She is?"

Risa nodded and pointed across the room. Molly followed her gaze and paused. There was Jordan, speaking quietly in the corner with one of her elderly aunts.

Except it wasn't Jordan, not exactly.

This Jordan was…different. Not at all the kid Molly projected in her mind whenever she thought of her. She was so grown up. It was startling.

In reality, she knew that time had passed and Jordan was no longer a wayward teenager. Hell, she'd seen her several times throughout her college days, but the young woman before her now was so much more than all of that. Somewhere along the way, Jordan had gone from attractive to absolutely stunning. Her long dark hair was pinned back on one side, keeping her bangs from falling into her face. She wore faded designer jeans and a V-neck dark green T-shirt that somehow made her look cooler than all of them.

As Molly absorbed the confident carriage, the easy smile, the finesse with which Jordan moved and spoke, she couldn't help but feel a little proud of Cassie's little sister. It was then that Jordan lifted her eyes and smiled at her.

And there she was, the Jordan she knew.

Molly gently lowered Risa to the ground and closed the distance between them, grinning and pulling Jordan easily into a hug. "Well, look who decided to grace us with her presence at long last."

"You know me, Mol, always forgetting the time."

As Jordan released her, their eyes met and something moved between them. An understanding. An acknowledgement of the difficult years that had passed since they'd last joked in this way. Jordan's smile faltered briefly, her eyes brushing the ground before she raised them back to Molly's soberly. "I should have called you more. Or been here. Something."

Molly squeezed her hand. "It's okay, Jordy." And it was. The accident had changed life as they knew it, and everyone had reacted in different ways. "You're here now and sure to unleash all sorts of trouble on the unsuspecting citizens of our small town."

Jordan narrowed her gaze. "Who told you?"

"We've met, remember?" That earned a grin. This was more like it. They'd all spent too much time being sad. "Hope you brought your appetite. Your parents ordered the menu eighteen times over."

"My kind of meal."

They settled down to dinner. The seventeen adults present were seated at a long table and the children at their own circular table off to the side, allowing their parents easy access. It was whenever they all got together like this that Cassie's absence was noticed the most. Almost like a gaping hole that no one quite mentioned anymore, but everyone still felt. Molly offered up a silent smile to let Cassie know she was remembered and missed on the day of her sister's homecoming. She found if she made Cassie a part of her everyday life, it made her feel somehow closer.

Molly was ushered to a chair next to Mikey's wife, Teresa, and across from Jordan. The early stages of the meal involved lots of questions about Jordan's job as a producer in the film industry. She seemed to field the inquiries as matter-of-factly as possible, but didn't give an abundance of information.

To accompany the prime rib, the family style platters of green beans, garlic mashed potatoes, and seasoned squash were flowing freely down the table now. Mikey loaded his plate. "So do you have a lot of famous friends now?"

"A few," Jordan answered. "The films I work on are not exactly blockbusters, but we do have some notable names on occasion. I worked with Jenna McGovern recently and she was nominated for a Golden Globe for our film. She's pretty great and we're still in touch."

Teresa grinned. "Ohhh, I love her. It all sounds so exciting."

Her mother-in-law took a sip of wine. "It does, but there are plenty of exciting careers that are a bit more stable. And allow you to stay in one place. Like at home. I wish you'd give that some thought, Jordan." *And here we go.* While the heads of the Tuscana family were warm people, they certainly came with a lot of opinions. Molly knew Amalia's thoughts on Jordan living apart from the rest of the family. She also made no secret that she didn't love her chosen career path. If it were up to her, all her children would have followed in her footsteps and gone into medicine. Mikey had done just that and now had his own practice, while also working two days a week alongside his parents at their clinic. Cassie had come close and studied medical management. But Jordan had showed little interest, and that had disappointed her parents outright.

"It would be nice to live in town," Jordan conceded cautiously. "But it's just not as easy with my line of work. In fact, it's near impossible."

"We could always use your help at the clinic," her father-in-law, Joseph, pointed out. "You could look into medical school. We'd be willing to support you financially in the meantime. You've had your fun. Maybe it's time to settle down, get serious. You're so smart, Jordana. Don't you think you've wasted enough time as it is?"

Molly resisted the urge to roll her eyes, though it was hard. They'd put the same kind of pressure on Cassie, who, in contrast to Jordan, would have done anything to please her parents. She'd earned her business degree, settled in town, and took over the managing of Applewood Primary Care. Under her watchful eye, her parents' clinic had grown to an overwhelming success, drawing tons of patients from neighboring towns.

But Jordan was different, and there was nothing wrong with that. It was just a shame the rest of the family didn't seem to agree.

"I don't think that's the direction I'm heading, Dad. But I appreciate the offer. I honestly do." Her gaze fell to her plate.

"Where's Jordan heading?" Great-aunt Irene asked in a loud voice. "I don't understand." This was not unusual.

Jordan looked up. "I think I'm trying to sort that all out. Can I get back to you?" And then she offered Aunt Irene a genuine smile, making Molly root for her all the more. In that moment, she decided to jump in, see if she could get everyone back on track.

"Well, I for one am thrilled you're here. It's great to share a meal with you." She raised her glass and met Jordan's eyes sincerely. "To Jordan."

The table followed suit and toasted happily, the touchy subject forgotten in light of the true meaning of the evening. Family.

The dinner came to a close, and as Molly shrugged into her jacket at the door, Jordan stopped her. "Hey, you. I just wanted to steal a moment and say thank you."

Molly shook her head. "I don't know what you're talking about."

"Yes, you do."

She felt the tug of a smile at her lips. "Maybe a little. Not a big deal."

Jordan nodded. "How's the bakeshop?"

Molly felt her spirits dip at the mention. "Uh…we're hanging in there." That was a good word for it; she just didn't know how much longer they could hang. She estimated maybe a month or two until she'd have to close the doors permanently, but that might be a bit optimistic judging from the most recent numbers. She hadn't told anyone yet, including her three loyal employees. She didn't have the heart. "Hey, come by tomorrow for coffee. We're not as cool as Starbucks, but we make a mean muffin. Plus, we can catch up. I may or may not make you pay."

"Risky. You're not going to put me to work, are you?"

"I can't make any promises. How are you with an industrial-sized mixer?"

"I've won awards for my mixing."

Molly studied her. "Impressive."

Jordan laughed and Molly relaxed, her troubles forgotten for a moment. There was something about being around Jordan again that eased her spirit. Maybe it was that she reminded her of Cassie. But no, on closer examination that simply wasn't the case.

First of all, they looked nothing alike. Cassie had been blond with pale blue eyes she'd inherited from her father's side of the family. Jordan, on the other hand, was all her mother. Her eyes were a much deeper blue, which contrasted nicely with her dark-as-night hair that fell just past her shoulders.

Then there was the intense difference in their personalities. Cassie had always been a bit more serious, a take-charge kind of girl others looked up to in admiration. Jordan was much more laid back, a friend to everyone, and always on the lookout for a good time. It was her fly-by-night attitude that used to frustrate Cassie to no end, but Molly had always found it rather endearing. "So tomorrow then?"

"How could I miss it?"

"'Night, Jordy. Don't get arrested."

"'Night, Mol. No promises."

❖

Jordan watched through the window as Molly got into her car. She'd expected her to look different somehow, either older or altered by loss. But that simply wasn't the case. Nothing about Molly said widow. She swallowed hard. If anything, Molly looked more vibrant, more beautiful than ever before. Her light brown hair was now accented with subtle blond highlights. It was a tad shorter, but she'd worn it down, which showed off a few sassy layers that added a whole new hip quality she hadn't seen on her before. But her chocolate brown eyes still danced.

And thus, she was stuck.

She hadn't made a plan for how she'd handle the Molly situation and the complicated layers that came with it. She'd meant to, but she'd hoped it would be a nonfactor. It was a schoolgirl crush once upon a time that was fun to reminisce about in her head. That was all.

As the gathering came to a close, Jordan declined rides from everyone who offered and opted to walk home that night instead. Enjoy the stroll. The streets of Applewood were generally pretty quiet after ten. Small towns tended to close up early. The stars gleamed brightly overhead and fresh air filled her lungs. As she passed The Owl Tree, the town's token bar, music drifted faintly from inside and she could make out a few shadowed figures knocking back a couple with their buddies. She contemplated heading inside for a beer when a voice behind her snagged her attention.

"Jordan Tuscana? Am I hallucinating on the sidewalk or are you actually standing here in front of me?"

She turned and smiled. "Hey, Summer."

Summer Siller closed the short distance between them on the sidewalk, stopped in front of Jordan, and took her in. "Wow. The water in Chicago is to be commended. Bottled even. You look great."

Jordan rolled her eyes. "Come on."

"When did you drop back into town, and more importantly, how long are you staying?"

"Today and I'm not sure. A little while, at least. No exact plans on that."

Summer nodded, still drinking her in blatantly. It was actually kind of amusing. They'd gone to school together. Summer had been two grades ahead, and into boys for only the first half of her time in high school. Kind of like Jordan. "You look good. Even better than the last time I saw you, which says a lot."

"You're sweet."

"Prove it and buy me a drink. We should catch up." But she didn't wait for answer and was already tugging Jordan in the direction of the bar.

"Actually, I was just heading home. Long day."

Summer turned back, her heavily made up face fell dramatically. "If you humiliate me now, I may never recover."

She held Summer's gaze and contemplated her next move. A little distraction couldn't hurt. She could unwind a bit from the day, shoot the breeze with Summer, see who else she might run into from the old days.

She slid Summer an easy smile. "Why not?

Except an hour later, when she had to peel Summer off of her like a fruit roll-up, she could have easily answered that question.

"What did you think of me in high school, Jordan?"

"Uh, quite honestly, you terrified me in high school. I watched you chase after my sister like it was your job."

Summer laughed. "We were just kids back then. If I had known you were an option, I might have chased after you. Everyone kind of thought you were just trying to be like your sister when it came to dating girls."

"Yeah, including my parents. Fun times. It took them years to believe this is actually who I am." Taking a last swallow of her beer, Jordan turned to Summer, whose chin now rested on her shoulder while her hand wandered a bit too boldly inside Jordan's jacket. "You know what? It's getting late. I think I'm going to call it a night."

Summer refocused her attention on Jordan's ear and purred softly into it. "I live a block from here."

Any other day, Jordan would have accepted such an obvious invitation, but for whatever reason, tonight just wasn't the night for it. Summer was nice enough, attractive too. Probably it was the drive, or the head trip being back in Applewood brought on, but she'd much rather just head home and curl up in bed. Forget the way her parents had once again marginalized her career and her life choices.

She caught Summer's hand and pulled it from its audacious placement on her stomach and kissed the back of it. "Another time. But thank you for the company." She dropped a twenty on the bar to cover their drinks.

"Sweet dreams, Jordan Tuscana. We'll talk soon."

"I bet we do. Thanks for the company."

Chapter Three

Flour Child was fairly peaceful when Jordan rolled in just before eleven that next morning. There was an elderly couple at the table in the corner, but the rest of the place sat empty. Molly was occupied in the back, but after hugging her to pieces, Louise set her up with breakfast and some coffee on the house. It wasn't long though before Molly appeared, half covered in flour, but smiling as if she'd had the best morning. She easily warmed up a room. "Morning, sleepy head."

Jordan leaned back in her chair, jumping right past morning greetings to the heart of the matter. "Who made this?" The cinnamon roll she was currently inhaling was unreal, beyond that even. "I need to look this person in the eye."

Molly beamed and snapped Jordan playfully with the towel she carried. "I did. Who did you think made it?"

She rubbed her arm. "Ouch. Mean. For real?"

"Yes, for real. Why do you doubt me?" She pointed to the little girl on the logo above the counter and then back to herself. "Flour child. Nice to meet you."

"I remember this place being good, but not this good. Have you sold your soul for baking secrets? Is that what's happened here?"

Molly slid into the chair across from her and rubbed the back of her neck. She'd probably been up since o'dark thirty, which made Jordan feel a little sheepish for the nine hours she'd just stolen. "That would be a better story, but no. The truth is that I've been experimenting a bit. Tweaking some of our older recipes and developing a few new ones. With all the Starbucks popping up like Whack-a-mole, we have to step up our game, and even that hasn't been enough. When the newest store opened right at the edge of town, our morning traffic took a real hit. Take a look around."

Jordan did and a sinking feeling came over her at the implication. Only the one other table was occupied. Her voice was quiet. "So are you in trouble?"

"We'll be all right." Molly smiled, but it didn't reach her eyes. Jordan sensed that wasn't the whole truth. While she was worried, this didn't seem like the moment to push. Instead, she changed the subject.

"How's the new house working out?"

"Well, it's not exactly new, which is kind of the problem. Turns out 'charming older house' is actually code for 'hope you like home repairs.' The newest casualties are the shutters. It's quite tragic."

Jordan quirked an eyebrow.

"I had a jumper."

"No."

"Yes, and don't look so horrified. Don't think I don't know when you're making fun of me. I think I taught you how."

Jordan laughed. "I forgot that part." A pause. "I could fix it for you, you know, if I thought you'd be eternally grateful. Maybe we could negotiate a back alley cinnamon roll agreement of sorts."

Molly studied her curiously. "Back alley cinnamon rolls I can do, but since when do you know anything about home repair?"

Jordan raised her shoulder and let it drop. "You can learn a lot on a movie set. One of the perks."

"Apparently. But I don't want to pull you from your much-needed R and R. I thought that was kind of the point of your whole sabbatical back here."

"Yeah, among other things. But it's either help you with your tragic shutters or shuffle papers for the dueling doctors at the clinic. I need to stay busy, and I'm thinking the shutter thing sounds pretty good. Plus, I enjoy the sun time. I look good in a tan."

"Done. Hired. In return, all the baked goods you can eat."

"So incredibly dangerous."

"My middle name." They shook on it and Molly stood. "Maybe day after tomorrow? In the afternoon?"

"Cool. I'll get the address from my parents."

Molly headed back to work and Jordan lingered, nursing the last of her coffee. She felt lighter somehow and she thought she knew why. Life as she knew it had a way of changing quickly. She rarely worked in the same place from day to day, let alone the same city. Producers, directors, budgets, and even the women she dated came and went. It was nice to know, however, that some things *didn't* change. Molly was still the same kindhearted, whimsical girl she was when Jordan was nine years old and her family first moved to town.

Molly and her father had lived several houses down for their growing up years. She remembered the day they'd first met vividly. She'd lost control of her soccer ball and chased it down the sloping street, losing ground as she ran. There'd been a teenager in a driveway washing a car. She'd stepped ahead of the ball just in time, stopping its progress. The girl popped it into her hands with her foot, smiled widely, and handed the ball back to Jordan. *"I think you lost this."*

Jordan, still breathless from her pursuit, grinned up at the girl with the light brown ponytail and halter top. "Thanks. Do you live here?"

"I do. This is my house. And I'm guessing you must be the new neighbor I saw moving in."

Jordan nodded eagerly. "We got here yesterday from California. My name is Jordan. What's yours?"

"Molly. Nice to meet you, Jordan from California. I'm sure I'll see you around. Take it easy on that ball, okay?" She waved once and went back to washing the car. But Jordan wasn't quite ready to leave her new friend. So far in Applewood, she'd yet to lay eyes on anyone younger than her parents.

"Hey, um...need any help?"

Molly considered the offer, then reached into the bucket and tossed an extra sponge her way, dribbling water across the driveway and a little onto Jordan. "You can take the right side if you want."

She dropped the ball in the grass and eagerly went to work on making the blue Volvo shine. For whatever reason, she wanted to impress Molly, and it seemed to work.

Once they finished drying, Molly walked around the car and stood beside her. "Wow. Nice job, kiddo. I'm guessing you've done this before."

"I help my dad sometimes. He's a doctor."

"Cool."

"So's my mom. I might be too one day."

Molly nodded. "Ambitious. I'm gonna have some lemonade. Want a glass? You've earned it."

"Definitely."

They sat in Molly's front yard drinking their lemonade and trading stories about Applewood and California. Jordan was having the best time and felt incredibly worldly hanging out with her new, older friend. Molly was pretty cool, she decided easily. She may like this place after all. "So what's school like here?"

Molly considered the question. "Pretty laid back. I think you'll like it. I'm going to guess third grade?"

"Fourth. What about you?"

"Tenth."

"Like my sister."

"Oh yeah?" Molly seemed to perk up at this new information.

And just the mention of Cassie seemed to conjure her up. "Jordy!" she yelled as she jogged up the sidewalk." Mom's been calling you for the past ten minutes. It's time for dinner. You need to come home."

"Hey," Molly said, standing.

Cassie paused. A slow smile formed on her lips as she stared. "Hi."

And that was the moment Molly stopped being hers.

She wasn't complaining. At least not entirely.

Cassie and Molly had connected from that first moment, and she believed that things had worked out the way they were supposed to. They'd been friends first and started dating late in their junior year. All three parents were concerned at first and even held a few meetings, but as time went on, they grew to accept Cassie and Molly for what they were. The perfect couple.

But none of that changed the special place Molly had in Jordan's heart. She'd been a gentle influence on Jordan over the years, listening when she needed advice and never judging her too harshly for some of the poor decisions she'd made as a teenager. Instead, she'd talked things out with her in a way no one else would. Pointed out how the things she did and said affected others.

Molly had meant a lot to her and still did.

Yet another thing that hadn't changed.

Chapter Four

The next day was about as beautiful as they came. It was April, and in Applewood that meant an even seventy-one degrees with a pleasant breeze moving the trees in delicate patterns. Jordan looked forward to spending the next hour or two outdoors. Already she could tell it was going to be a great day. There was just something about it.

She set out for Molly's house just after four. While she'd never been there before, she knew the neighborhood well enough, so it didn't take long to locate Molly's block. The quaint street felt lived in, comfortable, and screamed of backyard barbeques and block parties. She kind of liked it. Along her route, she passed overturned tricycles beneath shady oak trees, sturdy houses with colorful doors, and more "welcome" signs than she thought to count. It was a happy place and it fit Molly to a tee.

Upon arrival, she didn't knock immediately and instead took a moment to study her task. The dilapidated shutter, while a pretty powder blue, sadly needed more than just a re-hanging, as did its three neighboring counterparts. The finish was cracked on all four and there was evidence of sun bleaching. Not to mention the fact that the hinges were rusty and would need to be replaced entirely.

"So what's the verdict?"

Jordan turned to see Molly standing on the porch behind her. "I don't think I have the heart to break it to you."

Molly sighed. "I can be big about this. Give it to me straight."

Jordan walked to the nearest window and ran her hand across the wooden shutter. "I think if I just re-hang this one, you'll be right back here again in a few months."

"So they have to be replaced entirely?" She sat in defeat on the steps of the porch. "I lied. Not feeling big about this at all. How much is that going to cost, do you think?"

Jordan could sense Molly's immediate hesitation when money became a question, confirming her suspicions. "You know, I think we could save a few dollars if we just did a little rehab on these guys. Save their little shutter lives. It seems the humane thing to do. What do you think?"

"I think a pardon's in order. So we can actually do that?" Molly asked in an adorably hopeful voice. "The rehab thing?"

Jordan took the spot next to her on the steps. "We can. Well, I can at least. You can tell me jokes that aren't exactly funny and I'll feign amusement at your attempts."

Molly shot her a look of outrage. "I'll have you know that I'm incredibly funny and half this town will back me on this."

"They're laughing because they like you and you do this thing where you light up on the punch line. Regardless of the bad joke, it's kind of cute."

Molly considered this scenario before seeming to reject it entirely. "Uh-uh. I'm funny. You're jealous. End of story."

"See? You're even kind of cute when you're angry. Well done."

Molly slugged her hard in the shoulder. "Stop patronizing me."

"Ow. I'll definitely try. Color me intimidated." She rubbed her upper arm.

"Thank you." She paused and floated back down to sincerity. "But back to the shutters. It sounds like more work than you originally agreed to. I don't want you to feel obligated to—"

Jordan pointed at her. "Back alley agreement, remember? Don't you dare renege now. I don't know how we'd get past it."

Molly nudged her shoulder playfully with her own. "You're right. We wouldn't. But how much work are we talking about?"

"Not as major as you're probably projecting. I'll pick up some supplies today and see how far I get before dark. I can always come back tomorrow to finish up if need be."

Molly nodded. "I guess I should be honored. Once the news that you're back in town hits the masses, I won't have you to myself anymore. Everyone loves you, you know. It's kind of annoying."

"Nah, I'm pretty boring. No one will pay me much attention."

"Are you kidding? Attention is one thing you'll never be without. People notice when you walk in a room, Jordan. You must know that. Then you turn on the charm and they're gone forever. It's always been that way."

"Those were my wild child days. Things are different now. I'm different."

"If you say so." They stared out at the street and watched as an elderly woman walked her Yorkshire terrier past the house. "So... are we going to talk about it?"

Jordan squinted. "I think you're going to have to be more specific."

"This used to be easier." Molly turned to her more fully and took a moment to study her, her soft brown eyes full of concern. "How are things *really*? And please remember who you're talking to."

Jordan pulled her eyes from Molly's and stared hard at her hands. She could still see right through her and whether Jordan wanted it to be or not, her guard was now officially down. Molly had a way of doing that to her. She broke through all the barriers to just...her. "So things have been a little all over the place. Not so great, actually."

Molly leaned back on her hands patiently as if she had all the time in the world. "Okay, tell me."

And she would because that's what she did with Molly. "The short version of a long story is that I feel a little, what's the word... lost? God, that sounds so cliché that I can't believe I just said it. Erase the word lost from this conversation. I guess I just don't know what I'm doing anymore." She raised her hands in helpless wonder and let them drop, then sat quietly for a moment thinking how to best explain. "I work day and night because that's what it takes. Shooting schedules, contracts, location scouting, talent management, and long hours on set. But I'm not shy about putting in the time. I've ascended the studio ladder ahead of schedule, which should feel great, but it doesn't and I don't know why. I should be reveling."

"So revel. What's stopping you?"

She shook her head. "It feels hollow. I have friends that I tolerate, and women…well, let's just say the revolving door's had quite a workout, and you know what? I'm too old for that. What exactly is my purpose in life? Because it's all wearing a little thin."

Molly grinned in amusement and tucked a strand of hair behind her ear. "You're twenty-seven."

"What?"

"You're only twenty-seven years old."

"Exactly. And what do I have to show for it?"

Molly laughed. "A pretty impressive résumé to start with."

"Yeah, well, the studio has placed me on a temporary leave of absence. Did I forget to mention that particularly flattering part?"

"Okay. Wow. What prompted that?"

Jordan hesitated, not sure she wanted to share what had been a tragically weak moment for her. "They might have taken issue with the fact that I poured a pitcher of ice water over a high profile actor's head in front of an entire working set."

Molly covered her mouth, though the smile was hard to hide. "Jordan, you didn't. You can't do things like that." But she was now laughing, which only made Jordan laugh too.

"Listen, that guy had it coming. He'd been hitting on me since day one of the shoot, and no matter what I did or said, politely I might add, he wasn't getting the message. It was time he learned to keep his damn hands to himself."

"And you thought the ice water would—"

"Make it a bit more clear. Trust me, it did."

Molly shook her head, trying to regain composure. "You could have gone to movie jail."

"I still might."

"Will this hurt your career long-term?"

Jordan considered this. "Maybe. I don't know. It'll definitely be hot gossip for a few weeks." She stood, strolled to the suicidal shutter, and turned back. "If I apologize profusely and fall on my sword, that kind of thing, I should be able to get back in the studio's good graces. I would just have to, you know, find the motivation to actually *do that* and I'll be honest, it's eluding me in this moment."

Molly shook her head in amazement. "Only you, Jordan, only you."

"I'm a work in progress. This is not news to me."

"And thus, you're here. To regain your bearings, to steady the ship—"

"To spend time with the people who are important to me," she said seriously and inclined her head to Molly as an example of that. "Whom I never should have stayed away from for so long." She hesitated before pressing forward because it was a delicate subject matter for both of them. "When her plane went down...I didn't know how to be here anymore. Nothing felt right." Molly nodded solemnly, her eyes a little haunted at the topic shift. "I think it was a way to cope with losing my sister, but in hindsight, it was so incredibly selfish of me that I can't stand myself for it. I mean, my parents, you."

Molly got up and moved toward her. "Don't do that. Everyone deals with grief differently. I stopped eating for eight months. Your brother felt the need to fix every broken appliance in a twenty-mile radius. And the town erected a commemorative plaque. So you took some time away from us all, I don't think anyone holds it against you. I, for one, don't. There's no manual for dealing with loss, and we all had to find our own way through it. But you know what? You're here now and it's pretty great. Why don't we leave it at that?"

The sentiment alone, the fact that Molly understood, infused her with such gratitude, such relief that it was all she could do to nod mutely and fight the damn lump in her throat. They stood in silence for several moments, each lost in thought. Finally, Molly looked at her tentatively as if trying to make a decision. "Can I tell you something?"

Jordan tilted her head. "You can tell me anything."

"I've decided to start dating again." She ran a nervous hand through her hair. "What do you think about that? And you can be totally honest. Even if it's to tell me I'm insane."

Jordan paused with the information before offering Molly her most encouraging smile. "I think that's great, Mol. Sincerely."

"You do? You're not just trying to make me feel okay about it? Because the prospect of telling your parents is more than I can process at this point, and it was one thing in theory, but now that the day is here, I'm having all kinds of doubts and thinking maybe I should just call her and—"

"Whoa, whoa, whoa. Slow down, tiger." Jordan grabbed Molly by the shoulders and steered her back to the steps where she sat them both down. "First of all, breathe. That would be step one."

Molly took a deep inhale. Probably more than she actually needed which was endearing.

"You good?"

She nodded. "Better."

"Then let's back up a little bit. When is this date you speak of?"

"Tonight. Eden's friend set it up. I work with Eden at Flour Child. I don't think you've met her yet. She's pretty wonderful. And Southern. Totally Southern. I'll introduce you."

"I can't even wait. Stop stalling."

"You're good." A pause. "So…I'm supposed to meet this *woman*."

"Your date."

"Right, my date, for dinner tonight. She sounds incredibly accomplished, put together, and from what Eden says, attractive, so I'm pretty sure she's going to hate me."

"Because you're the opposite of all of those things."

Molly narrowed her gaze. "I see what you did there. Very slick."

Jordan took Molly's hand. "Just try and have a good time. Keep it simple. You never know."

Molly seemed to mull things over. "When did you become the smart one between us?"

"Can I have that in writing?"

Molly briefly considered this. "Definitely not."

She headed inside and Jordan spent the next hour gathering the supplies she needed from her parents' garage a few blocks down and set to work power washing, then sanding down the shutters to remove any chipped paint. She was losing light and contemplated calling it a day when Molly emerged from the house once again, and the image sucked all the air from her lungs. Molly stood there in a simple midnight blue cocktail dress, nervously clutching a handbag. Her hair was partially clipped back and the rest shimmered loosely down her back. She wore subtle heels and a small solitaire necklace. She looked, in a word, beautiful. No. More than that. As Jordan stared, time seemed to stand still, which was strange, and at the same time ridiculous, because when did time ever stand still?

❖

Jordan was staring at her oddly, which made Molly start to doubt the evening all over again. Clearly, the dress was all wrong, and who was she kidding? She was trying too hard. She wanted to turn back around and call the whole thing off, but that would be rude and she hated to be rude. "Is it too much? You should just tell me if it is. Say it. Say it's too much." Damn it all. Why was she so nervous?

Jordan set the sander on the ground, the odd expression morphing into a puzzled one. But she still hadn't said anything because she was probably working on a really crafty arrangement of words that wouldn't hurt her feelings. "It's not too much."

Molly narrowed her gaze. "Don't humor me. These are desperate times."

"You're giving me too much credit. It's a great dress. Trust me, Molly. I vote yes."

"What if she goes for casual? Then I'll look ridiculous in comparison."

"Valid concern. Where are you having dinner?"

"The Lodge in Andersville, one town over."

Jordan whistled low. "That's a five-star restaurant. Jeans wouldn't exactly cut it. Trust me, you're good."

Molly exhaled, feeling somewhat better and for the first time since coming outside, took in the scene in her front yard. Supplies were scattered across the lawn, her now naked shutters were laid out in a smart little row, already undergoing surgery. In response to the temperature, Jordan had pulled her dark hair into a ponytail and stripped down to just a tank top, a hint of perspiration dotted her chest. Molly shook her head slowly, taking her in. "You look like you should be in a calendar right now. A sexy one. I'd hate to see this go to waste. Should I take a photo for your Facebook page and your adoring fans?"

"If you do, I'd have to kill you. Besides, I was going for sweet and unassuming. Is there a calendar like that?"

"Oh, unassuming is not a word I would use to describe you, Jordy." Her eyes widened in realization. "But you do look thirsty, and damn it, I made you lemonade. *Forgotten* lemonade. I'm a bad person. Hold that thought."

"I was hoping you'd find a way to reward me," Jordan called after her happily.

Molly raced back into the house and poured a full glass of her homemade lemonade, added a handful of ice cubes and topped it off with a fresh strawberry from her garden in back. She raced back outside and presented the glass to Jordan, who was now waiting on the front porch and dabbing the back of her neck with a bandana. "Voila. All is now right with the world."

"You are an angel. Thank you." Jordan took three generous swallows of the lemonade before staring longingly at the glass, mystified. "Are you kidding me? Did you make this too?"

"Guilty. It's not like I'm going to serve instant."

"You're like Martha Stewart on crack; you realize this, don't you?"

Molly placed her hand over her heart. "I think that's the nicest thing you've ever said to me."

"Continue to regale me with your confectionary genius and you might find yourself surprised at some of the things that'll come out of my mouth."

"Such a tease." Molly checked her watch. "I hate to cut our time short, but I have to leave you here and go on an honest to goodness date. Is that okay?"

"It is. I'll put in another twenty minutes or so before I lose the light entirely and then we can reconvene…maybe tomorrow?"

"Sounds perfect. There's a spare key under the mat if you'd like more forgotten lemonade. You're also welcome to store those tools here so you don't have to lug them back and forth."

Jordan looked at her like she was crazy.

"What?"

"You keep your key under the mat? Tricky."

"Look around, smart aleck. This isn't exactly the hood. I think we're safe."

"Famous last words." Molly shot her a look that meant business and Jordan held up her hands in acquiescence. "But it's your place."

"Thank you for getting that. Very perceptive of you. Any last minute advice?"

Jordan thought for a moment. "Take it for what it is. A first date. If it goes well, fantastic. If not, you've lost nothing."

She tilted her head to the side, seeming to take in the words. "Got it. Nothing to lose. I'll remember that. See ya, Jordan." She exhaled slowly as she descended the steps, her stomach already a series of butterfly races at the prospect of the evening ahead of her. "Wish me luck."

Jordan stared at her, that unreadable, odd expression back on her face. "You don't need it."

❖

Once Molly's car disappeared from sight, Jordan set back to work sanding the last shutter and trying hard not to think about the reaction she'd just had to Molly as she emerged from the house. It was an adolescent aftershock of a schoolgirl crush that never should have been. Plus, it had nothing to do with the fact that it was Molly, and everything to do with the fact that a beautiful woman, *any* beautiful woman, had just walked out of that house.

Of course she'd noticed her. She wasn't dead.

She worked until the darkness enveloped her, stored her supplies in Molly's garage, and headed home...after one last glass of killer lemonade.

❖

The lodge was beyond bustling when Molly walked in. Nicely dressed folks chatted animatedly with one another as they waited for a table in the entryway to the restaurant. There wasn't a ton of space to walk, and Molly now had regrets about the way they'd arranged to meet. How exactly was she supposed to find her date, Heather McLucken, the tax attorney? She studied the faces of those around her for any sign of dexterity with numbers. Unfortunately, no one was exactly walking the restaurant with an adding machine and a W4. Typical. It was then that someone tapped her lightly on the shoulder.

"Excuse me. You wouldn't happen to be Molly, would you?"

Saved. "I am, yes. Hi."

"Hi, I'm Heather McLucken."

Molly accepted the woman's extended hand and smiled widely. Heather was striking. A tall blonde with twinkly green eyes and a warm smile. Tonight might not be so bad after all. She felt herself perk up almost instantly. "Nice to meet you. I'm Molly O'Brien."

Heather squeezed her hand, her eyes lingering on Molly's for just the right amount of time for Molly to momentarily lose herself in their impressive shade. Suddenly she was so looking forward to dinner.

"Shall we? I think they have our table waiting. I pulled some strings and got us seated in a quieter part of the restaurant so we can get to know each other. I hope that's okay."

"It sounds fantastic. Thank you."

As Molly moved toward the main dining area of the restaurant, Heather opened the door for her, earning a thousand points for good manners. She began brainstorming ways to thank Eden for this. A hug. A day off. An entire tray of truffles. Her firstborn.

As dinner got underway, things only seemed to get better. The conversation flowed easily, and Molly noticed that the faux confidence she had initially put forth was starting to feel authentic. It was actually kind of fun, this dating thing. Why had she held off for so long?

Heather took a delicate and rather sexy sip of her wine. "How's your food? The chef here is one of the best in the state."

"I'd have to say that's evidenced here. The chicken's cooked to perfection and the marinade accentuates the flavors nicely without overpowering. I'm kind of in heaven over here."

Heather leaned her chin onto her palm. "I like the way you talk about food. I'm told you own a bakery."

"That's right. It's just a small little place in Applewood, but people seem to like it."

Heather nodded and covered Molly's hand with her own. "I hope I'll get to check it out sometime."

Molly's heart rate noticeably sped up. *Me too, Heather-the-tax-attorney. Me too.* "Well, you're welcome anytime. What about you? You must be thrilled now that tax season's over."

"Well, with the exception of all of the extensions we've filed, sure. I'm thinking that by next week—I'm sorry." She held up one finger. "Can we pause this for a minute? I'm getting a call that might be important. So rude, but I need to take it."

"Oh, of course. Go right ahead. I can wait. Don't mind waiting." So she was a babbling fool, but Heather was attractive and charming and well-spoken. Who wouldn't have been?

It was then that Heather pressed a button on her phone and switched into take-charge mode. "Hi, Sal, yeah, I need in on the Celtics/Knicks action. I'll take the Celtics for a dime." Pause. She looked furious. "Just extend my credit, you asshole! I'm good for it. Don't do this to me, Sal." Pause. "Forget it. I'll call Jimmy. Oh, and, Sal? *Fuck you.*" She placed the phone back in her purse, turned back to Molly, and assumed the same serene smile from several moments prior. "Anyway. Yes, next week will be about tying up loose ends at the office."

Molly tried to pick up the conversation, really she did, but the person she'd just watched take that call was pretty much terrifying and not at all who she'd just had dinner with. "I'm sorry, I don't mean to get off topic"—she gestured tentatively to the phone—"but is everything all right?"

Heather sighed. "It will be in a minute. Do you mind if I just…" She picked up her phone and pointed before proceeding to dial.

Molly raised her eyebrows and slowly went back to her chicken, doing her damndest to ignore the incredibly loud warning sirens going off in her head.

"Sammy, it's Heather. I need the Celtics for a dime. You know what, on second thought, make it three." Pause. "You're the greatest. Just put it on my tab. I can settle with you in a week or so. I should have some cash coming in if all goes well with the playoffs on Sunday. Ciao." She leaned into Molly and practically purred. "Now where were we?

Molly shook her head slowly in wonder. "I couldn't tell you if I wanted to. Are you into…gambling?"

Heather held her thumb and forefinger close together. "A minor hobby. Excuse me, sir?" she asked a passing busboy. "Can you get me the Lakers score?"

He leaned in discreetly. "Two minutes ago they were down by twelve."

"Damn it!" she screamed at the room in general, inciting several glares from nearby tables. She grabbed for her phone and dialed angrily. "Bobby, can you get me the halftime betting lines? Now, asshole!" Molly wanted to die. To crawl under the table and die. Instead, she signaled the waiter for the check.

As she signed the credit card slip for *both* of their meals, Heather leaned in flirtatiously. "So explain to me how a woman as attractive and seemingly intelligent as you is still single?"

Molly sighed and set down the pen. "You know what? Single's not so bad."

Later that night, as Molly replayed the details of the date that had gone so terribly wrong, she wondered if it was some sort of sign that it was a bad idea. And for whatever reason, there was comfort in that. Her life wasn't so bad, she reminded herself. She had her routine, her small group of friends and her family. That should be enough.

She checked the time. It was late and she was opening the next morning, but she knew what she wanted to do before bed. She snuggled under a blanket on the couch and reached for the remote. Images of their trip to Jamaica, hers and Cassie's, flickered across her television, and she sighed into the comfort the home video provided. It was her go-to and she stole moments with it whenever she could.

"Why are you looking at me like that?" Molly asked from behind the camera. Cassie sat on a beach towel in the sand.

"Because you're adorable when you're concentrating on working that thing." The breeze caught her blond hair and lifted it. "Put that thing down and come in the water with me. We can stay where it's shallow if you want."

"Wait. Say where we are and what we're doing first."

Cassie smiled and looked straight into the camera. Because she couldn't help herself, Molly paused the video and stared at the frozen image. The room was silent as Cassie smiled back at her from the screen. The features were so familiar, so beautiful, and full of life. It was when she watched this particular video that she felt closest to Cassie. They'd been so happy on that trip. She hugged the blanket to her and unpaused the DVD. Cassie's voice filled the room. "It's June. We're in Jamaica. And we're in love. Can we go in the water now?"

"We can. Blow me a kiss."

And she did. Molly rewound it and watched the kiss again. And then the video went dark and she sat in the blackness, already feeling better as she drifted slowly to sleep.

Chapter Five

The next day didn't turn out as planned for Jordan. She woke up early, but the pitter-patter of raindrops on the window was only a sneak preview of the great big storms that would roll in and stay for most of the morning. She knew early on that she wouldn't be able to finish the shutter job over at Molly's so instead she headed for the clinic to make herself useful. They were down a receptionist and she'd volunteered to help out whenever she could. That seemed to make her parents happy, which was kind of her goal as of late.

She spent the morning organizing patient charts and scheduling, skills she'd picked up in high school and slid easily back into.

Her dad joined her midday in the break room for lunch, cutting his sub sandwich in half for them to split. He still wore his very official white coat she'd admired as a child, the pocket outfitted with a few token lollipops for the younger patients and a few demanding older ones. His hair was entirely gray now, and he'd shaved off the moustache he'd had for much of her childhood. "It's nice having you around again, Jordana. I could get used to this."

She smiled. She and her father didn't always see eye to eye, but she enjoyed spending time with him one-on-one. He was a good guy. "You say that to all your kids." But then that sounded strange because really there was just her and Mikey now.

He must have seen the realization flicker in her eyes. "Don't look that way. I still have three kids, you know. Five, counting Teresa and Molly."

Jordan nodded solemnly, knowing it was true. She played absently with the corner of her sandwich.

Her father slid her an inquisitive look. "So how are things with Molly these days? You two do much talking since you've been back?"

"A little. She seems okay. Why do you ask?"

He grabbed for a chip. "Your mother and I worry for her sometimes. She has a lot on her plate with her father's declining health and managing the bakery all by herself. She's there at five a.m. each morning and doesn't leave sometimes until well past dinnertime. She doesn't let us help enough, and for Cassie's sake, we should. We should all be watching out for Molly."

Jordan nodded and contemplated telling her father about the financial trouble at Flour Child, but decided that Molly had confided in her alone. She should respect that. "I guess I didn't realize she pulled so many hours. But I think she's managing." However, as soon as the words left her mouth, she knew she wasn't at all convinced.

"And what about you? When does the studio need you back in the saddle? Or have you decided to listen to reason and leave that world behind?"

It was no secret that her father found the entertainment industry frivolous in comparison to the rest of the family's noble work. She was the family black sheep, and she was used to her part. But for whatever reason, she needed to be honest with him in this moment. And she needed for him to understand.

She bit the bullet and recounted the details of her less than dignified dismissal from the set the week prior. When she finished, she met her father's eyes, and any hope of understanding or compassion on his part left her immediately. Instead, she only saw disappointment.

And, as always, it was crushing.

"That's no way to conduct yourself, Jordana." He shook his head in disapproval. "That's not how you were brought up."

"Yes, sir. I know. I lost my temper and had a momentary lapse."

"And look what it's cost you. If I have a momentary lapse when working on an important case, someone could lose his or her life.

There's no room for that kind of behavior if you want to succeed in life. Time for you to grow up, Jordan. I don't want to have to worry about you so much."

She nodded. "You're right. Of course, you're right."

They finished eating in silence before he went back to work. But the air was thick with tension. She put in two more hours in the reception area before packing it in. Her morale was a little low, but she ordered herself to snap out of it as she headed out into the drizzly afternoon. So she was still disappointing her father, she just suffered through it a little quieter these days. Maybe she had grown up.

❖

Jordan watched Molly anxiously from the corner booth as she pulled down the shades and flipped the Open sign to Closed. "Are you going to tell me how it went last night or make me sit here and wonder? The suspense is too much. I may die." It was close to five and that meant closing time at Flour Child.

Molly shot her a look. "Trust me. You won't die."

Jordan sighed dramatically, but truth be told, she felt better hanging out at the bakeshop. It had been a good move to swing by after work. Something about the place was cheerful and light and pulled her out of the mood she'd been in since lunch with her father. Or maybe it was just spending time with Molly, who was strangely very tight-lipped about the whole evening prior. Try as she might, Jordan hadn't been able to gain much ground in the way of sordid details regarding her blind date. She did, however, manage to score a fluffy blueberry muffin, which she'd polished off quicker than was probably polite. Lucky for her she had a great metabolism or she'd be in real trouble.

"Good night, all." Louise puttered by on her way home for the day. "I'd stay and chat, but I gotta make it to my place before *Jeopardy* starts. Alex Trebek is my sweet boyfriend."

Jordan shook her head. "You're out of his league, Louise."

Touched, Louise grinned and moved to Jordan, squeezed both of her cheeks, and then pulled her into a great big hug. "I knew I missed you. You're too adorable for words and you know how to make an old lady feel good. Come by tomorrow and I'll set you up with my special cinnamon coffee. I don't make that for many people." She squeezed Jordan's cheek again and headed for the door.

"You're on."

Molly rolled her eyes but was smiling as she went back to work, refilling the sugar dispensers one at a time.

Once they were alone, Jordan turned back to Molly. "Please tell me." She then offered her most hope-filled expression complete with wide eyes and a pouty mouth, which earned her a laugh from Molly. Jackpot.

"You know what? It was bad. Let's just leave it there."

Oh, that was entirely too little information. Jordan pressed on. "Okay, I can work with bad. Let's dissect a bit, shall we? Are we talking we-just-didn't-click-at-all bad? Or I-might-need-to-take-out-a-restraining-order bad?"

Molly sighed and sank into the booth across from Jordan. "It was more like you-have-a-gambling-problem-and-you're-not-taking-me-down-with-you horrible."

Jordan's mouth fell open. "Whoa. You got that from a first date?"

"You have no idea."

Jordan reached across the table and covered Molly's hand, joking now aside. "I know you were hoping it would be painless. I'm sorry it wasn't." Molly nodded, and when she looked back at her with those caramel brown eyes, Jordan felt herself melt a little, an uncomfortable pulling now present in her stomach. *And here we go...*

"It's not that. It's just…I'm starting to think I'm not cut out for this. The whole dating thing. I don't have the thick skin it seems to require, and let's be honest; I'm too old to try desperately to impress someone I've never met."

"Agreed. You're well into elderly. I know that when I hit my early thirties, I plan to just pack it in immediately. In bed by eight each night. No exceptions."

Molly shook her head, glaring. "It's different for you and you know it. You've got this presence, this effortless charisma. And then there's the fact that you're just, well, gorgeous, which is just not fair. The rest of us have to try, Jordan. Cut me some slack when I say that I don't know if I'm up for it."

Jordan let her mouth fall open. "You think I'm gorgeous?"

"Focus, please; we're talking about me."

"Selfish, but okay." Jordan sat up a little straighter, on a mission now. "I'm afraid it's time to get serious. Truth or dare."

Molly shook her head. "Uh-uh. We're not doing this."

"We are." Jordan knew when to use the big guns, and this was one of those times. Truth or Dare was the game Molly had used to get Jordan to open up to her when she was young, knowing full well that at the time Jordan thought of it as a sophisticated, older kids game and would therefore honor the rules reverently. Over the years, it developed into a thing they did, which had led to some very valuable conversations. The dare option was rarely utilized, however. It was just an unspoken understanding between them. Truth or Dare was about being honest with each other at all costs.

Molly's voice was quiet when she answered obligatorily. "Truth."

"Do you believe your life is over at thirty-three?"

She was silent and seemed to contemplate the question. "No."

"Do you deserve to be happy?"

The words must have affected Molly as her eyes filled slightly. She nodded. "I think so." And then more firmly, "Yes. I do"

"And doesn't it help to say it out loud?"

Molly relaxed back into the booth, the tiniest of smiles hinted at on her lips. "Surprisingly, it does."

Jordan brushed her hands together quickly. "Then my work here is done. I'll send you my bill."

Molly shook her head slightly. "Why does everything seem easier when you're around?"

It was a compliment and a commentary on the ease of their relationship. In this moment, she felt very connected to Molly, and the smile faded gradually from her face as she answered. "I don't know."

Molly held her gaze and the mood shifted. "Me neither."

There was a silence that hung in the air between them. Enough of one to make Jordan feel the need to step in and save them from the somehow weighted moment. "You know, rather than dissect the wonder that is me, can we talk about the rumor I heard at the clinic this morning?"

Her cavalier tone broke the spell, and Molly was again all smiles as she leaned in, resting her adorable chin on her fist. "If we must. What have you heard?"

"Jackson, the dueling doctors' seventeen-year-old errand boy, said that next Saturday happens to be Applewood's annual April Showers Festival. What say you?"

"I can confirm said rumor."

Jordan felt herself light up from the inside out as she scooted to the edge of her seat in excitement. "Listen, I love this festival. This festival is the stuff small towns are made of. It takes me straight back to when I was a kid. We have to go. Say we can. I want to ride the Ferris wheel."

Molly laughed. "I like it when you get all smiley like this. We can definitely go. But a) I hate the Ferris wheel and you know it, and b) you'll have to entertain yourself, I'm afraid. Or find some unassuming girl to fawn all over you per usual, as I will be working at the Flour Child booth like a good businesswoman should."

"Lame. But if you insist, I guess I can be big about this. What will you be selling this year?"

"That's just it. This is our chance to debut something noteworthy to a large crowd. People from all over come to this festival. It needs to be something good. Something new that could garner us some attention, and by attention, I mean cash." An idea sparked behind Molly's eyes. "You know what? Can I get your opinion on something?" But she didn't wait for an answer and was already up and dashing behind the counter. Jordan watched after her curiously when she returned just a moment later carrying a small plate with a solitary chocolate truffle in the middle.

"Taste this."

"Well, if you twist my arm." Jordan lifted the chocolate, took a small bite, and allowed the flavors to settle. And then they did.

"Wow. It's good, Molly. Are there more?" She threw an inquisitive glance behind her to the kitchen.

Molly gave her a long look. "But not perfect. I need it to be perfect and it's missing something. What is it missing?"

Jordan contemplated the question. "You might be asking the wrong person. I pretty much think everything you feed me is what heaven must taste like."

"Nice of you, but dig a little deeper and I'm betting you could help me figure this out. You have the outsider's perspective that I desperately need right now. Close your eyes and open your mouth." With an amused grin, she did so, and the last piece of the truffle was placed delicately on her tongue. She let the chocolate slowly dissolve in her mouth while listening to Molly's determined and kind of sexy voice speaking in a slow, even tone. "Now if you could add one thing, one quality, one *ingredient* that would make your mouth water…make you *crave* just a little bit more, what would it be?"

Jordan swallowed hard, fighting against the direction her thoughts were trying to lead her. Shaking herself out of it, she stumbled upon her answer. "Peanut butter?" It came out of her mouth before she'd even fully processed the thought. But there it was. She opened her eyes. "I pretty much like everything better with peanut butter."

Molly sat hard. "Huh. Okay, that's interesting. So you're thinking savory." She was lost in concentration and Jordan watched as she bit her bottom lip in a move that was so alluring she had to glance away momentarily. What exactly was happening to her here? Whatever it was, it was powerful.

Finally, Molly brushed the hair off of her forehead and caught Jordan's gaze. "You know something? It could actually work. But it wouldn't have to be a lot, just a hint of peanut butter so it doesn't overwhelm, but rather accentuates." There was a determination in her stare now and she was off, scurrying behind the counter, clearly in project mode and excited about it. "If this works, I owe you big time," she called over her shoulder.

"I like the sound of that."

And then from the recesses of the kitchen, "Come by the house whenever you're free. The shutters miss you. Plus, I hear there's complimentary lemonade."

"I can only hope the rumors are true," she called back.

Left alone in the cozy bakeshop, Jordan let out a slow exhale. Alone was good. It was safe. She could do alone.

❖

It was close to midnight by the time they were ready. Her third batch of the night. Molly stared at the tiny tray of individual chocolates and sent up a small prayer that this would be the time she got it right. "A little help here, Cas?" she whispered up to the air around her.

Taking a deep breath, she slowly brought a truffle to her lips and took a bite. And all at once, she knew.

This was it.

After weeks of tweaking and adjusting, tasting and accounting, she'd come up with the perfect balance of flavors. Her heart sped up and she raised one victorious fist in the air. There was no one there to see it, but she celebrated with her own silent happy dance through the expanse of the small kitchen. And she didn't just dance. She got down. She turned it out. She was a rock star of the kitchen in the crunkest sense, but that wasn't the point. This breakthrough was huge. Monumental. And it wasn't just about creating a new menu item to grace the display case; this was about finding a signature item that could put Flour Child on the confectionary map. This was about saving the store, her family's legacy, and for the first time in a long time, she thought she stood a chance at doing just that.

With the right marketing, that is.

She closed her eyes and sent a silent "thank you" Cassie's way. But then she paused in recognition. Because it wasn't Cassie who was responsible for the breakthrough, was it?

Jordan was the one who'd sent her down the path to success, and she was the one Molly should be thanking.

And she would.

In that moment, the hour late and her guard completely down, her thoughts floated to their exchange earlier. The image of Jordan smiling and tasting the chocolate bubbled to the surface, and a jolt moved through her. A powerful hit of something she didn't care to name. Interesting. Where had that come from? It was an odd and very unexpected reaction that she refused to analyze any further.

But it had been there all the same.

Moving quickly past it, she split the remaining truffles into two separate stacks and packed them in the bakeshop's signature pink box with a white ribbon. Knowing she would need to be back at work in less than five hours to prepare the next day's menu items, she headed home for some much needed sleep.

Chapter Six

I don't care what the stupid doctor says; I don't want that flavorless stuff masquerading as food in the dining hall." Jack O'Brien stared hard at Molly, his arms folded across his chest in a manner suggesting he wasn't going to budge. Her father was generally a pretty easygoing guy, but the stricter diet his doctor had him on was beginning to wear thin, as was his patience.

"So what exactly are you planning to eat instead?" It was close to lunchtime and she'd set aside time for them to eat together on her short break.

"I've ordered a pizza. It should be here any minute."

She sighed. "A pizza? Dad, that's hardly within the realm of the list of foods your cardiologist outlined for us."

Maybe it was the worried expression on her face, or the fragile tone of her voice, but in that moment, he seemed to soften considerably. In fact, he even looked a little sad, which broke her heart for a whole separate reason. "I'll just have one slice then. And maybe a little salad and fruit from the dining room."

He was trying to make her happy, even in the midst of his frustration. Molly met his eyes and took in his labored breathing. It seemed worse today. "I guess one piece wouldn't hurt. Maybe some rest after that though, don't you think?"

He nodded quietly, resolute now. "Maybe so."

In attempt to elevate the mood, she changed the subject. "So I think you're going to be proud of me. Or at least, I'm hoping so."

He eyed her suspiciously. "Explain yourself, child of mine."

"Well, you know how you always taught me to never give up when it came to generating new recipes? Keep those creative fires burning. Give up sleep if you have to."

That earned a partial smile. "Of course I remember. Never stop working at it, until it's just right. That's our motto."

"Exactly. Well, I did a little of that. I listened to your advice and it took a little time, but I came up with this." From her bag on the floor, she produced the small pink box. "Try one of these."

He gently tore the ribbon and took a small bite of the truffle. She waited, almost ready to come out of her skin in anticipation of what he might say. "So? What's the verdict?" she asked nervously. Her heart was racing now because his opinion mattered to her more than anyone else's. It just did. He wasn't just her father, he was her mentor. He taught her everything she knew, and if he was underwhelmed, it was probable that she'd missed the mark she thought she'd hit and... well, that would be quite a blow. "You're not saying anything. Why aren't you saying anything? Be honest with me. I can take it."

He took another excruciating moment. "I'm just trying to figure out how to explain to you that this is probably the best piece of chocolate I've ever tasted."

The smile that slipped onto her face started slowly and took a minute to get going. "Really? You're not just trying to be the supportive father, because I could handle it if you were. You can just admit you're being supportive and then tell me if something's missing or too overpowering or—"

"Haven't I always told it to you like it is?"

He had. Always. She blinked. "Yes."

"And this is what it is. You've got something great here. I assume you're going to roll these out at the shop?"

"I'd like to. The plan is to have several different flavor varieties, but this one would be our signature."

"Smart girl. Have you thought of a name for them?"

"I guess Molly's Kickass Truffles might be a little much for our younger customers."

The twinkle in his eye was back. "I think it might. What about naming them after you? MollyDollys."

MollyDolly was the nickname her father had given her when she was little. She moved it around in her mind. "Maybe. You know, that could actually work. It's cute and personal, and it would be a way to have my own stamp on them."

"True."

She smiled at him. "And they'd make me think of you." A lump arrived in her throat as she reflected briefly on his failing health, not a concept she allowed herself to think about too much. Congestive heart failure was a terminal diagnosis. There was still time left, but the days weren't exactly infinite and she felt them flittering away. He was the only parent she'd ever known, as her mother had passed from stage four leukemia when Molly was two and a half. The concept of life without him was a little more than she was willing to consider.

His eyes warmed and he squeezed her hand, clearly picking up on the direction of her thoughts. "Don't you go getting all misty on me. I'm a tough old guy, you know. Not getting rid of me any time soon."

She laughed and swallowed the lump. "I wouldn't dare presume."

A nurse poked her head around the corner into his room. "Mr. O'Brien? A pizza was delivered for you."

He slapped his hands together. "And the day just got even better."

❖

That afternoon at Flour Child brought with it four orders for delivery and a last-minute order of chocolate chip cookies for the clinic to be held for pickup. Molly set the cookies out to cool as Eden packed up the last of the deliveries. For the first time in quite a while, they had their hands full, and Molly liked the adrenaline rush the time crunch brought with it.

She lived for busy. It kept things interesting and gave the cash register a workout in the process. And right about now, dollar signs were her friends.

Her delivery guy, Damon, strolled in casually and consulted the clipboard on the counter. He'd worked part-time for Molly for the past two years and had slowly become part of the Flour Child family. She enjoyed his easygoing rhythm and the rapport he seemed capable of establishing with the clients. So he wasn't the fastest delivery guy on the planet, but many an old lady fell victim to his boyish good looks and placed an extra order or two, just so he'd deliver it. Not exactly bad for business.

However, there was one woman immune to his charm and noticeable biceps, Eden. The two of them went together about as well as oil and water on their most compatible day. They were like Batman and the Joker. Darth Vader and Luke Skywalker. Madonna and Elton John.

Damon leaned across the counter and peered at the stack of boxes. "So what do you got for me?"

Eden glared at him. "That's your greeting? 'What do you got for me?' Sugar, we're busting our asses back here. How about leading with a good afternoon or a hello. Or were you not brought up properly?" Her accent had a way of adding a whole new level of intensity to an insult.

Damon chewed his gum for a few token moments before smiling widely. "Good morning, sunshine." And then he dropped the grin entirely. "Now what have you got for me?"

Eden shook her head and moved to the first group of packages, muttering to herself. "Raised in a barn, I know what I'd *like* to give you."

"Well, that sounds promising," Damon called after her.

"Pig," she shot back.

Molly suppressed an eye roll. It was their daily banter. She'd had to intervene in their battles on more than one occasion when there had been customers present, but she was in too good a mood today to get caught up. Instead she packaged the cookies and took a swipe from the doughy spoon once she finished. Perk of the job.

Eden handed Damon the first order. "All right, now pay attention. A dozen passion fruit tarts and two dozen macadamia brownies to the library for book club."

"Got it."

"Then you're heading to the Allstate office next to the police station and dropping off the chocolate macaroons. Last, you're gonna loop around to the courthouse with the red velvet birthday cake for Judge Saunders. Think you can manage not to screw it up? Or shall I write it in permanent marker across your sweet little forehead?"

He took a step into Eden, eyes flashing. "Sounds pretty tricky. I think I'll just manage." With that, he lifted the stack of pink boxes and breezed through the door nearly colliding with Jordan in the process. He was pressed for time, but apparently not enough to resist giving her an appreciative once-over as she passed.

"Hi," Jordan beamed once she arrived at the counter. "Pickup for Primary Care of Applewood."

Molly was happy to see her. "Hey, you. I figured they'd send Jackson to pick up these piping hot, wonderful cookies."

"I volunteered. Trying to earn a few bonus points with the folks; you know how it is." Jordan's expression then shifted to one of amusement and she eyed Molly strangely.

Instantly self-conscious, she stared back. "What? Why are you looking at me like that?"

"Um." Jordan halfway pointed at her cheek. "Nothing. It's just you have some flour…"

"Oh." She swiped at her cheek aggressively. "Occupational hazard. Did I get it?"

"Wow, no. Not at all. It's pretty much everywhere. Like you've just returned from an all night flour rave and your reward was more flour."

Molly grinned. "Well, I have to have fun somehow."

"I can tell. You look, I don't know…" She shook her head. "Happy. Completely in your element."

"That's because I am. I love days like this. Not a cloud in the sky, the aromas from the oven wafting past every few minutes, and the cash register getting a good workout."

"Who could ask for more?"

They stood a moment, smiling at each other.

It was then that Eden cleared her throat. "Don't mean to interrupt, but I think these might belong to you." She slid a tray of oversized cookies across the counter to Jordan and extended her hand. "Eden Young. I don't think we've met."

"Pleasure. Jordan Tuscana."

"So you're the charmer everybody's talking about. Mr. Lacamore said you jumped his dead car battery yesterday in front of the library."

Jordan shrugged and looked skyward playfully. "I don't know anything about that."

"And modest too. Nice." She swung a dishtowel over her shoulder. "Well, I have some cleaning up to do in the kitchen. See you around, sugar." Eden turned and widened her eyes at Molly as she passed.

Jordan inclined her head in the direction of Eden's retreating form. "She seems fun."

"She is. But don't let the accent fool you. Even the cruelest of jabs can sound gentle with a 'bless her heart' tossed in at the end. It's her most notable skill."

"I'm incredibly jealous."

"Ditto. Will I see you later?"

Jordan made her way to the door. "You will. I'll swing by your place about four to finish the shutters. Maybe we can grab dinner after?"

At Molly's hesitation, Jordan paused and walked suspiciously back to the counter. "What? Don't tell me. You have another date?"

Molly dropped her gaze.

"Oh my, you totally do. You have another hot date to go on." She was grinning playfully, but the d-word alone was enough to make Molly's blood pressure spike at the impending drink she'd agreed to have with yet another stranger. Apparently, Eden's friend Paulene worked fast. The first setup had been difficult enough to muster the courage for. And after that whole traumatic experience, she didn't know how she was going to manage a second go-round. What if it went just as poorly?

"It's not a full date this time," she explained to Jordan. "Just drinks. A half-date. It's stupid, but I'm going and it doesn't need to

be discussed further because now I'm all...I don't know. Damn it."
She stared at the buttons on the cash register, studying their grooves
and attempting not to let herself freak out. Too late. The panic had
already set in, and her heart thudded rapidly in her chest and the
noise in the room was all sorts of deafening.

A minor panic attack. That's all.

She'd had them before and would get through this if she could
just, you know, find more air in the room. It was embarrassing and
she had no reason to get all worked up over a dumb half-date, but
alas, she was.

"Hey, hey. Look at me," Jordan said gently. Molly lifted her
gaze to Jordan who stared back at her with calm, understanding
eyes. "Inhale slowly, okay? Again. And one more time."

And then, Molly could breathe again. She never realized how
much she loved air.

Jordan paused, allowing her a moment to get back on track.
Her voice was quiet, reassuring when she spoke again. "It's okay,
Mol. We don't have to discuss it. But you're going to be okay, all
right? See you at four." And with a quick wink and a beautiful smile,
she was off. Molly stared after her, wondering how with just one
reassuring look and some kind words, Jordan had managed to steady
her lilting ship. Her heart rate slowed and the annoying ringing in
her ears drifted away.

She took another deep, much needed breath and reminded
herself why. Because that's what Jordan did. She made everything
seem within the realm of possibility, even the most enigmatic. It was
her gift. It was the way she approached life and it was contagious. It
had always been that way.

"So *that* was little sister?" Eden began the process of moving
warm oatmeal cookies from the silver tray in her hands to the display
case.

"Uh-huh."

Eden whistled low and Molly regarded her with a long look.

"What? What does that mean? Explain your pointed whistling."

"Well, she's ridiculously dreamy is all. Strikingly beautiful.
A looker. I see what Summer's been going on about now." Eden
picked up the empty tray and sauntered back into the kitchen.

But something about the comment didn't sit well with Molly and she was forced by an act of nature to follow. She pushed open the swinging door and sidled up next to Eden at the sink where she stood washing the tray.

"What do you mean? What did Summer say exactly?" She tried her best to be nonchalant, but wasn't sure how effective she was. So she picked up a mixing bowl and began to wash. Keeping busy would help.

Eden paused in the midst of washing. "Would take less time to tell you what she didn't say, if you catch my drift. Can't say I blame her. I'm straight as the day is long, but I know a gorgeous woman when I see one, and trust me, I just saw one."

"So you're saying Summer's *interested*? In Jordan."

Eden threw her a curious glance. "That's what I'm saying. I'm also saying that if you scrub that bowl any harder, we're gonna have a plate on our hands."

"Huh?"

Eden turned the water off. "It's clean. Give me that." She placed the bowl on the top shelf of the cabinet and turned back to Molly. "You don't like this at all. Just look at you, all worked up and steely eyed."

"What? No. Summer and Jordan can do as they please. I was just curious about the gossip. You always seem to have it all before me. Never fair. How are we doing on apple scones?"

"We're fine. Are you?"

Molly settled in atop the small stepladder. "Of course I am. Jordan is capable of making her own decisions. But if you must know, I happen to think that Summer is all wrong for her and I can't help but feel, I don't know, protective." Molly sighed. "Jordan needs someone caring, someone sensitive who gets her and will let her be who she is. Summer's about as warm and cuddly as a pit viper, and that might even be generous."

Eden grinned at her widely, knowingly even, and it was annoying. "If you say so."

"I do. And don't look at me like that."

Eden snapped her on the backside with a dishtowel as she passed. "You're a complicated woman, Molly O'Brien. But it certainly keeps things interesting around here."

❖

It was after eight when Jordan made it home from Molly's place. Thank God daylight was holding on longer now that they were into spring. The shutters looked great if she did say so herself. It was entirely possible she had a future in home repair. Her arms were a bit sore from painting, and it was plausible she wore home a higher percentage of the dusty blue paint than was actually on the shutters themselves, but it was a worthy cause.

Molly hadn't made an appearance, but it was probably for the best. Watching her glammed up and hopeful as she headed out for the evening with some random woman was a memory she could live without. Though she did hope for Molly's sake that the evening went well. She deserved to be happy, more than anyone she knew. She wanted that for her.

"Hey there, sweetie. You're looking especially...blue." Her mom grinned at her own joke as she stood in front of the microwave heating something in a small dish. No doubt her dinner. She was still wearing her scrubs, which indicated she hadn't been home from the clinic long.

"Yeah, it's a new look I'm trying out. I call it Shutter Smurf. No Dad tonight?"

"He'll be along shortly. Mr. Rubenstein stopped in after closing with pain in his heel. Might be that bone spur acting up again. Your father agreed to stay and take a look."

"Nice of him."

"Some warmed up spaghetti?" Her mother held up the Tupperware bowl from the microwave. She looked tired. The day must have been a long one for her, as were most. Her parents had opened the one and only medical clinic in Applewood eighteen years prior and gave generously of their time to the members of the community. One of the many things she admired about them.

"Give me about thirty minutes and I'll gladly arm wrestle you for some of that, but I think I need a quick shower first." She pushed off the counter and started in the direction of the hall.

"Jordan, before you go..."

"Yeah?"

"You'll notice I put a box in front of your bed with some things for you to go through."

"No problem."

"Some things of Cassie's. We held on to them for you, just in case."

Jordan nodded appreciatively, but didn't say anything because the lump in her throat was in the way.

Her mother's face softened in understanding. "Take some time and see if there's anything you might want to keep for yourself. No rush."

And there it was.

That sinking feeling she got whenever she allowed her mind to acknowledge the accident. It was like all the color in the room faded at the reality check. However, she did her damndest to push through it. "Sure, I'll take a look."

But fifteen minutes later, as she sat on the floor of her childhood bedroom, wet hair from the shower dripping on the carpet, the box a few feet away was a little too daunting. So instead of moving through the items in the box, she stared at it, letting her thoughts travel where they may.

The soccer ball peeking out from on top was familiar to her right off. But it hadn't technically been Cassie's. It was hers, on loan to her sister from the night before Cassie'd left for college in Chicago so many years before.

That night was still so incredibly vivid in her memory. She had been fourteen then and it had been warm out, one of the last lingering days of summer. She was sad at the thought of Cassie leaving home, which had manifested itself into despondency. She'd never been good at dealing with heavy emotion. So instead of sitting around the kitchen table and having one last dinner with her family before Cassie left for school, she'd taken her ball, and without permission, headed to the soccer field at the high school.

The daylight was fading as dusk shifted to night, but she could still make out the lines on the field as she practiced her footwork. Anything not to think about the next day, and what life would be like at home from here forward. Her brother had moved out two years prior, but it hadn't carried the same weight. The age difference was wider, and her relationship with Cassie was, well, different. They did stuff together, played soccer, watched movies, hung out. Okay, sometimes she annoyed Cassie when Molly or her friends were around, but in the scheme of things, that was no big deal.

She'd be all alone now.

Maybe she was acting childish, feeling sorry for herself, whatever. But she couldn't help it. As she dribbled, she felt the tears touch her eyes.

"Don't get ahead of the ball."

She paused and turned at the sound of the voice. "What?"

Cassie stood a few yards behind her, arms folded as she watched, her blond hair pulled back in a ponytail. "Stop doing that. You always get ahead and it screws up your control. If you want to make varsity this year, you have to work off of technique, not just speed and tenacity."

No longer alone, she swallowed the emotion and quickly swiped at her cheek to erase any evidence of shed tears. "Yeah, well, we can't all start our freshman year."

"And that's the second thing that's going to get in your way."

"What?"

"Self doubt. You're good, Jordan. Hell, more than good, but you let your head talk you out of everything."

Jordan nodded, knowing it was true. "It's just that everyone wants me to be you. I can't do that."

"Because you're not me. And anyone who expects that is not seeing how great you are all on your own."

Jordan took in the words, letting them settle. "That's cool of you to say." In that moment, she was feeling all sorts of sad again. She and Cassie had a typical sibling relationship full of daily arguments, hanging out, and lots of mutual interests. Mainly because Jordan looked up to Cassie. A lot.

"Tell you what. You make the team and I'll make sure I'm there for your first game."

"Seriously?"

"Seriously. It's only a two-hour drive. What? Did you think I'd never come home again? It's Chicago, Jordy, not Mars."

"No, it's just awesome that you'd come, you know, for me. My game, I mean."

"Like I'd miss it. Wanna knock it around for a while?"

"Sure." In actuality, nothing could have cheered her up more, but she played it cool. Jordan shot the ball to Cassie and they spent the next half hour passing it back and forth, dribbling up the field as they talked about anything and everything.

"Check in on Molly for me, okay?"

"Definitely." Molly had opted to stay in Applewood after graduation and take more ownership of the bakeshop alongside her dad. It was her lifelong passion, and Jordan couldn't have been more pleased to know that at least she'd still have Molly a few doors down. Not the same as Cassie, but it was still something to hold on to.

"And Mom's going to need you to step up more and help around the house. No running off with your friends after school before checking in with her."

"Okay. I can do that."

"I know. That's why I'm not worried." Cassie smiled and scooped up the ball. *"C'mon. It's dark now and Mom will worry you've run away and joined the circus. Not that you wouldn't fit in there."*

"Shut up."

"Just sayin'. I'm keeping this by the way; you have plenty of other soccer balls."

Cassie had kept her promise and attended the first game that season. They'd won. Jordan stared at the soccer ball and floated slowly back to the present. She shook herself free of the memory and wandered off numbly in search of a hairdryer.

All these years later and she never had measured up to Cassie. Not at school. Not on the soccer field, and definitely not at home. And the sad truth was that she probably never would.

CHAPTER SEVEN

Uncorked, the swanky little wine bar her date had selected, was half full when Molly arrived shortly before eight o'clock. She'd driven a good thirty minutes to Summitville, a moderately sized town that seemed to have a lot on Applewood in terms of sophistication. She could see herself spending more time in this neck of the woods, you know, if this whole thing were to work out. And it could work out. There was actually a tiny chance of that, she reminded herself, trying desperately to remain optimistic.

The lighting was fairly dim, but she was able to scan the tables for any sign of Diane, who purported to have dark red hair cut just shy of her shoulders. She didn't see anyone who fit that description, but she did pause momentarily on the man and woman feeding each other strawberries in the corner booth. Show-offs. But she couldn't help smiling at the cozy picture.

Easing into a table nestled in the heart of the room, Molly took a deep breath and waived the waiter off until her date arrived. Since she was only planning on one drink that night, she would wait so they could have it together over some getting-to-know-you conversation. That's how it worked, right? She was pretty sure at least.

But when eight twenty rolled around, she started to get a little restless. Eight thirty had her beginning to feel sorry for herself, and by eight forty, she was reaching for her bag and car keys just in time for a hand to land on her shoulder from behind.

"You must be Molly. My apologies for keeping you waiting."

She blinked a couple of times. Dark red hair. "Um, yes. Diane?"

"A pleasure to meet you. So sorry I'm late. I was with a client and couldn't get away. I'm normally quite punctual."

"Not a problem." She could get past the delay. Not a big deal in the scheme of life. A little rude, but not a total deal breaker. Plus, she liked the mention of the word client. Seemed corporate. Established. Sturdy.

"Tell you what, I'll buy you a drink to make up for it. What would you like?"

"Um…maybe a dry sav blanc?"

"Done." She signaled the waiter and ordered two glasses of wine, impressing Molly with plenty of pleases and thank yous in the process. Points for manners. Nice.

Drinks arrived, and after some initial small talk about the town and the weather, Molly decided to jump right in and get the real conversation rolling. So far, all seemed very promising and the drink was beginning to relax her. "So, Diane, you mentioned a client. What is it that you do?"

"I see the future."

Molly nearly choked on her wine. "So sorry. I'm not sure I heard you correctly. What did you say?"

Diane made a slow twirly gesture in the air. "I witness the future. In my mind. Then I meet with individuals who need guidance and channel all of the energies around them to read what lies ahead, in essence, their future. Pretty cool, huh?"

"Oh. Yes. So you're a psychic?"

"I prefer the term seer."

"Seer? All right. That sounds so interesting and…unique." Do not judge. Do not judge. Do not judge. The chant in her head was all that was holding her neutral facial expression firmly in place. That and the fact that she was brought up to be polite.

"It is. You see, energy is very important to me and I'm picking up lots of positive energy from you right now. In fact, I see this evening going very well."

Molly couldn't be sure, but she thought Diane's left eyelid was twitching.

"You do? Well, that's good news." She sipped her wine for no other reason than it would buy her time before she had to figure out what to say. Luckily, Diane grabbed the reins.

"Have you ever met with a seer before? Invested the time in exploring what lies ahead for you?"

"Hmm. No, I can't say I have." Yep, definite twitching going on.

"I can do a demonstration for you right now."

"Oh, you know what? We don't have to. Why don't we just enjoy the evening and—"

"Listen to my words carefully." Molly swallowed and listened obediently as Diane was now leaning into her space rather aggressively and speaking in a low-pitched voice. *Not at all creepy. Not at all creepy. Not at all creepy.* "In less than a minute, our waiter will stop by and check on us."

"Okay."

"Are you listening?"

"So listening." And she was because she was scared to death not to.

"Marking my words?"

"Marked." But really, it was a small place and their waiter had just visibly emerged from the kitchen moments before the whole proclamation. The odds were pretty much in Diane's favor.

The moment was upon them. The waiter approached. Diane shot her a knowing look just as he passed their table for one two down.

In response to the misstep, Diane rubbed her left temple rhythmically, and was that humming? Oh, baby Jesus it was. She was humming. Fantastic. Molly tried to ignore the inquisitive stare from the guy next to her, but what she really wanted to do was get the hell out of there because the humming was growing in volume and intensity.

"He's going to pause here on his way back to the kitchen. I can see the vision more clearly now."

But he didn't.

In fact, their waiter didn't shoot them so much as a glance for the next fifteen minutes, because he was probably as freaked out as

Molly was. Luckily, to fill the gap, Diane proceeded to forecast all sorts of exciting things that were definitely going to happen to Molly in the coming months including taking a trip, spending quality time with a loved one, and falling in love most unexpectedly. All fairly generic, though probable mentions. Well, except the love one. Turns out that one wasn't probable at all.

Molly stood, feigning reluctance. "Well, this has been fun, but I think I better get going."

"So soon? I haven't even shown you my crystals yet."

"Oh no. That is a shame, but I'm not feeling so great." Not a total lie. Her mood had taken a nose-dive and she was desperately in need of a large bowl of chocolate ice cream and her cozy gray sweatpants so she could feel appropriately pathetic about her new job, mayor of Loserville.

Diane took a step in. "Well, can I get your number? This has been just great. One of the best dates I've had in a while."

Molly sighed through her smile.

❖

Rover made three lazy laps around the fishbowl. Molly watched hopelessly, her face resting in her palm next to the glass. She was back from her date. It was just after ten and she was now home alone on a Friday night, the way she'd be for the rest of her pitiful life.

A spinster.

"Well, at least we have each other," she said solemnly to Rover, who chose that exact moment to swim away from her to the other side of the bowl. "Traitor," she mumbled, pushing herself up and wandering aimlessly into the kitchen. There was ice cream in there and copious amounts of it too.

Her thoughts drifted to where they usually did when she needed to feel better about things. "What'd you think of my date, Cass? I imagine you got a few laughs out of that. You have to give her points for originality." She stared at the carton in front of her. Cassie used to scoop the ice cream for her when she was depressed. And now she was older than Cassie ever would be. Sobering.

She missed her old life. When she had someone to come home to, discuss her day with, and to pick her up when she was low and laugh with when she wasn't. Life had been good then. Yes, they'd had their share of problems and there had been some arguments about the future and kids, but eventually they'd have figured it all out...if it weren't for the crash.

She believed that. Just as she believed they were robbed of what should have been their life together.

Molly took a bite of the double chocolate crunch, blinking back the tears in her eyes for only a minute before giving in and letting them fall in a ridiculous cascade down her face. Great. Now she was pathetic *and* emotional. Such a catch. With a lump in her throat, she continued eating her ice cream. Hell, maybe she'd gain another six pounds.

But you know what? That wasn't right. She set down her spoon with purpose. It wasn't fair to sell herself short and call it quits on any kind of meaningful existence because of a couple of horrible dates.

She decided to look at things another way.

She needed to get out there and have some fun. Take control of things. And damn it, she was going to start right now. She scanned the room for the remote control to her stereo system and stalked over to it on a mission now.

A flick of her wrist brought the living room to life with the vibrant sounds of some artist on the radio she'd never heard of. But the music was fast. It was loud. It was current, and she danced. She danced with a wild abandon she'd never felt before, moving across the room in a flurry, bopping her head, arms in the air, the music moving through her.

And it was good.

She felt alive, vibrant...dizzy. Whoa, okay, so maybe one too many turns around the sofa. Perhaps if she stood here for a moment, the room would stop spinning and that ringing would quiet down. That's when it registered that it was her phone that was ringing. Yes, definitely her phone. She located it just in time, glancing quickly at the readout before answering.

"Hey, Jordan."

"Oh, hey. Wasn't expecting you to answer. I was just planning on leaving a voice mail." And then in a hushed voice, "Oh, and sorry if I'm interrupting your half-date."

Molly looked around her empty kitchen. "Nope. No interruption happening here. Just maniacal dancing. What's up?"

"Um…just wanted to make sure you thought the shutters came out okay. I finished them up earlier. So when you get home, check them out and let me know."

It had been dark when she'd returned home, but how had she missed this? "Hang on. Let me take a look." She scurried down her front porch and across the sidewalk a bit. The luminous moon lit up the front of the house nicely. She took a breath. "Oh, Jordan, they're gorgeous." She placed her hand over her heart because they were. The fresh blue offered a perfect contrast to the white stone. It was amazing what just a small pick-me-up had done for her little house. Gone was the chipped paint and limp structure. The shutters were good as new, and Molly laughed at the obvious metaphor for her life. The shutters, as crazy as it seemed, gave her hope.

"So you're happy? I've earned my keep?"

"And more. Thank you. I needed this."

A pause. "Hey, you okay?"

Molly nodded into the phone. "I will be. Kind of a crazy night."

"In what way?"

She sighed. "Let's see, there was supernatural suspense, an overindulgence in ice cream, a self-involved fish, the crazy dancing previously mentioned. Oh, and I cried. I shouldn't forget the pathetic crying. Yeah, that about covers it."

"I'm coming over."

"No, you're not. I'm back together again. Promise. You do not need to come over."

"Yes, I do. There's ice cream."

Molly couldn't contain her smile, suddenly feeling not so alone. "There is ice cream."

❖

Jordan knocked on Molly's door ten minutes later. The nearly full moon poured light across the porch and the word "welcome" glowed brightly from the doormat. It was a peaceful night on the sleepy street, and the shadows the moon created played softly in the trees.

She'd spent the evening shooting the breeze at The Owl Tree with the bartender, Little Bobby, her closest buddy from high school. Little Bobby, six feet three inches and two hundred and ten pounds, wasn't really little at all, but he was named after his father and the town had to differentiate. She'd been having a good time catching up with many of the locals and could have stayed there most of the night if it hadn't been for the obvious emotion in Molly's voice.

It was clear she could use a friend, and Jordan didn't like the idea of her alone and depressed. So she'd dropped a ten on the bar for Little Bobby and abandoned the second half of her beer.

It was only a few moments before Molly appeared at the door. She was smiling, but the semi-red eyes indicated that all was not as well as she tried to play off. She wore gray yoga pants, a light blue T-shirt, and had pulled her hair up into a ponytail.

"You didn't have to come, you know. I'm sure you were wrapped up in something way more exciting and I've gone and ruined it."

Jordan followed her in. "I think your idea of my life is a lot more exciting than the actual reality of it."

"You're trying to make me feel better."

"A little. But it also happens to be true. So why the rough night? I take it the date didn't go so well."

"If you like lunatics it did."

"Oh no."

"Oh yes."

"Tell me about it now or later?"

"Definitely later."

"Done. But I feel strongly that we should take advantage of this opportunity."

Molly plopped onto the couch and pulled her feet underneath her in the most adorable move. "What opportunity is that?"

"The feel-sorry-for-ourselves, veg-out-on-the-couch opportunity, of course. They don't come along all that often. I'm boldly suggesting a movie. I love movies."

"I'm aware. People pay you to make them."

"Oh, you noticed. Can I check out your collection?"

"I'm not sure I could stop you." But she was smiling so Jordan pressed on to the shelf lined with DVDs and perused. "You actually have quite an impressive little group here. I never would have guessed."

"I feel there's a veiled insult in there somewhere."

"Not true." She held up the case for *The Godfather*. "Did you know Sofia Coppola appeared in this film as Michael's baby daughter in the christening scene?"

"I do now, movie person."

"Hey, are you feeling dark and violent or sweet and heartwarming?"

"I'm feeling dark and violent, so maybe sweet and heartwarming as a counteragent?"

"Great idea." She selected a DVD. "Eighties gold. Do you approve?"

Molly sat up straighter to read the title. "*Say Anything*. Perfect."

They settled in on the couch and watched as everyman Lloyd Dobler did his damndest to woo the smart girl in school. At several points, Jordan stole glances at Molly who seemed lost in the story, laughing and sighing appropriately at all the classic moments. As the credits scrolled, Molly pushed herself up into a sitting position, a dreamy expression on her face. "Can I just say that I love that movie? *That's* how it's supposed to be. Organic. You meet someone, fall for them, and do anything and everything to make it work, against all the odds and then…you know, live happily ever after."

Jordan smiled, enjoying the light that had sparked into Molly's eyes. "That's the idea."

Molly lifted the remote and turned off the TV. She stared pensively at the blank screen before turning back to Jordan. "But it never works out that way, you know? And I want it to. I want the movie."

"What was your favorite part?

Molly thought a moment. "I love that no one would have ever put them together. But they fit. In spite of the obstacles tossed in their way. Now you."

"Um, the big gesture. Radio in the air, heart on his sleeve, vulnerable as hell. It gets me every time." Because no one had ever done anything like that for her.

Molly stared. "I love how big a softie you are. Everyone thinks you're so tough, throwing elbows on the soccer field."

"That was only twice."

"But you're a complete romantic, you know that?"

Jordan looked skyward in jest. "I have no idea what you're talking about."

They laughed and then the room fell silent. "It makes me think of Cass and me. That movie. They're young, in love. Everything's easy."

Jordan's stomach tightened and the words tumbled out of her mouth before she could stop them. "But it wasn't always perfect. Between the two of you."

Molly's eyes widened slightly. "No, it wasn't. But it was love. We were in love. And now…"

"You look sad again."

She raised a shoulder. "I just think I'll never have that again. No one will ever love me in the same way."

"Don't say that."

"Well, it's true. I want to be with someone who lights up when I walk in the room, who wants to stay at home and cook pizza together and get in water balloon fights on the Fourth of July. But that person doesn't exist for me. At least not anymore." The emotion in her eyes was raw now, and Jordan, damn it, hated that.

"Hey," she said quietly, needing to do something, anything to help. "Come here." She moved to Molly who fell easily against her and held on, finally letting go of her emotion.

They stood like that for several long moments before Molly stepped back, slowly brushed away the stray tears, and took a calming breath. "Well, that was…completely indulgent."

"No, it wasn't. And you'll find love again. Just as soon as the time is right."

But that seemed to just garner another look of hopelessness. "It's worse than you think. I have two gray hairs and I've gained six pounds. Did you hear that? *Six pounds*."

"I'm going to level with you, Molly. You've never looked so good." Damn it, it was the truth. She was positively stunning and sexy for days, as much as Jordan wished to God she wasn't.

"Don't look at me like that. I don't need your pity looks."

But all Jordan could do was look at Molly. At how soft and thick her hair looked, at her incredibly long eyelashes, and then there was the generosity of her mouth. She wasn't sure what pushed her into action, but in that moment there had seemed like no other action to take. Before Jordan fully realized what she was doing, she leaned in and captured that mouth with her own.

And the result was so achingly wonderful that she lost herself.

It was a simple kiss and the warm press of her lips against Molly's only lasted a moment, but it was enough to push her into a haze of longing. As she pulled away, she found herself looking into Molly's eyes and the tiny traces of gold that danced in the brown.

❖

Hold the phone. Jordan had just kissed her.

As Molly stood in her living room, staring in utter surprise into vibrant blue eyes, that was the only thought her mind was capable of producing. *Jordan had kissed her.*

And though her intellect wasn't exactly working at the moment, her body seemed to be firing on all cylinders and had definite ideas on the topic, as the next thing she knew, she slid her hands into Jordan's long, dark hair and pulled her back in, meeting her mouth eagerly, searchingly and then some.

It was explosive. That was the word for it, explosive in so many ways.

Jordan responded immediately, her hands moving to Molly's waist and then pulling her in firmly. Once her lips parted, Jordan eased her tongue into the warmth of her mouth and she felt the results everywhere. Her heart raced and a dull ache moved from her center downward with alarming speed.

It wasn't enough.

She aggressively walked Jordan backward toward the sofa, breaking the kiss for only a heartbeat as she eased Jordan into a seated position and followed her down, straddling her lap and settling her mouth decidedly on Jordan's once again. It was a runaway train that continued to pick up speed, and she couldn't help but let it roll on. It was crazy, breathless, and Molly lost track of everything.

That's when hands began to move.

Jordan's were first and settled on the small of her back before slipping under her T-shirt to the skin beneath. Her insides fluttered at the contact and she felt herself pushing desperately against Jordan's stomach as the aching escalated. All the while, her mouth savored every moment of the tantalizing kiss. The flash of desire was staggering and her hands drifted from Jordan's face, to her neck, down her collarbone to her breasts. At the briefest of touch, Jordan took in air, pulling her mouth away. Her breathing was ragged, her eyes unfocused. "Wait a second, Mol. Wait."

And it all came crashing down.

At the sound of Jordan's voice, reality infused Molly's conscious thought and she tumbled back to the land of the present, the land of rational, and the land of what the hell? "Oh my God," she whispered. "What just happened?" She moved off of Jordan and backed away as if she'd been burned. She ran her fingers through her hair because she didn't quite know what else to do to erase the past three minutes. But somehow she had to erase them.

Jordan watched her from the couch. "Calm down. It's okay."

"It's *not* okay. It's not okay at all. You're Cassie's sister. You're Jordan, who's like ten years old. You're a child."

"I haven't been ten in a long time. We're both adults, Molly."

"You have to go."

Jordan stood and held up her hands. "Okay. I'll go. But please don't blow this out of proportion. Nothing unrecoverable happened here. We kissed. It happens."

"And it was a mistake." God, it was a mistake. What had she been thinking? What was wrong with her?

Jordan stared at her for a beat and then nodded once, her expression unreadable. "We'll just pretend this didn't happen then."

"Exactly. Because it *never* should have." She crossed her arms in front of her defensively and watched as Jordan made her way silently to the door. Alone in her living room, she sank in the chair as a multitude of self-recriminations surfaced and swirled.

She'd acted impulsively. She'd betrayed Cassie with her sister. She'd forever ruined her friendship with Jordan. And God, for a very brief time, she'd enjoyed it.

That was the part that upset her most of all.

Chapter Eight

W hat does a man have to do to get his coffee made to his liking?" Mr. Jeffries held his cup across the counter, just shy of Molly's chin. She took a breath because, man, she was not in the mood for him this morning. Channeling her inner Donna Reed, she forced a polite smile.

"I'm sorry, Mr. Jeffries. What exactly is wrong with your coffee?"

"Only one sweetener. I take two packets in my coffee. Everyone knows that."

This was true. She'd made his coffee every day for as long as she could remember, and she'd never once screwed up. But having not slept at all the night prior had her grappling for focus. "Sorry about that. But in good news, it's easily remedied." She took his cup and added the additional packet of sweetener. "Here you go. And tomorrow's is on the house."

"Well, it's the least you could do. Don't you think?" He shook his head in disgust and walked back to his favorite table. "Of all things," he muttered angrily to himself. Twenty minutes later, Mr. Jeffries placed his hat on his head and took off for home, leaving the place customer free. Molly slid into a booth and rested her cheek in her hand.

"You okay, sugar?" Eden wiped down the now vacant table. "You look a little glazed over."

Molly couldn't disagree. It'd been a rough twelve hours. She'd played back the night prior with Jordan a hundred times and still had very little understanding of how it could have happened. Those thoughts had kept her tossing and turning until it was time to head into work. Now, in desperation, she decided to seize the opportunity to talk it out. "Could we chat a minute in the kitchen?"

"You bet we can. Louise, sweetie, will you watch the counter for me?"

Louise didn't even glance up from the Pennysaver. "On it."

Once safely behind the swinging door, Molly pushed herself up onto the counter and stared hard at Eden. "Have you ever done something that you'd give anything to take back?"

A smile spread across her face. "Oh, I think I'm gonna like this."

Molly exhaled impatiently. "Shut up and focus. This is hardcore serious. Have you?"

Eden thought for a moment. "Sure, sweetheart. Of course I have. Let's see. I wish I'd never married Carl, the two-timing idiot from Oklahoma who stole my Chevy in the middle of the night."

Molly shook her head slowly. "I don't even know what to say to that. I think your life is a perpetual country music song."

"Call it whatever you will, but the cops caught up with him in Tuscaloosa and threw his sorry ass in jail. Wonder which one of us is crying now?"

"Again, just further proving my point."

Eden winked and slid herself up onto the counter across from Molly. "I guess you're right. Now you. What horrible thing do you regret doing?"

"Okay, but if I tell you this, it cannot leave this room. You have a tendency to share things with the free world, and while I love you anyway, this cannot be one of those things. Do you understand me, Eden Young? Top secret."

Eden seemed to sober at the serious tone in Molly's voice. "Of course, darlin'. You have my word. This stays between us."

Molly stared at the floor. "I kissed Jordan last night. Well, technically she kissed me, but then I made it worse and there was lots more kissing."

Eden's eyes were wide when Molly looked up and her mouth fell slowly open. "Well, color me impressed. Little Molly Hot Pants."

Molly pushed herself off of the counter and moved to Eden in a rush. "No, uh-uh. Don't say that. There can be no glorification in what happened."

Eden seemed confused. "So it was bad? The kissing?"

"No, that's not what we're talking about. I'm a horrible person. That's the main idea here. She's Cassie's little sister, Eden. A cosmic rule has been broken here. You don't kiss the sister. Ever."

"What if the sister is wildly attractive? Is there a clause for that?"

"Irrelevant."

Eden stared at her, clearly confused. "Let me make sure I understand. It's not that you don't like Jordan; it's that she's related to Cassie. Did Cassie hate Jordan or something?"

"What? No, of course not. It just feels wrong, what happened. And I don't know how to fix it. Tell me you know how. I need guidance here."

"I don't know that you *need* to fix it. Little sister is hot and Cassie would want you to be happy. Maybe this little spark is something worth exploring."

Molly couldn't believe the lunacy of what she was hearing. "You're crazy. Absolutely zero chance of that happening. But I can't avoid her forever and I don't want to. We have fun together, and things feel, I don't know, better since she's been home. A lot."

"Well, then you're going to have to be a big girl about this. Face her head on. Talk about what happened and get it out there on the table. Take the bull by the horns."

Molly nodded, marinating on the advice. "Take the bull by the horns. Got it. I just have to summon my courage and face her. Put everything on the table and get things back to normal."

"Or put *her* on the table and—"

"Eden!" Molly shouted, appalled.

The door opened and Louise held a ticket in the air. "Delivery called in for the clinic's staff meeting. Two dozen bombshell brownies. Damon should be back from the high school drop-off soon."

"Um, that's okay." Molly grabbed the ticket from Louise nonchalantly. "I can deliver this one."

"That-a-girl," Eden said. "By the horns."

She nodded and rolled her shoulders, warrior style.

She could do this. It didn't have to be that big a deal. She'd seen *Days of Our Lives*. People kissed all the time. She'd survive this.

❖

It took a certain amount of patience to work in the medical profession, and it consistently amazed Jordan how her family was able to do it. That morning alone, they'd treated upward of twenty-five patients with appointments, and another eight walk-ins. And instead of scooping up their prescription and heading out, they all wanted to chat about their week, their son, their wife, or how many football games the high school was on track to win this year.

Not only was it exhausting, it was starting to back up the schedule Jordan was put in charge of monitoring. She'd decided that while she was in town she would help out at the clinic as much as possible, and with a missing receptionist, she saw her opportunity. She could hang at the clinic for a few hours each day. She'd missed her family, and this was a great way to maybe reconnect, make up for the time she'd stayed away. So she was a rather successful producer in the film industry, she wasn't above answering a few phones for the dueling doctors.

"What's up, tiger?" Mikey asked, after saying good-bye to his latest patient. He pulled her ear as he passed behind the desk. Her brother practiced at a medical group in Andersville, but devoted two days a week to working in their parents' clinic. Good thing too, as having a third doctor in-house helped alleviate some of the pressure on their parents. Mikey was a good guy that way.

"Ow. Leave my ears alone."

"No way. As your brother, it's my job in life to tug on your ears. What's up next?" He leaned on the counter as Jordan consulted the computerized appointment book.

"You have Mrs. Fitzsimmons' sore throat at noon and then the staff meeting after lunch. That's when I make my crafty getaway. Jackson can take the desk."

"What? You don't want to hang out for clinic policies and procedures?"

"Sounds riveting, but I'm a volunteer. This right here"—she gestured to the room around her—"is out of the goodness of my heart."

"So benevolent."

Jordan grinned proudly. "Get it while you can."

The bell above the door rang and they turned. Jordan expected to see yet another patient or maybe Damon with the delivery they'd called in for the staff meeting. But she was wrong.

Molly's eyes held hers only briefly before fluttering to Mikey. "Hey, you two. What's with all the standing around? Shouldn't there be some work getting done around here?" She smiled at them, but it didn't quite take over her face the way Molly's smiles usually did.

When Jordan had left Molly's house the night before, she'd walked the neighborhood, working through the sequence of events. As many times as she'd imagined kissing Molly, the reality of it, of her, had been so much more than she'd ever planned on. She didn't know what had come over her and caused her to actually act on her impulse, but she did know that as their lips met, all bets seemed off.

Everything had faded away except for the sharp need that left her wonderfully breathless. She could still feel what it was like to have Molly's lips on hers, the weight of her on her lap, the intoxicating scent of the raspberry shampoo she used.

The exchange had rocked her. And though it had ended horribly, she couldn't quite get past the fact that for a few precious moments, Molly had kissed her back. In even more impressive news, she was probably the world's best kisser.

But as she'd walked on, she'd remembered Molly's words and the conviction with which she'd said them. *"It's not okay. You're*

Cassie's sister." And no matter how exciting those few moments had been, she could never change the facts in the scenario. Molly couldn't see her for who she was, only her connection to Cassie.

Mikey moved to Molly and kissed her cheek with a loud smack. "What is this? Have we moved up in the world? Since when does the esteemed owner of Flour Child personally deliver to little old us?"

"I make exceptions for special people." She handed him the pink box of brownies. "Out of the oven ten minutes ago. Still warm and amazing."

"You're my favorite sister-in-law. Have I told you that?"

"First time today."

"Then I'm slacking." He inclined his head to the break room. "I'll drop these off on my way to catch up on my charts. Thanks, Molly."

"No problem."

And they were alone.

Molly eyed her a moment. There was that slight smile again. "So, hey. How are you this morning, Jordan? I trust you're well."

I trust you're well? Were they now characters in a Jane Austen novel and she'd failed to be notified? Since when did they speak so formally to each other? Oh, this didn't bode well. "I'm fine. Just a little worried about the fact that you're talking to me like we're at high tea."

Molly exhaled and shook her head. "I know. That was weird. Agreed. But I don't want to be weird. Listen, Jordan, I don't know how we wound up…"

"Making out on the couch," Jordan supplied, when it was clear Molly couldn't actually say the words.

She winced. "Right. God. I don't know how that happened. Trust me, I fully accept my share of the blame, but I think we can both agree that it was a really bad idea." Jordan nodded because she could tell it was what Molly needed. "And the last thing in the world that I want is for things to be awkward between us. We're important to each other and I need that."

"I promise, nothing has to be weird. It's just me. Same old Jordan."

Molly held her gaze steadily and Jordan watched as those caramel eyes slowly softened. "Yeah, it is." The moment lingered, and no one said anything until Molly seemed to shake herself out of whatever trance had wrapped around them. "So we're okay, then? Business as usual?"

Jordan lifted a shoulder and regarded her seriously. "Unless you plan to renege on our baked goods arrangement. Then we have problems."

Massive relief washed across Molly's face. "No, I think I can come through on that one. Oh, and come by the bakeshop tomorrow. I want you to try something."

"You're on."

It was still there, Jordan noted. That crackle between them that had emerged so aggressively the night before, was still simmering just below the surface. She would ignore it if that's what Molly wanted, but that didn't make it any less real.

Molly gestured behind her to the door. "I guess I better get back to work."

"See you soon."

"Uh, yeah. Tomorrow." Molly nodded once and headed out into the world as Jordan watched after her.

So they'd go on like before. It meant stuffing the off-the-charts chemistry they'd discovered back in the box, but she could do that to keep from scaring Molly away altogether.

Because that wasn't an option.

❖

There was a chill in the air that was unseasonable for April. Some sort of cold front had blown in from up North. Molly pulled her hoodie more fully around her and shoved her hands into the pockets.

It was Wednesday, which meant she'd spend the late afternoon at the cemetery after work. After arranging some fresh flowers, she updated Cassie on the week's happenings and all the preparations for the big birthday party coming up.

"I also went on another date this week. I know. What was I thinking? You would have loved this one, by the way. If nothing else, I have a good story to tell one day." She leaned back on her elbows and stared at the sky. "I'm just looking for that click, you know? The one we had. And that doesn't just happen every day. So maybe it's okay that I'm picky. I should probably just be patient and someone nice will eventually drift along. If not, that's okay too."

It was a relief to talk things out with Cassie. Even if she did do all the talking. Wednesdays had a way of centering her when nothing else worked, bringing the world into some sort of manageable focus.

Wednesdays mattered to her.

Molly stayed for an extra half hour that day. She didn't bring up what had happened with Jordan in her living room. Nor did she mention the subsequent time they'd spent together or the ever-present tugging. Because to do so would give it more credit than it deserved. Talking about it on their Wednesday afternoon would make it real, and it wasn't. It was a minor blip on the radar. And this particular blip would soon be firmly behind them.

Chapter Nine

Molly glanced up as Eden sauntered into the kitchen and stared. "Did you invite an army of starving people over or do you just need a chocolate fix worthy of the *Guinness Book*?" She surveyed the truffle-covered countertops of the bakeshop's kitchen with a hand on her hip.

Molly went back to work. "Neither." She was on a mission and couldn't be deterred. It was the end of the workday, but she didn't care. She had to keep going.

"When you ducked back here to do a little work, I had no idea what you were embarking upon. This is a little crazy town, sugar. I'm not sure our refrigerators can hold this many truffles."

"I bake when I'm stressed, okay? It's a thing."

"Then you must be a stone's throw from a breakdown."

"It's been that kind of week is all. My dad's been depressed; business is hit and miss. Oh, and then the unforgettable blind date that I have you to thank for."

"Mhmm. And that's all that's got your mind scrambling?"

"Yep."

"All right. We can play that way. So what are we going to do with all of these?"

"You and Louise can take some home along with the copies of the recipe I laid out for each of you. I want you up to date on our latest menu item. Some will go to my dad, the Tuscanas, and then the leftovers can get us started on the inventory we'll take with us to the festival."

Eden snagged a truffle and took a generous bite. Molly watched as her eyes widened in delight as she sank into the taste. "You did it," she finally whispered. "You really did it."

Molly couldn't help the grin. "They're good, aren't they?"

"Best I've ever had and I know chocolate. Woo-hoo!" She offered Molly a high five and their customary hip bump.

"What's all this?" Louise asked as she entered the kitchen.

"Molly's stressed so she's baking for the free world."

"Because of Jordan? Nothing wrong with a little kissing, MollyDolly. You're only young and sexy once. Wish I'd remembered that when I was your age. I should have slept around more."

Molly gasped and shot Eden an accusatory stare. "You didn't? Eden Young, you're going to die. You have no concept of discretion."

"What? Louise doesn't count. She's bakeshop family. You don't keep things from the bakeshop family."

Molly glared harder. "By that logic, maybe we should notify Damon too. Where's the phone?"

Louise shook her head. "No need. I told him this afternoon when he picked up the muffins."

Molly glared. "Fabulous."

"They *were* pretty good muffins." Louise headed back out to the counter.

"Maybe we should just run my life by committee." Molly threw her hands in the air and went back to rolling truffles while Eden considered this.

"You'd definitely have more fun. Now that you're actually talking about it, did you smooth things over with little miss Jordan?"

"Yeah, we're fine."

"Your voice is flat. Sweetie, it's hard to believe you when sound like a pancake."

Molly stilled her hands, but kept her eyes on the bowl of cocoa powder. Her resolve to remain tightlipped was weakening. "When I went to talk to Jordan today, almost everything went exactly how I wanted it to."

"But something didn't. What didn't go according to plan?"

Molly sighed, finally turning fully to Eden and lowering her voice. "My eyes kept doing this thing where they'd dip down to her mouth and there was…"

"What? There was what?"

She lowered her voice even more. "This little tug. The whole time I'm talking to her, there's this pulling right in the center of my stomach." She shook her head at Eden. "I don't know what it is, but it's never been there before and now I need to find its off switch."

"Don't you dare turn it off. Run with it, sugar, like you've never run before. Sew your wild oats with the attractive young thing that's just sashayed into town. I've worked here for over three years and I'm ready to see you get back up on that horse, and this is the first time I've ever seen you near one."

"Yeah, that's not gonna happen with Jordan. She's important. I can survive a little tugging."

Louise stuck her head in. "Don't want to interrupt, Molly, but Jordan's up front to see you."

Eden grinned widely. "Let the tugging begin."

❖

"So you're telling me I helped make this little wonder of wonders happen?" Jordan held up a truffle and grinned. There was sincere happiness written all over her at having contributed, and Molly couldn't help but smile back.

"That's exactly what I'm saying and that's why I wanted to personally introduce you. It was your suggestion that got me there." In addition to the truffle Jordan was eating, Molly'd presented her with a pink box full to take with her to show her gratitude.

They were sitting alone in a booth by the window. Eden and Louise had quickly said their good-byes as soon as they'd finished with closing.

"So what's the plan now? For the MollyDollys. I like the name, by the way. Entirely fitting."

"Thanks, you. The plan is to make these little guys my superstars. Push them every chance I get. Debut them at the festival. Hope for large orders. Maybe even set up a way to take mail orders via the Web down the road. And then see if any of it makes a difference."

Jordan nodded but her eyes held concern. "And if they don't?"

"Then things get harder."

A pause. "Are you going to lose the shop?"

Molly leaned back against the booth and took a moment before answering. "Probably." God, she'd never admitted that to anyone. But she trusted Jordan, and somehow it felt okay. "I guess these truffles are my version of a Hail Mary pass in the fourth quarter. I just have to put them out there and hope to generate some buzz, even if it's just temporary."

"Have you thought about taking out a second mortgage on the place?"

"Been there, done that." She lifted her shoulder. "This is it, Jordan. I either get my head above water, or close up shop for good. And time is ticking."

Jordan shook her head. "You can't close down. That would kill you, Molly. You love this place."

It was true, and the thought generated a wave of emotion. "Which is why I'm not giving up. Flour Child is my connection to my family. It's my father's legacy, and one day, I'm going to be without him." Her eyes filled at the thought. "But I don't want to be without his shop, you know?"

Jordan took a deep breath. "Then you won't be." She looked around. "You know, things are getting entirely too heavy in here. Let's go."

Molly eyed her suspiciously. "And where are we going? I have more truffles to make for the festival."

"Plenty of time for that, and let's be honest, the truffles aren't going anywhere. Let's take a walk. I haven't had a chance to check out the town much, see what's new since I've been gone."

She had to admit it sounded nice. The sun was setting and the temperature would be crisp. She liked crisp. And she liked walks. "Okay, but I can't be gone too long."

"I know. Can you even imagine what would happen if you were?"

"Shut up."

"Okay, as long as we're walking."

They took the long way through the square, and Molly narrated a bit, describing the new businesses that had popped up in recent years. "Oh, and right here outside of County Market, we have our very own, wait for it, Redbox." She held up her hands as if to say "tada." "Tell me you're not impressed at our consumer progress."

"Color me shocked." Jordan shook her head. "God, it's all so different and yet not at all."

They passed Mr. Mueller, the mail carrier, just across the street. He must have been headed home for the day. As they waved, he offered a double take and came right over. "Jordy Tuscana. Well, look at you. A knockout if I ever saw one. Who would have thought that scraggly kid would grow up so well?" He pulled her into a warm embrace.

Jordan smiled at him that dazzling way she smiled at people. "Thanks. You're holding up pretty great yourself. How's Dustin? I miss him."

He smiled a little brighter at the mention of his son, a friend of hers from high school. "Just promoted to junior partner at the firm in Chicago. I'll tell him I saw you. Glad you're home. Say hi to your folks for me."

"Will do, Mr. Mueller. It was nice seeing you."

Molly shook her head as they walked on.

"What?"

"Everyone loves you. It's foregone. Some sort of cosmic rule."

Jordan smiled widely. "Well, of course."

That earned her a pointed nudge in the ribs. "Ow."

"Oh, please. Where to now?"

Jordan looked around, plotting their next move. "The soccer field?"

"Okay. A nostalgic glimpse of the glory days coming right up." Molly had to admit that she was feeling lighter. It turned out she needed to get out of the shop. She just hadn't realized it. Plus, the town seemed to sparkle extra bright today. Maybe it was just spending time with Jordan and putting things back in place between them. Who knew?

But it didn't matter. The sun was making its descent in the sky and the cooler temperature had her energized, up for anything. And with Jordan, you never knew what you were in for.

Ten minutes later, they arrived on the very pristine soccer field. The high school went to great lengths to keep it in tiptop condition, and the wide expanse of green grass was quite picturesque. Jordan put her hands on her hips and blew out a breath. "Totally and completely surreal to be standing here right now. Whoa."

Molly had to agree. She came out for a lot of the high school football games to support her alma mater, but soccer was somehow harder. It had been Cassie's passion, and without her, it had just seemed empty. Standing there with Jordan, however, carried with it a whole different purpose. She was a vibrant presence, and Molly felt the effect of her proximity. "A lot of your youth was spent right here on this grass."

Jordan took a few steps in. "Yeah, well, until I was kicked off the team."

"You always did think you knew more than everyone else."

"In shocking news, it turns out I don't. It just took a few years for me to figure that part out."

Molly stared, struck at the way the descending sun layered across Jordan's eyes, making the blue more vibrant than she'd ever seen it. "I think that's called acquired maturity."

"Don't give me too much credit. I'm about to break into that equipment shed over there and lose all sorts of mature points." Her grin was pure mischief as she backed away.

Oh, this wasn't a good idea. Molly was pretty much a rule follower, and the words "breaking in" so did not fit into that neat little square. "Jordan," she called. "Hey, maybe not. I'd rather stay out of jail, you know, if at all possible."

Jordan lifted her head from the lock she now examined. "Live a little, Molly. Nothing will happen, I promise. And who knows? You might even like it."

She didn't have a chance to protest further, however, as it only took Jordan two point three seconds to pop the lock. The door was now open, and moments later, Jordan approached dribbling a soccer ball proudly. "Wanna play?"

"Pshh, no. I'm not into anything that requires defense. I was a cheerleader in high school, remember?"

Jordan offered a lazy smile. "I have not forgotten. Do you still have the uniform?"

For whatever reason, a typical Jordan comment that she could have matched toe to toe just a few days ago now left her speechless, and, oh God, was she blushing? Yep, that was a full on blush she felt creeping down her neck. Jordan must have noticed too, and in a merciful move, let her off the hook.

"You don't have to answer that if you'll play with me."

She kicked the ball to her.

"Fine," Molly said and rolled her eyes. But the true source of her annoyance was at herself and her inability to behave like a normal human, not at Jordan. But who was counting?

She kicked the ball back.

And they were underway.

They started out in a side-by-side run, passing the ball between them as they went. But once they'd covered the length of the field once, their game turned into one of keep away, with Molly struggling with everything she had to steal the ball from Jordan, who was so much more adept at this, that it wasn't close to fair. Finally, out of breath and feeling like she might die, Molly collapsed onto her back in the middle of the field.

But she was smiling.

There was some aspect of the carefree play that loosened something in her and made her heart soar, even as it thudded wildly in her chest from exertion. True, she was more out of breath than she'd probably been in her entire life thus far, but there was a euphoric high there too. "I see why you like this," she said to Jordan who stretched out on her back alongside her. They both stared up at the darkening sky.

"Told you you'd have fun. You should listen to me more."

Molly turned her face to Jordan's and they shared a smile. "I should. You're kind of unpredictable though. That part hasn't changed."

"Yeah, I think I'm okay with that."

"Me too." It was true. She found it kind of refreshing. And a little hot. Damn it, she didn't mean that last part.

As if reading her thoughts, Jordan pushed herself onto her side and propped her head up with her hand. As she looked down at Molly, the amusement fell from her face and was replaced with sincerity. Molly felt her stomach tighten in reflex. "About earlier, I'm sorry if I made you uncomfortable, you know, with the cheerleader comment."

Molly nodded, but couldn't shake the reaction she was having to Jordan's proximity. "It's okay. I know you were just being playful. It's what you do."

"But after everything, I should be more sensitive to the... situation."

Ah, yes, the situation. She decided to play stupid. It was her best chance to sidestep whatever it was that was pulling at her, because if she allowed herself to think about the other night as she lay there, looking up at Jordan, well, the slope would become a lot more slippery. "I don't think we have a situation."

"No?" Jordan's gaze trailed lazily down her face. When her eyes lingered briefly on Molly's lips, she felt it all over. The air between them was doing that snap-crackle-pop thing.

"No," Molly said absently. Was she imagining it or had Jordan closed the distance between them? Because her mouth seemed extra close, and she had to admit, it was an incredibly sexy mouth. Jordan reached down and gently moved a strand of hair from Molly's forehead, and for the life of her, Molly couldn't remember why this kind of closeness was a bad idea. And then Jordan reminded her.

"Cassie and I spent her last night in town out here, before she left for college." She pushed herself into a sitting position and stared out at the field once again.

"Oh yeah?" Molly said, following her up.

"One of my favorite memories of her. After that, I used to come out here a lot, late at night, almost to this very spot. You know, when I had a lot on my mind, or just needed to be alone. It became my place."

It was almost completely dark out now and the stars were peaking through the night sky ever so slightly. As Jordan was sitting slightly in front of her, Molly couldn't see her face. "What do you like about it?"

"It's so quiet. Just listen." They did for several long moments. "Probably the quietest place on earth. This town, I don't know if you've noticed, has the most unique hum about it once everyone is tucked in for the night. But out here, it's different. There's nothing. Barely a cricket. When you sit out here, it's just you and the night."

It was beautiful, what Jordan just said. And as much as Molly thought she knew everything there was to know about Applewood, Jordan had just taught her something new. She hugged her knees to her chest and looked up at the pale moon. "Thank you for sharing this with me."

Jordan turned back and smiled and it was so genuine that Molly warmed instantly. "You might be the only one who'd get it."

She nodded, honored that Jordan would see that in her. They sat in silence for a while longer, enjoying the night, the company, the quiet.

Chapter Ten

W hat would you think about a marble cake with a cheese-cake mousse filling?" Molly looked up from her notes and regarded her mother-in-law, who smiled widely at the suggestion.

"I think Joseph will love it. With a happy birthday message, and make sure you get sixtieth in there. He's eight months older than me, and I want to make sure we point that out."

"Duly noted. Rub in his age aggressively. I think we can handle that." They sat across from each other at the Tuscana kitchen table, going over the details for Dr. Tuscana's sixtieth birthday party. Molly had, of course, donated the services of the bakeshop to provide the dessert options, which included the all-important birthday cake. The Tuscanas were her family, and one day would be the only family that she had. She would do anything for them. "Along with the cake, I think we'll do some chocolate covered strawberries and a truffle assortment. Oh, and caramel apple shots. He loves those. What do you think?"

"I think you know best is what I think. And I'm going to defer to you in all things food related. You have my official sign-off to go crazy."

Molly grinned. "Perfect. That's how I like it."

She was grateful to have the one-on-one time with Amalia, and nervous as she was, she knew there was no time like the present to discuss the recent changes she'd made in her life. It was a conversation she'd been dreading because she never in a million years wanted to do anything to hurt the Tuscanas. She'd go out of her way not to. But she owed it to them to hear it from her.

"Well, I think we've made some progress today, don't you?" Amalia stood. "Joseph's never had a great big birthday party. I think this is going to mean a lot to him, to have all his family and friends gathered in his honor."

"I think so too." She followed Amalia from the kitchen to the living room. Now or never. Finding the courage, she spoke, her voice a little louder than she'd meant it to be. "Um, there's something else I wanted to talk to you about before I go. If you have the time, I mean. I don't want to keep you."

"Of course, sweetheart. What do you want to talk about?" She took a seat on the antique sofa that she loved so much.

"It's hard to say this, and that seems strange because it's you, and you've always been like the mother I never had. Both you and Joseph mean the world to me."

"Is everything all right?" Amalia looked fearful.

She took a breath. She was handling this all wrong. "Yes, it is. Everything is fine. I didn't mean to worry you. I've just…I've decided to start dating again. I've been on two dates. Bad ones. But still dates and I wanted you to know."

Without saying a word or moving a muscle, Amalia was still able to communicate so much. It was all right there in her eyes. Disappointment. Sadness. Hurt. And it just about killed Molly.

But she pressed on, doing anything and everything to smooth things over. "I know this must be hard for you to hear, which is why I wanted to be sure it came from me." Amalia nodded and attempted a smile, but still had yet to say anything. "I loved Cassie very much. I still do and she will always be a part of me, but I think I should try and make a life for myself now, as hard as that may be."

"Of course you do," Amalia finally said and pulled Molly into a tight hug. "And I want you to be happy, Molly, both Joseph and I do." But there were tears shining in her eyes when she released Molly. "I won't lie and say it will be easy to watch you move on, because when I think of you or spend time with you, I think of Cassie. And it's like I have a piece of her still with me. But that's not fair to you, I suppose." Just as the tears in her eyes threatened to spill over, Amalia moved past her toward the bedroom. "I better get changed. We're meeting Mick and Barbara Luntz for dinner." And then over her shoulder, "I'll call soon. You can see yourself out?"

"Of course."

Hollow. That's how she felt as she stood alone in the Tuscana living room. Like she'd somehow let them down. She didn't want to cause any unnecessary pain in their lives. In fact, that was the last thing in the world she wanted to see happen. They'd been through too much already. And while she knew inherently that she was doing the right thing, the guilt that settled in the pit of her stomach argued otherwise.

❖

Jordan reached back and rubbed her neck, gently massaging the tight bunch of muscles that called out from hours of poring over the books spread out in front of her. She glanced at her watch and took note of the fact that morning had transitioned into afternoon while she sat in the reference section of the library trying to understand the ins and outs of small business ownership.

And there was a lot to learn.

Half a dozen books sat open around her, and her coffee had long gone cold. On her next break, she would remedy that situation, but for now she would live without the caffeinated pick-me-up in favor of progress.

She allowed herself only a moment to stretch before returning to her reading, taking notes on her laptop as she went. It was roughly twenty minutes later when her thoughts were interrupted by an energetic child's voice accompanied by that of a very familiar adult.

"How many books can we take? We should take a lot. They're free," she heard her niece, Risa, state as she rounded the corner into the room.

Molly smiled down at her, holding her hand as they walked. "How about four books since you're four years old?"

Risa considered this. "How about five? No, seven."

"You drive a hard bargain. Let's just see how it goes."

"Aunt Jordan!" Risa said happily, spotting her. She scurried across the short distance and climbed easily into her lap. Jordan hadn't spent much time with her niece and nephew in the past, but this trip was definitely making up for it. She enjoyed every second she could steal.

"Well, hey there, munchkin." Jordan pulled her in for a squeeze. She really was the cutest kid ever. "How did you know I needed somebody cute to brighten my morning?"

Risa laughed the genuine laugh that only kids could pull off. "I didn't, silly. Aunt Molly and me are spending our day together. We already had chocolate chip muffins and now we get to buy books and then we're going to the playground to swing."

Molly joined them, standing alongside the table. "I love to swing. But we're just going to *borrow* the books, remember?"

"Yeah, we're going to borrow some. Any ones we want." Risa nodded her head slowly in dramatic punctuation.

"Whoa. Libraries are pretty cool that way, huh? Trusting."

"Yep. What are you doing here?"

"Yeah," Molly said, surveying the scene. "What *are* you doing here? And when did you start wearing glasses? This is all very suspect."

Caught. Jordan took the glasses off and settled back in her chair. She didn't quite know how to explain, or even if she wanted to. "Right. The thing is I'm just doing a little research for a project and the glasses help me see the words."

Molly shook her head. "Incredibly vague. Details needed."

Jordan sighed. "Not sure I'm ready to divulge details to the world quite yet."

Molly glanced down at Risa. "Hey, button, do you think you could run ahead to the children's section and see if you can find any books with ballerinas in them?"

Risa scampered down, already in project mode. "I know I can. I love ballerinas. I am one." She twirled four or five times for them and after a round of applause headed into the adjacent room to start her quest.

Molly refocused her gaze on Jordan. "The world is gone. Just you and me left. So what do you have going here? International espionage? Code cracking?"

She decided to just go for it. "All right, I'll tell you, but don't laugh."

"Deal."

"Do you remember the short documentaries I used to work on in college?"

Molly sat down, instantly involved. "Of course I do. The one about the suicide forest stuck with me for weeks. That one won a local award, didn't it?"

"Two actually. It was that kind of project that made me want to work in film for the rest of my life. But the reality of a big budget studio is nothing like the days of working on something that mattered. The entertainment business pays well, but the intrinsic value is not exactly comparable."

Molly raised an eyebrow. "Okay. So what does all this equal?"

She met Molly's eyes tentatively, already feeling the weight of her scrutiny. "I don't want to go back to the studio once my leave of absence is complete. My friend George and I have been tossing around an idea for the past year or so. He's just been waiting for my okay, and I think I'm ready to give it. I want to start my own production company. With him on board, of course. Make the kinds of films that I want to make with the people I know I can make them with. And I want to start with documentaries."

"Wow."

"And before you say it's a long shot and that I should stay where the water's warm, I want you to know that I think I can do this. I've given it a lot of thought. It's going to take an incredible amount of work and time to get off the ground, and I'll start small at first, but I think the end result will be worth it. I want to make films that count for something." A pause. "Now you go." She exhaled, nervous as hell. Molly was the first person she'd let in on her idea, and her response mattered more than she was willing to admit even to herself.

A slow smile spread across Molly's face. "I think it's a great idea."

"But."

"That's just it." She leaned her chin on her palm. "There aren't any buts. I think you should do it. You're going to need capital. Have you looked into small business loans?"

Jordan stared at her in wonder. "You're serious?"

Molly narrowed her gaze. "Are you?"

"It's just that I was expecting something more along the traditional lines of 'stop dreaming, kid.' Or maybe the old standby, 'have you considered medical school?' That one's my favorite."

Molly's face softened in sincerity. "I would never say those things to you."

Jordan nodded because she was right; she wouldn't. And the extra shot of encouragement was just what she needed. Suddenly, she was excited about her prospects all over again. "Thank you."

"No problem. Now back to business. How do you plan to fund this venture of yours?"

Jordan bit her bottom lip. "I might have enough in savings to get us off the ground at first."

"Get outta town." Molly whistled low, which earned them both a disapproving glance from old Mrs. Robinson three tables over.

Jordan kept her voice low as she refocused her attention. "It's not a ton, but like I said, studio work does have some perks, and the paycheck is most definitely one of them. They took care of my food and lodging whenever I was on location, so my bank account reaped the rewards."

"You sure you want to give all that up? You could buy a lot of soccer balls with those dollar signs. Wouldn't have to break into sheds anymore. Think of that."

"Valid point, but I'm more than sure." She stared past Molly in surprise. "Oh. I think our niece is constructing the Eiffel Tower out of ballerina books." She tilted her head. "Who knew they had so many?"

Molly jumped up. "Yikes. On it. We'll talk later. Oh, and, Jordan?"

She met her gaze. "Yeah?"

"You look good in glasses. Really." The comment coupled with the weighted look in Molly's eyes hit her right in the center of the chest like a line drive. And for one second, she let herself enjoy that twisty feeling she had in her stomach as she watched Molly walk away. Yeah, it was hard to breathe, but she'd work that part out later.

After that exchange, her mind dreamily wandered elsewhere and it was nearly impossible to concentrate on the work in front of her. She closed the book in happy defeat. Oh well, the productivity had been nice while it lasted.

Chapter Eleven

As far as odds went, date number three was destined for success. It had to be, right? At least that's what Molly told herself as she approached the entrance to The Owl Tree. She'd grown smart enough over the course of the past few weeks to insist that her date travel into Applewood this time around. This would make her escape route that much shorter. But then again, with three times being a charm, she wouldn't exactly need one now, would she? Good thing too, as Eden's friend was running out of lesbians.

She had to admit she was feeling confident on this particular Friday. Maybe it was the excitement of the upcoming festival or her recent success with nailing down the recipe for MollyDollys. Whatever it was, she planned to use the extra swagger and was actually looking forward to whatever the night had in store. The optimism felt good.

On the sidewalk, she glanced down at her denim capris and black tank top. Sexy enough, without looking like she was trying too hard. Just the kind of message she was looking to send.

Before she could even make it inside the bar, she spotted a woman making her way up the sidewalk. This had to be her would-be date. She smiled as the woman approached and the woman smiled back. Short dark hair, slim cut jeans and a forest green top. Definitely attractive. One wouldn't call her drop-dead gorgeous, but she had a warm smile that would snag your attention.

"Molly?"

She extended her hand. "That's me. You must be Annaleigh."

"I am. Nice to meet you. I was so excited to hear you lived in Applewood. I've always loved it here and look for any excuse to visit." She blushed. "That sounded horrible. Not that you're just an excuse, but—"

Molly held up a hand, laughing. "Not at all. I get it. Shall we head in? I'll give you all the insider secrets."

Annaleigh smiled. "I came to the right place."

The vibe was already easygoing, and as Molly held the door open for her date, she didn't even try to hide the smile she felt creeping through. The night had so many good possibilities.

The Owl Tree was hopping as the town came out in droves to celebrate the weekend. Music played from the jukebox in the corner and a group was gathered around the dartboard in the back. As they passed through the crowded space, Molly paused to say hello to, well, everyone, introducing Annaleigh to her friends and neighbors. Finally, they snagged a table to the right of the bar, just underneath Owlfred, the bar's giant stuffed mascot. Molly gestured up. "Local flavor."

"He's quaint. Lots of character."

"Right?" They smiled at each other for a moment. She could be wrong, but there might just be chemistry here. Time would tell.

Little Bobby brought over a pitcher of Miller Light and a couple of glasses. "Hey there, Molly. Molly's friend."

"Hiya, Little Bobby. How'd you know we were drinking beer tonight?"

He shrugged once. "S'my job to know these kinds of things."

"Impressive," Annaleigh said, raising her eyebrows.

Little Bobby grunted, which Molly knew was code for thank you, and headed back behind the bar to tend to his waiting customers.

Annaleigh took it upon herself to pour them each a beer. "So what kinds of things does one do for fun in Applewood, USA?"

"Oh, the usual. Swap meets, recreational drugs, and lots of competitive gardening."

Annaleigh stared back at her wide-eyed.

"Kidding," Molly assured her.

Annaleigh leaned back in her chair. "Thank God. I guess I'm a little sensitive. You just wouldn't believe some of the dates I've been on lately."

Molly regarded her. "Trust me, I would. In fact, I might have you beat."

"Wanna bet?"

They went on to trade stories, and in a shocking turn of events, Annaleigh took the proverbial gold. "Wait, so you actually went to jail?"

She nodded. "That's what happens when the cops find a trunk full of marijuana plants in the car you just happen to be riding in."

"Oh, no!"

"Oh, yes."

Molly reached across the table and covered Annaleigh's hand with her own. "I'm sincerely sorry that happened to you and even more sorry that I cannot stop laughing about it."

"That's okay. I'm sure it's a story I'll tell my grandchildren one day, so there's that."

"My take on it exactly. Cheers to bad dates, present company excluded." They clinked glasses, and not long after, Molly poured them a second round.

Things were going well.

Annaleigh leaned forward tentatively. "Is it too soon to tell you that I'm having a really great time?"

Molly set the pitcher down and grinned. "Not too soon. And me too, by the way. This is nice."

She slid Annaleigh's glass across the table to her, just as her eyes landed on a cozy scene across the room. Jordan sat at the bar, her head dipped low, grinning at something Summer Siller was whispering in her ear. How had she missed them when she first arrived? She watched a beat longer because like a car accident, she couldn't seem to look away. Summer's hand moved from where it rested on the back of Jordan's barstool up the small of her back. Molly suppressed an eye roll. What was Jordan thinking? But she knew the answer to that question and it was spilling generously from Summer's overly low cut top. Summer Siller was not only easy, she was manipulative and shallow too. And if that's what Jordan was after, who was Molly to stop her?

"Friends of yours?" Annaleigh asked, following her gaze.

"One of them."

"We can invite them over if you want."

Worst idea ever. "You know what? Let's not. I'm enjoying hanging out with you." Annaleigh smiled, and was that a blush? It most definitely was. A cute blush too. "So second grade, huh? Tell me how you got into teaching?"

"I think it's what I always wanted to do. From the time I was old enough to appreciate school…" Annaleigh was still talking, but Molly's attention was snagged by the sight of Jordan moving to the jukebox with Summer plastered to her side like a second skin. Classy.

As Jordan turned, their eyes connected, and she seemed to take in the scene. It wasn't long before she headed over, wisely dropping Summer at the bar first. Thank God for that. Molly refocused her attention on Annaleigh and her story, doing her best to ignore Jordan as she approached. It was juvenile, but it's what she was going with.

"Hey. Wasn't expecting to run into you tonight," Jordan said. She grinned at Molly before shifting her attention to Annaleigh and extending her hand. "We haven't met. I'm Jordan."

Annaleigh accepted the handshake. "Annaleigh, a pleasure."

"So what are you two up to tonight? A little Miller Light action?" Jordan was laid back and friendly, and damn it if something within Molly didn't react to all that annoying charisma and confidence.

"Actually, we were trying to get to know each other a little better one-on-one." Molly's tone was a little less friendly, and Jordan seemed to notice.

"Oh. I'm sorry. Didn't mean to intrude."

"Not at all," Annaleigh said as she glanced uneasily from Molly to Jordan. "I was just telling Molly how much I enjoy Applewood. I remember coming here for the festival when I was a kid."

Jordan pulled up a chair and shot her a victorious glance. Molly wondered what in the hell she thought she was doing. "One of my favorite events. You'll have to come back next week for this year's. I hear it's going to be bigger and better than ever."

"Really? In what way?" Annaleigh asked.

Molly sighed as they continued. Her date had been hijacked.

But what made her even angrier was the fact that her eyes kept tracing the open top button of Jordan's blue Henley and the olive skin that peeked out from beneath. Damn it, why did she have to look good in everything she wore?

As the conversation droned on, and on, and on, her frustration only grew. Instead of listening to Jordan describe how much she loved indie rock, all this new version of Molly could think about was the shiny lip gloss Jordan wore and how her mouth was almost heart shaped and full. *Fuck.* And now she somehow had a new penchant for swearing. Fabulous.

It was time to get herself out of this, and she saw the perfect opening.

Molly inclined her head and smiled sweetly. "Jordan, I don't want to interrupt, but I think your date is trying to catch your eye." It was true. Summer was falling all over herself to look alluring enough to attract Jordan back over to the bar. It was annoying and helpful at the same time.

"I guess that's my cue." Jordan offered them one last devastating smile and headed back to Summer.

❖

The evening had definitely taken a negative turn. Jordan stared into her empty glass and contemplated the wisdom of a second beer. A no-brainer, given the circumstances. "Hit me, Bobby."

For the better part of an hour, she'd watched Molly and her date du jour, Annaleigh, chatting cozily in the corner of the bar. It was whatever. She'd told herself from the get-go that she wanted Molly to find happiness, so why was it so ridiculously hard to watch it all go down? Summer's warm breath tickled her ear. She was chewing gum, which was typical for Summer, but for some reason Jordan found it less than endearing in this moment.

"We should dance," she purred.

Jordan looked around. The bar did have a small dance floor, but no one used it. "It's not really that kind of bar."

Summer tilted her head. "Since when do you play by the rules? This can be any kind of bar we want it to be."

To hell with it. She had a valid point.

Jordan took a long swallow of her beer and allowed Summer to pull her onto the dance floor in the back of the room. The song that played was bluesy, something from way back. They moved together slowly, earning an interested glance from a patron or two, but it felt oddly welcome, dancing close to someone.

Jordan leaned in next to Summer's ear. "So did you hear about the kidnapping in the park?"

Summer pulled back, wide-eyed. "No, what happened?"

"It's fine now. They woke him up."

A beat of silence hung in the air, before Summer's face relaxed into a grin. She laughed loudly and slapped Jordan playfully across the shoulder. "You had me goin' there for a second."

They laughed together as the song wound down.

The dance hadn't lasted long, but it had been a welcome distraction. Summer was uncomplicated, friendly, and not exactly hard to look at, especially when she went to such lengths to put it all out on display like she had that night. And there was definitely a lot to display. What was even better? There were no highly sensitive, guilt-ridden feelings involved. And she needed a serious break from those.

As they made their way back to their spot at the bar, Jordan lifted her eyes to the arctic freeze of Molly's stare. As she met her gaze questioningly, Molly looked away. Okay. What the hell was that about? Molly was allowed to go on any number of dates, but she wasn't allowed to enjoy herself with a friend without blatant judgment?

Unbelievable.

Summer turned to her. "Wanna get outta here?"

"Definitely. What do you have in mind?"

"We could go for a drive, but given the drinks we've had, maybe it's better if we just walk to my place. Talk about old times or something." The sultry look in her eyes made it clear the "or something" was the operative part of that sentence. And you know what? Summer was exactly what Jordan needed tonight. Summer was easygoing, fun, and more importantly, wouldn't view kissing her as a colossal mistake.

"Let me settle up."

"Bobby, make that two of us." Molly leaned over the side of the bar adjacent to theirs.

"Date over already?" Jordan asked.

"Something like that." But Molly was refusing to look at her and that made her all the more heated.

"Something on your mind, Mol?"

She shook her head once, staring at the wall as she waited for her check. Still no eye contact. "Nope. You?"

"No, I'm great. Better than."

"Clearly."

"How's the little bakery?" Summer asked.

That did it.

Molly turned fully and regarded Summer as if she were a teacher dealing with a not so bright student. The patrons who sat between them watched the exchange like a tennis match.

"The *little* bakery is fine. You should come in sometime."

"Yeah, I'm more of a Starbucks kind of girl, but thanks."

Ouch. Even Jordan cringed.

"Somehow I could have guessed that. Tell you what, Bobby. Keep the change. I have an immediate urge for a shift in scenery." She dropped two tens on the bar and headed for the door where Annaleigh was waiting. Jordan watched her go. To say she looked devastatingly beautiful when angry was an understatement.

❖

In a stroke of great timing, Annaleigh's cab arrived just as they exited the bar. Shaking off the exchange inside, Molly offered her a smile. "So I had fun tonight."

"Me too." Then she seemed to hesitate. "And while I'd love to see you again sometime, Molly, it seems like you might already have a lot on your plate."

Molly stared back at her curiously, until realization flared. "Oh. If this is about Jordan, it's nothing. Trust me."

Annaleigh placed a gentle hand on Molly's forearm. "I don't want to overstep my bounds here, but it didn't seem like nothing.

Your eyes were trained on her all night like some sort of gravitational pull."

Molly's gaze dropped to the concrete. She felt defeated, exposed. "No. It's not like that. My partner died four years ago. Jordan is her younger sister. It's…complicated."

Annaleigh straightened, her eyes wide. "Yeah, I'd say. Tell you what." She took a small notebook from her bag and scribbled something on a piece of paper. "Here's my number. Someday, if you figure it all out, call me. In the meantime, maybe have a conversation with her. Or level with yourself."

Molly stared numbly at the small blue square of paper. "Thanks. I'll think about it." With that, the most promising date she'd had in years slid into the waiting cab and sped back out of her life.

And she was reeling.

The door to The Owl Tree opened and the boisterous sounds from the bar spilled onto the sidewalk along with Jordan and Summer. Molly didn't even try to hide an eye roll this time. She about-faced and headed down the sidewalk in an attempt to get home and put the whole failure of an evening behind her. And getting the hell away from Jordan was step one.

"Molly, wait up."

Damn it all. No. She kept walking. *Pretend you didn't hear her.*

"Are you purposefully ignoring me?"

She paused and turned abruptly to face Jordan who was only a few paces back. "Apparently not with a lot of success. What is it that you need exactly?"

"Insight, I guess. You want to tell me what happened back there?"

Molly lifted her arm and let it drop. Her anger only growing the longer she looked into those vibrant blue eyes. "I crashed and burned with Annaleigh; that's what happened. Nice job."

Jordan narrowed her eyes. "This is somehow my fault?"

She felt her blood pressure shoot up at notch. "Oh yeah, I'd say you had a hand in it. Joining us at our table, gathering as much attention for yourself as you possibly could. It's what you do. Oh, and then there was the little show on the dance floor. That was a nice touch. Totally sophisticated. I hope you're proud of yourself."

Jordan's eyes flashed hot. "Believe it or not, Molly, not everything is about you. It's not a crime to have a little fun. I was just trying to enjoy the night for whatever it was or wasn't."

Molly had to laugh at that one. "Exactly my point. You're such a player, Jordan. You always have been. Why not just admit it? Speaking of which, isn't Summer waiting for you?" She craned her neck and peered around Jordan, but the sidewalk was empty.

"I told her I would catch up. Wow. You really don't like her."

"Please. She's been out for me for as long as I can remember. The first day I drove the car my dad got me for graduation, she let the air out of my tires at the movie theater. I had to roller skate home. Good thing I had them in my trunk."

"Roller skates?" Jordan asked quietly.

"Yeah, roller skates," Molly shot back.

"That's…horrible." But there was the tiniest hint of a smile on Jordan's face.

"Don't laugh. It *was* horrible. I even got a blister." But damn it, she was smiling now too because it sounded so ridiculous played back now. They stared at each other a moment, the tension somehow cut in half.

Jordan then shifted her focus to a nearby tree as if figuring out what she wanted to say next. Finally, she slid Molly a hesitant look. "Can we maybe admit that there's something clouding the issue here, something between us?"

Molly was quick to answer because it was easy. "No, we can't. I'll see you around, Jordan." She turned to go. And just when she thought she was home free, she wasn't.

"Molly?"

She blew out a breath. "Yeah?"

"What if there was no Cassie? Would it be different?"

It was a loaded question and the answer had the power to change everything. There was distance between them on the sidewalk, but she met Jordan's eyes squarely. She looked so effortlessly beautiful that Molly almost forgot the facts. She could drown in Jordan if she let herself. But the trick was not to let herself. Instead, she answered the question as honestly as she could, because she owed Jordan that. "But there is. There was. And I wouldn't change that."

She walked on.

When she got home, she slipped into her pajamas, fed Rover, and crawled into bed. But sleep didn't come easily, which further annoyed her because if there was one thing she excelled at, it was getting a good night's rest.

So she stared at the pattern the moonlight shed across her ceiling and contemplated her predicament. She couldn't admit to Jordan that there were feelings circling, but after what happened at the bar, it was maybe time she admit it to herself.

She was attracted to Jordan and it was affecting her in a way she wouldn't have thought possible. And acting on those feelings would introduce a myriad of complications into her life that she simply didn't need.

It was a bad idea, plain and simple.

So she'd tolerate the way her mouth went dry when Jordan walked into a room, or the slow roll her heart did when they laughed together. She would ignore the perfect mouth and the body that looked like it was straight out of a movie. And when Jordan tossed her dark hair, she wouldn't imagine what it would feel like to run her hands through it and pull Jordan's lips to hers.

No, she just wouldn't do that.

❖

Jordan hit the bag once, twice, and really let loose on the third punch, which she echoed with a roundhouse kick. Her hair, which she secured in a ponytail, was beginning to escape the rubber band and long strands fell along the sides of her face. Sweat dotted her neck and chest. Her lungs were beginning to burn. None of these details interested her. She kicked the bag again, hard, and followed up with a series of jabs.

It was late. Probably close to twelve thirty. Jordan hadn't gone back to Summer's place as they'd planned. She'd called her and made a lame excuse about having to get up early. The YMCA closed at ten, but Mr. Standish, her old gym teacher, left her with the key when he headed home.

With the place to herself, she'd let go, releasing every pent up emotion building within her. For a while, her thoughts centered on Cassie, and the grief that'd overwhelmed her that first year after she'd died. Then they somehow slid into how cheated she felt over losing her sister, coupled with guilt surrounding how she'd allowed herself to go MIA on the people she loved thereafter. Finally, as she kicked and pounded the bag, practiced her footwork, and shaped her technique, she thought of Molly. How it had felt to kiss her, laugh with her, and of all that would never be between them.

But that last part didn't seem right.

She sat down hard on the gym floor, breathing heavily as she reasoned her way through her warring emotions. In the midst of all of it, there was one thing she knew for sure. Life was precious. Losing Cassie had taught all of them that lesson, and she, for one, wanted to live her life to the fullest. Milk every last drop from what the world had to offer her. It sucked that Cassie wasn't here anymore, but she and Molly were.

So it wasn't ideal, the scenario with Molly. So the hell what? It was the labels that came automatically attached to them that stood in the way of any proverbial next step.

And it was stupid.

She'd seen the look in Molly's eyes as she walked away from her earlier that night, and she knew that Molly felt it too, whatever it was that was simmering between them.

Life was too short. Now she just had to make Molly see that. And she would. She jumped to her feet and toweled off.

New plan.

She wasn't giving up that easily.

CHAPTER TWELVE

A ll right, folks, next on the agenda, we should talk about the dishwasher." It was after closing a few days later, and Molly surveyed the attentive faces of her three employees. It was their once a month staff meeting and they sat around a table in the center of the bakeshop munching on the pizza Molly had ordered in keeping with staff meeting tradition. "It's been pretty hit and miss lately, so if you're closing, it falls to you to take care of the remaining dishes."

Louise sat forward. "I've found that if you kick it real hard on the bottom, it gets going pretty good."

Eden nodded and popped a pepperoni in her mouth. "I slam my hand down real good on the top portion. Like I'm squashing a bug or something terribly upsetting. That also seems to get it started."

Molly grinned at the description. "Well, we shouldn't have to beat the hell out of it for too much longer. I've scheduled Reginald to come out and take a look. Hopefully, it won't cost too much to fix, but I'll need to get an estimate."

Damon raised his hand. "I could take a look at it."

Eden rolled her eyes. "Please. What do you know about fixing anything? From what I've seen, you just break stuff. Broke two dishes just this week."

He glared at her. "Excuse me, princess high horse, but why don't you take a step back and worry about things in Hee-Haw while I try and save this place a few extra bucks."

Eden took a deep breath, but before she could wind up for round two, Molly stepped in. "Whoa, whoa, I think we're getting off track. Damon, that would be great. Thank you. Eden, it can't hurt to let him take a look. You never know." She shrugged in punctuation just as the bell above the door chimed. They all turned in unison in time for Jordan to appear.

"Oh, sorry, guys. Didn't mean to interrupt. I was just stopping by to see if Molly was free." She was wearing workout clothes and looked like she'd come from a run. Her hair fell around her shoulders as if she'd just taken it down from a ponytail. Then there was that just-exercised glow about her that only added to that ultra beautiful thing she always seemed to have going. Catching herself, Molly jerked her eyes back to Jordan's face after they had absent-mindedly trailed down her body.

Too late. Jordan's eyes widened in recognition of what she'd just done, and a slow smile took shape on her face. Molly sighed internally.

"Actually, we're in the middle of a staff meeting," she said.

"I like staff meetings," Jordan countered.

"Well, you're in luck then," Eden chimed in with way too much excitement. "Sit here with us, sugar. We'll be done in just a bit."

Damon pulled out the chair next to him and Louise grinned up at Jordan adoringly.

Molly wasn't having it. No way. "Jordan, maybe I can call you later? I'm sure you have a million things to do."

Jordan ignored the hint and smiled that devastating smile. The power it carried annoyed her. "I really don't mind waiting if none of you mind."

Louise stood. "Absolutely not. How about a brownie, Jordan? They're fresh from the oven just thirty minutes ago, laced with caramel too."

"Oh. I guess if it's no trouble. That sounds fantastic. I'm a total caramel fan."

"No trouble. Oh, and there's milk," Eden said, hopping up to get it.

Molly shook her head slightly, but swallowed the frustrated comment on the tip of her tongue. What exactly was Jordan trying to accomplish with this? She waited patiently so Jordan could be appropriately fawned over and attended to like a long lost member of the royal family and then moved on to the next topic on her agenda. As she spoke about the spring menu items, her eyes continued to brush past Jordan. She seemed to be listening attentively, happily even. Damn her. It had been a bold move, crashing their staff meeting, and she seemed quite pleased with herself for having done it.

"And that's about everything," she said in conclusion. "Does anyone have any questions about the schedule for our booth at the festival? I've tried to work it so that everyone has some available free time to enjoy the fair."

"Looks good to me," Eden said, making obvious eye contact with Louise.

Louise stood and elbowed Damon. "Yep, me too. I better head out. C'mon Damon, you can give me a lift home."

"Sure thing, Ms. Lou-Lou." He tipped an imaginary cap to Jordan and headed for the door.

"I'll walk out with you," Eden said without so much as a look back.

Molly stood in awe. Never had she seen three people clear out of a room so fast in her entire life. Traitors. All of them.

Jordan sat back in her chair. "I was hoping maybe we could see a movie tonight. What do ya say?"

Molly gathered the empty pizza plates. "You crashed my staff meeting."

Jordan blinked. "Yeah. I'm sorry. I didn't think you'd mind. You always let me get away with stuff."

Molly raised one shoulder. "Well, I did mind today."

"But in bonus news, you seemed to like my outfit," Jordan said, totally calling her out.

Molly glared at her. "Yeah, you look great. I especially like the attitude and over confidence you're wearing. Nice touch." Hips swaying, she carried the plates through the swinging door to the kitchen, leaving a chilled room in the process.

❖

Jordan didn't know why she was baiting Molly so much. Maybe because ever since they'd kissed, Molly went out of her way to pretend she was invisible. But the once-over Molly gave her when she'd walked in the door said otherwise, and Jordan didn't plan to ignore those signals any longer.

She pushed up from the table and followed Molly into the kitchen. She found her kicking the hell out of a dishwasher, which was mildly amusing. "Well, you two clearly aren't getting along. Everything okay?"

Molly shot her a death look. "Yes, Jordan. Everything is fine other than the fact that the damn dishwasher won't kick into gear." As Molly geared up for a second assault, Jordan held up a hand and stepped in.

"May I? I don't think it can take much more."

Molly blew a strand of hair off her forehead in defeat. "Might as well."

With gentle hands and one firm push, Jordan was able to reseat the dishwasher and smiled widely at Molly when the sounds of rushing water answered back. "Tada."

"Congratulations. Even the dishwasher gives you whatever the hell you want." She didn't mean it, but Jordan smiled wider, enjoying the game.

"I'll take that as a compliment. So about the movie?"

"You're not listening. No movie."

"Because you're avoiding me."

"Because I'm exhausted."

"We can watch one together at your place. Or mine, but seeing as how it's a couple hours away in Chicago, it might make it a long night. So maybe yours."

"I think I need some alone time tonight."

Feeling alive for the first time in so long, Jordan took a step into Molly, effectively trapping her between the counter and her body. Molly's eyes widened and she inhaled noticeably as Jordan placed her hands on her waist, her thumbs possessively across Molly's abdomen. Her eyes took a pass at Jordan's mouth and she knew, just knew, Molly was thinking about that kiss. "Are you sure?" Jordan asked quietly, dipping her head, already so close to Molly's mouth. She remembered how it felt on hers just a few nights ago.

Molly nodded slowly, but the way her eyes fixated on Jordan's lips left room for question. They hovered there for a moment, breathing in the same air. The tension was thick. Jordan felt it all over.

Molly spoke just above a whisper. "I can't do this with you, Jordan. What would that say about me? What kind of person I am?" Slowly, Jordan slid her hand into Molly's hair. It felt like spun silk on her skin.

"That you're human. That you feel things. What are you feeling right now?" She returned her hands to Molly's waist and inched them slowly up her rib cage, stopping only when her thumbs came just beneath her breasts, tracing the curve below.

Molly's lips parted slightly in surprise and she hitched in another breath. "You know what I'm feeling. You always seem to know."

Jordan was surprised by the admission and how quickly her body was responding to Molly's. The electricity was like nothing she'd ever experienced. Off the charts, actually. Jordan moved in closer until their bodies touched fully. They were both breathing a little erratically. Jordan stared into Molly's eyes and watched as the tiny flecks heated to gold.

Yep. They were on the same page.

"The thing is, I feel it too, Mol." She lingered there for several wonderful yet torturous moments before finally taking a slow step away.

She made her way to the swinging door that led to the front of the bakeshop. "You know what I want. Ball's in your court."

Chapter Thirteen

Soft rock played quietly from the iPod dock in Molly's green and white kitchen three nights later. She loved her kitchen. It was probably her favorite room in the entire world, homey and smelling of fresh spices she kept on the rack. It was nearly eleven that night, and even though she had to be up at four the next morning, she was in project mode and very little got in her way when that happened.

Baking had always been her security blanket, and after the week she'd had, the kitchen called out to her. Instead of dwelling on the things that bothered her, she could lose herself in the creation of something sweet and wonderful and the world would be a better place when she was done, wouldn't it?

Peanut butter cups were the mission du jour and she was up to her arms in flour. Encouraged by Pink Floyd and the way her mind got all soft and slow when she baked, Molly kept her head down and her hands moving as she sashayed her hips in time to the music. Therapy, she thought.

She danced her way to the too high cabinet above the stove and felt blindly for the jar of peanut butter she kept there. But damn, it was empty because she'd needed therapy the week before too, when she'd stayed up all night perfecting her chocolate chip pound cake and then the five thousandth batch of MollyDollys she'd need for the festival.

Derailed and furious at herself for forgetting to pick up a new jar at the grocery store, she stood in the kitchen weighing her options. This was not an ideal situation, this peanut butter crisis, but it wasn't insurmountable. When one needed peanut butter, one should venture out into the world and get some. So she grabbed her keys and headed to the bakeshop. Once there, she quickly flipped on the lights and scanned the shelves of the walk-in pantry until she located the large jar they kept there. In another horrifying peanut butter blow, they were virtually out there too. She checked the paperwork, and sure enough, Eden had added peanut butter to this week's grocery order.

Well, damn it all to confectioner's hell.

She checked her watch. It was after eleven thirty and Conyers Grocery would be closed for the night. But she was this far in. Why not take the drive to Franklin? It was only one town over? It would take her eighteen minutes each way, but it was a matter of principle now.

She wasn't going down like this.

She hopped back into her car and set out on the winding, dark farm road. Surprisingly, she found herself actually enjoying the late night drive. As the Eagles sang about Hotel California on her radio, her mind drifted to the very thing that had her baking in overdrive.

When Jordan left her standing alone in the bakeshop's kitchen three days ago, she'd drawn in a shaky breath and struggled desperately to regain her equilibrium. When it came to Jordan, it seemed her mind and body were in a war for the ages. As Jordan had pressed up against her in those shorts and thin work out top, she'd felt it all the way down to her toes. She now understood that she was more attracted to Jordan than even she realized. The very person she *could not* be attracted to by the laws of the Universe.

But she knew the power they carried now. The two of them.

She'd felt it full on in the kitchen. And all she had to do was avoid moments like those, delicious as they may feel, at all costs. Because there was guilt involved, a whole hell of a lot of it, and Molly had spent the rest of the week bathed in it. Not to mention what it would do to her relationship with the Tuscanas. It was hard enough for Amalia to hear she was interested in dating again, but her becoming romantically involved with Jordan could devastate the balance and ruin their relationship forever.

On the other side of the coin, she hated what this newfound dynamic was doing to who she and Jordan were to each other. Jordan was important and by pushing her away, she was losing her altogether and that didn't feel right either.

Because when Jordan arrived back in town, something shifted into gear for Molly. The shop was going under, but just having Jordan around again made her feel that there was hope for Flour Child. For the future. For her.

And yet here they were, stuck in neutral.

And she had not a clue what to do about it.

Hence, she baked.

The twenty-four hour Walmart in Franklin didn't let her down, and to prove a point to the cosmos, she almost bought the whole wall of peanut butter. Instead, she settled on three jumbo jars of the good stuff, paid the bored with life cashier, and climbed back into her car.

Victory. Peanut butter crisis averted.

She was singing along to Bob Dylan ten minutes later and doing fifty-five on the farm road when her car began to choke and sputter until it was jerking forward in random spurts. *Oh God. Oh God.* Flashing back to her high school driver's ed class, she relied on instinct, held firmly to the steering wheel, and kept her foot from pumping the gas too vehemently. As her heart hammered away in her chest, she whispered the words, "please, please, please," until the little-car-that-could gradually decelerated altogether, and slowed to a stop on the side of the very dark, very lonely road.

Damn it all again.

After thanking baby Jesus for her life, she got out and surveyed the scene. Except there was really nothing to see. She popped the hood but had very little idea what she was looking at. An attempt to start the car again just produced more sputtering.

Maybe that victory declaration had come a little too soon.

She called for roadside assistance, but due to the late hour, and her out of the way location, she was informed it could take up to two hours before they could have the one guy on duty out to her. Seriously? Just the one guy? The script reading phone operator advised that she not head out on foot and instead encouraged her to remain in her vehicle with the doors locked until help arrived.

She hung up and did the next best thing. She called Mikey.

"Why hello there, Molly," he said upon answering. "What's up in your world?"

"Hey, Mikey. I'm sorry to call so late, but I have kind of a situation here and was hoping you might be able to play big brother-in-law and help me out."

"No problem. I'm great at big brother-in-law and I was still up. What happened?"

She explained the embarrassing sequence of events that now sounded more ridiculous than any words could justify as she paced rapidly back and forth in front of her car.

After a pause and chuckle, "Give me twenty minutes."

"You have no idea how many kisses I plan to pepper your cheek with. Thank you so much!"

"See you soon. Hang in there and—"

"Lock the door," she said with him in unison.

❖

Jordan closed the door to Risa's bedroom. "Okay, she's out like a light. Just needed a little reassurance that there are, in fact, no sharks swimming on her floor when the lights go out. Common mistake."

She settled back onto the couch and pulled her feet up to her chest, all set to finish the film she'd started with Mikey three hours before. It was rare that they got much one-on-one time, but with Teresa out of town on a girl's trip, she was taking advantage of the opportunity to bond with her brother and his kids. It was only a minor inconvenience that their movie was interrupted every twenty minutes when one of the kids needed something. She kind of enjoyed being the one to step in and help out. Plus, they really seemed to like her so the old ego wasn't exactly suffering.

Mikey stood and turned to her apologetically. "I hate to extend the longest movie in the history of film even further, but—"

Jordan stared at him pathetically. "Et tu, Brute?"

"Afraid so."

She decided to cut him a break. He did seem to have a lot on his plate with Teresa out of town. "So what's up?"

"Molly's car broke down halfway between here and Franklin. I need to get out there and pick her up."

Jordan shot a glance at the clock. "What the hell is she doing out this late by herself?"

He shrugged. "Got me. Something about a peanut butter crisis. Your guess is as good as mine. Can you stay with the kids until I get back?"

She stood and headed for her keys. "I'll do you one better. I'll go."

"Bad idea. I don't like the idea of you out this late either."

"Please, Mikey. I live in downtown Chicago."

"Point taken."

❖

She put the top down on the Beetle because it was that kind of night. The wind in her hair felt good as she sped along the twisting farm road. It took her twelve minutes to reach Molly's car. When she arrived, she could just barely make her out in the driver's seat.

She parked on the opposite side of the road and headed over. As she approached the car, Molly stared at her through the window questioningly. Finally, she exited the car wearing cutoff denim shorts and a hooded gray Rutgers sweatshirt. She looked incredibly confused and equally adorable.

"What's going on? I thought Mikey was coming."

"He wanted to, but he had an existing date with a couple of small people. Hence, you get me."

"Yeah, hence," she said neutrally, but Jordan could tell she was relieved someone had come to her rescue. The night was dark and the road was pretty desolate. She was glad she'd gotten there when she did.

"So will the engine turn over at all?"

"It tries and tries but never really gets there."

"It could be the spark isn't making it to the spark plugs."

Molly looked hopeful. "Do you know how to fix that?"

"Not a clue. Let's get out of here and let roadside tow it to Gibson's."

As Molly walked around the passenger's side of her bug, Jordan surveyed her across the car. "So. Peanut butter."

Molly shot her a glare as she slid into her seat. "Shut up."

"If you insist. Top down okay?"

"Sounds nice, actually."

Jordan smiled and pulled onto the road. As they drove, the cool air rushed past them, lifting their hair as the stars twinkled brightly above. The air smelled smoky, as it always seemed to on those country highways. They rode in silence for a while. Finally, Molly leaned her head against the seat and turned. She gazed at Jordan steadily, those soft brown eyes now gentle.

"Thank you for coming out so late. That's what I should have led with when you got here. I seem to forget my manners with you lately, so let me try again. Thank you."

"It's okay. I didn't mind coming. And you're welcome."

Molly glanced over her shoulder. "So this car, how long have you had it? Last I remembered, you were driving a *green* Beetle."

"True. When I hit twenty-five, I decided it was time to get a little more serious about life and swapped in the bright green for dark blue."

"Because blue is infinitely more refined?"

"Well, objectively."

She laughed and Jordan felt it right in the center of her chest. It was nice to laugh with Molly again. It had been days since she had, and it was apparently her new favorite pastime. "So outside of the infamous peanut butter breakdown, how was your day?"

She lifted a shoulder. "Oh, you know, baking cookies and saving the world, that kind of thing."

"Multitalented."

"Aww, you noticed."

"I notice a lot. I love you in the cutoffs, by the way."

Molly's cheeks colored and she glanced down at her shorts. "Thanks, but maybe let's not flirt. It just causes problems."

"I wasn't flirting." She tossed Molly a serious glance and watched her turn an even deeper shade of red.

"Oh, right. No. I didn't mean—"

Jordan held up a hand as she watched the road. "Kidding. I was totally flirting."

Molly exhaled slowly, her tone measured. "I don't know what to do with you sometimes. It's like I don't know whether I'm coming or going."

"Right. And that's bad?"

"I don't know."

They drove in silence for a few minutes, the radio playing quietly as they made their way into Applewood. Finally, Jordan turned it off.

"Truth or dare."

It took Molly several moments to answer. "Truth."

Jordan's eyes never left the road. Her words were slow and even when she asked the question that she had to know the answer to. "Do you think about that night as much as I do?"

They turned onto Molly's street. "You know what? I don't want to play."

"Why do you always do that?" Jordan asked, her voice mirroring the frustration she felt. "Why do you refuse to participate in what's happening around you?"

"It's so easy for you to say that, Jordan. But you don't know what it's like to be me. I lost the love of my life. My world was turned upside down. It's hard enough to move on from Cassie, to find a way to wake up and start again, but if I feel like I'm betraying her at the same time, I don't have a chance." With that, Molly exited the car and headed up the walk.

Jordan got out and stood next to her car, calling after her. "I didn't ask about Cassie. See, that's the thing. I only asked about *me*." She heard her voice break and she held out her hands helplessly. "Why don't you see me, Molly?"

Molly turned around. "What are you talking about? Of course, I see you."

Jordan shook her head. "You never have. You've always been there for me, Mol, but you've never really seen me. Do you know that I've compared every girl I've ever dated to you? It's true. You were always the unattainable ideal." She studied the sidewalk before raising her gaze to Molly. "I get that it's not easy, the concept of you and me. I just wish you thought I was worth it."

Molly stared at her, her eyes wide, full of emotion. But she didn't say anything, and it was all the response that Jordan needed.

She reached for the door handle to her car. "Okay, then. Glad you're home safe. I guess I'll talk to you soon."

"Ask me again."

"What?" Jordan turned back.

Molly blinked. "The game. Ask me again."

"Truth or dare."

"Dare."

Jordan took a breath. "Kiss me."

This time Molly didn't hesitate. She didn't stop walking until her mouth was on Jordan's and her arms firmly around her neck, pulling herself in, going up onto her tiptoes for better access.

When their lips met, Jordan closed her eyes. Molly's lips were so soft and wonderful that she let herself be pushed up against the car. It was as if all of the cool air had been sucked from the night, leaving only heat. She kissed her back hard, possibly too hard, but it wasn't like she could stop herself. Molly let out a murmur of contentment and angled her head for the best fit, deepening the kiss. Jordan's hand slid into Molly's free falling hair and gripped gently as Molly's mouth, the intoxicating scent of her soap, and the skill with which she now owned Jordan assaulted every inch of her. This was the moment she had been daydreaming about for days, and it lived up to every expectation and then some. Then, just as quickly as it had started, the kiss was over. Molly now held Jordan's face in her hands. Her breathing was heavy as she stared unabashedly into Jordan's eyes.

"I see you," she said quietly. "Believe me. I do." Her thumb stroked Jordan's cheek gently as she lowered herself back onto her heels again. Molly let her go and took a step backward. "Good night, Jordan." She turned, not waiting for an answer.

Struck, amazed, and mesmerized by what had just taken place, Jordan stood there motionless, rooted firmly to the cement of the driveway. She watched Molly let herself into the house, and once the kitchen light glowed brightly through the window, she floated ever so slowly back to Earth. With her hand now touching her still swollen lips, she relived the kiss she would be up all night thinking about. Because it was the kind of kiss you didn't forget. It was the kiss you compared all other kisses to for the rest of your adult life. The kind that left you wanting so much more, yet satisfied you immensely at the same damn time. If that was even a real possibility. But where Molly was concerned, she was beginning to understand that there was no limit to what she didn't know.

It was with a slight smile on her lips that she climbed back into the car and headed for home in the wee hours of the morning.

Chapter Fourteen

There was something about the April Showers Festival that made the word feel infinitely more exciting. Perhaps it was the fact that the whole town came together in celebration. Or maybe it was the cover bands that played in rotation on the stage at the back of the fairgrounds, the ones that made Molly want to dance the whole time she was there. Or even more likely, it was the amazing food booths that she took pleasure in hopping between, sampling all the sinfully wonderful options. Whatever it was, she looked forward to it all year, even if it meant a ton of work for the bakeshop.

As was tradition, Flour Child had a small but dignified booth at the center of the concessions section. This year, they were selling caramel apple wassail, white chocolate macadamia nut cookies and, of course, MollyDollys. The truffles were making their grand debut that afternoon. And after only being open an hour, the booth was already picking up buzz.

"I'll take a half dozen of the truffle thingies named after you," said Mrs. Welch, Molly's elderly neighbor from two doors down. "The ladies from my bridge club said I had to come try them out, and I always listen to them."

"Coming right up." Molly handed the chocolate to Mrs. Welch in their customary wax paper bag with the bakeshop's name stenciled along the bottom. "Let me know what you think, and if you like them, tell your friends."

But before she could move on to the next customer in line, Mrs. Welch bit right into one and grinned. "Amazing," she breathed. "Don't worry, Molly. I'll tell everyone I know." She looked down at the truffle in her hand, shook her head in wonder, and headed off with her remaining chocolates. Another satisfied customer.

"Sugar, you think we made enough of these things? We're an hour in and already hitting our stash pretty hard."

"No worries. There are more at the shop." She grinned triumphantly, and though it was still early, that's kind of how she felt. Triumphant. Bold. She was taking control of her life lately and if felt good.

Eden slung an arm around Molly's shoulders. "My, my. It seems our fearless leader has thought of everything. When bonehead gets here, we can send him back for more inventory."

"Eden, can we maybe not call Damon a bonehead? He's a member of our staff and just as deserving of respect as the rest of us."

"If you say so. And out of loyalty to you, I will try not to call the bonehead a bonehead."

"Thanks for going out of your way."

Eden placed a big smacking kiss on her cheek. "Anytime."

As the hours rolled by, the bright blue sky dimmed and made way for the twinkling of stars. The crowds increased exponentially as did the line at the Flour Child booth. In good news, her shift was almost over and she could head out into the world to enjoy the festival. The carnival rides were now lit up with neon, and as she handed Mr. Walker his change, she stared at the towering Ferris wheel in the distance. Her nemesis.

The great big circle of terror.

Satan's bicycle wheel.

The symbol of all her fears rolled into one.

Saying she was afraid of heights was an understatement. And after a widely witnessed freak-out on the ride when she was twelve years old, she steered clear of the thing. Even the sight of it sent a terrifying shiver through her. Every once in a while, she'd start to feel a little courageous and wonder if she could ever give it another go. You know, conquer that fear once and for all. But the answer was always no, she'd decide most matter-of-factly. She could not. Her fear of heights and rides and all things scary was just something she'd have to live with.

"Hey, proud business owner."

Molly shot a look over her right shoulder and found Jordan leaning over the side of the booth. Her hair was swept partially back and she looked incredibly fresh faced and vibrant. This time a shiver moved through her for an entirely different reason.

They hadn't seen each other since the kiss in the driveway. The kiss she'd initiated in one of the most daring moments of her entire life. The thing was, the kiss they'd shared that first time in her living room had been great. No, more than great. But the second kiss had completely devastated the first one. How? She wasn't quite sure. It was a mystery—as was the fact that she forgot the rest of the world existed when Jordan's lips were on hers. She didn't know exactly where they stood, but a door was definitely standing open. It was just a matter of whether she chose to walk through it. And she had a feeling she'd know the answer by the time the night was over. "Hey, you. Enjoying yourself?"

Jordan grinned whimsically. "You have no idea. I've been here an hour and barely scraped the surface. Done soon? There's festivating to partake in."

"Festivating?" Molly arched an eyebrow.

"Festivating. Don't look at me like that. It's a word."

"Give me five minutes."

"Okay. Meet me at the bandstand?"

Molly considered this. "Only if you have a cold beer waiting for me. I'm working pretty hard here." She offered up a pathetic facial expression for effect.

"I'll see what I can rustle up." And she was off, with Molly watching in appreciation as she walked away.

"You should take a picture. Lasts longer," Eden whispered in her ear.

"What are you, seven? I haven't heard anyone say that since elementary school."

"What can I say? I like the classics." Eden gestured in Jordan's direction with her chin. "You hittin' that yet?"

"Excuse me?" Molly said, shocked, but okay, not entirely. It was Eden. Molly took off her apron and handed it to Louise, who was taking over for her, and headed to the booth's staging area.

Eden followed, close on her heels. "Don't play innocent with me, Miss Molly. You have blatant lust scrawled across your forehead in giant red letters."

Molly decided to drop the lame protestations. It's not like Eden was wrong. "Okay, the blatant lust exists, yes. But blatant lust is not always smart lust, you know? Does lust *have* to be smart or can it just be fun? Fun lust." She took a deep breath. "What do I do here?"

Eden stared at her as if trying to work a difficult puzzle. "What do you want to do here?"

"Hit that."

Eden laughed loudly and pulled Molly into a hug. "I love you. And let's be clear. Fun lust is not a crime and you could definitely use some fun. Get outta here and enjoy your night. I think you're in good shape. Please do everything and anything that I would and that's an order."

Molly offered a small salute.

The area around the bandstand was overflowing with people when Molly arrived. The band onstage played a cover of "Neon Moon" and the vibe was laid back fun. Just what she was in the mood for. The dance floor was packed, but Molly was able to spot Jordan off to the side, sitting on the grass with the more mellow festival goers, taking in the music, the ambiance, the evening.

"I hate to interrupt, but is this seat taken?"

Jordan glanced up and smiled. The lights from the dance floor caught her eyes and the pleasant tug showed up right on time in the center of Molly's stomach. "Well, I was waiting for this charming and attractive small business owner, but I guess you'll do."

"You're so good to me."

Jordan handed her a beer. "Look at that. I really am."

She took a seat in the grass next to Jordan, and for the next few minutes they listened to the music as Molly enjoyed the chance to get off her feet for a little bit. It wasn't long before out of the corner of her eye she noticed Jordan studying her. "What?" she asked, self-conscious. "Is there flour on my face again?" She swiped at her cheek.

"Nope."

Molly glanced down at her hands then back at Jordan. "Then what?"

"I just can't seem to stop looking at you."

"Oh," she said quietly. She looked back at Jordan and smiled. The gaze they held seemed to communicate so much. Jordan's eyes were soft, kind, and through that stare Molly understood fully that she was safe. Jordan knew what she'd been through because she'd gone through it herself. Whatever it was she was afraid of, that kept her from letting go, slowly evaporated in the span of that exchange.

It was just Jordan, whom she'd known most of her life, looking back at her. There was nothing to fear, and the realization was like a cool glass of water on a thirsty day. She was all of a sudden energized and eager to live life. "Come to the fun house with me?"

Jordan looked at her dubiously. "The fun house?"

"Mhmm. I don't do rides, as you know, but the funhouse has always been my favorite. It's a different one this year so I don't know the maze yet. We can figure it out together."

"Well, if you insist. But will there be clowns? I hate clowns."

"I'll protect you."

Molly paid for their tickets and led the way through the psychedelic red and white door. Once inside, it was pretty hard to see and crazy loud rock music filled the space. A flash of light lit the small room every five seconds or so and they used the brief illumination to find their way to a long hallway. "Careful. The floor in here is sloped."

"Sloped up or down? Whoa." Jordan said, stumbling.

"Up *and* down. Here take my hand." She reached just behind her and found Jordan's hand and held tight. They laughed as they made their way down the uneven path together, and Molly found herself on an adrenaline high from the combination of fun and the overt sexual tension that just holding Jordan's hand was apparently able to elicit.

The second section of the funhouse was a rather complicated maze of mirrors. "Get ready," Jordan offered. "I'm kind of a maze prodigy." They maneuvered corners and squeezed through tight spots that forced them close together. But as is typical when dealing with a maze, every few minutes, Molly found herself stopped short up against Jordan's warm body. As time went on, she started to anticipate it, hope for it. Long for it.

A rapid succession of inappropriate thoughts moved through her mind and she couldn't say it bothered her. Her libido was clearly alive and well and trained alertly on Jordan and the incredibly sexy black top that dipped just low enough in front. The faded jeans she wore looked like they were made for her near perfect body.

They heard loud voices from up front as a group of kids entered the fun house. Jordan held a finger to her lips to indicate silence and gestured with her head for Molly to follow her into the darkened room that shot off the pathway at the end of the maze. Stealth was the name of the game and it was fun. Molly wasted no time and joined Jordan in the dim room, the only illumination a black light that caused the white tic-tac-toe marks on the wall to glow subtly.

Once they were inside and alone, Jordan gently pushed her up against the wall. "I thought we could steal a moment," she murmured. "Want to steal a moment?"

Molly met her gaze. "Is that what this is called?"

"Something like that." The sexy sound of Jordan's voice coupled with the way she was holding her let loose another tidal wave of sensation that Molly felt all over. It was the worst kind of physical torture, yet completely welcome at the same time. She was drowning in need after the sly touches, rubs, and bumps of the last few minutes in the fun house. She leaned in to capture Jordan's lips with her own, only to have her pull away at the very last second.

"Not yet," Jordan whispered.

"No?"

"No. I just want to hold you right here for a minute, because *this* feels really good." As she spoke, her hands drifted slowly down Molly's waist, over the curve of her hips and around behind her until Jordan's hands slid down and across her ass, pulling her in slowly, tightly. Molly's mind went completely blank, but oh, God her body didn't. It was alert and thrumming. She took in air and realized that she wouldn't be able to take much more of the intense aching. "God, Jordan," she murmured.

Warm lips covered hers, silencing her. And it was perfection, that feeling. She kissed Jordan back with a wild abandon that she didn't know she was capable of. She accepted everything Jordan gave, but wanted more still. Jordan melded her more firmly against the wall, holding her tightly as their tongues danced and hands moved. But it wasn't long before Molly reversed their positions, needing that give and take, the push and pull. She reached her hand up and around Jordan's neck, then into her hair, loosening it from the clip entirely. But her knees were melting and she wasn't sure how much more she could take. She knew she was rocking into Jordan and losing the last bit of control—

"Whoa. Check out this one, Justin. Tic-tac-toe time in here." As the trio of preteen boys entered the room, Molly took a step back, though her eyes held fast to Jordan's. It was quiet except for the distant sounds of music and the shallow breaths they took as they stared at each other. Molly took a moment to right herself, find her proverbial footing again. Because in all honesty, she was having trouble remembering her own name after the last few minutes.

Jordan took her hand and leaned in next to her ear. "Let's get out of here."

They maneuvered the rest of the funhouse clumsily, their limbs no longer as agile. They made fun of themselves as they went, bumping into mirrors and occasionally each other until they finally spilled out into the crisp night air, laughing as they always seemed to laugh when they were together.

Jordan smiled at Molly as their laughter subsided. "So it turns out I like funhouses."

"So that's all it takes?" Molly said, inclining her head in the direction of the funhouse.

"I'd hardly minimize the experience."

Molly sobered and held Jordan's eyes. "No. I wouldn't either."

Silence hung between them. Apparently, neither one of them seemed sure where to go. It was a tangled web they were weaving, but Molly just couldn't seem to stop herself. In actuality, she wasn't sure she wanted to, so she ignored the voice of reason in the back of her head.

Jordan took the initiative. "Do you want to—"

"There you are," Louise said, semi out of breath. She'd appeared out of nowhere and grabbed Molly's hand. "We've been looking everywhere for you. There's someone who wants to talk to you. "

"Can it wait, Louise? We were just—"

"No, it can't. It can't! You'll want to meet this guy. Trust me." Louise tugged on her arm more forcefully and Molly looked to Jordan in apology.

"Maybe we can talk later."

"Yeah. Definitely. Go take care of whatever it is you need to." As Molly backed away, Jordan flashed the amazing smile. "I'm going to hit up the Ferris wheel, because Lord knows you wouldn't go with me."

There was that tremor again at just the mention of the ride. She swallowed the reaction and instead called over her shoulder to Jordan. "Show-off."

❖

Jordan did ride the Ferris wheel. Twice. Not only did she love the exhilaration of being up so high, but quite honestly, she needed to cool off. The interlude with Molly had carried her somewhere between amazing and torturous, and the cold air rushing across her skin helped bring her back to earth.

She was happy though, and it must have showed.

"What's going on inside that head of yours?" Little Bobby asked, as they exited the car. She'd run into him at the base of the ride, and he'd eagerly offered to go up with her. They'd been friends since they were kids, and Bobby just seemed to get her. He didn't say a whole lot to other folks, but with her he always seemed to relax.

"Long story."

He slung an arm around her waist and pulled her in. "It wouldn't have anything to do with that Flour Child booth over there, would it? Or its proprietress?"

Jordan stopped walking and turned to Bobby, unsteady by what he might have picked up on. Whatever it was that was transpiring between her and Molly, she knew one thing for sure. Molly wouldn't want it up for public consumption, and that meant she needed to do damage control. Just the idea of word drifting to her parents...well, she didn't even want to imagine that moment. "Um, no, actually, it doesn't. Why? What are you alluding to?" She hated lying. She really did, but it was the best course of action.

"Just feels like there's some friction there. The good kind."

Jordan raised a shoulder. "We're friends. We always have been. That isn't going to change."

"Fine. But if you break her heart, you know I'll have to kill you. The whole town will. That girl's been through enough and we collectively have her back. Got it?"

"I wouldn't let that happen. Besides, like I said, you're misreading the situation."

"If you say so." But he didn't seem convinced. Bobby had always been an intuitive guy.

She decided to turn things around on him. "What about you? The murmurings about you and a Miss Felicia Reid are a bit out of control these days. She sits at your bar and bats her eyelashes while you work. It's all very adorable. Interested?"

"Nah. You know me, Jordy. I prefer to be on my own. Felicia's a nice woman. Hell, she let me cheat off of her in algebra back in the day, but I'm not in the market for anything. I have the bar, my Monday Night Football. I'm a happy guy. See?" He pointed at his face and smiled a tiny smile.

Jordan studied him. "That's the most pathetic smile I've ever seen. Don't close yourself off to anything, okay? Just because you're used to being on your own doesn't mean you're happier that way."

Bobby's eyes widened and he gave her a little shove. "Look at you, getting all sentimental on me. All right, Dr. Phil, I'll keep an open mind."

"That's all I'm asking. I'll send you my bill."

Jordan and Bobby parted ways when he ran into his more boisterous buddies. Jordan wasn't in the mood. She walked the fairgrounds, saying hello to friends and friends of friends and even stopping in for a dance or two near the bandstand. Her spirits were high and the night just seemed to thrum with energy. She kept a lookout for Molly, scanning faces in the crowd, but came up short each time.

"Aha, just the girl I've been searching for." Celia Foster, the town librarian, smiled at her conspiratorially. Oh, that couldn't bode well.

"Hey, Celia. What's up?"

"Library fundraiser is about to start. And since you've spent more than a little time there on your trip home, I thought you might be willing to help us out. We could use the funds."

Trapped. "Of course. What can I do?"

Celia smiled widely and Jordan knew she was in trouble.

Chapter Fifteen

Molly looked on as the middle-aged man in the five hundred dollar boots sampled his fifteenth gazillion truffle. The man, introduced to her as Grant Tranton from Chicago, took a moment to think, or study the stars. She wasn't sure which.

"Who else has this recipe?" he finally asked.

"Um, no one outside of Flour Child. It's my own. I mean, I developed it."

He stared at her intently. "It's remarkable. I have to tell you, and I know chocolate."

Molly felt her cheeks color. "Thank you."

He consulted his phone. "Are you free a week from Thursday for a meeting?"

"I guess that would depend on what we'd be meeting about."

He practically rolled his eyes at her. She wasn't sure how she felt about this guy. "I'd like to discuss how we might work together on these amazing little things. Get them into the hands of lots of people. What do you call 'em again?" He popped another. Kind of greedy.

"MollyDollys. Wait, so let me make sure I understand this. You're saying you want to—"

"Mass produce them. But we can discuss the details Monday. You're interested?"

Was she interested? This was a back handspring kind of moment. She hadn't done one since she was eighteen, but she was considering it right now. What kind of crazy question was that? "I think I could be interested. I'd like to hear the details though." Well played, Chocolate Jedi. Don't show your hand quite yet.

"Perfect. Here's my card." She took the glossy green rectangle. "I've already taken one of your brochures from the booth. How about we meet at this, uh, little place you have?"

"Sure. We can meet at the little place." She could put up with his patronizing, big city tone, just as long as he could back up what he was saying. And somehow she had a feeling he could.

They shook hands and Grant Tranton headed off into the hustle and bustle. As he was absorbed into the crowd, Molly couldn't help but smile as she looked down at the shiny green card. Her heart swelled at just the sight of it.

Good things were starting to happen. Who would have guessed?

❖

Celia Green stood at the podium that had been wheeled out onto the bandstand. Most of Applewood had gathered at the base of the stage, and Jordan was wondering why exactly she'd agreed to this. Because it was for a good cause, she reminded herself. She should shut up and be a good sport.

"You all ready to rustle up some more cash for some new books?" Celia called into the microphone. She'd transformed herself from quiet librarian into animated emcee without much difficulty. It was a little frightening. In response to her question, there were some serious hoots and hollers from the crowd. It was pretty clear that the alcohol was now flowing as the festival moved into the later stages of the evening. Tipsy townsfolk yielding money wasn't a bad combination as far as charity was concerned.

Celia continued. "Next up for auction is one of Applewood's homegrown favorites. Jordan Tuscana is now a famous moviemaker, who's making our small city proud. The winning bidder gets three hours of around the house handiwork from Jordan, who from what I hear is handy in more ways than one."

What in the hell? Perhaps Celia had indulged in an adult beverage or two herself. Or maybe she just wanted to spice up the bidding. Jordan began to understand her role and smiled widely as she joined Celia onstage.

"I'll start the bidding at seventy-five dollars. Who will give me seventy-five for Jordan?"

"Seventy-five," called a familiar voice from the left side of the crowd. She narrowed her eyes at her brother, who grinned proudly up at her. Oh no. This was not good. She didn't even want to entertain what sort of hazing Mikey would have in store for her if he won.

"A hundred," called Mr. Huskill, her parents' elderly neighbor. She blew out a breath in relief. This was good. If he won, they'd probably spend the time over a game of chess and some coffee. She decided to root for him. Go, Mr. Huskill. The odds were on her side, as Mikey wouldn't want to go over a hundred.

But damn it all, in a shocking turn of events, he countered. "One fifty."

She shot a warning glare at her brother, who was enjoying this way too much. She would pummel him later.

"One seventy-five." That's right, Mr. Huskill, take that guy down. You got this.

Mikey lifted his ball cap. "Two hundred. My floor needs some washing with a toothbrush."

Oh no. He was kidding. He had to be kidding. Seriously, someone had to put a stop to this. But Mr. Huskill wasn't saying anything. In fact, Mr. Huskill was tragically silent. He was some distance away from Jordan, but she did her best to give him her puppy dog eyes. Anything to keep her out of the hands of her merciless big brother.

"Two twenty-five," a female voice called out. Jordan swiveled and Summer smiled up at her from a few rows in. This was good. Summer would flirt with her mercilessly, but she'd be kind. She'd be hospitable. There would be no torture or humiliation involved.

"Two twenty-five going once." Celia surveyed the crowd. "Going twice." She pointed her gavel at Summer. "Going three times and—"

"Three hundred." The bid came from the back of the crowd, but Jordan knew without looking. She located Molly, who calmly held Celia's gaze, at the edge of the lawn. The crowd seemed to enjoy the new development and murmurs of "uh oh" and "Mikey's got a sidekick" rippled down to the front row. If the town thought Molly was in cahoots with her brother, it made the scenario all the more perfect. But Jordan knew differently and the secret she shared with Molly made things exceptionally alluring.

"Three hundred going once, twice, and sold to one Molly O'Brien. Sorry, Jordan. There's no telling what lies in store for you."

She tried her best to look appropriately nervous. "I can hardly wait to find out."

❖

Several hours later and Molly, once again, couldn't sleep. Instead, she tossed and turned and marinated on the events of the day. There was the fun she'd had at the booth with her coworkers. The fact that they'd sold out of MollyDollys hours in advance of the close of the festival. The unexpected meeting with Grant Tranton that could lead to so much more. And of course, tucked in the middle of all of that had been her interlude with Jordan.

And let's be honest, she'd surprised even herself with that impulsive bid.

The slash of jealousy that had cut across her at the thought of Summer spending hours of downtime with Jordan took precedence over her more reasonable side. Her bank account couldn't really take the hit, but she'd figure out the logistics later, which seemed to be how she was operating most of her life these days. Without a net.

She hadn't seen Jordan after the auction. She'd slipped away on purpose, helping with the last of the booth cleanup before heading for home. The heat between them had been unmistakable that night, and she didn't want to do something she'd regret later.

Her feelings for Jordan were complicated.

And she'd have to sort them out in due time. But what was wrong with enjoying whatever this was for a little while first? She didn't consider herself a selfish person, so for once, she'd like to do something just because she wanted to.

One thing was for sure when it came to Jordan. She had a way of creeping into Molly's thoughts with a persistence unlike any other.

Like now.

Their tryst in the funhouse had rocked her in a way she hadn't been prepared for, and as she lay there, staring up at the ceiling, her body latched on to the memory of Jordan pressed up against her, all soft and demanding at the same time. She'd worn shorts and a tank top to bed, but as the memory took over, the covers were becoming too much. She threw them off of her and let the cool air move across her skin as her mind continued its very detailed recollection. She closed her eyes and let the movie play on as the rest of her responded with a slow burn. God.

There was a clinking sound.

She turned onto her side, and resumed her daydream, chalking it up to her aging house.

But there was that sound again.

Clink.

She sat up and surveyed the window in confusion. It wasn't raining was it? It didn't sound like rain.

Clink. Clink.

She moved to the window, just in time to see something fly up and hit the glass. What in the world? She peered down and her mouth fell open when she saw the culprit. It took her only a moment to lift the window and hang her head out. Jordan stood beneath with the wind in her hair. For a moment she just stared, because it was a breathtaking image. "What are you doing?" she finally whispered.

"Just making sure you got home okay," Jordan whispered back. She was smiling and Molly couldn't help but smile back.

"I did. Look. Here I am." She rested her chin in her hand. "It's after midnight, you know."

"I know. I couldn't sleep. I wanted to say good night."

Molly stared at Jordan, the air around them heavy. She made a decision. "I'll come down." She closed the window, considered putting on a robe, but decided against it. She descended the stairs and opened the door.

And there she was.

Blue eyes, full lips, glossy, windblown hair. But it was the way Jordan was looking at her that stole her breath and sent the ripple of longing through her. Her body responded noticeably, as if Jordan had already touched her. What happened next was clear to her.

They moved to each other at the exact same time, their mouths colliding, no preamble needed. It was hot, bewildering, and hazy. Molly slid her hands into Jordan's hair, holding her in place as her lips and tongue began to explore. Somehow, they stumbled inside and that was good. That's what she wanted.

Jordan kissed her back like she was starving, but Molly was right there with her. Kissing, tasting, reveling. Then hands got into the fray. Jordan grasped her waist and lifted Molly onto the small entryway table. Her palms moved up Molly's ribcage to the outsides of her breasts. There was a moan. Hers.

"God, you're sexy," Jordan murmured into her skin.

The adjective stopped Molly short because no one had ever used that word to describe her before. Girl next door, maybe. Cute or pretty, on occasion.

But not sexy.

"Something wrong?" Jordan breathed, pulling back and studying her face.

She shook her head. "Just the opposite." And she captured Jordan's mouth in a searing kiss, encouraged in a way she couldn't quite explain. She felt confidence for days and it was liberating.

Jordan's lips found her neck, her ear, and circled back to her lips again. God, it felt good, but she wanted more. She wanted things she couldn't even name and she wanted them now. Their pace was fast and that was okay too. Once the fire between them took hold, she wasn't sure it could be any other way.

Molly pulled her lips from Jordan's just long enough to unbutton Jordan's shirt and free her of it. She dipped her head to kiss the tops of breasts peeking out from the black bra. Sensing Molly's need, Jordan reached behind and unclasped the bra, letting it fall to the floor. Molly sighed in deep appreciation then, because Jordan was that exquisite. She didn't have the luxury of dwelling, however, and settled her mouth first on one breast and then the other, giving each the much-deserved attention until Jordan was writhing beneath her touch.

"Upstairs," she breathed, helping Molly off of the table.

She nodded wordlessly and pulled Jordan by the hand up the stairs. When they hit the top step, they fell together again, kissing and stumbling their way into the bedroom where they landed at the foot of Molly's bed.

And they were underway.

Molly wanted Jordan more than she'd ever wanted anything in her life.

She set to work unbuttoning Jordan's jeans and sliding them off of her. The slinky black underwear she revealed was just icing on the cake. Leave it to Jordan to be sexy in every sense of the word. She stood then and ran an appreciative hand from Jordan's shoulder, across her breast, down her stomach, and settled ever so gently between her legs, pushing upward just a tad. "Christ," Jordan gasped, closing her eyes.

With only Jordan's underwear now separating them, Molly let out a long, shuddering breath before sliding them gently down her hips. Jordan sucked in air.

Control shifted to Jordan and Molly's tank top was the next thing to go. She kissed Molly onto the bed and removed her shorts and the panties underneath before settling herself on top.

When they finally came together, skin on skin, Molly's desire had tripled. Lust was a very powerful thing, she decided, as her body rubbed up against Jordan, searching for any sort of purchase. Some kind of relief. Her center pressed against Jordan's thigh and she began to move, arching upward, as Jordan focused her attention on Molly's breasts, her tongue tracing first one nipple and then the other.

"Jordan, please," she whispered. It was all too much. She couldn't take any more of the throbbing, the sensations that were racing through each and every part of her. She'd never experienced anything like it in her entire life. It was like electricity, this thing between them. Yeah, that was a good word for it. Electric.

Sensing her desperation, Jordan kissed down her stomach as her hand slipped between them, sliding with purpose to where Molly needed her most. As Jordan entered her, Molly's vision flashed white. On the second thrust, she climbed higher and then higher still as Jordan continued to move within her. Her body undulated, out of control now, but she didn't care. She cried out and clung to Jordan, her body erupting in a climax so powerful that it was all she could do to just hold on as powerful wave after wave after wave shot hard and fast through her. She was aware of the fact that she was still calling out, which was rare for her because she never called out during sex.

But it wasn't that way tonight. Not with Jordan. She should have known Jordan would be thorough. With her hands. Her mouth.

Jordan rocked her through it until their bodies stilled against each other.

"Oh my God," she breathed when it was all said and done. She stared at the ceiling in wonder, trying to make sense of the magnitude of the pleasure she'd just experienced. "That was so good. How was that so good?"

Jordan stared into her eyes from above. "Yeah?"

"Yeah, really, really good. Did I say good already? I should have because I don't even—" She kissed Jordan in appreciation, but the kiss was like a drug that grabbed hold of them once again, and the passion that had subsided built to a steady rhythm as their kissing continued. Molly slid her hands down Jordan's back and cupped her from behind, pulling her in, which elicited a quiet moan from Jordan. Encouraged, she rolled them over, a new determination overtaking her. She'd been preoccupied with thoughts of Jordan's body for weeks now, and she finally had the chance to do something about it. It was excitement layered with anticipation.

Her mouth was on the move and she settled first at Jordan's collarbone, licking across its expanse. As she moved lower to Jordan's breasts, she let her hand trail lightly across Jordan's stomach and down to her thighs. She placed feather light caresses across their insides. Jordan tossed her head against the pillow and moaned quietly. She began to move her hips in attempt to connect better with Molly's hand, but that wasn't what Molly had in mind. Taking the cue, she kissed her way across Jordan's perfectly toned stomach, parted her thighs gently, and allowed her mouth to play. She avoided the one spot that would send Jordan over the edge, kissing around it teasingly until the sounds from above gave her all the encouragement she needed. And she took Jordan more fully.

Jordan jerked and Molly felt fingernails dig firmly into her shoulders. In response, she slid into Jordan, closing her eyes at that feeling of complete envelopment and began to move. She looked up and watched as Jordan threw her head back and rode out the release in beautiful rhythm. God, she was gorgeous. It was quite possibly the most picturesque thing she'd ever watched happen.

Once Jordan collapsed back onto the bed, Molly crawled up beside her and traced the outline of her jaw softly. "Hey, you," she said quietly after a few moments.

"Hey, yourself."

"That was incomparable."

Jordan turned onto her side so she faced Molly more fully. "I can't believe we just did that."

Molly laughed. "Me neither. We're crazy."

"I think I love being crazy." Jordan began to absently play with her hair. It was soothing, and she lowered her head onto Jordan's shoulder and settled in. She could easily fall asleep to this.

"What made you stop by and, you know, throw things at my window?"

"I tried to sleep, but I couldn't stop thinking about you, us, earlier." It was nice to hear she hadn't been alone.

"The funhouse," Molly said.

"The funhouse," she agreed. "I'll never look at one of those things the same way again."

Molly absently traced a pattern on Jordan's stomach and squinted to better make out the numbers on the digital clock next to her bed. "Geez, it's late."

"Should I go?"

It was an important question.

They hadn't established anything. Discussed what it was that they were doing. It had been all action with very little logic. But regardless of what the future did or did not hold for them, when she looked at Jordan, Molly felt genuine affection. They had a history. They were friends. Friends who were apparently more than a little compatible in bed, which brought up a lot of questions. "No, you're welcome to stay. I just made the comment because I have to be up at four thirty. Baker's lot in life and all."

Jordan looked at her skeptically. She sensed Molly's unease. That much was clear. "You know what? It's probably better that I'm not missing in action when morning rolls around at Tuscana headquarters. Fewer questions, you know."

But in actuality, she wouldn't be missed. They both knew the doctors would be too focused on their morning rituals and getting the clinic up and running to check in on Jordan. It had always been that way. They were loving parents, just not always hands on.

"Jordan, you don't have to—" But Jordan was already up and gathering her clothes one piece at a time. Molly pulled on a robe and followed her silently down the stairs. She waited patiently in the darkened entryway as Jordan pulled on her shirt.

A space had opened up between them. The mood had shifted.

It wasn't carefree and fun, the way it had been just minutes before. The air was full of uncertainty, protocol, doubt.

From the doorway, Jordan held Molly's gaze for several seconds before she said anything. "Tell me we're not going to pretend this never happened." She stared skyward as she continued. "Because I don't think I could handle that."

She looked so entirely vulnerable that Molly closed the distance between them. She lifted a hand to Jordan's cheek, stroking it with her thumb. It was meant to convey how much she cared and that what they'd just shared mattered to her. "You know, I don't think that would be possible even if I tried." She brushed Jordan's lips with hers. "Sweet dreams."

Jordan nodded solemnly and headed off down the sidewalk.

Molly went back inside and sat at her kitchen table, alone with her thoughts. And there seemed to be a lot of them. Her mind became very active, and with lust out of the way, the volume of what she'd just done hit home with staggering candor.

It had been good between them that night, more than that even. But what would this mean for their already established relationship? And where exactly was it that they were heading? Because quite honestly, she didn't know. She reminded herself of the bottom line here.

Jordan lived in Chicago.

She was just a kid.

And she was Cassie's *sister*, she told herself for the five hundredth time. The facts were against her, no matter how much fun she'd had or how wonderful Jordan felt beneath her touch.

Her thoughts drifted more fully to Cassie, which unleashed so much more on her already delicate psyche. As she sat there, flashes of their life together played across her mind like the images in a film. She saw Cassie's smile, which radiated, heard her laugh. She relived the first moment she fell in love with Cassie, after the Homecoming football game their sophomore year. The quiet nights they'd spent watching their favorite TV shows together. Popping popcorn for Cubs games. All of it.

Their life together had been everything to Molly. Tears sprang into her eyes right before the first sob tore from her throat. She covered her mouth, but they continued to wrack her body. Relentless.

The guilt, the overwhelming guilt at what she had done, was simply too much.

"I'm sorry," she whispered to the air around her. But this time, it felt like there was no one there to forgive her.

Chapter Sixteen

When Jordan woke the next morning, nothing felt the same.

And really how could it? The night before was unlike anything she'd ever experienced, and she couldn't wipe the smile from her face if she'd tried.

As she showered, she recalled each moment she and Molly shared in explicit detail. She couldn't get past how well they'd fit together. Then there was how hot it had been. But that wasn't even the best part. With Molly, she'd felt excited and secure all at the same time. It was the most wonderful combination, and she knew it was because they had their friendship, their history to build on.

They still did.

But there'd been a lot unsaid, and it concerned her.

She'd left when she did because she could tell that would make Molly the most comfortable. If there was even a chance of anything between them, and she knew it was slim, it was going to have to be in small steps. She could do small steps. She'd welcome any kind of step where Molly was concerned because she mattered too much to screw this up.

And while there was nothing she wanted more in life than to pick up the phone and call Molly, or even one better, take a little morning trip to the bakeshop, the Molly she knew would require space. Time to process the new level of intimacy between them. And she could give her that. She'd give her whatever she needed.

She studied herself in the mirror, deciding to leave her hair down today. She applied a tad bit of cranberry lip gloss and grabbed her messenger bag. She was due at the clinic for her volunteer shift in ten minutes. She swung open the door and—"Whoa."

"Hey there, sexy kitten." George grinned at her like the Cheshire cat he imitated on a regular basis. Her mind scrambled, because he was supposed to be in LA. It was just like him to show up unannounced on the doorstep of her childhood home, but damn it, he was a sight for sore eyes so she hugged him anyway.

"What in the world are you doing here?" she asked as she squeezed him tight.

"I missed you. Plus, you told me I was welcome anytime. It was a lie? You lied to me? What kind of best friend are you?" He feigned shock. Always the drama queen.

"I didn't lie. You're welcome here."

He placed his hand over his heart. "I should hope."

"Wait, what about my cat? You're supposed to be taking care of Francis Ford Coppola until I get back." She took her cat most everywhere with her, but with her dad's allergies, she'd had to set up a caretaker for the trip.

He rolled his eyes. "It's so pretentious when you call him that."

"Fine. Frankie. Where's Frankie, George?"

"Your next-door neighbor agreed to feed him. I left him the key to your apartment. I hope that's okay."

"Seriously? Paul? That guy's had his eye on my place ever since he moved in. He's probably taking measurements as he plans my accidental drowning." She locked the door behind them.

"I wondered about the tape measure."

She slugged his arm. "Walk with me. We're going to work."

"We are? I didn't know we had a job. I'm moving up in the world."

They walked to the car. "Don't get too excited. We work for free."

"Well, you win some, you lose some."

"Sing it, sister."

As they drove through town to the clinic, George whistled low. "When you said Mayberry, you meant it." He squinted at a woman outside the post office. "Is that Aunt Bea? Oh my lord, I think it's Aunt Bea. Pull over. Let's pause and say hi."

"Stop that. I warned you what it was like here. You gotta admit though, it's quaint. Not exactly a hipster dwelling, but cozy."

"It's more than quaint, Jordy. It's downright adorable. How have you never brought me home with you before? I could find a nice boy and live here forever."

"I haven't been back here in years. This is not news to you."

He nodded knowingly and then turned to her from the passenger seat, joking forgotten. "And you've been okay since you've been back?"

And then she understood. He wasn't here on whimsy, to sightsee in the little-town-that-could. He was genuinely concerned for her and was here to make sure she was all right.

It spoke volumes to Jordan about their friendship. She reached across and scratched the back of his head. "I'm okay, Georgie. I promise."

He nodded. Sincere moments like this one were rare between them. He then shook himself free of the emotion with an upshift in energy. Typical George. "Good. Because I want you to be. Now take me to work so I can earn my proverbial keep."

❖

It was just past noon and they were just hitting the traditional lunchtime lull at the bakeshop. Molly loved the lull. It gave her a chance to have a cup of coffee and regain her footing. Business would pick up again in about an hour or so, but they generally used the down time to catch up on whatever was running low in the display case and prep more dessert items as they moved away from breakfast pastries.

Molly drizzled some butter over a tray of blackberry pie bars and slid them into the oven. When she turned around, Eden was studying her with unusual focus. She glanced around, self-conscious. "Um, want to tell me why you're looking at me like I'm your perplexing science project?"

"You're different."

Molly moved to the sink to wash her hands, shaking off the declaration. "I'm tired. Is that what you're picking up on?"

"That could be part of it. Why are you tired, Molly? Tell the kitchen." She gestured to the empty room.

Molly squinted in confusion. "You're the only one here."

"Work with me, sugar. What's with the relaxed demeanor, the casual swagger, and the extra glow? Did you have sex last night? Is this sexed up Molly? Because I've never met her."

She opened her mouth to answer, but the fact that Eden so had her number precluded any sort of protestation she could come up with. Instead, she stared. Lamely. Because that's what she apparently did now. Gave in to herself and her every whim.

Eden extended her hand as a slow smile spread across her face. "Nice to meet you. I'm Eden."

Molly swatted her hand away. "Fine. Yes. There was sex."

Eden danced in a circle Rocky-style as Molly looked on.

"Are you done? Are you done dancing?"

"Almost." She danced in a second circle. "Was it as good as you thought it would be? Was it as hot?"

She felt the small smile form on her lips.

Eden punched her in the arm gleefully. "Well, color me happy. It was, wasn't it?"

"Better," she said shyly.

Eden arched a highly interested eyebrow. "And everything's good? You survived a very big step. Proud of you, you know."

"Well...not entirely. I had kind of a breakdown afterward."

Eden's mouth fell open. "Not in front of Jordan?"

"God, no. After she left. There was this moment when it hit. The realization. And I crumbled." She leaned against the counter as she tried to figure out how to better explain. "You have to understand, I've never been with anyone other than Cassie. And that's forever changed now. Last night was kind of monumental, and I didn't roll with the punches as well as I hoped I would."

"Is it because you were with someone else? Or because you were with *Jordan*?"

Well, if that wasn't the million-dollar question. "Both. I think. I've always been a rule follower, Eden. You know this. I don't cheat at Monopoly. I wait for the walk sign before crossing the street even when there aren't any cars coming. I've never tried an illegal drug in my life. And sleeping with *the sister* feels like breaking a rule. There's bound to be a no sleeping with the sister clause."

Eden thumbed through an imaginary book in her hands. "Good news. I just checked and there's not."

Molly rolled her eyes. "It's something I'm working through."

"One thing at a time, honey. You can do this." She pinched Molly's cheek affectionately and went back to the salted caramel snicker doodles she was mixing. "I'm going to put on some music while we work. That cool?"

"Sounds great."

Sixty seconds later, when the song "Let's Talk About Sex" filled the room, Molly couldn't help but laugh. And shake her hips subtly to the music.

As the day at the bakeshop came to a close and the sun began its slow descent in the sky, Molly sat on the bench outside watching the world head home around her. She looked down at her cell phone and smiled. She dialed quickly but got voice mail. That was okay; a message would do.

"This message is for a Jordan Tuscana. Sorry to bother you. This is Molly O'Brien, also known as the illustrious auction winner. That's actually how I prefer to be addressed, by the way, 'illustrious auction winner.' I was calling to politely inquire about setting up a date and time to collect my winnings. See, I have a car that needs to be washed and a back porch that could be stained, and word on the street is that you're surprisingly handy. I hope the street is right. Please get back to me at your earliest convenience. P.S. There's possible lemonade. I emphasize the word possible."

It was several hours later, while Molly was in the bathtub, that the reply must have come in. Wrapped in her cuddly white robe, she listened to the voice mail.

"Illustrious auction winner, thanks so much for your message. I wondered when you'd call in your winnings. In good news, the street doesn't lie. I've won multiple car washing competitions. I made it to state in car washing when I was younger. If I remember correctly, I learned from the best. How do I know if this lemonade is any good?"

Molly dialed immediately and grinned when she got the outgoing message. "I'm going to let that lemonade comment go, as I actually *won* state in lemonade. I know. I'll pause for your required reverence. What about tomorrow?"

She waited for her phone to buzz and when it did, she let the call roll over.

"I'd love to do manual labor tomorrow, but my schedule is bit tied up with a friend. Not that kind, auction winner. I know where your mind goes. How about the day after? Looks to be a good car washing day. Tag. You're it."

She dialed back. "There's nothing more I hate than being it. The day after tomorrow is perfect. I'll start the lemonade. Four o'clock? Please confirm. I can't stop tapping my foot until you do."

"Calling to confirm. Cease the tapping. People will stare. I can't even wait, by the way. And I mean that with the utmost of sincerity. Sweet dreams, auction winner."

Molly smiled at the phone for a few moments before moving on to feed Rover. Things were looking up. She had a meeting with a possible distributor for her truffles, her dad had a good week and seemed to be on board with his diet, and she was carefully figuring out how to navigate the dicey Jordan scenario. It wasn't the easiest of situations, but maybe it was because she was putting the cart before the horse. It wasn't like she had to be in some sort of hardcore committed forever relationship with Jordan. They were enjoying each other's company, and sewing a few wild oats in the process. And you know what? Sometimes oats needed to be sewn.

"Sewin' a few oats," she said to Rover to keep him in the loop. "That's all." But it registered somewhere in the back of her mind that it was Rover she was talking to nowadays, and not Cassie. She didn't allow herself to dwell. As soon as the thought entered her head, she erased it.

Not something she was ready to deal with.

She was holding her own, and she intended to stay that way. In fact, she caught herself humming a tune as she headed down the hallway for bed. It was almost ten and she needed her sleep. And as she drifted off, she felt the presence of a small smile on her face.

Hope. That was the last cognizant thought she had before slumber took over. It turns out, there was hope.

CHAPTER SEVENTEEN

When Molly arrived home from work the next day, Jordan was waiting on the front porch. It had only been a couple of days, but she was definitely a sight for sore eyes in a mouth-watering kind of way. She wore faded jeans with a hole in the left thigh, a white tank top underneath a pale blue shirt, that she wore open. And it just so happened to bring out the color of her eyes vibrantly.

After stealing a minute to take her in, Molly checked her watch. "Am I late? I thought we decided on four. I hate to be late."

"Then you're in luck because I'm early. I was free, so I thought I'd head over. I didn't mind waiting. It's such a gorgeous day. Just look."

Molly took in her surroundings. Jordan was right. Applewood had offered up a pretty nice one. A total of two clouds in the sky, and just a slight breeze that happened every few moments. Spring was in the air, quite literally, and temperatures were rising.

"So, hi," Jordan said, was that shyly? Jordan was never shy. It was adorable.

"Hi." And for whatever reason, she didn't quite know what was expected of her. Should she hug Jordan, pull her in and kiss her? Neither felt entirely right, so she stood rooted to the top step and smiled. Okay, so it was possible she was feeling a little nervous herself.

So stupid.

But then again, really it wasn't.

Because this *wasn't* Jordan the way she knew her. This was a new Jordan, and there was this unfamiliar dynamic between them that required finessing.

Jordan lifted a hand to shield the sun from her eyes. "I hear there's a car that needs to be washed?"

"Oh, it most definitely does. And I should confess, it's been a while. You came at the right time."

Jordan trotted down the stairs and circled the car once. "Prepare to get your money's worth. Where can I find supplies?"

Molly pointed to the garage. "Yonder."

Jordan stared at her for a beat.

"What?"

"That was a cute moment for you. Very Molly."

"Stop teasing me."

"I might." Jordan shot her a killer smile as she lifted the door to the garage and headed in. And we're back, Molly thought with a sigh of relief. Just like that, they'd picked up their old give and take.

As Jordan got set up, she headed into the house, changed into jeans and a T-shirt, and brought a pitcher of lemonade and two glasses onto the porch. That's when she took a seat on the steps and took in the view.

And what a view it was.

After giving it a good spray down, Jordan leaned across the front of the car and lathered the hood with generous amounts of soap and water that also covered her arms and parts of her shirt. Her hair was pulled back in a ponytail, but as always, it wasn't holding, and loose strands fell haphazardly around her face. Uncontrollably, her eyes drifted down Jordan's body, taking in her low-slung Levi's and the hole that offered a glimpse of the smooth skin beneath. Jesus, how was it that a woman was allowed to look the way Jordan did? It should be forbidden really, because it wasn't fair to all those she came in contact with.

She watched for a while longer before Jordan turned and seemed to catch her in the act. Molly feigned sudden interest in the cracks in the sidewalk. "Well, what do you know? There are little pieces of grass growing in there. Amazing."

Jordan tilted her head to the side. "You were so not staring at grass. I think you were checking me out."

Molly blew out a breath to point out the lunacy of that comment. "Uh, no, I wasn't."

"You totally were. You were staring at my ass."

Molly was quickly aware of the fact that her mouth had gone dry. "Maybe. But there's no need to point that out." In an attempt to move on from the topic, she poured a tall glass of lemonade for herself and one for Jordan who quickly headed over for it.

"Thanks," she said, accepting the glass. She drank it down slowly as a tiny droplet of sweat made its way down her neck. So not helping her cause.

"You were right about the lemonade."

Not finding her voice readily available, Molly nodded instead. Jordan shot her a questioning glance and headed back to work. Ten more daydream-infused minutes later, and Molly knew she'd be in trouble if she didn't snap herself out of her lust-filled haze. She scrubbed her face in an attempt to wake herself from the blatant daydream that had overtaken every inch of her. And she did mean every inch. Multiplication tables maybe. *Eight times seven was fifty-six.*

But it wasn't working because academics just made her imagine Jordan in the sexy glasses from the library, which took her to a whole new fantasy.

Time to take control. "Want some help?" Movement would be good. An aerobic distraction.

"Nope, I don't have much left. Plus, you paid for this, remember? All you have to do is sit back and watch."

And watch she did. Jordan looked like a cover spread for *Details* magazine right there in Molly's very own driveway.

"What?" Jordan asked, in regards to her overt stare.

"Nothing, you just look…" Edible, her brain supplied. "Like the sun might be getting the best of you. Maybe you should take off that outside shirt. Just wear the tank top. Might be…more comfortable."

Jordan glanced down and grasped the front of her open shirt. "This one?"

"Yeah, it might help you cool off. You know, hot day." Molly fanned herself for effect.

"Thanks for looking out for me." Jordan shot her an amused smile before sliding the shirt off her shoulders and going back to work in her tank top, which only made things so much worse.

But Molly couldn't have turned away if she'd wanted to. Not that she did. In a last attempt to stay sane, she concentrated on Jordan's car washing technique instead of how great she looked. That was a lie. She was doing both because, in horrible news, she was an excellent multitasker.

At long last, Jordan dropped the sponge back into the bucket. "And I think that's a wrap. Care to inspect my work?"

Molly walked down to the driveway and did a once around the car. She'd planned to compliment Jordan's work under any circumstances because she'd put a lot into it, but the end result was actually quite remarkable. The car gleamed.

"You're good at this."

"It's your job to be nice. You're Molly."

"No, I mean it. You did, however, manage to get about as much water on yourself as you did on the car, but I guess everyone has their own method."

Jordan gasped. "That sounds like judgment." And with lightning fast speed, she pressed the sprayer's nozzle, and a steady stream of water hit Molly straight in the shoulder. She stood there in utter shock, water now dripping from her shirt.

"I cannot believe you just did that. You got me all wet."

Jordan raised an interested eyebrow, which caused Molly to play back that sentence in her head. She felt the flush on her face almost immediately. "I meant the hose. The water you just—Ah, hell. You look really hot right now."

A slow, sexy smile took shape on Jordan's lips. "Yeah?"

She let out a breath "You have no idea."

Jordan laid the hose down on the driveway and closed the distance between them. With measured determination, she placed her hands on the car, on either side of Molly, effectively boxing her in. They weren't touching, but Molly would never have known that from the humming she felt across her skin and the aching that she felt lower. Jordan's eyes never left her mouth in a move that affected her all the way down to her toes. Damn it all, she was captivating.

"We can't kiss out here," Molly whispered. "There are neighbors, you know. It would be all over town by sundown."

"But I really want to."

Molly inclined her head to the house. "In there. There can be kissing in there." She ducked under Jordan's left arm and headed casually for the front door. She had no way of knowing if Jordan would follow her in, but she had a feeling.

❖

Jordan went still and stared after Molly as she walked into the house. Who knew a car wash could be such great foreplay? She'd felt Molly watching her, and it had her completely and utterly turned her on.

She found Molly in the kitchen, putting away the lemonade. She approached her from behind and carefully swept her hair to the side, and exposed the back of her neck. She took it in for a moment, that neck, the simplistic beauty of it. She kissed it delicately, drawn in further by the warmth of her skin. Molly turned around, and the look on her face caused Jordan's stomach to clench. Her eyes were hungry and it looked good on her.

Molly stepped into her space, her lips parted slightly. She cradled Jordan's face in her hands and pulled her in slowly. The kiss was equally slow, and God damn it, beyond good. She loved the way Molly kissed. It was thorough, tantalizing, and in this particular moment, it tasted sweet, like lemonade.

The couch was a few feet away, and Jordan angled them in that direction, the kiss unbroken. It wasn't even an option really, to break that kiss. Molly palmed her breast through her shirt in a move that made her hitch in a breath. Molly's thumb circled the nipple she could feel straining against her bra. Not satisfied, Molly pushed her tank top up as she settled Jordan onto the couch and slid on top, all soft, determined, and sexy. With each breath Molly took, her breasts rose and fell against Jordan.

Yeah, this.

This was the moment she'd needed since she'd arrived at Molly's house. It was quite easily, perfection.

She was perfection.

After one last searing kiss, Molly pushed the cups of Jordan's bra up, and with her tongue began to trace circles around first one breast then the other. As she pulled a nipple more firmly into her mouth and sucked, Jordan moaned quietly. She reached around and pulled Molly firmly up against her, needing so much more and not wanting to wait for it. But Molly gently grasped her wrists and placed them next to her head in a signal that she was in charge, a move that upped Jordan's level of need about three notches. The expression on her face was one of such earnest intent that it was all Jordan could do to surrender to her touch.

God, this woman. She was dying.

Molly kissed lazily down her stomach to her abdomen and began to unbutton her jeans slowly, excruciatingly so, and when it just about seemed like her world had stopped on its axis, there was a knock at the door. They both went still. When the sound of a doorbell followed, their eyes met. "Just stay quiet and they'll go away," Molly whispered.

Jordan nodded and held her eyes, trying desperately to maintain her breathing with Molly's hands still on the zipper of her jeans. Several seconds passed.

"MollyDolly, you home?" Another knock. "Your car is in the driveway."

Molly's eyes widened and she pushed herself up. "Dad?" she called. "How did he get here?" she murmured and made her way quickly to the door.

Jordan took the cue and put herself back together again, attempting to resemble a normal human being going about life. No crazy almost-sex here. She followed Molly to the entryway where she found her ushering her father into the house.

"Hi there, sweetheart," he said, kissing Molly's cheek and squeezing her tight.

Molly looked incredibly concerned. "Is everything all right? What's going on?"

"No, no, everything is fine. Just thought I'd pay my daughter a visit. Oh, hello," he said, noticing Jordan for the first time.

"Dad, it's Jordan Tuscana. You remember Jordan."

He looked harder and broke into an enormous grin. "Why, it sure is. Well, would you look at this girl? I haven't seen you in years." He closed the distance between them and pulled Jordan into a warm embrace. She'd always liked Mr. O'Brien. There was something about him that spoke of kindness, and there was always that contagious twinkle in his eye. Plus, he used to give her a free cookie when she'd stopped by the bakeshop growing up.

"Hi, Mr. O. It's so good to see you."

"You too." He turned to Molly and hooked a thumb at Jordan. "This one's turned into quite a looker."

"She has," Molly agreed conservatively. "All grown up, it seems."

"Doesn't it just seem?" Jordan said playfully, sliding Molly a private look. Molly responded with widened eyes, a silent warning for her to behave.

"You don't look much like Cassie," Mr. O'Brien said, studying Jordan. "But I suppose you always favored your mother's side of the family and Cassie your father's. Wouldn't you say, Molly?"

Jordan caught the obvious tension that entered Molly's body at the mention of her sister and deflated a little at the sight. It was still there, that silent barrier between them. Maybe it always would be.

"Yeah, I'd say that's about right." But her eyes had lost the vibrancy that had been there just a moment before, and Jordan felt the hit.

She'd spent her whole life being compared to Cassie. Why would this be any different? The only thing was, it was too important to pale in comparison when it came to Molly. She couldn't live with falling short in this instance. So what did that mean for them?

"What have you girls got going tonight?"

Molly shook her head at him. "Wait. You haven't explained how you got here." She threw a curious glance out the entryway window. "Did someone from The Manor drive you? Why didn't they call?"

"I walked," he said, and strolled past them into the living room.

"Dad!" Molly said, following him. "That's like fourteen blocks. Please tell me you didn't. You know better."

Mr. O'Brien took a seat and sighed deeply as he settled into the chair. "Relax. I made it here in one piece."

"And what if you hadn't?" Molly looked horrified. "Your heart can't take that kind of exertion anymore. The doctors have been through this with you. Why won't you listen to them?"

"Molly, I'm a sixty-eight-year-old man who wanted to see his daughter. And I decided to do just that."

"I would have come to you. Or picked you up."

Mr. O'Brien looked frustrated and a little sad. "I have to be able to do things for myself. Why won't anyone let me? I'm more than capable—" But he was coughing now, and it didn't sound good. Molly moved to sit beside him and Jordan sought a glass of water from the kitchen.

When the rattling cough subsided, he drank a few swallows from the glass. "I'm sorry," he said to Molly resolutely. "I don't like upsetting you, but I needed to get out on my own this afternoon. I needed to feel like a person again. Like myself."

Molly nodded, but tears touched her eyes. She hugged him then, and Jordan felt a sentimental pull at the display. They'd always had such a strong bond, Molly and her father. For years, she'd watched their relationship with envy. She didn't have very many gentle moments with her own father. He just wasn't built that way. A ruffling of her hair, or a quick half hug. He meant well, she knew that, but it had never been easy the way it was for the two people in front of her. They were a team and it showed.

"Why don't we all go to dinner?" Jordan asked. It wasn't exactly her place to make such a suggestion, but it was out of her mouth before she could stop herself. Mr. O'Brien just seemed so sad and she wanted desperately to cheer him up.

He seemed to perk up a bit at the offer. "I don't want to ruin any plans you might have."

Molly shrugged. "We don't have plans and I'm starving. Do you feel up for it?"

An enormous smile broke across his face, as if he were touched at the invitation. "I'd really like that."

"Great," Molly said. "Let me call over to The Manor and let them know what's going on. I don't want them sending out a search party for you." As she passed Jordan, she squeezed her arm. "Thank you," she said quietly, meeting her eyes.

Jordan nodded, happy to hear she hadn't overstepped her bounds.

❖

Molly listened to the two of them in awe. They were like long lost best pals.

"I think *City Lights* might have been his best work." Her father set down his fork. "The opening scene where the tramp meets the flower girl, now that was a masterpiece."

Jordan nodded, her eyes sparkling in excitement. "Did you know Chaplin shot that scene three hundred and forty-two times? He couldn't figure out how the blind girl was going to mistake the tramp for a wealthy man. Can you imagine the mood on that set?"

"I wouldn't want to."

"Cheers to that." They clinked glasses and Molly regarded them. They'd been chatting about movies for the past thirty minutes and seemed to be having a great time. It was fun to watch them exchange stories, each so involved in what the other had to say. She could listen to them all night.

It turned out that Jordan's idea had been a good one.

They'd decided on Angelina's, a quiet little Italian restaurant just on the perimeter of Applewood. They'd shared a bottle of Chianti, though her father limited himself to one glass. The homemade lasagna was to die for, and Molly had been eying Jordan's spaghetti and meatballs ever since their food had arrived. When her father excused himself to the restroom, she made her move.

"Hey, isn't that Mrs. Trimble, the hateful algebra teacher from high school?"

Jordan turned in her chair and Molly slyly stole a meatball and popped it into her mouth. Jordan whirled back around and shot her a look of feigned shock. "I can't believe you just did that."

"So incredibly worth it," Molly managed as she finished chewing the most wonderful meatball on the planet.

"Totally blatant."

"Yeah, well, I'm a daredevil. They actually call me that around town. Daredevil Molly."

Jordan laughed. "First of all, no one calls you that, and second of all, you're really cute when you have sauce all over your face."

"And that would be?"

"Right now. Yeah."

"Oh," Molly said, appropriately embarrassed. She grabbed her napkin and went about scrubbing the side of her mouth.

"No, it's actually over—Here, I got it." Jordan delicately dabbed the corner of Molly's mouth, smiling. Her voice was now low, intimate. "I can't believe the same girl who was systematically taking my clothes off just two hours ago is now blushing over a little marina sauce."

Molly felt her face heat further along with other parts of her. "You cannot say things like that to me in a restaurant. Besides, I was…in the moment then." But just the mention of their interlude on the couch took Molly right back there.

"But not now?"

Molly could faintly smell Jordan's perfume. Some sort of intoxicating vanilla fragrance that was affecting her ability to think clearly. Before dinner, Jordan had run home and changed into her alter ego, fashionable supermodel. Her outfit of designer jeans, a royal blue cuff shirt, and modest heels, was in great contrast to the one she'd worn earlier. One of the qualities that made her incredibly intriguing. Not to mention alluring. So many interesting layers to explore. Molly's eyes dipped to Jordan's mouth, and her stomach did a roll. It took her a minute to find her voice, her body now thrumming. "No, I'd say now too."

Jordan's expression took on the heat Molly felt. "We're kind of—"

"Combustible," Molly supplied, without even having to think about it.

"What's combustible?" her dad asked as he settled back into his chair.

Molly laughed, totally caught. "Oh. The, um, what's it called? The chocolate lava cake they rolled by."

He shook his head. "I wish I'd saved room."

"Next time," Jordan said.

The mood from earlier was recaptured easily as they settled in and waited for the check. It had been a fun night. Her dad looked a little tired, but the laughing, smiling, and time out seemed to have bolstered his spirits noticeably. In fact, she didn't understand why she hadn't thought of it sooner. Visiting him daily was all well and good, but she should have been taking him out more, even if it had to be for short spurts. He was a gregarious type who needed to feel connected to the world. She decided to make a point to plan things for them to do together outside of The Manor.

As they drove back to Molly's house after getting her father settled back in, Molly felt herself at a loss.

What now? She didn't know the proper protocol here and didn't want to assume anything. There was Jordan's car parked along the curb, and there were the steps that led to her house.

Her bed.

So many options with so many repercussions.

Jordan turned to face her on the sidewalk outside of the house. "It was fun tonight. Catching up with your dad. Smart guy."

The warmth in Jordan's eyes caused Molly to relax. "He is. Thanks for being so wonderful tonight. You knew what he needed when I didn't. He had a great night tonight because of you."

Jordan raised a shoulder and let it drop almost shyly. "I don't know what you mean. We all had a fun night."

"Yes, you do." Molly took a step into her and tugged lightly on her shirt. "You've turned into a pretty great person, you know that?"

Jordan appeared genuinely touched. "Thank you." They stood on the sidewalk starring at each other lazily before Jordan took a deep breath. "I guess I should say good night."

"Yeah." And then, "Is that what you want?"

Jordan took a minute and shook her head.

"What we're doing here, Jordan, it can't be—"

She held up a hand, but her eyes held understanding. "I get it. You don't have to explain. I won't develop any grand ideas about the future. I'm a big girl, Molly, and I know the score here."

But Molly felt the need to explain. "No, it's not like that. There's no score. I care about you, Jordan, a lot. It's just that this is a tricky situation and, God, when you look at me like that I can't even think straight."

Jordan's lips parted in surprise. She moved in slowly and kissed her, causing Molly's head to spin right on cue. "Can we go inside?" Jordan said quietly. "Forget the world for a while? Even if it's just temporary?"

"That sounds about perfect." And it did. They were on the same page and all was well.

When they came together that night, their pace was slow. Wonderfully so. Molly savored each tender touch, excruciating as it was to not race ahead. They enjoyed each other in a whole new way that Molly found intoxicating. She let herself get lost in Jordan, and it was the most satisfying feeling in the whole world.

Letting go.

She marveled how adept Jordan seemed to be at just about everything, and that included sex. She knew exactly when to be sweet and coaxing and when she should be neither of those things. It was a powerful combination.

"You have some impressive moves," she said later as they lay there exhausted alongside each other. She traced the outside of Jordan's breast with her finger.

Jordan propped her head up with her elbow. "You haven't seen all of them yet."

The sentence shot a powerful thrill through her center. "I can't even imagine what you're referencing."

"You don't have to imagine. Because there's always later." And then she smiled. And there it was, that connection, that little click that they'd always had between them. In spite of all the changes, it was alive and well and had only been added to by what they just shared. Because she just had to, she leaned in and brushed Jordan's lips with hers.

"Later it is. For now, we should get some shuteye. I hear the rooster crows early around here."

Jordan eyed her with amusement. "You sound like one of the Waltons. A very alluring Walton, but still a Walton. And please tell me that was just something to say and that there's not a rooster in your backyard."

Molly looked at her quite seriously. "I guess you'll just have to stick around and find out."

"God, I think I have to now."

"That's good news," Molly said and held her gaze.

They snuggled in, limbs tangled, Jordan's head tucked under Molly's chin. It was easy between them, the way they fit together. She never would have imagined it could feel this easy.

"Night, John-Boy," Jordan whispered.

Molly laughed and pulled Jordan in tighter. It wasn't long before deep, even breathing indicated Jordan had drifted off first.

She was grateful for the quiet moment because she didn't have the right words to describe what it was she was feeling. As she lay there staring out her window with Jordan asleep in her arms, she watched the moonlight play in the trees and shook her head in wonder.

Something slow and steady was beginning to take root within her and spread out. It was an odd feeling, discovering someone that you've known for most of your life.

It was so much more than she'd figured on. She'd expected fun and maybe even the intense chemistry. Instead, she'd been swept away by so much more than all of that. Everything in her had surrendered to Jordan that night.

When her alarm went off at four the next morning, she snuck out from underneath Jordan's arm, feeling the loss of the warmth against her. As she made her way to the shower, she heard Jordan mumble quietly.

"Not a rooster."

She smiled and turned back, but Jordan was already fast asleep, her hair across the pillow. She looked peaceful, angelic even. She walked back to the bed and pulled the sheet across her, covering her breasts, tucking her in. The morning air carried a chill after all. It had nothing to do with the unexplained feelings she felt swirling within her.

Nothing at all.

Chapter Eighteen

The next morning, Jordan took a tentative sip of the Starbucks latte she knew she shouldn't be holding. George had picked up coffee for them on what would be his last morning in town, but she could see imaginary Molly glaring at her in the recesses of her mind. The beverage was, quite simply, contraband.

She and George walked up Main Street en route to the library for Jordan to show him the business plan she'd been working on. George had some connections in the venture capital world, and though she had a decent nest egg, it wouldn't be enough to get the production company up and running without outside financial assistance. They'd worked on films together before and had such a harmonious creative energy that she was thrilled he'd agreed to come on board.

"So how's the inn working out for you?"

He lit up at the question. "Oh, it's adorable. Maureen, the innkeeper, will be hosting a tea later. I plan to hit it up before I head back to the city. I don't know if you heard me, so I'll say it again. An actual *tea*. And *I'm* invited." George looked so incredibly excited that Jordan had to laugh.

"She likes to keep things fun over there."

"Fun doesn't do it justice. I feel fancy and I love it."

"Thinking of moving to Applewood, are you?"

He looked thoughtful. "Well, you never know."

"Whoa. Hold the phone. What does that mean? And there's a coy little smile on your face. What are you not saying?"

He took a deep breath. "I met someone last night when you ditched me for requisite manual labor."

"First of all, I told you I had an obligation that I had to keep, and second of all, who did you meet? Seriously, this town is like the size of a shoebox and not exactly overrun with gay men in a conga line down Main Street. Though that could be fun."

He laughed sardonically. "Shows how much you know."

They settled onto the bench in front of the library to finish the discussion. "Seriously, Romeo, who?"

His eyes sparkled. "The quiet bartender over at that owl place."

She laughed. "Please. Little Bobby?"

"That's him. Unfortunate nickname though, don't you think?"

"Not gay."

"Gay."

"Nope. I've known him for years. You couldn't be more off."

"Wait and see."

"Fine. But I'm rarely wrong. And I'm sorry, but I can't drink this." She handed him the latte. "I'm on a one-way guilt train to hell if I do."

George studied her with interest. "Suddenly developed an aversion to your favorite morning pick-me-up? Interesting development."

She sighed. "Long story. My sister-in-law owns the bakeshop around the corner from here and—"

"That's who you were with last night, right?"

"Yes. Focus, ADD. We're talking about Starbucks and how it's ruining lives."

"Drastic, but okay. Plus, I'd rather talk about the sister-in-law and why you turned all squirmy when she came up. Go on. Squirm again. I enjoy it."

Jordan exhaled slowly. "I'm sleeping with her."

"Duh. But since when does that kind of thing ever get under your gorgeously moisturized skin?"

"Exactly. It's kind of the ideal situation. Amazing sex. A noticeable lack of strings. My dream scenario, right?

"Right. Perfect."

She met his eyes. "Except it's not perfect. It's not even close." She lifted one shoulder and let it fall helplessly.

Her mind drifted back to earlier that morning when she'd woken up at Molly's house. The sun peaked at her through the window and she turned over to meet it, very aware of her body. As details from the night before tumbled back to her, she stretched languidly on and ran her hand across Molly's pillow.

She knew she should get up and go about her day, but she had to hold on to it just a short while longer, this little bit of wonderful. So she closed her eyes and reveled for a moment, and it felt great.

Finally ready to face the day, she strolled to the bathroom and paused at what she saw sitting there on the dresser. The frame held a simple snapshot that looked as if it were taken on New Year's Eve. Cassie beamed at the camera while Molly smiled adoringly at Cassie. It was the most natural thing in the world, that photo. But Jordan felt as if she'd been punched in the stomach. She picked up the wooden frame as if drawn to it by a magnet and ran her thumb gently across her sister's face. As she stood there, reality came crashing down around her, and she was reminded of just how impractical the circumstances were.

Real life was still out there, waiting for her to return. Nothing had changed.

She looked at George. "It's different with Molly. Everything is different with her."

His eyes took on understanding. "Wow. I was waiting for this day. Just didn't think it would come in this complicated little package. So what's the plan, Stan? What are you going to do?"

It was quite simple. "I get my heart broken, I guess. That's the plan. There's no good ending to this one, George. I should run like hell before I'm in any deeper. I really should."

"Because?"

Where should she even begin? "You'd have to go back quite a ways to understand. I've spent my whole life trying to reach the bar my sister so expertly set and failing miserably. It's the story of my life. My parents wanted me to be more communicative and helpful, like Cassie. To go into the medical profession, like Cassie. At school, it was always, 'your sister never would have gotten a B. Why don't you try harder? Your sister was all-state in soccer, but it's like you don't want it bad enough.'" She took a moment and then met his eyes. "But I did want it bad enough, George. That's the thing. I just fell short. And I don't think I could bear to fall short when it comes to Molly. For her to see me that way, as some sort of consolation prize, that would be too much for me to take."

"But if the world were perfect?"

She smiled, but her eyes filled. It took her a moment to form the words. "She would look at me and see someone she could possibly, maybe, one day fall in love with. I would measure up this time. That's the unattainable fantasy."

George put his arm around her and pulled her in tight. "Well, you do measure up as far as I'm concerned. I happen to think you're pretty great."

"Thank you, George." She gave him a squeeze.

"Ready to go make these numbers happen?"

She pushed herself up and took his offered hand. "Let's make some awesome movies together."

❖

Jordan woke the next morning to the buzzing of her phone. She checked the clock. It was just past seven a.m. Who in the world would be—and then she grinned as she realized *exactly* who was wide-awake and had been for hours.

Molly's text message was simple. "You up yet, sleepyhead?"

She walked into the living room as she typed her response. "Of course. Got an early rise. Cows fed. Chickens walked. They're getting good on the leash."

"Impressive. Meet me in the park for lunch later?"

"I think I can swing it." Jordan smiled as she typed, already thinking about Molly's chocolate chip cookies. "I'll bring lunch. You bring dessert."

"The real kind? Or proverbial?"

Jordan swallowed and exhaled slowly before she answered. "I think I'm a bad influence on you."

"The worst. I'll bring both. See you at noon by the picnic tables."

At eleven fifty-five, Molly rounded the corner into the recesses of the park. Jordan sat atop a picnic table and watched her maneuver the winding sidewalk. She wore faded jeans that sat low and a snug, short-sleeved turquoise scoop neck that had her radiating color and energy.

Molly stopped a few feet away and tilted her head. "Waiting for someone?"

"Nope. Just counting leaves. But since you're here, we could hang out."

"Serendipitous."

"Big word. You must be smart too."

"Oh, I am."

Molly took her in. "Riding boots, aviators, and lip gloss. A fascinating combination."

Jordan let her mouth fall open. "You don't like my look?"

"I love your look. I'm in awe of your look. I would never have guessed how good those things would look together. Edgy and soft at the same time. Kind of like you."

Jordan realized that she was being complimented and her heart did a little roll. She climbed down from the table, removed her aviators. "So, hi."

"Hey," Molly answered softly.

They took each other in a moment before Jordan produced a blanket. "Tables are overrated. Are we agreed?"

Molly slid her an amused look. "Oh, definitely. I don't know why we put up with the things."

"Great minds."

Molly grinned and followed her to a patch of grass, delicately shaded by a generous oak. In a stroke of luck, the place was entirely theirs. There was a mother with a couple of small children at the playground near the entrance, but that was quite a ways back, and Jordan hadn't spotted a soul this far into the park. They were completely on their own, and the privacy was a nice touch.

"So how's your week going?" Jordan asked as she unpacked the contents of the large brown paper bag. She handed Molly an apple.

"You first."

"My friend George came to visit. We worked on some details for the production company. It was great to see him." She stopped a minute to watch Molly eat the apple, because really, it was a pretty great visual. "I'd love for you to meet him someday."

"Me too. You should have brought him to Flour Child."

"Next time. Now you go."

Molly tossed Jordan the apple. "My week's been pretty great. In the midst of all the commotion surrounding the festival, my dad breaking out of The Manor, and well, us, I never got to tell you my big news."

Jordan took a bite of the apple. "Oh, I love big news. Let's hear it."

Molly took a deep breath. "The festival came through. A businessman from Chicago is interested in partnering with me to mass-produce the truffles. We have a meeting next week. If it goes through, I may not lose the shop. I know it's not a done deal yet, but I can't help feeling hopeful that this is the thing that will turn it all around."

"You're kidding. That's wonderful. That's more than wonderful. It's—come here." Molly laughed as Jordan reached across the blanket and pulled her into an embrace. Jordan couldn't have been more excited if it had been her own amazing accomplishment. In fact, she knew this felt better.

Molly pulled back enough to meet her eyes. "Thank you for being my sounding board through this. It was nice to feel like I had someone in my corner."

"I'll always be in your corner."

Molly nodded. "I'm starting to get that." Her eyes dropped to Jordan's mouth. She moved in slowly and then paused just a whisper away from her lips, almost as if she were giving Jordan the chance to stop her.

That wasn't going to happen.

The second she saw Molly that day, all the reasons she'd been avoiding her, the doubts, the concerns flew immediately from her head. Her heart be damned.

Nothing with Molly was simple, but it wasn't really like she had a choice.

Molly claimed her mouth in one hell of kiss, all soft and tentative at first, but ever deepening. She ran her hands from Molly's shoulders, to her arms and intertwined their fingers. There was a light breeze blowing now that lifted their hair and swirled the branches above them. The chill it caused mirrored the one that was already moving through her at the soft feel of Molly's skin. As they broke apart, Jordan stared at Molly, amazed at the snap, crackle, pop of the air between them.

"Someone promised me lunch," Molly murmured, stealing one last kiss before sitting back on the blanket. "Unless our shared apple is the main course." She took another bite, and Jordan marveled at the way she delicately licked the juice from her finger.

"You give good apple."

Molly smiled the kind of smile that made Jordan want to kiss her some more. "Focus, you. What do we have for lunch?"

Jordan shook herself back into action. "Right. For lunch, we have a couple of to-go sandwiches from Sammy's. Fresh chicken salad with grapes for you and roasted chicken with arugula for me. Oh, and kettle chips. Cannot forget the kettle chips." She dropped the bag between them so they could share.

"You're kind of awesome at lunch. I forgot it was chicken salad day."

"Lunch is one of my better times."

As they ate, they chatted about the ever-growing popularity of MollyDollys, the new receptionist at the clinic, and George's lead on funding for the production company. By the end of it, they were full, happy, and ready to relax before heading back to work and the world.

"So it actually looks like it's going to happen?" Molly lay on her side with her head propped up in her hand looking down at Jordan, who watched the trees from flat on her back.

"It does. George has set up a few meetings with some potential investors, but according to him, they're really excited and already on board. A friend of his owns a newswire agency in San Diego, but has shown interest in doing something more creative with her millions. George swears by her and is going to set up a meeting when she's in Chicago next month. I also have a few grant proposals I need to start working on. There's lots of funding for this sort of thing out there."

"I can't wait to see your first film. You're going to make documentaries, Jordan. Can you believe it? Important ones too. I know it." She traced a circle in the palm of Jordan's hand.

"I don't know why it took me this long to understand that this is what I should be doing, driving my own projects. I do my best work when there's passion involved." Molly raised an eyebrow, causing both of them to smile at the implication.

"Today was fun," Molly said, sobering. "It makes me want to have more days like this."

The comment took Jordan by surprise, and she realized something. Molly's face was far more relaxed, more open than she'd probably ever seen it. "Me too." And because she simply had to, she reached out and swept the stray hair from Molly's forehead. It *was* a great day. She couldn't agree more.

Molly pushed herself into a seated position and looked back at Jordan, studying her almost as if she were trying to make her mind up about something. And then, she was all too serious. "Go on a date with me," she said quietly.

Jordan sat up, unsure of what it was Molly was saying. "As in?"

"For real this time. I'll be honest, Jordan, I don't know that it can work between us, and we should both be prepared for that. What your parents will think terrifies me, but we have to level with ourselves about this, about us, and that means—"

Jordan felt a surge of something swell within her and she kissed Molly. She wanted to listen to her list all the reasons they deserved a real shot, because it was like music to her ears, but she couldn't resist another minute. It was that kind of have-to.

When they came up for air, Molly stared back at her breathless. "That wasn't an answer."

"Oh right, that." Jordan looked skyward in mock contemplation, which made Molly poke her in the ribs. "Ow, not if you're going to do that a bunch. I can't date you then."

"No promises."

Jordan sighed and allowed herself to drown in Molly's eyes for a moment. "It seems I'm willing to risk it."

They stared at each other as the weight of what they'd just decided settled over them. Jordan would be lying if she said she wasn't worried. Molly was a lot to lose if things didn't work out, and there was lots of opportunity for things not to work out. And the look on Molly's face told her she was just as scared. "One day at a time, okay?" Molly said. "When do you go back to Chicago?"

"Four days."

She whistled low. "Way to make this dramatic."

"It's my job to be dramatic. I want to live the movie, remember? Don't you want to see what happens next?"

"I can hardly wait to see how this thing ends."

"Good. Chicago's only a little more than two hours away, and I like driving. Sometimes I sing really loud. It's awesome."

Molly laughed and brought her forehead to Jordan's, cradling her cheek. "Is this completely crazy?"

"Yeah. But sometimes crazy pays off big, and I'm betting on us."

❖

"So a partnership?" Molly asked. She looked across the table at Grant Tranton while struggling to understand his proposal. It was after three on Thursday, and she'd closed the bakeshop early for the meeting and gave her employees the afternoon off. There was a plate of Knock Yourself Out Blueberry muffins sitting between them on the table, two of which Grant had already wolfed down.

"Exactly. I'll, of course, hold controlling interest of the venture, as it's my capital that will get the production up and running. I'll also be the one handling the business side of things. In return, you'll retain forty percent ownership of MollyDollys, which also means you'll receive forty percent of any and all profits. He slid a sheet of paper across the table to Molly. "This is what I'm thinking we can do in sales next year. That bottom line would be your take."

Molly lifted the sheet and did her damndest to mask her surprise at the figure.

He held up a hand. "It's a projection, but my projections are right more often than not."

"Okay." She swallowed and looked again at the really nice number. She wanted to frame that number. Maybe take it out for dinner sometime. "Can you walk me through how all of this would work?"

"Essentially, we go into business together. Sign a few documents. You bring the truffles. I bring the distribution channels, the know-how, and my connections with several well-known retail outlets. Together, we make lots of beautiful money together. Sound good?"

She shook her head slowly. "But to produce that many truffles, I'd be working night and day. I don't think—"

He laughed out loud, and there was something about it that made her feel foolish, like she knew so very little that he thought it was cute. "Understand we'd have to commercialize the process a bit. Produce the truffles on a grander scale at a facility in Chicago. We'd hire a group of workers. Correction, I'd hire them."

"Mass production? The recipe isn't designed to work that way."

"Not to worry. They'll still be handmade, just as they are now. Just in larger volume. We'll actually be cutting costs in the end. By a lot."

Molly tried to take it all in. "And what would be my role in all this?"

"That's the best part. You've already done it. You've created the recipe. Added a cute little name and a story. I might need you for PR now and then and to sign off on an occasional business decision. But essentially, you get to sit back and reap the rewards."

Reap the rewards. That could be nice. She could definitely get behind reaping. It was time for a little reaping in her life. She thought of the past due notices that were piling up, the letters from the bank. "How long?" she asked. "Before we actually see money coming in?"

"Well, it'll take time to get deals in place. We'd have to find a facility and get it up and running. Plus, there's packaging to think about, Web design. I would love to have MollyDollys out to the world in six months."

Six months.

The back mortgage payments wouldn't wait six months. Felix at the bank had already granted her extension after extension. He couldn't shield her from foreclosure much longer. She asked the question she didn't want to have to ask. "Is there a possibility of a cash advance?"

He tilted his head and frowned, grappling to understand. He looked around. "Is this place in trouble? Level with me. If we're going to work together, I need you to be honest."

She nodded. "I'm a bit behind."

He sighed and she somehow felt as if she'd let him down. "How much do you need to get by?"

It was a number she hadn't divulged to anyone, but it was time to swallow her pride. Do or die time. "Seventy-five thousand."

He whistled low but didn't say anything. He sat there looking pensive as the tension in the room grew exponentially. This was her last shot. Whatever came out of this man's mouth next would decide the fate of the shop, her family's legacy, and her hopes for the future all tied into one. It sounded dramatic but it was all very true. It was one of the most terrifying moments in her life.

Finally, he gave her a long look. "Understand that this money will go against your share of the profits until it's repaid in full. It would be an advance, not any kind of signing bonus."

"I understand completely."

Another never-ending pause. "We have a deal. I'll put the advance in the paperwork," he said and extended his hand. They were the most glorious words in the history of words.

"We do?" She felt the most amazing smile break across her face as she stood. Relief flooded her senses, and her body felt so much lighter, like she could easily float away. She shook his hand, but it wasn't enough. She full on hugged the guy and jumped up and down a few times afterward.

He laughed at her antics and eyed her strangely at the same time. "I'll leave this paperwork with you and be in touch soon regarding the advance." She was still rocking out to the imaginary victory music when he left.

Things were coming together. They were going to be all right. She looked at the photo of her parents on the wall and felt such gratitude for what they'd built for her. And she hadn't let them down. She hadn't. And with MollyDollys to put Flour Child on the map, business would return to how it had been in the pre-Starbucks era.

When her dancing mellowed to a controlled hopping, she no longer knew what to do with herself. Except that she did. She fumbled for her phone. There was one person she had to share this with.

❖

Flour Child was seemingly deserted when Molly came into work that next day, but with the new plan in place, she tried not to let that bother her. She'd given herself the late morning shift so she could enjoy a quiet, celebratory morning at home after the events of the day before. Deserted, of course with the exception of Mr. Jeffries, who was nursing his coffee a bit longer than usual and watching the world go by from his seat by the window. She greeted him, which earned her a customary scowl in return.

She made her way to the back of the shop to put on her apron and get to work. She'd be off by six, and that left plenty of time for evening plans, about which she had a lot of ideas.

She should probably go over the morning's receipts to see how they did and—"Holy hell!" She was ripped abruptly from her thoughts at the sight of Eden and Damon engaged in a heat infused lip lock for the ages. She covered her eyes out of respect and because these two hadn't been just making out. They'd been climbing all over each other in some sort of aggressive, passion-filled groping session that they clearly did not intend for her to see. Holy hell, again.

Okay. What in the world was she supposed to say here? Carry on? Nice technique? Her brain wasn't working. Better just to talk sans the thinking. "Sorry. I didn't mean to interrupt your making out. Sorry. Your time, I mean—HOLY HELL! What is happening right now?"

Because quite honestly, she was at a loss on every count.

They'd stepped away from each other as soon as Molly walked in, and now Eden seemed to be sending Damon secret signals with her eyes. But he wasn't understanding, which only complicated things, so the three of them stood there in the most awkward triangle of confusion as Molly prayed the floor would open and swallow her up and away. She was tempted to jump and see if she could make that happen.

Eventually, Eden inclined her head in the direction of the door. "Scram, hot sauce. Let me talk to Molly." He nodded a few times too many and finally left them in the kitchen with a quick "sorry about that" thrown in Molly's general direction as he passed.

Once they were alone, Eden turned to her calmly. "I apologize you had to walk in on that, sugar."

Molly was still reeling. The world was upside down. Eden and Damon, mortal enemies, had just finished a round of tonsil hockey in her kitchen, and damn it, there had better be an explanation so life could make sense again. "Don't apologize. No apology needed. Just explain, please. How long has this been going on?"

Eden shrugged. "Three months or so."

"Three months! And you're just now telling me? Correction. You weren't telling me at all, were you? When were you planning on doing that, exactly?"

Eden sighed and took off her apron. "I've been trying to, but it's hard, you know. Damon and I, well, we're...about as easy to explain as a two-headed rooster."

"Trust me. I get that. Not the rooster thing, but the complicated part. So all that fighting, that was an act?"

"Hell no. He drives me crazy and then some. But that's where it all comes from, I think. We argue, we fight, and then there's all this tension in the air and then we have to just"—she made a grabbing gesture with her hands—"tear each other's clothes off and have at it."

"It's foreplay?" Molly asked in disbelief. "You two put us through all your crazy knockdown, drag outs so you can ravish each other later?"

Eden looked at her guiltily. "Yeah, I guess that's about it."

"And you legitimately like him?"

"At first, it was just the sexy sex, and who doesn't love sexy sex? But, you know, he's actually kind of sweet to me. Does thoughtful things other men wouldn't think of. Leaves me little notes and takes the trash out before he leaves, you know?"

Molly stared at her, liking the new shade of pink that dusted Eden's cheeks. She seemed more embarrassed by her last admission than the scintillating scene Molly had just caught her in. It was telling. "Well, look who's got it bad? Come here." She pulled a clearly bashful Eden in for a tight hug. "I like you in vulnerable. It totally counteracts your feisty disposition."

"This does not mean we're gonna run off and get hitched. At least not right away."

"But I look stunning in red so keep that in mind when you pick out your bridesmaid dresses." Which was a perfect coincidence because Eden's face was now scarlet.

"What about you?" Eden asked, clearly trying to deflect. "How's your red hot love life?"

Molly thought back to the picnic in the park and felt the smile break out across her face. "You know? I don't have too many things to complain about this week. And"—she held out one arm to punctuate—"I have an honest to goodness date tonight."

"Whoa. With Hotty McHotpants?" Molly suppressed an eye roll at Eden's new favorite nickname for Jordan.

"With Jordan, yes."

"Oh my dear Lord in heaven, alert the media. Molly O'Brien has taken the big step in living her life to the fullest."

Molly held up a finger. "Except, let's not alert anyone. It's imperative that my in-laws don't hear anything about this until we decide we need to tell them. And we haven't decided that yet. It's too early and there is no reason to get everyone involved until we're sure. Capiche?"

"I think I can manage that as long as you can promise the same about the smooching display you saw here today." Eden slid her a sidewise stare in challenge and extended her hand to seal the deal.

Molly accepted it just as the bell up front signaled a customer. "I'll get it."

"It's probably Mrs. Peterson picking up her triple order of MollyDollys. I tell you what; these little truffles are going to put us in the lap of luxury. They're flying out of here faster than a glob of butter melts on a stack of hotcakes."

Molly took a minute with that one. "So, fast?"

"Hell, yeah. Fast."

Molly felt a burst of pride. "Well, they may not put us in the lap of luxury, but they will keep us in business. Let me help Mrs. Peterson and then I have a story to tell you. I received some very important papers today."

❖

"So Eden was excited?" Jordan asked, taking another sip of her champagne. They'd wound up at a little French place Jordan knew about not too far from Applewood. She'd insisted they celebrate Molly's news over crepes and a little bubbly, which had made for a fantastic dinner. She'd made note of the restaurant when she'd discovered it and planned to come back one day.

Molly leaned her chin on her hand. "She was thrilled. Turned out they'd all pretty much figured out that the shop was going under. They just didn't have the heart to let on, so they played dumb. All three of them. They're about to be out of a job and they're worried about *my* feelings. Can you imagine that?"

"It's a great group you have there."

Molly smiled as she thought about it. "We're a little family, in a way. It's nice to care so much about the people you work with." She reached across the small table and threaded her fingers through Jordan's. "I have a lot of great people in my life it seems."

Jordan looked at their hands and then back at Molly. "There's a reason for that, you know."

"And what would that be?"

"Because of who you are, Molly. Your kindness. Your warmth. It sounds like a cliché, but you're the heart and soul of the whole town, and what you do at the bakeshop makes a difference. The way you take time with everyone and the care you put into the amazing food. It goes a long way. When people walk out of Flour Child, their day is a little bit brighter. I, for one, happen to think that's a pretty amazing thing. I hope to make that sort of a difference one day."

Her words were simple, but they resonated. Hearing what Jordan thought of her, that what she did mattered, moved something powerful in Molly. She took a sip of champagne to allow the weight to settle. "Thank you," she said, lifting her eyes to Jordan. "And I don't quite know what to say after that."

The small candle that sat between them flickered gently, and Jordan tilted her head to the side, biting her bottom lip in a move Molly found incredibly attractive. "Don't say anything. Just know it's true."

They moved on to lighter topics then. The changing weather and the longer days. How much they looked forward to summer and the fireflies that would dance through the trees at night. And they laughed a lot. That was Molly's favorite part about spending time with Jordan. They always had such fun together. Time seemed to fly by.

And it was easy. Just *easy* in the most wonderful way.

Later, they walked back to Jordan's car leisurely, hand in hand. As they neared the car, Molly tugged Jordan's hand bringing them to a stop. "Tonight was wonderful. Dinner. The conversation. And then there's the fact that you look amazing." She did too. When Jordan had knocked on her door earlier that evening, Molly had needed a moment to take her in. Dark jeans and an off red V-neck top that dipped just low enough, capped off with the standard boots, this time with a small heel. Not overly fancy, but killer when it was Jordan wearing it. Her mouth had gone dry at the sight.

Jordan stepped into her. "Then I hope you won't mind if I do this." She dipped her head and kissed Molly, a slow gentle kiss that left her skin tingling and alive.

"You kiss pretty good, Hotty McHotpants."

"What did you just call me?" Jordan whispered against her mouth, the corners of her lips curving in amusement.

"You heard me," Molly said, leaning in for more and sliding her arms around Jordan's neck in the process. Yeah, this was a pretty good date, she thought lazily, as they kissed some more. Finally, she pulled back and looked into Jordan's eyes. "Now take me home. There's homemade Oreo ice cream."

Jordan's mouth fell open a little. "Sometimes when I think you can't get any better, you somehow do. How did you know I like Oreo?"

"Everyone likes Oreo. It's a law of nature."

"I love nature."

❖

Back at Molly's house, Jordan fed Rover while Molly scooped the ice cream. "He's a happy little guy," Jordan remarked as Rover sprang into action, doing laps around the tank as if he knew he had an audience.

"He's a little obsessed with dinner time. A fish after my own heart, I'm afraid."

"I like his fish spirit."

Molly handed Jordan a bowl and made her way to the couch. She'd taken off her shoes and wore just the green print sundress that preoccupied Jordan all through dinner.

Molly slid her a look. "Stop all that grinning and come sit with me."

"On my way and doing my best stern face."

Molly laughed. "Oh, that's much better. Well done on stern. Really."

"Thanks. It's one of my better looks. I added in a little sultry. I don't know if you picked up the sultry."

"Trust me. I did."

But Jordan had to then switch gears because the ice cream she'd just tasted demanded her full attention. "Oh, my. Hello," she said to the bowl as she sat.

"Yeah?" Molly asked. She was clearly intrigued by Jordan's mystification and sat a little taller.

Jordan held up a hand and pointed at her bowl. "Can't talk to you right now. Busy." She went back to the ice cream because really she just wanted to experience it fully. It was heavier than store-bought and the vanilla tasted more full-bodied. The large chunks of Oreo seemed luxurious in comparison to the tiny pieces most brand names mixed in. Quite simply, it was heaven on a spoon. Five bites later, she turned to Molly.

"Sorry. We were bonding."

"You and the ice cream?"

"Right. Ice cream bonding. It's a thing."

Molly scooted closer to Jordan, enjoying this. "So you like this ice cream?"

"I would lay down my life for this ice cream."

"Wow. That's an endorsement. If I ever decide to mass produce, I'll have to put that quote on the carton."

"With my picture please."

"As long as you work for free. Funds are tight."

She raised an eyebrow. "Well, I accept other forms of payment."

"Yeah? Lucky me."

Jordan looked at Molly, and there was that prickle of awareness that started low and crept up her spine whenever she was in close proximity to her. Her eyes dropped to Molly's mouth just in time for Molly to take her bowl into the kitchen.

"No way," she said as she passed. "I know that look, and there can be no getting naked tonight."

Jordan stared after her. "What do you mean? You've already decided this? Not even a tiny getting naked chance? I don't think we should take the *chance* off the table."

"Uh-uh. This is a *first date*. What kind of girl do you think I am?"

"The kind who enjoys a *really good* first date?" Jordan's laughter faded and she covered her mouth when she realized Molly wasn't joining in. "Oh. You're serious?"

"As a heart attack, movie person."

And Jordan got that she truly was. "Okay. So we'll just hang out. And not think about getting naked at all."

Molly glared at her as she took her empty bowl back to the kitchen. "Stop saying *naked*. That adds a whole new level of difficulty."

"You said naked first. I don't want to point fingers, but—"

"Neither of us is allowed to say it anymore," Molly practically yelled.

"Got it. Geez. No saying the forbidden word."

Molly took her spot back on the couch across from Jordan and stared at her as if struggling. She lifted one shoulder weakly. "But you are pretty far away. Maybe there's no rule against, you know, proximity."

"Well, you seem to be way more into rules, so I trust your judgment. I vote you come here." Jordan swung her legs onto the couch between them and lifted an arm for Molly, who slid beneath it perfectly. With Molly-of-the-amazing-sundress up against her fully, Jordan felt every erogenous zone she had come to life and some she didn't realize existed.

But she could do this. She was an adult.

"So tell me about your last relationship?"

An interesting turn in conversation. "You want to hear about me and other women?"

"It's not so much that I want to. But I think it's important I fill in the gaps. Plus, it will keep me from thinking about…other things."

"Forbidden words?" Molly tickled her ribs in punishment, forcing her to laugh and squirm. "Sorry. Right. Other relationships." Jordan sighed and settled back in. "Not a lot to tell. Last real anything was with a woman who lived in my building. We went out a couple of times, and it became a little more about the hook-up. We didn't have a lot in common, though I think she wanted to pretend we did. Made her feel less guilty about the whole thing."

"That's rough when there's no real common ground. Is that the main thing you would change?"

"I guess. She also didn't get my sense of humor. Could never pick up on when I was joking and when I wasn't. It was a problem for me. What about you? What would you change?"

Jordan felt Molly tense in her arms, clearly uncomfortable at how the tables had been turned. "Oh, about me and Cassie?"

"Yeah." Jordan knew she was treading on dangerous ground, but she also knew it was somewhere she had to go. Before answering, Molly pushed herself into a seated position, breaking all contact, her gaze on the wall. "Um. That's a hard one. Maybe her deep-rooted obsession with the cap on the toothpaste?"

"Wow. That's pretty generous of you. There's really *nothing*?"

"You know, I guess maybe there isn't. I'm going to get some water."

Jordan wanted to drop it there, badly she did. But she was up and following Molly before she could help herself, her frustration growing by the moment. Through it all, she understood Molly's thought process. She understood why Molly needed to remember Cassie in the most favorable light possible.

Yet it simply wasn't fair. It was stacking the deck against her.

"Why do you act like everything was perfect with Cassie? That she was?"

"Of course she wasn't perfect. No one is. But what we had, it was more than what most people have. It was—"

"Incomparable apparently." Okay, that sounded overly sarcastic.

Molly went still, the glass in her hand suspended as she scrutinized Jordan. "Whoa. What's with the attitude?"

"Because you set up this wonderful ideal of a relationship which is, A. bullshit, and, B. impossible to compete with." Okay, now they were off the tracks entirely and Jordan didn't seem capable of reining herself in.

Molly stared at her hard, defensive. Angry. "Who the hell are you to judge? And why is it that you feel you have to compete?"

Jordan was too far in to stop. "Just look over your shoulder, Molly. There are three pictures of you guys looking young and in love on the refrigerator."

"You want me to take the photos down?" It wasn't the question itself that got to Jordan, but the way Molly said it, as if it was an illogical idea. It was infuriating.

"I don't think you could handle it if I did."

"Well, it's not your call anyway."

"I guess my question is will it ever be yours? Because I'm starting to wonder, Mol."

Molly shook her head in mystification, taken aback. She looked incredibly uncomfortable. "I don't think you understand what it is that you're talking about at all and maybe we should just—"

"If I had asked you if you were free after work on Wednesday, what would you have said?"

"That I'm not. You know that Wednesday is—"

"Set aside for Cassie. As is a large part of your life, and probably part of your heart, and that's not a pattern I see ending anytime soon. That's the only point I'm trying to make here. She'll always be a part of our past, Molly. She was important to both of us. We both loved her. And we both miss her. But does she have to be such a big part of our present?"

Molly's eyes flashed. "The photos, the Wednesdays, they're important to me. After everything, they're all I have."

"All you have. Ah, well, that certainly puts things in perspective. Thank you."

"That's not fair. You know that's not what I meant."

"Do I?"

"We're talking about a relationship that took up half of my life. And this"—she gestured between them apathetically—"whatever the hell this is, should have at least earned me your patience in trying to sort it all out."

The words Molly had just used to describe their relationship were telling, and she felt the effects of the blow all over. "Whatever the hell this is. Nicely put."

Molly glared. "You know what? I don't want to do this with you. You should go."

It was a runaway train at this point, and Jordan couldn't stop it. The fight had taken over and it felt like they were no longer in charge of it. She was angry. More than angry, because this is exactly what she knew would happen. "That would be your solution. Take the easy way out and avoid dealing with any kind of conflict. It's what you do best, after all."

"Says the girl who fled town for four years," Molly bit out. "Take a harsh look in the mirror, Jordan. I don't think you have a lot of ground when it comes to standing tall and dealing, do you?"

"Low blow."

The look on Molly's face was glacial at best. "Leave, Jordan. I don't want you here. I don't know how I can make that more clear to you." Her voice was terrifyingly final. Jordan felt the blast of those words and something else too. Hurt. And it was far more devastating. She turned and headed for the door.

As she drove home, her mind replayed the argument over and over again. And while she was still worked up, she was also leveled by the way Molly had so easily dismissed their relationship. Who they'd become to each other. And now, it felt like it had all crumbled around her.

God, she hated that feeling.

But it was hard to stay pissed off when your heart was hurting the way Jordan's was. What had started out as one of the best nights ever had spiraled into something she would give anything to undo.

She shouldn't have pushed. Molly was right.

As she drove, it occurred to her that it was time to face some hard facts. If she and Molly couldn't so much as have a conversation to work through some of the obstacles between them, well then, maybe it was better if they were done.

She sighed.

She could lie to herself quite well when she wanted to. It was one of her best talents.

❖

It turned out the clinic's new receptionist was the real deal. Her name was Alyssa, and Jordan had her pegged at about twenty-three or twenty-four years old. But the girl was definitely competent. The waiting room was as busy as Jordan had ever seen it, but Alyssa had everyone informed, happy, and moving along at a steady pace. This was good news for Jordan, as now she could devote more time to getting the details of the production company in order and start to make arrangements to head home.

Given everything that had happened recently, it was definitely time.

Behind her, Jordan heard Alyssa addressing a patient. "I apologize, sir, we'll do our best to get you back soon, but without an appointment, it could take a little time."

"Sweetheart, do me a favor and tell Mikey that Luke is here and that my fuckin' hand hurts."

Hearing the language, Jordan spun around in her chair from where she'd been categorizing charts. She recognized Luke Treyhorn. He'd been a friend of her brother's in high school. From the rumor mill and Facebook, she'd heard he'd picked up an alcohol problem that cost him his marriage and quite a few friends. She watched as he stalked back to his chair, muttering to himself under his breath.

"Everything okay?" she asked Alyssa quietly.

"I'm pretty sure he's drunk," she whispered. "I'm trying to work him in, but your brother is booked solid."

Her mother was out of the office on a speaking engagement in Springfield. That didn't leave them a ton of options. "What about my father?"

"Overbooked. Even more so."

Jordan nodded and shot a glance at Luke. He was mouthing something she couldn't make out and rhythmically hitting the back of his head against the wall where it made a quiet little thud each time. Fantastic. And not at all intimidating. "Let me talk to my brother."

Jordan waited outside of exam three for Mikey to finish up with his sprained ankle. When he emerged, he bopped her on the head with his clipboard in typical Mikey fashion. "What's up, doc?"

She frowned at him. "Should be my line, no?"

"Semantics. Everything okay?"

"Um, bit of a situation, actually. Luke Treyhorn is drunk in reception. I think he banged up his hand somehow. He's demanding to see you."

Mikey shook his head in annoyance. "So what else is new? He's in here once a week, angling for pain meds and I'm not going to do it this time."

"Can you at least talk to him? The waiting room is full and he's pissed, Mike. We need to get him out of here."

He sighed. "Fine. Send him to exam one. I'll be right in."

"Got it. Thank you. You're a rock star."

"That's *Dr.* Rock Star."

"Yeah, it is."

Fifteen minutes later, Jordan checked her watch. Only three more charts to get through and she was out. Alyssa seemed to have everything under control and it was a weight off her shoulders. She had the afternoon.

Part of her wanted to casually swing by the bakeshop to see Molly. Lay eyes on her, make everything feel okay again, because it was eating away at her the way they'd left it. But another part of her, the self-preserving part, thought it was smarter to hit the gym, do a little kickboxing, and work off some of the stress externally. On her way there, she'd call her neighbor, Martin, and check on her cat. Let him know she'd be home by the end of the week.

She was on the very last chart when the shouting erupted from down the hall followed by a loud metal crash. She exchanged a look with Alyssa and they took off down the hall.

When she threw open the door to exam one, Luke had Mikey up against the wall, his forearm across her brother's neck. "You think you're better than me, you piece of shit? You think you can lord over all the rest of us because you have a fucking pad in your hand? Huh?" Luke's voice was scratchy and out of control.

Her eyes shot to Mikey, who was red and gasping for air and Jordan's stomach dropped at the sight. She reacted instinctively and charged Luke, tugging with everything she had on his forearm, but it was like pulling on a fixed slab of asphalt. Unmoving. She heard Alyssa quietly talking into the phone. "We need the police at 282 Comburg Castle Way. The clinic, that's right. We have an assault in progress."

Luke pulled Mikey forward and then slammed him into the wall again hard. A nearby painting fell to the ground and glass shattered near their feet. Jordan changed her strategy and grabbed Luke by the back of the hair, effectively pulling his neck back. His eyes locked on hers and the fury there sent a chill through her. She saw his elbow as it flew through the air and then darkness.

Nothing.

Everything was quiet.

Chapter Nineteen

Molly hung up the phone and covered her mouth and the smile that tugged. Her strategy session with Grant had gone better than expected. He'd received the signed paperwork cementing their partnership, and had taken a successful meeting with a very interested distributor.

She couldn't believe this was really happening.

Things were looking up, indeed.

And she knew instantly who she wanted to share the news with, but then she sighed as she remembered the reality of why that wasn't so easy. The fight she'd had with Jordan had come out of nowhere. And its effects left her shaken, as did Jordan's assertions that Molly didn't seem capable of living a life without Cassie in the forefront.

But the thing that got to her most of all was the underlying fear that Jordan might be right. As she'd pulled milk from the refrigerator that morning, she'd come face-to-face with the photos in question, the ones that had inserted themselves into the most wonderful evening she could remember having in a long time. And as strong as the feelings she had for Jordan were becoming, she still couldn't bring herself to take the photos down. It was too final. Too concrete an action.

Instead, she'd stared at them as doubt circled.

But somehow, in the wake of her fantastic mood, the issues they needed to sort through could wait. She missed Jordan. Besides that, she knew Jordan would be thrilled for her news despite their fight, because that's the kind of person she was. She grabbed her keys and headed out with purpose in her stride.

As Molly approached the clinic, she saw the lights. Two cop cars and an ambulance. She cringed at the sickening red and blue swirl that forever haunted her memory, a reminder of her darkest day. But why were they here? It didn't make sense to her less than rational mindset. And then the fear crept up on her. Her heart pounded out of her chest and she had trouble inhaling, almost as if she'd forgotten how.

It was the beginning of a panic attack.

She gripped the steering wheel and began to talk herself down. The clinic had minor emergencies all the time. Patients that needed to be transported quickly to a hospital or the occasional case that was too big to be handled locally. It wasn't that unheard of. Probably it was something along those lines.

At least that's what she kept telling herself.

She parked her car across the street as a police cruiser blocked the entrance to the clinic's parking lot. She was moving quickly because, well, she had to. There was a small grouping of curious onlookers standing along the perimeter the police had set up.

"Does anyone know what happened?" she asked the group in general.

Jack Asher, the mechanic from the body shop across the street, looked her way. "Jordan Tuscana is hurt and unconscious inside. Not sure how yet. At least, that's what the rookie cop said."

Her feet were moving before her mind could fully process what she just heard. Oh God, no. Her body went numb with dread. A million crazy and terrifying thoughts streaked across her mind in rapid succession and she found herself scarcely able to feel her legs but she forced them forward anyway.

Crazy Luke Treyhorn was in handcuffs in the waiting room when she entered the clinic. She'd never liked the guy. He was the type who would blatantly leer at a woman on the sidewalk, make inappropriate comments, and then high five his buddies about it in plain sight of everyone. And that was when he was sober. "Where is she?" she managed to ask the young cop standing next to Luke. Travis something was his name. He came into the bakeshop once in awhile.

"Ms. O'Brien, you can't be in here right now. I'll need you to wait outside."

But it wasn't like she could exactly listen to him.

She was already halfway down the hallway, glancing into exam rooms with Travis-something calling after her when she found them. Two police officers were taking a statement from a young woman Molly didn't recognize. Her father-in-law seemed to be straightening up the disheveled room, and Mikey was leaning over someone on the exam room table.

"Where is she? Is she okay? Mikey!"

He turned at the sound of her voice, revealing Jordan lying on the exam room table peering at her from around Mikey's body. "Hey, it's Molly," she murmured.

Relief. It was a wonderful thing. She took a moment to breathe because she'd forgotten to on the way in. She'd been terrified, more so than she could wrap her mind around in the moment. And as she'd made that alarming trek from the parking lot into the hospital, something had come loose within her. But she would deal with that later. The important thing was that Jordan was conscious and sitting right here in front of her.

She inhaled again and held the doorjamb to steady herself as life floated back into the reasonable column.

"Jordan, I told you to hold still," Mikey instructed her.

Molly moved into the room. "Is she okay?"

He concentrated on Jordan's forehead and applied a stitch. "She will be. Because I happen to be good at my job."

Jordan waved him away, her attention on Molly. "How did you know I wanted to see you?" She smiled lazily as Mikey applied a series of Steri-Strip bandages to an angry looking gash on her forehead that was already swollen and purple.

"What happened?" she asked, moving to Jordan's side.

Jordan raised a delicate hand to her head. "Asshole throws a mean elbow. Just as I was ready to clock his ass too."

Mikey threw a glance to Molly. "Treyhorn got a little out of hand. Don't worry. Besides the gutsy kid sister here, no one else was hurt. She was out for a few minutes and came to with a nasty little wound that is going to smart for a couple of days. Needed a few stitches too."

Jordan closed her eyes. "I saved Mikey's life."

Molly raised an inquisitive eyebrow and turned to her brother-in-law for explanation. Jordan wasn't herself.

"She was a superhero. That's true. Now she's a *drugged* superhero," he supplied. "In case you couldn't tell."

Aha. That explained the extra exuberance. She surveyed Jordan who lay back on the exam room table and stared upward. "Room is kind of spinning and it's sleepy in here."

Joseph set down the tray of instruments he'd gathered from the floor and surveyed his daughter. "We had to loosen her up with a few Valium before we could numb the area and stitch the wound. She's always had an aversion to needles."

"I like the stuff you gave me though," Jordan murmured. "More of that please. Put it on my tab."

"I think you've had enough, Jordana," Joseph said, smoothing her hair. "We should get you home. We'll need someone to watch her though, after such a powerful blow to the head."

"Uh, I can knock off early and take her over to your place until Mom's home," Mikey said to his father. "Alyssa can reschedule the rest of my afternoon."

"Molly can take me," Jordan said quietly.

Joseph turned to her in question. "I don't want to inconvenience you. But if you don't mind,"

"She doesn't," Jordan answered, sitting up. "We get along really well."

Molly took a step back as the panic flared once again. "Actually, I can't. I have to run some errands. I'm glad you're okay." She nodded once and turned for the door, but not before she saw the look of hurt flash in Jordan's eyes. It sliced through her, but it was nothing compared to what she'd have felt if the afternoon had turned out differently. Those moments, on her way into the hospital, when she didn't know…

It was too much. All of this was just too much.

And she couldn't do it.

CHAPTER TWENTY

There was an annoying throbbing at her temple Jordan couldn't quite explain. She squinted in an attempt to shake it off as she pushed herself into a sitting position, awake but a little confused. It was morning; that much she could tell. She raised her hand to the side of her forehead and discovered the bandage.

Right, drunk guy in the clinic. Fun times.

There was a bottle of aspirin and glass of water next to her bed with a Post-it from her mother instructing her to take the pills upon waking. She did, and shortly after her shower, felt immensely better. She applied her customary lip gloss and checked her phone for any communication from Molly. A text. A voice mail. Anything. She wasn't surprised, but she was sadly disappointed.

The look on Molly's face as she'd fled the scene yesterday resonated with her. Terrified. That was the best way to categorize it. She thought of the scenario from Molly's perspective, having already lost so much in her life, and understood her freak out. But that didn't mean she wasn't hurt by it, by the way she walked out of the clinic.

On her.

There was really only one thing left to do. She pulled the suitcase from beneath her bed and started to pack.

❖

She'd overreacted with Jordan.

Molly knew that now. It had taken her a good twenty-four hours to come down from the emotional rollercoaster the day had her on, but in that time, she'd gained perspective on a few things.

And while it took her a couple of days to figure that out, she knew that now. She'd been so caught off guard by the possibility of something happening to Jordan that it took her right back to that horrific time in her life, and she'd fled the scene in response. It was a defense mechanism and one she wasn't exactly proud of.

In the wake of their fight, she'd pulled herself back emotionally. She'd spent the last couple of days going through the motions of her day-to-day life and feeling incredibly hollow in the process. It was time to fix what had gone wrong and navigate the very dicey waters that may still be ahead.

While she didn't exactly know how, she had to find a way to make it right with Jordan.

She rang the bell and waited nervously on the front porch of the Tuscana house. Her heart sank at the realization that Jordan's Beetle wasn't in the driveway. It was possible she'd already left for Chicago and she was too late. She hoped that wasn't the case.

Amalia beamed upon opening the door. "Well, this is a nice surprise!" She kissed Molly's cheek. "You look tired, sweetheart. Is everything okay? How's your father? Is he doing all right on the Atacand I prescribed?"

The succession of concerned questions was really nothing new. Amalia and Joseph made a habit out of worrying about their family, and she was grateful to be included. "We're both fine. He seems to be adjusting to the new medication well. Thank you for taking such good care of him. Is, um, Jordan home by chance?"

Amalia sighed. "She said good-bye twenty minutes ago and headed out. She said something about taking some time to clear her head before getting on the road to Chicago. She seemed to have some things on her mind, but didn't bother to tell me about them. I feel like I have to be a mind reader with my own daughter."

"I'm sure she wants to. It's hard for her sometimes. She doesn't want to upset you."

"I'd rather she upset me than shut me out."

She decided to go out on a limb. "Does she know that?"

"Of course she knows that. She's my child." But Molly knew it was something Jordan needed to hear.

"Maybe she could use reminding?"

Amalia nodded in a rare moment of concession. "Maybe so. Do you want to come in? I have a roast that should be ready in a half hour. Stay for dinner." Molly's stomach raised its hand in wholehearted acceptance, but her heart was elsewhere.

"I wish I could, but I'm afraid I have some things I need to get done." Molly offered a wave as she descended the porch steps.

"Molly, wait," Amalia called after her. She descended the steps and placed her hand on Molly's forearm. "There's something I've been meaning to tell you. A couple of weeks ago, when you told me you were ready to date again, I…" she paused to gather her thoughts. "I reacted badly. I guess I just wasn't prepared for those words, which is silly because it's been over four years." Her expression clouded with what Molly could only guess was residual pain. The kind that never did go away no matter what the grief counselors promised. "I want you to find happiness again, Molly. That's what both Joseph and I hope for. I guess I just need you to know that we support you. You will always be a member of this family."

It was everything. Molly covered Amalia's hand and met her eyes in gratitude. "Thank you for telling me that." She headed to her car. "Did Jordan say where she was headed before Chicago, by chance?"

Amalia shrugged her shoulders. "Only that she needed to be alone."

That's when it clicked. "Thanks, Amalia. I'll see you soon to finalize the menu for Joseph's birthday party." She didn't so much as wait for an answer.

Five minutes later, she parked her car and made her way to the soccer field. Dusk was hanging on, and the temperature was dropping. She fleetingly wished she'd brought a light jacket with her, but the thought faded to the background when she saw Jordan's silhouette. Her stomach clenched and her chest warmed, and for a moment, Molly just had to stare at her.

She was midfield and her hair, which was pulled away from her face in a clip, blew lightly in the breeze as the yellow turned to pink in the sky above. There was a bandage across the corner of her forehead and she felt guilty at just the sight. When Molly finally sat in the grass next to her, Jordan turned and studied her, before looking back out over the green grass and waning sky.

Okay, so Jordan didn't look overly excited to see her, but she didn't exactly glare at her either. If anything, Jordan's eyes seemed pensive, almost sad. Understanding the need for solitude and enjoying the quiet herself, Molly chose not to say anything just yet. Instead, she reached for Jordan's hand and pulled it into her lap. It felt really good, the warmth of Jordan's hand in hers as they watched the sky. Actually, just being near her made the stress of the last two days start to slide away. There was something to that, she noted to herself. Being close to Jordan seemed to be an antidote to just about everything these days.

And then finally, when the very last of the light began to make its dip, she squeezed Jordan's hand. "I'm sorry." Jordan turned her face, and it was all Molly could do not to touch her cheek. But somehow she didn't feel like she had permission for that. There was something guarded about the way Jordan looked at her, like she could do real damage. And she knew it was true. They were dangerous together, the pair of them.

Somehow, it didn't deter her from what she was beginning to understand.

"I need to apologize too. I shouldn't have forced the Cassie issue. It was insensitive." Jordan said.

"I shouldn't have kicked you out."

Jordan played with the grass. "No, you shouldn't have. But you did what you needed at the time. I get that."

It was the politically correct answer, but she needed more. She needed *Jordan*, and that meant total and complete honesty between them. It wasn't going to be easy.

"Cassie and I didn't have a perfect relationship. We were normal people who fought over normal things like her work schedule conflicting with our plans. Or my tendency to be overly sensitive and resistant to change. I hated that she gave in to your parents and their every whim. But she was mine and I was hers and we had a good life."

Jordan looked at her, listening.

"And you're right. She's been gone four years now and she's still a big part of my life. I don't have the magic solution to make you okay with that. But I also don't know how to just let go of who I am because I've discovered feelings for someone new. Does that mean this other part of me doesn't exist anymore? That the first part of my life is null and void? And that leaves us in a difficult spot."

Jordan nodded and stared at the field. Molly would have given anything to know what she was thinking. But there was more to say.

"I do know one thing. When I thought that something had happened to you yesterday, my world felt like it had been torn wide open. And while I flashed back to the time I lost Cassie, it was losing you that panicked me yesterday. Yesterday was about you. And if I could do it over again, I wouldn't have left you at the clinic. I'd have been there for you."

Jordan turned to her then, and threaded her fingers through Molly's.

And she knew Jordan understood.

"Thank you for telling me that. I know it's not easy."

Molly nodded.

"You're not alone though," Jordan said. "I miss her too. I got so caught up with my life, my job. I didn't take advantage of those last few years that she was here. Now, I feel like I threw away the last bit of time I had left with my best friend. And I hate myself for it and I don't think I'll ever stop." Her eyes filled with tears and Molly's heart broke at the sight.

Molly scooted in closer. "Hey, hey. Stop. You can't think like that. If you carry that kind of guilt around, it will break you, Jordan. And you are too good a person for that." She then did what she'd wanted to do since she sat down. She leaned over, cradled Jordan's face in her hands, and looked her straight in the eye.

Jordan nodded silently as tears streamed down her face. With her thumbs, Molly brushed them away before wrapping her arms around Jordan from the side and holding on, her chin nestled on Jordan's shoulder. They sat there in silence for a long time as Jordan regained her composure.

Finally, Molly broke the silence. "Have you noticed the number eight popping up an extra lot?"

"Cassie's stupid Magic Eight Ball. I say that now, but I was so jealous of that thing." Despite the emotion, there was a tiny grin on Jordan's face at the memory.

"I remember. Well, I think eights are her way of checking in on us. Saying hey."

Jordan nodded. "Yeah. Maybe it's selective perception, but I have noticed it."

"See? She's still with you, Jordan."

"Maybe you're right." She wiped the rest of her tears away as they watched the edge of the pink sky slip away. "I'm not generally a crier."

"I know. We've met, remember?"

"Right. That whole known-you-all-my-life thing."

"In surprising news, there seems to be lots more to discover. I like that."

Jordan turned her face to Molly's. "Me too. I like discovering you." Her voice carried sincerity, and Molly found her incredibly attractive in this moment. Jordan's eyes dipped to her mouth, and she felt her stomach do that flutter that Jordan often set in motion.

"We should probably kiss or something. You know, to make up officially."

Jordan moved in slowly. "Yeah? I do think it's kind of a rule."

"Can't be breaking rules," Molly murmured before she descended on Jordan's mouth. And there was no arguing that it was a pretty awesome kiss. She sank into it, feeling it in her center and cascading downward, that wonderful flood of feeling Jordan always left her with. She moved closer, her hands running up the back of Jordan's neck, into her hair. Jordan's hands held her waist and pulled her gently onto her lap, where the wonderful, socks knocking kissing continued. They were alone under the great big sky, and though she didn't have answers to the important questions, Molly knew the connection between them was more than enough in this moment.

Before the spark between them caught fire right there on the soccer field, Molly made a point to slow their pace before pulling her mouth away entirely. It had been one hell of a good make out session and she was breathless as a result.

She turned in Jordan's arms and nestled her back against her, facing the soccer field. Jordan held her snugly from behind. "So all in all, it was a pretty good first date, right?" Jordan asked.

Molly laughed. "Well, yeah. I mean, objectively. In fact, I don't know how we're going to top it."

"I could kick you out next time. It could be our thing."

"I like it. Creative."

"I have many more ideas we could test out." Jordan placed a kiss just below her earlobe, sending a shiver right through her.

She covered Jordan's arms with hers and hugged them to her. "I'm almost afraid to ask, but do you *have* to leave tonight?"

"I do."

The wind fell from her sails a bit. It wasn't great news. "I was hoping you'd decided to put it off. Stick around a little. Soak up small town life."

"Trust me, I wish I could. And right about now, I'd give anything to stay right here and explore small town life with *you*, but George scheduled a meeting with Emory Owen tomorrow morning, the potential investor I was telling you about. I've put my life on hold these past few weeks. I'm afraid if I don't take this leap now, I'll miss my chance."

It made sense. "Then you should go."

"I'll come back. Or you can come to Chicago. You may like Chicago."

Molly turned in Jordan's arms and wrapped her arms around her neck. "I can't wait to come to Chicago."

"You know." Jordan stared skyward. "I don't *actually* have to hit the road for an hour or two."

"Whoa. That's a lot of time," Molly said seriously.

"A proverbial lifetime."

"Suggestions?"

"Xbox Live?"

Molly laughed. "Could be fun. I'm pretty good."

Jordan held up a hand. "Wait. Something has occurred to me. Technically, this isn't our first date anymore. We're *past* the first date mark which opens up…other exciting options."

Molly grinned mischievously and kissed Jordan. "Do you want to drive or should I?"

❖

It was one thirty-three in the morning when Jordan finally acknowledged the clock. She'd thus far pretended it didn't exist and let herself get lost in Molly. The warm feel of her skin, the amazing scent of her shampoo, it was right where she wanted to be.

They'd lost their clothes fairly quickly after arriving back at Molly's house and spent the evening in tantalizing exploration of each other. What began hot and fast had ended slow and sensual in just about the best mixture she could have imagined.

But it hadn't ended there. They'd talked for a long time afterward, which made it that much better. And while it was true that they'd avoided the difficult topics, Jordan's family, their future together, and Cassie, they'd found plenty of other interesting subjects to cover.

Molly looked down at Jordan, her head propped up on her hand as she traced lazy circles across the plane of her stomach. "So if you were stranded on a desert island, what would you do with your time?"

"Perfect the great American cartwheel. No question. You?"

"Wow. You didn't even have to think about that one. Um, I might try the cartwheel thing for a while, but I'd probably spend time creating recipes from the naturally occurring foods there."

"Well, then I win."

Molly's mouth fell open in equal parts shock and offense. "How do you figure? My thing is practical and serves a purpose. Your cartwheel, while festive, won't keep you alive."

"But think how impressed they'll be when they find me. They'll make me mayor of cartwheels. They'll give me the key to Cartwheel City. You can visit."

Molly shook her head in bewilderment and rolled on top, beginning to tickle Jordan mercilessly in a move that had her squirming and laughing to escape the assault. But in good news, Jordan was stronger and eventually won out, reversing their positions. She captured Molly's wrists and held her down while she now wiggled and laughed beneath.

"Say I'm the mayor of Cartwheel City."

Molly's eyes danced. "You are so eccentric, it's scary."

"I'm charming. Say it."

She softened. "You, incredibly beautiful person, are the mayor of Cartwheel City."

She released Molly's wrists and rolled to her side. "Aww. I like the way you said it. It was really nice."

Molly slid against her in a move that had her breath hitching. She lifted Jordan's chin with one finger and met her gaze softly. "I can be nice sometimes."

"I love it when you're nice." And then there was her mouth. God, that mouth. She kissed it leisurely until finally, Molly curled into Jordan like she belonged there. And it felt like she did.

Jordan fought sleep, wanting to savor each moment until she had to get on the road. Technically, she could stay the night and drive in the early morning hours to still make her meeting, but she was practical minded enough to know she wouldn't be at her best then. But as they lay with their limbs tangled, Molly's face tucked into her neck, she seriously considered blowing off the whole meeting altogether. It was worth it. This.

Molly must have sensed her reluctance and whispered against her neck. "You have to go, don't you?"

She kissed her temple. "Probably."

Molly pushed herself up, looking adorably concerned. "Do you think you can stay awake for the drive? Let me make you some coffee."

She sat up across from Molly. "I won't need it. I think you've given me a lot to think about. Reflect on. Relive." She raised an eyebrow in seductive punctuation.

"Good." Molly leaned in and brushed her lips in a feather light kiss. "Was kinda the goal. Now let's get you on the road to cinematic history before I change my mind about giving you up."

Jordan dressed silently and Molly slipped into a robe. As they said good-bye in the doorway of Molly's house, Jordan felt the lump form in her throat. She'd be back in just two weeks for her father's birthday, but that seemed like an eternity. She didn't want to leave Molly. And how ironic was that? She was the girl who always hoped the women she was with wouldn't get attached, and here she'd gone and done just that. More than that even, because she wasn't just attached, she was in deep.

Molly touched her cheek. "Call me when you get there so I know you're safe."

"I will."

Molly went up on her toes and kissed her, lingering just a bit. "Bye, Jordan. Please be safe." And as she pulled back, Jordan felt the loss.

"Sweet dreams, Molly." She walked backward a few steps, memorizing the way Molly looked in that moment. Standing on the porch in her robe, still swollen lips. Sexy as hell. She'd done a lot of difficult things in her life, but leaving Molly that night had definitely been somewhere at the top of that list.

But they had plenty of time, she reminded herself as she pulled onto Main Street. Plenty of time.

Chapter Twenty-one

Yes, hi. This is Molly O'Brien calling for Mr. Tranton again." She shifted the phone to the other ear so she could better stir the brownie batter. The advance check he promised her should be ready soon and she needed to arrange for delivery or pickup, whichever would be faster. The bank continued to call on practically a daily basis now and she no longer had the luxury of that little cushion of time.

The curt woman on the other end of the line sighed. "Yes, Ms. O'Brien. Mr. Tranton received your messages and instructed me to tell you that your advance check would be ready by the end of next week. He was hopeful you'd have time to discuss a few details of the Walgreens deal. It's almost in place."

Praise baby Jesus.

She'd held the bank off as long as she possibly could, and the minutes were beginning to matter, a place she'd never thought she'd be. Even though she was growing further and further behind, if the check was ready when his assistant professed it would be, all would be well.

It was Tuesday. She could make it to Monday. She could. Big sigh of relief. "Thank you so much."

"Mr. Tranton will be in touch within the week to set up the planning session."

"That sounds great. I appreciate your help."

She hung up the phone and turned to Eden and Louise who stared at her like a couple of beauty pageant contestants, awaiting the results.

She let out a breath. "The check will be ready on Monday. We're still good."

The tension left their bodies immediately as they released one another, but Eden tried to play if off. "I told you, sugar! You worry too much! Pass me that salted butter!" But the covert look she exchanged with Louise coupled with the fact that she was now speaking in exclamation points tipped her hand. She'd been every bit as concerned as Molly had.

They were in this together, she realized. Her little group. They were a makeshift Flour Child family, and she was so grateful for them it almost hurt.

But in newly fantastic news, the bakeshop family was going to be okay. She'd just been assured of that. She took a moment to call Felix over at the mortgage department and let him know that the check was on its way. He'd seemed conservatively happy to hear it, and she knew she owed him her firstborn for all the interference he'd run for her over the last six months.

Content that her job was no longer at stake, Louise headed to the front of the shop to work the counter. "I'm off to greet the customers and hopefully dodge Mr. Jeffries' grumbling."

Molly turned to her. "That man adores you, Lou. He just doesn't know how to show it."

"Well, he should try smiling once in a while. You know, prove he has teeth. You never know at his age."

Eden laughed. "Tall order for that man."

Molly and Eden went back to their respective projects, brownies and croissants, working in quiet tandem.

Eden shot her a look across the island. "You hangin' in there, sugar?"

She glanced up. "Sure. I'm getting by."

Eden leaned her hip against the counter and folded her arms. "You miss her, don't you?"

"Who?" It was a lame attempt to sidestep a conversation that would make her think about Jordan, because when she thought about Jordan, all she did was think about Jordan, so she rationed it out in small doses. The truth of it was she missed her more than she would have thought possible.

"Don't play dumb with me, missy. You've fallen for her and we all know it. It's written all over your pretty little face when you get all daydreamy and smile at nothing."

"I do miss her. A lot, actually."

Eden's eyes sparkled with excitement. "So you're in this for real? Inching toward the big L-O-V-E? White picket fence and all?"

And there was that hesitation. As much as she was feeling for Jordan, there were obstacles holding her back when she considered anything too permanent. Because there was the bigger picture to consider. Among other issues, there were the Tuscanas, who would hate the idea of she and Jordan together by design. And the concept of losing them was almost too much to think about. They were the only family she had outside of her father. It would crush her if they were no longer a part of her life. And what if she devastated them with this relationship, and she and Jordan didn't work out in the end. The risk was exponential and she wasn't generally a risk taker.

"I think love is a lofty word."

"Okay, so you're playing it conservative. I can get behind that. But it's good? Things are progressing?"

"They are, and most of the time I'm incredibly happy about that. But it's different. She's...different." Molly slid the brownies into the oven and pushed herself up onto the counter.

"And that's a problem?"

"It's..." She hesitated, not knowing quite how to explain the thoughts that had her consumed with guilt for the past couple of days. "It's a problem for me, I guess. Yeah."

Eden narrowed her eyes, trying to understand. "Wait. So you're comparing her to her sister?"

Molly took a moment and nodded. "I wish I didn't, but yeah. And when I do compare them, I feel horrible. Hence, the problem."

Eden took a breath. "You're gonna have to decode this one for me."

Molly sat up straighter thinking of another way to explain. "Cassie was goal oriented, dependable, and sweet, but fairly serious.

Jordan is funny, wild, and unpredictable. She's the life of every room she's in. Sometimes it's hard to believe they're even sisters."

"Still not sensing a problem."

"There's more." And here we go. "With Cassie, things were sweet. They were comfortable, right where you'd want them to be."

"And with Jordan?"

She shook her head slowly. "We click in a way I've never experienced. It's like this thing that overtakes me when I'm around her. I just want to talk to her, laugh with her, stare at her all the time. It's a lot to take in in a really wonderful way."

"Different is okay, Molly."

"Different *is* okay. But what if it's more? *More* doesn't feel okay."

Eden's face softened as realization struck. She moved to her quickly, taking Molly gently by the shoulders and rubbing her hands up and down. "Oh, sweetie. You're worried that you fit better with Jordan than you fit with Cassie? You can't do that to yourself. You can't beat yourself up for what you feel. That's not something you're in control of. I get that you don't want to betray Cassie's memory, but that's not what's happening here. You have to move on with your life and forgive yourself for what's happening between you and Jordan, no matter how strong your feelings are."

Molly raised her gaze to Eden, her voice laced with fear. "I don't know if I can."

❖

It was the end of the day Wednesday and Jordan flopped onto her couch and turned on a little jazz to take the edge off her aching neck muscles. She'd spent the day researching office space and pricing equipment, and now her brain felt fuzzy, and really, who could blame it?

In some ways, Jordan was happy to be home. It felt good to see the familiar walls of her downtown apartment and scratch Frankie under his chin again. He still hadn't totally forgiven her for leaving, but they were baby-stepping their way back to a respectable cat-human relationship. She fawned over him and he acted like he could perhaps put up with it. It was a start.

The meeting with the investors had gone well and after taking a look at some proposed projects and a reel of Jordan's work, it seemed they had a tentative deal. And that meant cash. This production company was actually going to happen and there was a lot to be done.

But she had to hand it to herself. It'd been a productive month. She'd figured out her next career move, something she had a true passion for, and had even reconnected with her family. Yet, for the past week, her life felt incomplete and she knew why. Molly wasn't there, and that made everything seem a little less vibrant.

She wanted the vibrant back.

It was a problem she didn't see going away easily, if ever. But the space between them this past week had offered her perspective. She knew what she wanted one hundred percent, and it was Molly. And though that didn't exactly come in a nice neat little package, she no longer cared. How brave was that?

She slid a look to the digital clock on the microwave and her heart did a little leap of excitement, acrobatic heart that it was these days. Three minutes until the phone date she and Molly had scheduled earlier in the week. She'd been looking forward to it all day. She stood for a quick second and checked herself in the mirror, which was ridiculous because it was a phone call. But then there seemed to be a lot of ridiculous lately.

"What?" she asked Frankie, who only yawned in cat judgment. "You haven't met her. You have no basis on which to weigh in." He looked at the wall in boredom.

She and Molly had exchanged a couple of phone calls and a few scattered text messages since she'd been home, but it had fallen drastically short of satisfaction for her. While on one hand, they'd both been busy, on the other, they were both probably a little cautious about the relationship. But as the days sans Molly added up, she felt her cautious side slipping away more and more.

The phone in her pocket started to vibrate. Right on time. She felt the smile on her face take shape and grow. "Hey, you."

Molly sighed into the phone. "So it's really nice to hear your voice."

"It is?" Jordan got up and walked to her kitchen table because the zip of energy talking to Molly gave her required movement.

"You have no idea."

"How was your day? Give me the scoop."

"Five trays of blueberry muffins, a hundred million MollyDollys, three fancy birthday cakes, and that was just my morning. Now a segue. When do I see you exactly? Because that's what I'd like to focus on."

Jordan grinned into the phone. "I like that you announce your segues. Not enough people do that. And three days from now. I thought I'd come a couple of hours before the party to help out. My mom would like that."

"I would like that."

"All the more reason."

"How's Chicago?"

"Busy. I feel like I haven't stopped since I've been home. But the deal's in place. It's time to start putting plans in motion for my first project, which I think might be an extension of the short film I did in college about the suicide forest in Japan. Do you remember that one? It would be a more full-length version now that I have the means."

Molly took in air. "I loved that film. It was absolutely chilling. That's when I knew that you were gifted at this, when you could elicit that kind of response in me."

The compliment resonated, and she took a minute to let it wash over her. No one from back home had showed that much interest in her college work. Her family had definitely downplayed it, probably afraid to encourage her too much in that direction. "Thanks. That film meant a lot to me when I made it. One of the reasons I want to make more like it."

"And you will." A pause. "So as we talk, I'm trying to picture you at your place, all urban and ultra cool. What's it like? A person's home says a lot about them, you know?"

"That sounds like a lot of pressure. Not sure I want to tell you now."

"Then don't. Let me give it a shot. Okay, so I'm imagining brick walls in the living room, steel lighting fixtures in a rather open kitchen, and then a large bedroom with not a lot of furniture. You're kind of a minimalistic kind of girl."

Whoa. It was shockingly accurate. "Um. Yeah. Except the bedroom is pretty standard size. Other than that, you're spot on. How exactly did you do that?" She glanced around curiously for the hidden cameras.

"I just thought about you and what you like."

"Impressive, and I mean that genuinely."

"Well, if I remember correctly, you're really good at knowing what I like."

Heat flooded her face and she wandered aimlessly back into the living room. "You're too far away for a line like that. You'll keep me up all night thinking about it."

Molly chuckled quietly. "I was referencing chicken salad and romantic comedies, but we can talk about the other things I like, you know, if you want to."

The insinuation made her stomach tighten reflexively as memories of their most recent night together flashed across her mind. Plus, there was the fact that she just loved Molly's voice. She loved it even more when she dropped her tone and sounded super sexy, which was in complete contrast to her everyday good girl persona. It was thrilling to say the least.

She sighed deeply. "Exactly how many more hours until I see you again?"

Chapter Twenty-two

By late in the afternoon on Friday, Molly's kitchen looked like a confection tornado had blown through it. And why shouldn't it? She'd spent the entire day at home, baking away in preparation for her father-in-law's birthday party the following day. She left Flour Child in Eden's trustworthy hands in the meantime and only called in to check on things three times. She was working on easing her status as control freak when it came to the bakeshop she loved so dearly.

She let out a breath and surveyed her work. There were plates full of a half dozen different flavors of truffles. Oversized white chocolate dipped pretzels dried on the rack next to coconut macaroons, which were hanging out with a platter of giant chocolate chip cookies. Now those had come out nicely. And the pièce de résistance, the chocolate marble birthday cake, was baking snugly in the oven. Or at least the third layer of it was.

No one at this birthday party was going to find the dessert table lacking in any capacity. Fully aware of the reputation she planned to live up to, she had conquered sugar township and all the surrounding territories.

To accompany her efforts, she'd put on some sultry blues from her iPod, and the tunes inspired her to sway her hips ever so slightly. And to reward her hard work, she celebrated with a glass of Tempranillo, her new favorite red wine blend. It was true she still had the chocolate covered strawberries to make, followed by some clean up, but she allowed herself a few minutes to revel in her success.

"Check it out, Rover." She indicated the stash of goodies with a tilt of her head. "Bet you couldn't have done all of that." He continued to swim laps. She raised a shoulder. "Well, you couldn't."

She slid a glance at the clock. It was a little past four o'clock, and if her calculations were correct, Damon should be finishing up his other deliveries and would be by soon with the apple caramel shots Louise had prepared for the party. She would need to make room in the refrigerator in her garage if she wanted to—

The sound of the doorbell stopped her mid thought. Perfect. Right on time.

She swung the door open to the tray of small shot glasses, but as she raised her gaze, her breath caught. Because it was Jordan who stood there, offering the most welcome smile in history. Her hair was pulled into a stylish ponytail that looked the perfect addition to her slim fitting jeans and the dark red thermal top. "Delivery," she said with a little tilt of her head.

Molly's mouth fell open and her heart stuttered in her chest. Because it really was the most fantastic surprise ever. They stood there smiling at each other stupidly before Molly found her voice. "How did you—What are you doing here?"

"Bringing you these." She glanced down at the tray. "Whatever these are."

She took the tray from Jordan. "Caramel apple shots. Now get in here right now so I can make a big deal out of you."

"I've always liked attention."

Molly followed Jordan into the house, her insides doing a happy dance at this latest development. She set the tray on the counter and turned in time to find herself pulled into Jordan's arms for a scorching kiss. She was grateful Jordan had a firm hold on her because her knees just about went to Jell-O.

"Sorry. I've been waiting to do that all week."

"True story?" Molly murmured against her mouth, going in for more.

"Mhmm," she said. "And worth the wait."

Molly tilted her head and studied Jordan. "But really, how is it that you're here right now? Explain yourself."

"I pulled a couple of all-nighters and made a satisfactory dent in the planning for the company, which I should tell you has a name now."

"And you're just now mentioning this? You should have called with news like that. What is it?"

"Journey Production Group. Because essentially, that's what this whole thing has been for me, a journey. And these last two months have been what I hope is just the beginning."

Molly nodded as she took it in, understanding the meaning. "I love it, Jordan. I really do."

She smiled. "Thank you. But as far as my early arrival goes, I do have one request. Don't tell my parents that I came to town early. They'll be pissed I didn't spend the time at their place and right now, I just—" She broke off as something snagged her attention. She looked past Molly in mystification. "What in the world have you been doing in here to make it smell so wonderful? Are you harboring Keebler elves?"

"No elves. There are elfin labor laws. You're probably smelling chocolate chip cookies, truffles, macaroons—" She didn't get to continue her list because Jordan was already gone, investigating the overflowing trays like a six-year-old on Christmas morning. "Halt right there. Back away from the tasty treats."

Jordan froze with a cookie halfway to her lips. "No cookie?"

"Nope." Her face fell, and Molly forced herself not to laugh because it was possibly the most adorable look she'd ever seen. "Sorry, Charlie. Those are strictly for tomorrow."

"But I drove a long way and these are still oh so warm."

It was too much. The large sorrowful puppy dog eyes, the pouty mouth, the little furrowed brow. It wasn't like she was made of steel. She took a deep breath as her resolve crumbled. "Okay. You can have one. But then I close up shop until tomorrow at the party. Are we agreed?"

"Mhmm," Jordan said through her mouthful of cookie. She hadn't exactly waited.

"So what's the verdict?" But Molly already knew. She'd mastered the art of the chocolate chip cookie when she was sixteen and never looked back. She could make them in her sleep. And when they were served warm, they were like circular crack.

Jordan leaned back against the counter. "I love this cookie. This cookie and I were made for each other."

"Well, don't forget I was instrumental in your meeting."

"You can be in our wedding."

There were still strawberries that needed to be dipped, but in the moment, Molly didn't find them so important. She wanted to spend time with Jordan. Talk to her. Touch her. All of it. So they did what they loved to do. Picked out a movie and snuggled in on the couch together. Jordan let Molly do the choosing this time, and she selected one of her all-time favorites, *Serendipity*. There was something about the concept of two people fated for each other that she found utterly captivating. So they settled in and watched as John Cusack and Kate Beckinsale navigated the world's obstacles until they could finally come together the way they were always meant to.

As the movie played on, they'd moved closer and closer together on the couch, until Molly lay with her head tucked into Jordan's shoulder. Cozy was an understatement. Comfortable was too common a description for the perfect way they seemed to fit together, even in these casual moments. With Jordan there with her again, Molly felt her whole world perk up.

As the credits scrolled the screen, she pushed herself up and looked back at Jordan, gently brushing a strand of hair from her forehead. "Do you believe in that stuff?"

"What stuff are we talking about?"

Molly tossed her head in the direction of the screen. "Fate. The concept that two people can be destined for each other?"

She thought for a moment. "I think I do believe that. What about you?"

"It's a nice idea, but I don't know, maybe it's just a grand romantic notion that someone once thought up." She thought about it for a moment. "But even if that's the case, it's nice to think about, isn't it? Pretend."

"Hey, don't count out romantic notions."

Molly smiled and stole a slow kiss. "I like that you're a romantic. A dreamer type. Very sexy."

Jordan looked skyward. "Yeah, well, I dream *a lot*."

"And while I hate to break this up or move from this incredibly wonderful spot, I have a little more work to do tonight. Is that okay?"

"Of course. Is there anything I can do?"

"Um, maybe in a little bit. Why don't you bring your stuff inside, get settled? Relax." And then a thought occurred to her. Maybe she was being too presumptuous here. "That is, if you were planning to stay here tonight. I didn't mean to assume, and you don't have to feel—" She blew out a breath. "This is stupid. Go get your stuff. You're staying."

Jordan shot her an amused grin. "Be right back."

Molly set to work reheating the chocolate, and the sound of running water caught her attention from the bedroom. Fifteen minutes later, Jordan emerged in short shorts and a tank top. Molly stopped stirring mid-stroke because her brain stalled out. Took its break. Grabbed five. Whatever brains did.

Jordan took her spot next to Molly at the counter. "I stole a bath. Long day and the quick soak felt like heaven. I hope that's okay."

"Bath stealing is fine," Molly said, forcing herself to concentrate on the strawberry in her hand even though she was totally preoccupied with Jordan and the fact that she smelled wonderfully of cucumber soap. And looked beyond awesome in that outfit.

"What can I do to help?"

Molly tossed a look behind her. "Uh, you can stir the chocolate, and in a few minutes we'll get you set up with some strawberries of your own. Think you can handle it?"

"Are you kidding? I'm a natural at this kind of thing."

But Molly slid her a glance twenty minutes later, and she wasn't a natural at all. There was chocolate pretty much everywhere. On the tray between the strawberries. Across the countertop in large drops. And all over Jordan.

Molly leaned a hip on the counter next to her. "Feeling a little free with the chocolate?"

Jordan looked back at her with sad eyes. "It won't stay where I want it to."

"It does that."

"I guess you make it look easier than it actually is."

"Yeah, well, that's my job. But I have to say you look extra good in chocolate."

"Well, that's a plus. I was kinda hoping you'd like it."

Molly leaned in and delicately kissed the spot of chocolate off the side of Jordan's cheek and took her time doing it.

She sighed and closed her eyes. "I knew there was a reason I was bad at this."

"Want to watch a pro in action? I have a couple strawberries left over there."

Jordan looked to her in relief. "I was hoping you'd ask."

❖

Jordan watched, captivated, as with smooth precision, Molly dipped the strawberry up to its stem in the chocolate, and with a slow turn of her wrist, pulled it back out and onto the wax paper. There wasn't a drop of chocolate anywhere. It was a picture-perfect strawberry, out of some sort of food magazine.

The move, that little twist of her wrist, had been so simplistic. So elegant. So ridiculously hot.

Molly picked up a second strawberry and repeated the action, biting her bottom lip in concentration. Jordan's mouth went dry at the sight.

"And that," Molly said, placing the strawberry with the others on the paper, "was the last one." She picked up the tray and whisked it off for storage in the refrigerator so the chocolate could cool onto the strawberries.

"What do we have to do now?" Jordan asked.

"Clean up." Molly returned to the counter.

"But there's chocolate left," Jordan said innocently, sliding behind Molly at the counter. She swept Molly's hair to the side, leaned down, and kissed the side of her neck. Molly hitched in a breath.

"There's always, um…a little left over. You don't want to run the risk of, oh wow, running out."

Jordan continued to slowly kiss her way up Molly's neck to just below her ear. "You're good at that, you know. Strawberry dipping," she said between kisses as she ran her hands down the side of Molly's body, tracing the subtle curve of her hips. Jordan could have resisted if she didn't look so cute and so effortlessly sensual at the same damn time.

"Mhmm. Pretty good." Molly leaned back against her in surrender.

Jordan reached around and began to unbutton Molly's blouse. She pulled it back and eased it off her shoulders, leaning down to taste the skin there in the process. She turned Molly around to face her and her eyes caught slightly parted lips. She descended on them in a kiss so unhurried she luxuriated in its unravel.

She needed Molly, but she was going to take her time and enjoy this.

As she pulled her lips away, Molly stared up at her, eyes dark with desire. She reached behind Molly and unclasped the navy blue bra that stood in the way. She took a minute to take her in. Because standing there before her, she was just that stunning. And then delicately, she took a spoonful of still warm chocolate and drizzled it carefully across the tops of Molly's breasts in a move that had Molly gasping. Jordan lowered her mouth and began to do what she'd been fantasizing about since she set foot in the kitchen after her bath. She tasted the chocolate, licking at first, and then sucking gently once her mouth found its way to Molly's nipple. The quiet sounds Molly made only fueled her determination and she sucked harder, savoring the sweet taste of the chocolate and the warmth of Molly's soft skin. Molly's hands were in her hair as she held on for the ride, pushing against her, looking for some kind of release. It was easily the most turned on Jordan had been in her whole life.

Molly's heart pounded beneath her fingertips, beneath her touch. This woman enraptured her, and the feelings she was able to elicit in Jordan were so unique, so much more than she would have thought possible. And that didn't even begin to touch on the physical longing.

Once every last bit of chocolate was gone, Jordan refocused her efforts. She unbuttoned the denim capris Molly wore and watched them slide easily to the ground. She traced a hand from between Molly's breasts and down her body, across her stomach, her abdomen, and stopping just short of the light pink panties Molly wore. "Please," Molly breathed at her slight hesitation.

She slid her hand inside and marveled at just how ready Molly already was.

"Oh God," Molly managed at the touch, moving against her hand. But Jordan wrapped an arm around her waist and held her still.

She massaged at first, which caused Molly to part her lips and close her eyes as she took one shallow breath after another. Jordan slid into her then, into warmth and wonder, and began to move slowly. She opened her eyes then and met Jordan's gaze where they locked onto each other. Molly reached back and gripped the countertop for support as Jordan picked up speed. Finally, Molly clenched around her and called out, tossing her head back yet again. The image captivated Jordan as she looked on in reverence. When it was over, Molly sagged against her for support, burying her face in Jordan's neck as she rode out the last few shockwaves. She wrapped her arms around Jordan's waist, and finally, smiled against her. "You make me totally lose myself, you know that?"

"I think I have an idea."

Realization crossed Molly's face. "We just did that in my kitchen."

Jordan looked around, confused. "Yeah, we did. You've never had sex in a kitchen before?"

"I don't think I've ever had sex outside of a bedroom now that I think about it."

"Well, I think all that's about to change."

Molly laughed and nuzzled Jordan's neck.

"So the chocolate?" Jordan asked.

"Massive points for creativity. Did I say massive? Because I meant to."

❖

Molly opened her eyes and blinked them clear, focusing on the green numbers that stared back at her from the digital clock on the bedside table. It was a little before five a.m., and even though she didn't have to go into work that morning, it never seemed to matter to her internal clock.

She cradled her head in her hand and stared down at Jordan who slept next to her peacefully. She took a deep breath and savored the way she was feeling in this moment. Fulfilled. She watched her sleep for several moments and remarked to herself that Jordan really was the most beautiful woman on the planet. And because she just had to, she cradled her cheek and placed a kiss at her temple. "Uh oh," she whispered, as Jordan's eyes fluttered open. "I didn't mean to wake you. I'm sorry."

A slow smile spread out across Jordan's face when their eyes met. "You are?"

She thought for a minute. "No. Not really." She slid down the bed so she was face-to-face with Jordan. "I love watching you sleep. I could do it for hours. But now that you're up, I can do this." She leaned in and caught Jordan's mouth in a slow and sensual good morning kiss.

Jordan slid her arms around Molly's waist and pulled her in close. "I would like to be woken up in this manner every day. Maybe a couple of hours later, but everything else should be exactly the same. What time is it, very alluring bakery person?"

"Too early. Occupational hazard."

Jordan stole a look at the clock. "So this five a.m. wakeup could be a reoccurring thing?"

Molly scrunched one eye guiltily. "It will be a reoccurring thing. My body decides it's up and there's no turning back. No matter how hard I try to go back to sleep on days off, it never works."

"You're kind of sexy in the morning. Have I told you I love your morning voice?"

"Oh yeah?" she said, purposefully allowing it drop.

"Mhmm." A pause. "So it seems we're both awake."

"We are."

"Kind of a shame to let such an opportunity go to waste. You're here. I'm here."

Molly grinned. "It's like you're able to read my mind." She slid on top of Jordan and edged a thigh between her legs.

Jordan closed her eyes and swore quietly, which only encouraged Molly as she moved slowly against her. It wasn't long before she crawled down the bed in exploration of the body she could just never seem to get enough of. Addictive.

It was shaping up to be a fantastic morning.

Several hours later, Molly lifted her head from a very deep sleep. The kind that made your body feel disconnected and weighted down in the most heavenly way. Then she stared at the clock in disbelief. It was after nine, and in record-setting news, she was just waking up. How was it possible that she'd fallen back asleep? And not just any kind of sleep. The kind you write home about. She shook her head in wonder. Jordan threw her entire universe into a tailspin, and apparently, the five a.m. rendezvous was just what she needed to conquer her early morning rise time. The missing ingredient, she thought to herself with a smile. She'd found it at last.

She closed her eyes indulgently, but remembered that she had an important day ahead of her. She forced her fuzzy brain to focus and thought of each item on her to-do list for Joseph's birthday party. There was a lot to accomplish, but she'd get to it later. She stretched, enjoying the way her body felt both energized and rested. It really was the best combination.

She rolled over intent on wrapping her arms around Jordan and kissing her into next week, but found the other side of the bed empty and cold.

Had she left already?

Molly climbed out of bed, and a quick glance to Jordan's oversized duffle bag on the floor let her know that Jordan had, in fact, not fled the scene. She put on her silk robe and wandered down the hall. And that's when it hit her. That amazing aroma of fresh coffee and bacon frying.

Yet another fabulous combination.

She loved bacon. It might be God's greatest gift to man.

As she rounded the corner, there was Jordan standing over the stove, already showered and ready for the day. How had she slept through that? Jordan wore her hair down today and her long bangs fell loosely just shy of her left eye. She had on jeans, a short-sleeved white shirt, and Molly's green smiley face apron tied around her. A morning news show played nearby on the television.

Jordan smiled upon seeing her standing there. "You're up."

"I can't remember the last time I slept this late."

"It's good to do that once in a while, you know. I worry about you not getting enough sleep."

The sentiment touched her, and she took a moment with that as she made her way into the kitchen. "Thank you for worrying about me. It's nice to have someone do that." Molly pulled her in for a lingering kiss. "So, good morning," she murmured.

"Morning." Jordan took a deep breath and smiled. "I love the sound of that. It should be on some sort of Hallmark card or decorative sign. It's that good."

And Molly liked the sound of it too, so she stayed right there, leaning up against Jordan for a moment longer.

Just because.

She tugged on the green cloth. "You look cute in this apron." And then she remembered how Jordan had looked in the sleep shorts the night prior and out of them later that night when they'd adjourned to her room.

"Why, thank you." Jordan glanced down at the apron. "I'm doing my best Molly impersonation. I thought it only fair that I prepare something for you this time. And breakfast it must be, because it's all I'm good at. In better news, I happen to rock at breakfast."

And she wasn't lying.

Their meal of bacon, omelets, and toast was a nice surprise. They ate leisurely while they talked about the events of the past week and even watched a little bit of the *Today Show* together on the couch.

As they cleared the dishes, Molly stole a glance at Jordan, enjoying the domesticity of the morning. It felt so natural, so everyday.

And yet so wonderful.

Suddenly, she could see this as their Saturday every week, and the thought just about knocked her over.

Because she wanted that. She was in for those Saturdays.

Without a doubt, she wanted Jordan around. She missed her when she wasn't. It was so clear to her now. So easy. She wanted a full-on future with Jordan and would work to ensure that happened. She smiled as the revelation washed over her in a wave of equal parts excitement and relief. For the first time in long while, she knew what she wanted and it felt pretty great.

"What?" Jordan asked, catching her stare. "You look like you're in a world of your own over there."

Molly nodded slowly, the smile never leaving her face. "Kinda am."

"You want to tell me what's going on in that head of yours? Because it looks like a lot of fun."

Molly went up onto her toes and placed a kiss just below Jordan's ear. "Nope. But I'm thinking maybe we can talk later tonight. After the party? When there's more time."

"Okay." Jordan smiled back at her curiously. "We'll have to do that."

CHAPTER TWENTY-THREE

Molly set down her glass of champagne on the white linen tablecloth and surveyed the place. She had to hand it to her mother-in-law. The once generic ballroom of the Applewood Country Club had been transformed into stunning elegance with no expense spared.

Twinkly lights dipped down from the ceiling and an eight-piece orchestra played from the corner of the room as Applewood's best and brightest mingled, sipped champagne, and collectively wished Joseph Tuscana a happy sixtieth birthday.

All in all, it had turned into a pretty fancy affair, and the turnout was more than they'd hoped for. It would be the most talked about event in Applewood into next year. Molly knew that much.

It was two hours into the party and everyone seemed to be having a marvelous time. Herself included. The thing about Dr. Tuscana was that everyone in town knew and loved him. He was hardworking, playful, and sympathetic to his patients. And in contrast to the relationships he had with his children, he withheld judgment throughout the course of their care. It was the town's steadfast appreciation of their doctor that accounted for the just over two hundred guests there to celebrate his birthday.

Molly checked the dessert table and noticing the truffles had dwindled, headed to the kitchen for more. "For the hundredth time, sugar, I've got this," Eden said as she rounded the corner with a whole new tray. "Now would you get out from under my feet and enjoy your family's party? You're more annoying than a fly at a picnic."

"I'm not a fly. I just want to make sure everything is perfect."

"And it is. Do you trust me or not?"

"Of course I trust you."

"Then for the love of all things sexy, get out there and have a good time for both of us. Shake hands, kiss babies, dance a little."

"Yes, ma'am." Molly offered a small salute and scurried away from the dessert table in search of her father. She'd spoken to him briefly on his way into the party and wanted to make sure he was feeling all right. She'd arranged for one of the nurses to accompany him tonight just in case he got to feeling weak and needed assistance. But there was no way she was going to let him miss the party, no matter how nervous it made her. He needed time among his family and friends.

"Hi, Daddy." She kissed his cheek from behind and slid into the chair next to his at one of the round banquet tables. He smiled over at her as he bopped his head along to the swing dancing taking place on the dance floor a few feet away.

"This is some party." His eyes twinkled when he said it, and that made her swell up inside. "You all did a fantastic job helping put all this together. It shaped up to be pretty fancy in here."

"Thank you." She threw a glance around at the decorations she'd help put up earlier in the afternoon. Jordan had been there too, and out of respect for her family, they'd kept a small distance between them. There would be a time and place to talk to the Tuscanas, but it was the furthest thing on her to-do list at the moment. In fact, due to terror, she planned to put it off as long as possible. When the time came, she'd have to plan it out carefully. Strategize. It would require a great deal of finesse. Even thinking about the concept had her feeling a little sick to her stomach. She pushed the whole idea from her head. This was a party.

"Are you feeling okay, Dad?"

"Never better. It's nice to see all of these smiling faces in one place. I'm having a great time. Don't worry about me, kiddo. Why don't you go find your friends and have some fun. I'm gonna go talk to Chuck Cupper a bit. See if his golf score's improved any."

"Okay, but save me a dance a little later."

He squeezed her hand. "I look forward to it."

Molly made her way through throngs of friends and neighbors, stopping to talk every so often. All the while, she scanned the room for Jordan. And she wasn't hard to find. It was as if a part of her was always trained on Jordan's proximity.

She watched her from across the room as she laughed at something her old soccer teammate said. That smile lit up her whole face, and it was a stunning visual. Quite simply, she radiated tonight. Jordan wasn't much for dressing up, so she'd gone for sleek and sophisticated. She wore a simple black dress, cinched with a thin red belt. The medium heels made her legs look long and luxurious. The outfit looked like it was made for her, and she easily stole the room.

Molly headed that way, intent on spending a little part of the evening with Jordan, because, well, she really, really wanted to.

"Molly O'Brien, I need to talk to you!"

She stopped. "Mr. Jeffries, hi."

"You weren't at the shop this morning." He glared, his eyes full of accusation.

"I know. I had some things to do to get ready for the party. I'll be back in the morning though. Back on schedule."

"Well, good. Just seems if it's your shop, you should be there each day. People depend on their routine not being disrupted." He was still glaring hard, but she knew that what he just said was code for "I missed seeing you," and she felt a smile touch her lips.

"You're right, Mr. Jeffries. I'll try and remember that in the future. 'Be there every day.'"

"See that you do," he huffed and headed off in search of someone else to snarl at.

She lifted her eyes to where she'd last seen Jordan, but she was gone.

❖

The terrace was quiet when Jordan made her way out there. Guests had come and gone throughout the party, enjoying the view and the quiet tranquility of the night. She rested her forearms on the railing and looked out over the expanse of treetops that surrounded the country club. It was a picturesque overlook and she took a minute to soak it in.

She was enjoying the party and the chance to see everyone together in one place all in celebration of her father. It was a good night. Admittedly, she spent much of it stealing glances at Molly, but that was pretty much the norm these days.

"Well, well, what do we have here?" She turned. Summer sauntered her way over to the railing with two glasses of white wine. One of which she handed to Jordan. "You looked a little lonely."

Jordan held up the glass. "Thanks. Just catching my breath for a minute is all."

"Glad you're back in town. Boring around here without you. How long are you staying this time?"

"Couple more days."

Summer eyed her and smiled leisurely. "Which is plenty of time."

Jordan stared at her curiously, very much on guard about where this was going. Summer seemed to be in perpetual game mode and it was important to stay one step ahead, exhausting as that was. "Plenty of time for what?"

"For you and me to finally spend some one-on-one time together." She leaned in close to Jordan's ear. "Clothing is optional. Though this outfit is a favorite." She ran her hand the length of Jordan's body from shoulder to thigh, inching up just under the hem of Jordan's dress.

Bold. Summer never was one for subtlety. And if she didn't opt out now, she had a feeling this cat-and-mouse game would never end. She turned to her. "As nice a time as I'm sure we'd have, I'm going to have to decline."

"Because you're seeing someone?" Summer stared at her evenly.

She decided to just level with her. "Yes."

Annoyance flickered across her face. "Molly. Then it's true. I wondered when I saw your car parked outside of her house at two a.m., but I gave you far too much credit for that, Jordan. "

Whoa. "My car? What were you doing on her street at two a.m.?"

"Just checking out a theory, and this is one I am so sorry to have been right about. Molly O'Brien? Seriously, what are you thinking?"

Jordan shook her head and took a step back. "You don't know what you're talking about, Summer." She turned to go.

"She'll never love you for you."

The words froze her in place. She felt as if she'd been punched as she turned back.

"You and I, Jordan, are the also-rans of this town, and it's important that people like us stick together. And that's why I'm looking out for you. You'll never matter to her the way Cassie did, and when she looks at you, she'll always think of her. *Always*."

Jordan took a minute because the words hit home. "You don't know that."

Summer offered an overly sympathetic smile. "Don't I, though? I have something you don't right now, Jordan, and it's called perspective. You're second place in this scenario no matter how many different ways we run it. And trust me, that isn't going to change."

"Stop. It's not like that with us." And she believed that, mostly. Well, at least she wished she did.

"It's lose-lose, Jordan. If you're not willing to consider yourself, think about Molly. Her life was torn apart when she lost Cassie. She deserves a fresh start, and she can't have that with you. You come with baggage, with reminders. You're just an extension of her loss. Another way for her to hold on to Cassie, and if she stays with you, she'll never get that clean slate. How do you not see that?"

Jordan met her gaze and held on. There was so much logic in those words, as twisted as they seemed. But Jordan wouldn't let herself admit it fully. "You're wrong."

Summer tilted her head to the side. "I'm rarely wrong." She laid a hand on Jordan's shoulder as she passed and headed back into the party.

Jordan was reeling.

She didn't want the words to affect her, she really didn't. Because what Summer had professed about her, about Molly, was resonating with her no matter how much she fought against it. She stared into the darkened trees and talked herself down one minute at a time.

Things were good in her life.

Hell, they were better than good. They were great, and it was important that she remember that. She heard the door to the terrace open and she turned. And in that moment, everything seemed to right itself.

"Hey, stranger. I've been looking for you. That's some party."

Molly stood a few feet away, her eyes shining brightly. She wore a yellow cocktail dress with thin straps. It came in at the top of her waist and fell loosely to just above her knee. Quite simply, it was stunning on her.

She held up a hand. "Before we go any further, I have to tell you how pretty you look. In fact, I don't think I've ever seen anyone look prettier."

A soft smile touched Molly's lips and her cheeks colored just a hint. "Thank you. I was saving it for a special occasion and tonight felt like the night."

"Another good decision."

Molly took the spot next to her at the railing. "I thought by now the party would be winding down, but trust me, no one seems to be going anywhere any time soon. Your brother's about to start a conga line, I can feel it."

"Mikey always liked a good time." Jordan smiled and stared out into the night.

"Hey, look at me." Molly placed her hand on Jordan's chin and gently turned her face. "You have the most faraway look. Everything okay?"

She met Molly's eyes and exhaled. "It feels better now. I'm just enjoying the quiet. The crickets are beginning to chirp. It's one of my favorite times of night."

Molly took in their surroundings. "It is pretty beautiful, isn't it? The emergence of spring. Everything about it seems so promising. So hopeful."

Jordan studied Molly's profile. "It would be even more promising if I were able to kiss you. Because that's what I really want to do right now."

Molly's looked at her and her lips parted ever so slightly. When she spoke, her voice was quiet, just between them. "What kind of kiss would it be?"

It didn't take much thinking. "Soft. The kiss would be soft and slow, like the night around us right now. I would ease my hands into your hair and pull you in even closer against me." Molly closed her eyes. "I'd feel how warm your skin was and lose myself in how wonderful you taste. And then…there would be no stopping us."

Molly opened her eyes and held Jordan's gaze for several long moments as the heat they felt but couldn't express hung between them. Finally, Molly glanced behind her and then back to Jordan as if an idea were taking root. "Come with me."

And, of course, she did.

They followed the terrace as it wrapped around the building and stopped at the outside door that led to the adjacent banquet room, empty for the night. Molly tried the handle. "Locked. Stay right here." Jordan watched her as she disappeared around the corner. It was only a minute or two before she appeared on the other side of the door and let Jordan in. Molly then took her hand and led her silently to the nearby coat closet and Jordan began to understand.

"Okay. So we're just—"

"Stealing a moment. Exactly."

"Stealing a sexy moment, you mean."

"I do."

Once safely inside the small walk-in closet, Molly flipped the light on and backed herself slowly to the wall, a small smile breaking across her face. "I remember you mentioning something about a kiss?"

Jordan smiled back as she moved to Molly. She leaned in and paused just a breath away from Molly's incredibly enticing lips. "I think I said it would be soft at first." She brushed Molly's lips with hers once, and then deepened the kiss on the second go-round. "I think I also said it would be slow." She slid her hands from

Molly's face into her hair and pulled her in again. And she kept that promise, luxuriating in the kiss, taking her time with it. Savoring the wonderful experience that kissing Molly inevitably was. She felt so alive when they were together like this, like no other time in her life. It was quite possibly—

There was a gasp from the doorway. She pulled her lips from Molly's just in time to see her mother place her hand over her heart, her other hand on the open door. Her father stood just over her shoulder. "We were just looking for a quiet place to…" Her mother's gaze flew from Molly's face to Jordan's. "I don't understand. Would someone please tell me what is happening here?"

And in that horrible moment, she didn't quite know what the words should be. But Jordan did. She straightened and stepped toward her parents in earnest.

"I know this was probably a surprising sight to walk in on, and I'm so sorry for that."

But her father wasn't listening. He was staring intently at Jordan, disappointment written all over his face. "What in the world are you doing?" he whispered harshly. "You've pulled some insane stunts in your time, Jordana, but this is too much. You've gone too far."

"We weren't doing anything wrong, Dad."

"But weren't you?" he bit back.

Her mother placed a steadying hand on his arm. "Some things are sacred, Jordan. You of all people should understand how upsetting this is. Cassandra was your sister. Your *only* sister. Have you no respect for her memory at all? Either of you?" Her mother's eyes filled with tears, and in that moment, so did Molly's.

"It's not Jordan's fault," Molly managed.

"I would never have expected this from you, Molly," her mother said, as if her heart was broken.

"But you would have from me?" Jordan quipped.

"That's right, we would have," her father shot back. "You always wanted everything she had and look at you now."

Molly held up a hand. "Okay. Let's not say things we're going to regret later. You're all family."

Jordan tilted her head. "Yeah, just some of the members of the family are less impressive than others, right, Dad?"

"Don't," Molly murmured to Jordan, placing a hand on her shoulder.

"Let her say it. It's true," her father growled. "If you're looking for another Cassie, Molly, you're not going to find it in this one here. They're nothing alike."

Jordan swallowed the anger, the pain that comment inspired and focused on diffusing things. She made sure her voice was calm and even when she spoke. "As much as I wish to God it wasn't the case, Cassie's gone now. And this"—she gestured between herself and Molly—"has nothing to do with her." But as the conversation shifted to Cassie, Molly noticeably withdrew, her eyes now fixed on the ground.

"How long has this been going on? How long exactly have you been taking advantage of your sister's—" Her father then held up his hand. "You know what? I don't want to know the details." He shook his head slowly and walked away. It was clear he was upset. She could only hope that with time, he would understand.

Jordan turned to her mother. "Mom, I feel like I should apologize, but that doesn't seem right. Because what I feel for Molly is very real, and I'm not going to stop seeing her because of our past. It's time for us all to move forward."

Her mother turned to Molly in question. "Is that how you feel too?"

Molly raised her eyes to her mother-in-law and then turned helplessly to Jordan, her eyes swimming with desperation. She opened her mouth to say something and then closed it again. "I'm sorry," was all she managed. "To everyone, I'm sorry."

The words hit Jordan hard. What did that mean, she was sorry? She was backing down. Why was she choosing not to stand up for them? Summer's words echoed in her ears. *You'll never matter to her the way Cassie did.* Self-doubt was a powerful thing and it systematically ate away at Jordan as she stood there.

Her mother nodded solemnly and straightened, raising her hand and letting it drop. "I don't even know what to say to you two. I should get back to the guests."

Left alone, Jordan turned to Molly. "Are you okay?"

"I'm fine." But she'd wrapped her arms around herself almost as if in protection and took a step back. "Do you think you could give me just a minute?"

"Sure. Whatever you need."

And she left her there, even though it went against every instinct she had.

As Jordan crossed the empty banquet room, her limbs felt heavier as she realized that things were much more precarious than even she had acknowledged. The feelings they'd all just exchanged were so unguarded, so raw. She was still reeling from their effects. It had been a horrible scene back there, and there was nothing she could do to undo it. The worst part had been the haunted look in Molly's eyes as it all went down. It was an excruciating sight. It tore at her still. And it wasn't just the look. It was its implication.

"Jordan, wait."

She turned just in time for Molly to throw her arms around her neck and hold on. She felt the tears against her neck as she wrapped her arms around Molly's waist and pulled her close. "Why does it have to be this hard?" Molly whispered in a strangled voice.

"It's going to be okay. You know that, right?" Molly released Jordan.

"I don't know that it is. I can't lose them, Jordan. I just can't. It's all so much more than I imagined it would be."

Jordan nodded, because she felt the same way. And would it ever get easier? She was beginning to wonder.

❖

It was close to midnight when that marathon of a birthday party finally came to a slow conclusion. As much as Jordan wished the thing would just end, the guests seemed to have other ideas. She'd been tempted to offer the band a thousand dollars to just cut out early and put them all out of their damn misery. Instead, she'd played dutiful daughter, and she and Mikey stayed until the final partygoer eventually trickled out. Throughout it all, she remembered to smile and laugh and play her part with a flourish. She was a Tuscana after all.

It was an act. Inside, she was a mess and amazed that she'd held it together as long as she had.

Molly had stayed as well, but in contrast, spent most of her time busy in the kitchen helping Eden with cleanup. It was a coping mechanism that Jordan recognized easily in Molly.

Escape.

Instead of dealing with problems head-on, it was Molly's instinct to avoid conflict altogether. She was a pro and she did it better than anyone Jordan had ever encountered.

Her parents had been cordial to her in front of their friends, but there was a veil of tolerance in the way they looked at her that told her they were still wallowing in disappointment at what they'd uncovered. And she felt the effects of that disappointment right in the center of her chest. She'd experienced this kind of rejection from her parents many times in the past, on a smaller scale, but it didn't soften the blow. Molly, on the other hand, was a different story. She'd never been anything if not loved and adored universally by the Tuscanas. This would be a difficult pill for her to swallow, and for that reason, Jordan was worried.

She caught up with Molly in the parking lot. She carried her heels by their back straps and walked barefoot on the pavement. "You weren't going to say good-bye."

Molly turned, just shy of her car. She met Jordan's eyes and then dropped her gaze to the pavement. "Sorry. I meant to. Just tired. Both mentally and physically." She wasn't lying. Everything about her looked exhausted. But there was something else there too, and it tugged unpleasantly at Jordan.

Sadness. Molly looked undeniably sad.

"Do you want me to come by for a little while? We could put on a movie. Forget the world." It was a Hail Mary attempt and she knew it.

Molly offered a smile. "You're sweet. But I think I'm ready to call it a night." Everything important to her seemed to be slipping through her fingers and like some God-awful dream she couldn't wake up from, there was little she could do to stop it.

"Will you text me and let me know that you got home okay? It's late."

She nodded once. "I will do that."

Jordan leaned in to kiss her good night, but just as their lips met, Molly took a step back, ending the kiss abruptly. She covered by tossing Jordan a reassuring smile.

"'Night, Jordan."

"Good night."

But it wasn't. It was the worst kind of night.

Molly was hurting. She was in distress, and her presence only seemed to make it worse. And she had no clue how to fix it. Except that she was starting to feel like she did.

For everyone.

Everyone except herself, that is.

Chapter Twenty-four

It was raining the next morning as Molly set out for the bakeshop. She decided to walk anyway because she needed to inhale the fresh air, feel the thick, wet drops on her skin. She needed to remind herself that the life she was so excited about just two days prior was still there and waiting for her.

Truth be told, it had shaken her, the way Amalia and Joseph had stumbled upon them the night before. She'd planned on handling the situation with a delicate turn, introducing the concept of her and Jordan a little bit at a time, and now that opportunity was gone. Completely blown.

But something else had shifted also.

She'd seen the situation through their eyes and what she was doing with Jordan was a big deal. Was she exactly ready for that and everything that came with it? She nodded. She was. She knew she was, so why was she now sidestepping what was the best thing that had happened to her in a long time? She amended that. Maybe ever.

She was running again. And she hated herself for it.

Sunday mornings at Flour Child brought in pretty steady traffic. It was one of their better days of the week as far as foot traffic went. They'd sold several dozen trays of buttery croissants, and more muffins than she could remember. They were completely out of the orange raspberry coffee cake, but Louise was at work in the back trying to make up for it. If they could keep this kind of business going in the middle of the week as well, the shop would be in much better shape financially. It was those before-work runs to Starbucks that were the difference. In contrast, the leisurely Sunday morning pace invited family and friends to luxuriate a bit more, and that meant a trip to Flour Child.

She smiled widely as she handed Mrs. Dumphey her change, sliding the pink box across the counter to her. "Enjoy your breakfast."

"Thanks, Molly. See you next weekend." And there it was. Another indicator. She blew out a breath. In just a few more days, her financial woes would at least be temporarily quelled and she could focus on revamping the shop. With the check from Grant, she could settle her bills and maybe even have enough left over for an espresso machine, a concept she'd been tossing around in her head for a little while now.

Quaint little bakeshop or not, she needed to keep up with the big boys, and that meant fancy coffee drinks in large cups. It was time to jump into the twenty-first century and win back some of those weekday customers.

"You're lost in thought."

She raised her gaze to find Jordan smiling back at her from across the cash register. And there was that crazy mixture of feelings again. Happiness to see her. There was always that. And the undeniable guilt that the happiness brought with it, stronger now, so much sharper after the events of the night before. She didn't know quite how to reconcile the two.

"Sorry, just thinking through some things. What can I get for you?"

"Uh…" She surveyed the display case, perhaps caught off guard by the business like question. "Just coffee, I guess. I'm not really hungry."

"Coming right up." Jordan reached into her back pocket for cash. "Stop. You don't pay for things here, remember?"

"Right." She put the money away.

But Molly understood the gesture. Because somehow, nothing felt certain anymore. Norms that once flowed easily now felt shaky and suspect right along with everything else.

She'd known it wouldn't be just be the two of them in some secret romance forever, and now reality was very much present and accounted for. The world at large now intruded upon what had been just theirs, and they had to find a way through it. They could do that, right? She wished she had more confidence.

She handed Jordan the coffee.

"Thanks. I know you're working, but is there a chance we can talk for a few minutes? I can come back if now isn't good."

Molly tossed a glance over her shoulder. "Uh, let me just grab Louise to mind the counter."

The sun broke through the clouds as they emerged from the bakeshop and naturally veered in the direction of the park. Jordan sipped her coffee as they walked. "I was worried about you last night when you left. You seemed, I don't know, shaken up."

Molly nodded, her eyes tracing the cracks in the sidewalk as they walked. "I don't know how to explain what happened when your parents opened that door. It was like I had been working this very tricky puzzle, you know?" She looked up at Jordan. "And just as I had the pieces close to being where I wanted them, they were somehow tossed into the air and landed in a heap all around me." She sighed. "I can't believe I'm talking to you in analogies, but I want you to understand how it felt when they said those things. About us. When the people most important to me in the world accused us of—"

"You felt guilty. It made you question everything between us all over again."

Molly nodded, once again in awe of how Jordan just understood. As always, she just got it.

Jordan didn't look at her when she asked her next question. "And now? Are you still questioning now?"

They were at the entrance to the park when Molly grabbed Jordan's hand and tugged her to a stop. "I don't want to be. When you're here right in front of me like this, I feel like it's you and me against the world and we can do this. But—" Her eyes filled with tears and she turned away. "There's a lot to sort through."

Jordan's gaze never wavered. There were very few times when she was unable to tell what Jordan was thinking, but this was definitely one of those times.

"Molly, that's kind of what I wanted to talk to you about."

❖

Some things in life were hard. But Jordan knew what she was about to do was for the best, even if it didn't feel that way. Even if it felt like a horrible decision. And the only way she was going to get through it was to remind herself of that fact over and over again like the worst kind of broken record.

Seeing Molly in such distress the night before had been hard, but seeing that anguish still in her eyes today was the tipping point. Hell, she could barely look at Jordan. She was the cause of that pain and she wasn't willing to be any longer. As outlandish as Summer could sometimes be, she did make another valid point out on the deck of the country club.

Molly deserved a fresh start.

And what she brought to the table was a minefield of a relationship. And she loved Molly too much to make her try and navigate it.

She ran the word over again in her mind.

Love.

Because she knew undeniably that she was in love with Molly, and those feelings changed the way she approached the situation. She could do for Molly what Molly couldn't do for herself. Because Molly was too noble, too loyal to look out for her own needs. But Jordan could do that for her.

She turned to Molly, steadying herself against the big brown eyes that seemed to be searching hers. "It's, uh, just that we both have a lot on our plates. Me with the start-up, you with the new distribution deal. It's not exactly an ideal scenario. The timing kind of sucks, you have to agree."

Molly tucked a strand of hair behind her ear and tilted her head ever so slightly in mystification. "Jordan, what are you saying right now?"

"It's too much. Let's be honest. You said it yourself. It's harder than we thought it would be."

Molly's voice held a quiet intensity. "And? Say what you're going to say, Jordan. Don't leave it there."

Jordan took a fortifying breath. "I think it's best we end things here. I go back to Chicago. You pick up your life in Applewood. You know, maybe over time give Annaleigh a call." Okay, that was hard to say.

Molly's lips parted in surprise and she shook her head slightly. "*Annaleigh*? Did you really just say that to me? This isn't you talking."

Jordan stared at the sky and pushed on. "Except it is. I care about you, Molly, and that will never change, but we're probably heading in different directions in the long run. Surely you feel that too."

"Don't you dare tell me what I feel." There was fire in her eyes now. "Why are you doing this? Because of your parents?"

"That's part of it. But I'm not exactly good at the whole tied down thing. I never have been." A lie. She'd give up everything she had for that kind of life with Molly. If only it were the right thing for Molly too.

"Tied down? Wow." The blow registered on Molly's face, but there was something else there too. Defeat. And it just about killed Jordan. "I don't know where this bravado is coming from, but at the same time I don't have the energy to fight you on this, Jordan." She raised one shoulder and let it drop. "I guess I'm fresh out of fight. If this is what you want, I guess I'll see you around. Have a safe trip home." She turned and headed off down the sidewalk.

And Jordan watched.

She watched Molly walk back out of her life and it hurt like nothing she could have imagined. "Molly?" she called, because she just had to.

She looked back over her shoulder. "Yeah?" That's when Jordan saw the tears. The words caught in her throat until she finally managed them on her second attempt.

"Take care of yourself."

Molly didn't say anything. She nodded once and headed back down the sidewalk.

Once she was safely back at her parents' house, Jordan packed her things. She slung her bag over her shoulder and found her mother in the living room reading a book.

She set the book down when she saw the bag. "What's going on? Are you leaving?"

"I need to get back. I have a lot of work waiting for me."

"Don't go yet. I know we're all on edge after the argument last night, but I've been looking forward to your visit all week. We don't have to talk about last night if you don't want to."

"Have your feelings changed?"

Her mother stood as she considered the question. "I wish I had handled things better in the moment. It was a shock to say the least. But I'll be honest; I don't think I like the idea of a…relationship between you and Molly. I'm not sure you're the right fit for her, Jordan."

"And by right you mean good enough?"

"No, that's not at all what I'm saying. But Molly's been through a lot, and she's vulnerable."

"Well, it's not something you're going to have to worry about any longer. It's over. A done deal."

"Oh, Jordan. I know you think that makes me happy, but that's not true. I just want everyone to be all right. That's all I want."

Jordan closed the distance between them and hugged her mother. "I'm fine. I love you, Mom. But I have to go now. Say good-bye to Dad for me. I'll call soon."

And with that, she walked out of the house, got in her car, and headed out of Applewood. It was once she was safely out of town and alone in her car that she let the tears stream freely down her face.

She'd done the right thing for Molly.

It didn't matter that her heart was broken in the process.

Chapter Twenty-five

It was just after two a.m. on Tuesday night and Molly sat alone at her kitchen table. Her window was open and she listened to the sounds outside.

Crickets, the soft rustle of the leaves, the quiet hum of serenity.

If she didn't know better, the everyday sounds would have made her think all was well, offer her the comfort of their normalcy. But everything was, in fact, not okay.

It was the opposite of okay.

She felt more alone than she had in her entire life.

When she couldn't sleep, she'd played the vacation video, reaching desperately for any comfort she could find in Cassie's vibrant smile, her teasing laugh. But it didn't reaffirm her the way it normally did. Something was off.

And as she sat in her darkened kitchen, she didn't know where to turn for comfort. She should call Eden. Her father. But it wasn't what she needed. The one person who could help, who could talk her through this, make her feel better with just the sound of her voice wasn't an option anymore.

She stared at the cell phone in her hand and willed herself to set it back down.

She'd refused to let herself think about Jordan much, because when she did, she came apart altogether. So, she once again pushed her aggressively from her thoughts. It was a wound she had to keep her fingers off of, at least for now.

There was too much on her plate.

But it didn't mean she wasn't keenly aware of the loss. Almost like a recently discovered piece of herself was now missing.

She purposefully left herself off the schedule the next morning, taking the time off for her meeting in Chicago with Grant. At least she had the advance check and the planning session to look forward to, to distract her.

She followed the GPS to the address on Grant's business card and solemnly rode the elevator to the eleventh floor. She'd made a point to dress the part and traded her casual bakeshop attire for a skirt and blouse. Her hair was pulled up for effect. She felt businessy and a tinge excited for the meeting, despite the fact that the rest of her life lay in tatters.

When she reached the appointed suite, she paused and double-checked the number on the plaque outside with the business card in her hand. The door stood ajar. The floor of the office was covered in file boxes, and a man in a suit stood over a desk packing another. Two other men were similarly occupied.

"Excuse me. I'm so sorry to bother you." She took a tentative step into the office and held up the business card. "I'm looking for Grant Tranton, but I think I might be in the wrong place."

The man looked up but only briefly. "I'm sorry, ma'am. He's not here."

A pause.

"But this is his office?"

"Unfortunately so."

"Okay. Do you, by chance, know where I could find him? I have an eleven o'clock appointment."

He sighed and straightened. "I wish I did. The contents of this office have been seized as evidence. Mr. Tranton is wanted on several charges. We'd be interested in any information you may have about his whereabouts." The man covered the distance between them and handed Molly his card.

She stared numbly at the letters. Federal Bureau of Investigation. "He's wanted on charges?"

"Quite a list of them. Money laundering, fraud, identity theft among others. And that's only the most recent string. He's made a career of it. I'd like to get a statement from you about your interaction."

She stood there, shell shocked as the information settled. On impulse, she dialed Grant's number, but the singsong notification that informed her his phone number was no longer in service was the tipping point. The grim understanding caused most of the color to fade from the room.

She just kept hearing the words *this can't be happening* repeated on some endless loop in her head. It made her dizzy. She prayed to God it was all just a misunderstanding, but she was smart enough to know it probably wasn't.

The ramifications of it all occurred to her one at a time, tumbling down on her like the contents of a messy closet. Grant Tranton was a criminal. He was probably on the run. There would be no partnership. No advance check. And, God, no bakeshop.

It was over.

She grasped the doorjamb for support, feeling lightheaded and so very, very stupid. "Thank you for your help."

"Ma'am, are you all right?"

She met his gaze. "No. I don't think so."

❖

Jordan checked her watch. She was eight minutes late, which was pretty good for her. The restaurant George had picked for dinner was one she'd never been to before, but had all the foodies in the area raving. She didn't have much of an appetite these days, but she'd try to eat something to be polite.

She'd been back in Chicago for a couple of weeks now and hadn't spent much time with George outside of work. But then again, she hadn't spent time with *anyone* outside of work.

She pushed her sunglasses onto her head and squinted as her eyes adjusted to the dim interior of the restaurant. As she headed to the hostess stand, she was quickly intercepted.

"There you are, beautiful person." George pulled her in and kissed her cheek loudly. "We weren't expecting you for another seven minutes."

"Because I'm generally—"

"Running fifteen minutes behind schedule, yes. It's my job as your friend to be acutely aware of your shortcomings and love you despite them. And voila, I do. Are you ready to meet the love of my life?"

She smiled at George because his eyes were dancing with excitement and it was adorable. "I am. You've been talking this guy up for weeks. I have to see if he measures up. You know, in my job capacity as your friend. See how that works both ways?"

"You're very astute. Right this way. Our table, and the very handsome Robert, await our presence. Be nice, whatever you do."

She batted her eyelashes. "I'm always nice." Plastering a smile on her face, she followed George to their table. Robert's back was to them as they approached, but when he saw George, he stood politely and turned.

She froze. Absolutely speechless, that's how she felt.

He, on the other, looked nervous. "Hey, Jordy. Good to see ya."

"Little Bobby." She turned to George in shock. "You're dating Little Bobby? Robert is Bobby?" Worlds were colliding. She swiveled back to Bobby. "You're seeing George? I didn't know you were—Wait. We have to rewind. That makes you gay. You're *gay*?"

Bobby offered a small smile and shrugged. "No one knew except me. And, well, George. He seems to have a way of just knowing things." He exchanged a private look with George who motioned for them all to sit.

"So all of this time you two have been seeing each other? Since your stay in Applewood?" Jordan looked from one of her friends to the other. Her mind was still scrambling to catch up.

George offered her an apologetic look. "Guilty. But in all fairness, we were taking things slow."

"At my request," Bobby supplied. "I've known who I am for some time now, but I never acted on it in any sort of *official* capacity like this. And until I met George, I thought I never would. I was planning on bachelorhood for life. This is so much better."

Jordan shook her head. "I don't know what to say. I'm floored." Except as she saw the happiness between them, the genuine warmth of their stares, she found the words. "I love both of you dearly, and once the shock subsides, will be so very happy you've found each other. I'm mystified, but in a really good way. To new beginnings." She raised her glass to the two wonderful men in front of her, who clinked their glasses and beamed back at her.

And for the first time in weeks, the smile on her face felt genuine. "I'm still the best friend though, right?"

"Right," they answered in unison.

The rest of dinner consisted of talk about Journey, location scouting, and an agreement on some last-minute equipment purchases. They were scheduled to start shooting their first project in just five short weeks, and Jordan couldn't have been more ready. Anything to distract her mind from the very acute sense of sadness she'd been inundated with these past few weeks.

George settled his chin onto his hand. "There is one more thing I've been meaning to tell you."

"I don't think anything you could say will shock me more than you already have. Go for it."

"I'm moving to Applewood." He raised a hand to preclude her from interjecting too quickly. "Robert's got the bar to run, and I'm perfectly capable of commuting. It shouldn't change my role in the shoot at all, as most of it will be on location anyway. It just means on office days, I'll have to wake up a little earlier to make the drive to the city. I'm capable of driving. I'll even sing in the car."

She thought it over in amusement. "George Underwood living in small town, USA. Someone should make a film about *this*. Who needs suicide forests?"

Bobby slid her a hopeful look. "You could move home too, Jordan. Make your parents happy."

"That it would. But I think I'm best right where I am."

George studied her. "You're not over her, you know. Molly. And don't look so surprised. I filled Robert in on all the details, and he brought to the table a few details of his own. We're on to you. You act like it was just a little fling, a blip in your history, when we all know it was much more than that."

"It was more than that. But it's done now. The movie's over."

"It doesn't have to be. Why are you running?"

She tossed her napkin onto the table. "You know what? There's a lot there and I'd rather not get into it."

"But look how miserable you are," Bobby pointed out. "It's written all over your face. Molly's too. And now that Flour Child's closing, she's been even more withdrawn. Barely shows her face anymore."

Jordan paused as her stomach dropped out from beneath her automatically. "What do you mean it's closing? When did this happen?"

Bobby studied her curiously. "Molly put the word out a couple of weeks ago. Thursday is the shop's last day. You didn't know?"

She shook her head. Her parents hadn't mentioned anything, but then Molly seemed to be a subject matter they purposefully avoided. She turned to Bobby as she tried to piece it together. "I don't understand. She had a plan, a business deal with a distributor that would fund the business, get it back in shape."

"I heard it fell through," Bobby said. "The whole town's broken up about losing the shop. Wish they'd thought of that before they gave so much of their business to that stupid Starbucks."

George reached for her hand. "You're not gonna leave her out there on her own on this, are you? Sweetheart, she could use some moral support about now."

She pulled her hand away, her mood having taken a horrible hit after the news she'd just received. The concept of Molly without Flour Child was unthinkable, and it made her sick to her stomach just thinking about how Molly must be feeling. She could no longer concentrate on the conversation. Her brain had taken a sharp detour. "I don't know what I'm going to do. It's important that I not upset her life right now."

George gave her a long look. "And dropping out of it completely isn't upsetting for her?"

Damn it, he had a point.

❖

Jordan was pacing, which was so cliché and straight from some sort of Perry Mason movie that she couldn't believe she was doing it. Yet, somehow it helped her think, or not think, which she thought might be a better alternative.

It was after ten. Too late to call. That and the fifteen other million excuses she'd dreamed up argued that she should skip the whole thing and watch boring late night television to dull her senses, possibly pour herself a scotch.

But, no. Absolutely not. She was more mature than that, and it was time to start acting like it. She decided to just go for it. Before she knew it, she'd dialed the number and held her breath as it rang a second, a third, and a fourth time. Finally, there she was.

"Hello."

She closed her eyes at the sound of Molly's voice. The voice she'd spent the past few weeks attempting, rather unsuccessfully, to push from her thoughts.

"Hey. I hope I didn't wake you."

"Uh, no. Just in time though."

A long pause. "How are you?

"Getting by. You?"

"I'm fine, I guess." She kept her eyes closed against the onslaught of emotion she was already feeling. God, this was hard. "I heard about the shop today, and I wanted to call and tell you how sorry I am."

"Thanks. Me too." Molly blew out a breath and Jordan could tell she was settling into the conversation. Despite everything, they still seemed to be dialed into each other. "The deal fell through. It was all a sham. At least I think it was. Probably some sort of front for Tranton's behind the scenes business transactions. He was arrested last week in Florida. He's a criminal."

"That's horrible. I can't even imagine what you're feeling."

"It's been hard. I had to tell my dad yesterday. That was the worst part."

"How did he take it?"

"Just as you would imagine. He says all the right things. He's the best dad ever, but underneath, I could tell it crushed him. I could see it right there in his eyes. He and my mom started the business in their early twenties. He trusted me with it and I—" Her voice was strangled when she broke off, and Jordan could tell that emotion had gotten her.

"Molly, listen to me. You did everything you possibly could. Everyone loves that place, and they just took for granted that you would always be there."

"Thanks for saying that. It helps, I don't know, to hear that from you." A pause. "I guess I should go. I'm glad you called."

"Me too. Hang in there."

"I will."

God, she missed her. "Molly?"

"Yeah?"

"Are we going to be okay?"

Another pause. "Maybe over time. This is a start. I suppose I'll see you at the next family gathering. Fourth of July?"

"I love fireworks."

"I know."

"Good night, Molly."

"Night."

Jordan stared at the phone for a good twenty minutes before pulling herself off the couch and heading into her cold, empty bedroom.

Chapter Twenty-six

Early Sunday evening, Molly closed up shop for the day and headed off down the sidewalk to her car. She had four days left as a small business owner and then it would be time to decide what life had in store for her next. Deb Paulson, who owned the diner down the street, had offered her a position. She was hoping to spice up her dessert menu and was thrilled to have a chance to bring Molly in. That or she was just a nice lady who saw someone in need of a job. It could really be either.

She decided to pick up dinner for her dad. It would be a nice change from the cafeteria food. She carried the baked chicken into his room and found him staring intently at a chessboard midgame.

"Beating yourself again?"

He looked up and smiled. "I get so frustrated at how good I am. Look at this. I never seem to be able to take myself down."

"Funny how that works. I hope you're hungry. Fabulous daughter that I am, I've brought us chicken dinners."

"I hope it's fried."

"No dice, Daddy. But I hear the baked is just as good."

"You heard wrong," he grumbled, but it was good-natured.

She set up dinner for them in the corner of the room by the window and opened it, so they could watch the sunset. There was a serenity about the meal and they ate in companionable silence for a bit. Finally, her dad sat back in his chair and regarded her. "So have you decided? Are you planning to take the job at the diner?"

It was the twenty million dollar question.

She would probably have to, but the thought of not heading into Flour Child each morning still hadn't completely sunk in. She didn't want to consider other options. And she wouldn't have had to, if her life had only gone according to plan.

"I guess so. It'll be a change though. That's for sure. I'm more worried about my staff. Louise is planning to retire, but what's going to happen to Eden and Damon? They'll need a paycheck. I just feel so responsible."

"While that's admirable, I'm more worried about you."

"Well, you don't have to be. I told you. I'll take the diner job, come up with some amazing desserts, make that place famous and that's the end of it. I'll be just fine."

He gazed at her. "That's not what I mean."

She sobered because there was this knowing look on his face that made her feel instantly vulnerable, as if he knew everything that was going on inside her. "I don't understand."

"I'm talking about your heart. Something's happened. And if I had to guess, I'd say it has to do with Jordan."

She stared at her hands. Hearing the very intuitive words caught her off guard, but it wasn't like she could hide from him. She'd never been very good at that. She raised her eyes to his in question. "How did you know that?"

"Lots of clues. The way you talked to each other at dinner that night. How she looked at you when she thought I wasn't looking. The fact that you were acutely aware of her every move at the birthday party. Love's a hard thing to hide. Even an old fool like me knows that."

She nodded as tears sprang into her eyes. "I was in love. You're right. And I don't know why I'm crying now. I promise you, I've been strong this whole time. I've held it together."

"Because it's your old dad you're talking to now. I'm the guy that put Band-Aids on your scraped knee, remember? I calmed you down when you had a nightmare."

"And got me through the darkest year of my life." He was right. He had always been her soft place to fall, so of course she let go of emotion when she was with him. It's what they did.

"Tell me what went wrong."

Molly blew out a breath, wiped the tears from her cheeks, and explained the series of events at the birthday party. The complications they faced when it came to Jordan's parents, and the guilt she continually struggled with herself regarding Cassie. She raised a shoulder helplessly. "I pulled away from her that night. We were supposed to spend the weekend together, and I could barely look her in the eye after everything. The next thing I knew, she ended things. Said we were heading in different directions."

"Are you?"

"I don't know. I wish I did. We felt in sync in almost every way. At least that was my impression." She thought on it and countered. "No, it was hers too. I know it was."

He thought for a minute. "Maybe she sensed just how hard all of this was on you and did what she thought was noble."

She let the idea settle. "She was trying to let me off the hook?"

"It's possible."

She shook her head. "I screwed everything up, Dad. I held parts of myself back from her because I felt like they belonged to someone else. I didn't fully see it then, but I do now. Because I wasn't ready, I may have blown the best thing that's ever happened to me." She shook her head. Letting Jordan go was breathtakingly stupid and now she couldn't imagine why she'd done it.

He sat forward in his chair. "And what are you going to do about it?"

"I don't know that there's anything I can do."

He shot her a frustrated look. "You have to take control of your own life, Molly. I can't leave this world—"

"Dad, don't say that."

"Let me finish," he said sternly. The intensity in his tone shut her up immediately. "I know it's not fun to talk about, but this is what it comes down to. I'm sick, and little by little, I feel my strength slipping away." He reached out and clutched her hand in his. "I can't stand the thought of leaving this world knowing you're not okay, do you hear me?"

"Yes, sir," she said solemnly.

"You're a fighter, Molly, but sometimes you forget that. I don't want you to walk through life alone. Now, you've been dealt some tough blows along the way, but those trials don't define you. You can't let them hold you back from getting out there and living." There was fire in his eyes as he continued. "If you love this girl, damn it, you go out there and get her. The rest of the world will just have to deal with it. And if it's guilt that's eating you alive, well, then you figure out how to deal with that too because life is too short. Understand me?"

"I do." And she did understand. More than she ever had. His words washed over her in a call to action. Suddenly, she was feeling motivated.

She had work to do.

❖

There are some days that feel more important than others.

When Molly woke up the next morning, she knew that the day before her would be one of those. She'd scheduled herself on the second shift at Flour Child and took the morning for herself. She had a quiet cup of coffee and watched Rover swim his morning laps as she pulled her thoughts together and geared up for what was ahead.

She walked to the flower shop and enjoyed the bright sunlight the morning had to offer. Everything in her path just seemed to encourage her forward. The most noticeable encouragement being the date, the eighth of June. *Eight.* She hadn't planned it out that way. It had to mean something.

As she approached the graveside, she took stock. She'd spent a lot of time here over the past few years. It was her Wednesday and she valued her Wednesdays and everything that came with them. It was a place she came to for comfort, to talk, or to simply decompress from a long day. But standing here now felt different. She was nervous as she listened to the sound of her own heartbeat. Remembering her purpose and the importance of what she needed to do, she made herself comfortable in the grass next to Cassie's headstone.

"Hey, you," she said, arranging the flowers in the small vase and tucking it into the grass. "It's an absolutely gorgeous morning. The kind you used to love."

She closed her eyes and pictured Cassie's face, the soft breeze that would have played in her hair on such a day. "I wish I could say things have been easy lately. They haven't been and I'm beginning to understand why. That's kind of what I came here to talk about." She took a deep breath because this woman was everything to her once. The love of her life. But that somehow seemed like a different life now. "I've missed you so much these past four years, Cassie, but I've carried you with me every step of the way. Know that. Our life together wasn't perfect, but it was ours, and I loved you deeply. You were my first love, and that will never change."

She ran her hand reverently across the letters of Cassie's name, the date she was born, the date she died and willed herself forward as hot tears sprang into her eyes. "But the thing is, I have to take a new step in my life. And that means I have to move on from us. From you. It's time to tuck our pictures away and close that chapter of my life. I need to have my heart free."

She took a moment. "I've fallen in love with someone, which means in some ways, I have to say good-bye to you. I promise I'll be back here every once in a while, Cass, but it won't be the same." She closed her eyes as the full meaning of those words took hold. It was hard to move on from someone you loved, even when they'd been gone from your life for a while. Even when you knew it was the right thing to do.

The tears slid down her cheeks now, but she didn't wipe them away. There was an ache in her heart that she allowed herself to feel to its fullest. Because she needed to feel it. This was the end of something that had been a part of her for a very long time. It was a poignant and important moment in her life, and no matter how much it hurt, she would be present for it. As the tree branches rustled nearby and a sparrow chirped in the distance, she let herself cry one last time for Cassie.

But as she raised her face to sunlight overhead, something remarkable happened.

The pain receded.

And what washed over her in its place was a sense of peace and hope and excitement for what lay ahead. It was the most wonderful gift and she knew immediately who'd sent it. "Thank you," she whispered. "You'd be so proud of her, Cass. She's grown into the most amazing woman."

She kissed her fingers and placed them gently on the granite, whispering one final message. "I'm so grateful for the love we shared. Good-bye, Cassie."

She stood and wiped the remnants of tears from her cheeks. She took a deep breath and began walking toward her new life.

CHAPTER TWENTY-SEVEN

"Sugar, do you want the copper mixing bowls in the big box or packed separately?" Eden placed her hands on her hips as she awaited an answer.

"Big box is fine," Molly answered absently. She stared at the framed photo on the wall of her and her dad when she was six years old. Her face and hands were covered in flour, and she was standing on a step stool to reach the counter. Her father beamed at the camera from alongside her.

She loved that photo.

Her eyes brushed past it daily in the course of customers and recipes and deliveries. But that photo was what it had been all about.

Reverently, she lifted it from the hook on the wall and held it in her hands. It was so lightweight for the amount of value it carried within.

This was the end of an era. There seemed to be a lot of that lately. There were two days left until she closed the doors of Flour Child for good. She tried to imagine what it would be like, but she'd never known life without this place.

She felt hands on her shoulders and turned to face Eden who regarded her with sympathetic eyes. "Don't let yourself get caught up and sad. You had a lot of good years in this little shop. We all did. Concentrate on the good times. Meanwhile, we got a lot of work to do. So let's pack this place in two shakes of a sheep's tail. Got me?"

Molly stared at her blankly. "I have no idea what that means, but I'm up for the challenge of figuring it out."

They divided their time between the daily grind of running the shop and packed during lulls in customer traffic. "Eden," Molly said as she examined the various pans for what to keep and what to trash. "What do you think you'll do now?"

Eden stood from the box she was packing. "Well, I wanted to wait for the right time to tell you, but I think I'll be planning a wedding." She pulled the work gloves off her hand, and there, displayed in all its glory, was a small, shiny engagement ring.

"Whoa." Molly placed her hand over her heart. "Eden, it's so beautiful. Oh my God, come here right now." She held her arms out and Eden moved immediately into them. "Congratulations. When did this happen?"

"A couple of days ago. Damon shocked the hell out of me. Got down on his knee in the middle of my living room. Even made me cry. Can you believe that? Me crying?"

"I can't. But I love it. Vulnerability could be your new thing." She looked at her in wonder. "You're going to be a wife, Eden. I'm shaking with excitement right now, if you haven't noticed. Where will you live? Your place? His apartment? Your place is cuter."

"Jury's still out. Damon's got a job interview over at UPS in Andersville. If he gets it, we'll be good to go, and I think we'll shop around for a new place of our own. If not, we've talked about moving back home. Make things easier on us financially. My folks have a nice guest house on their property."

It was a horrible idea. The worst ever. "To Tennessee? Oh, Eden, no. You can't leave. You're my best friend. I've never had an honest to goodness best friend before."

Tears formed in Eden's eyes. "Well, you're my best friend too. And now I've gone and started crying again. What is this all about? It's these stupid hormones. That's what it is. I'm not a crier."

Molly's eyes widened as a whole new suspicion took hold. "Eden, are you hinting at what I think you're hinting at, because I'm about to freak out here."

A slow smile took shape on Eden's face and her hand drifted down to cradle her stomach. "I'm due in seven months."

A great big whoop escaped Molly's mouth and she did a celebratory leap. "That is the most fantastic news I've ever heard." She hugged Eden yet again. "You're going to be a mom. Do you understand how huge this is? There's going to be a tiny little baby Eden for me to kiss and dress up and play with and—" Her thoughts changed direction and her demeanor followed suit to ferociously stern. "There's no way you're moving away now. Damon *will* get that UPS job and you will stay right here so I can be a proper aunt to this baby and spoil him or her rotten. There's no other option."

Eden smiled warmly at Molly. "I'd like nothing more. Let's make that happen."

The news was just what Molly needed, and she wallowed fully in the excitement. The shop was closing, but life really would go on. This was the perfect example of that. There was so much good still to come. She was convinced of it now.

And maybe, just maybe, there would be a new beginning for her too.

She felt the butterflies flutter in her stomach as she remembered her four-part plan. It was time to knock number two off her list.

It was close to six that evening when she knocked on the door of the Tuscana household. She hadn't called first and now hoped she wasn't interrupting dinner. Not that the Tuscanas had much time for a sit-down dinner in the middle of the week, but manners were still important.

"Well, look who's here," Joseph said upon opening the door. "You don't have to wait to be let in, Molly. You know that. We're Italian. One big happy family, you know?"

She did know, and though the Tuscanas had been nothing but warm to her, even after the tension at the birthday party, she still felt that things were a little awkward between all of them. It seemed the Tuscanas thought it best to pretend the relationship with Jordan never happened. Everyone should just erase the whole thing from their memory so that life could move forward as originally scheduled. But that wasn't exactly something she could do. Hence, her visit.

"Is Amalia home?"

"Yeah, yeah. Come on in. You can have some chili and cornbread. I made it." He grinned like a kid, and she couldn't help smile back and accept the affectionate bear hug he pulled her into.

"You cooking? Impressive."

"And rare. How's the packing coming? Need any help?"

"Nope. I think we've got it all under control."

"Molly, sweet girl! We were just talking about you earlier. How are you holding up? I know this week must be incredibly difficult for you."

"In more ways than one. And that's actually what I'm here about. Can we talk in the living room?"

"Sure, sure," Joseph said and exchanged a glance with his wife. "Let me set the stove to simmer."

Once they were seated, Molly didn't waste any time. "I love you both very much. You've been there for me in good times and in bad and made me welcome in your home always."

Amalia clutched Joseph's hand. "We feel the same way, sweetheart. You're family to us. You always will be."

"But Jordan's your family too."

Joseph again looked to Amalia and back to Molly. "Of course she is."

Molly sat up a little straighter as she reflected on the woman who had come to mean so much to her. It wasn't hard to find the words. In fact, they flowed through her with ease. "She's caring, and smart. She has the wittiest sense of humor and conducts herself with class and integrity. She'd go out of her way to help a stranger and nearly always puts the needs of other people before herself. And I'm one hundred percent completely in love with her."

Amalia's eyes widened at the words, and Molly held up a hand to signal she had more to say. "It might be difficult for you to accept those feelings at first, and that makes complete sense to me because it's taken me a while too. But I can't let that get in my way. This isn't about you. It's about Jordan and me. Over time, I hope you'll see the good in this. But more importantly, I hope you learn to see the good in Jordan herself. She's so much more than you give her credit for.

I'm not looking to replace Cassie. I couldn't if I tried. But Jordan is every bit as worthy. It's my hope that you finally see that."

Amalia took a minute, seemingly struck. "You mean that? What you said before?" She looked genuinely touched at the notion.

"About loving her? I do. I've never been more sure of anything in my life. I love your daughter and I want to spend my life making her happy."

"Now what?" Joseph asked.

She eyed him with a calm confidence. "I go and get her back."

Chapter Twenty-eight

Life is kind of like a Ferris wheel. That's the conclusion Molly came to from the bench just a few feet away from the terrifying contraption. In fact, she'd been studying the thing for over an hour, trying to work up enough courage to buy a ticket. As she watched each car make the climb to the tip-top only to descend to the ground from which it came, she came to an understanding.

In life, like a Ferris wheel, you start your journey just as others are completing theirs. There was something very poetic about that and the parallel eased her fears, if only a tad. And this week had been about tackling old fears.

Part three of her plan involved facing what she found most terrifying in life. She'd made a habit of backing down from all that scared her, and it was time she put an end to that tendency. Riding this Ferris wheel wasn't necessarily something she wanted to do, but something she had to do.

So she'd made some calls and tracked down the closest Ferris wheel she could find and made the two-hour drive after closing time. From where she was now, it was only another hour to Chicago, her next stop. And if she could just convince herself to get on the stupid ride, she might get there before the cows came home.

It was a process.

"Last call for the big wheel," the ride operator called out. "Last call!" The amusement park closed at seven on weekdays. She'd known that going in. She'd just been dragging her feet, the fear crippling her.

Her stomach flip-flopped and her mind raced, but she forced herself to her feet. If she wanted to live life without regrets, she had to learn to be courageous. To go after what she wanted. This was training ground in front of her and she was ready. She wouldn't be held back by fear any longer.

"One ticket, please," she told the operator with confidence. She counted out the dollar bills and exchanged them for a blue ticket stub that she gripped harder than was necessary as she settled herself into the swinging car.

That's when it hit.

What the hell was she thinking? She couldn't do this. It had been a nice thought. Really. A brave overture on her part, and who didn't want to be brave? But yeah, no, this wasn't going to happen. The panic attack was in full force, and she struggled to catch her breath. The air around her felt unusually warm and she tugged at the collar of her shirt. She had to get off this thing. Now. She opened her mouth to signal the ride attendant, but her voice simply wasn't there. She gripped the bar in front of her in terror as her car rose higher and higher a little bit at a time as each new passenger boarded the ride.

This was bad. This was really bad.

She forced herself to breathe. Seven seconds in. Five seconds out. It wasn't long before her car eased to the top of the wheel and paused there. As a coping mechanism, instead of focusing on how far she was from the ground, she raised her face skyward and watched the stars.

And whoa. There it was, right in front of her. Clear as day.

Her eyes trained on a grouping of stars that, if she wasn't crazy, seemed to be concentrated in the shape of the number eight. She laughed out loud, tears and all. It was a sign if she had ever seen one. It meant she was doing exactly what she was supposed to be doing in this moment. She nodded her head and accepted the challenge in front of her just as the wheel began to circle.

On the first go-round, she clung to the bar for dear life, barely sneaking a look at the world as it passed. She would just wait this thing out and get out of there.

But on the second go-round, her hands loosened their grip and her breathing returned to semi-normal. That was something. The ride moved a bit too fast for her liking and it made her stomach drop in that way she couldn't stand, but she was managing. Score one for her.

Then something miraculous happened. As the wheel continued to circle, she began to enjoy the sensation. The wind in her hair was refreshing and the panic shifted into some sort of welcome exhilaration. She let go of the bar and sat back in her seat, taking in the panoramic view, the ever-changing neon lights of the park, and the night all around her. Music played from the speaker in her car and her spirits soared in victory.

It was over faster than she thought it would be. Before she knew it, the attendant was pulling back the bar and releasing her from the ride. She threw her arms around his neck and squeezed. Surprised, he patted her back awkwardly. But she didn't let go.

"You must have enjoyed yourself, huh?" he asked nervously. He probably thought she was a crazy person and maybe she was.

"It was the best ever. Very helpful. Thank you."

"Anytime."

"Do you mind if I ask your name? You're kind of part of this whole memory now."

He pointed to the letters sewn onto his shirt. "Leonard, ma'am."

"Leonard. Len. That's a great name. I have to go now, Leonard." She squeezed his hand.

"Okay. Have a nice night."

"That's the plan," she called over her shoulder.

❖

"Hey, Mom. It's me." Jordan adjusted her rearview mirror to soften the obnoxious headlights from the car behind her. God, she hated driving at night and much preferred mass transportation.

"Hi, sweetheart. How are you?"

"I'm on the road. Headed into Applewood, actually. A friend of mine is moving to town this weekend and I offered to help."

"A friend of yours is moving to Applewood?"

"Yeah, you remember George. Long story. But listen, it's kind of last minute, but I wanted to see if you and Dad were free for dinner. I know you all tend to eat kind of late, so I thought I'd risk it." It was a bold move to call and arrange to spend time with them, but she wanted to try to work on their relationship. They were good people. And they were hers. Why wouldn't she try to fix things?

Her mother's voice lit up at the invitation. "Jordan, we would love that. Your father's still at the office with a patient, but he shouldn't be that much longer. I'll give him a call. What time will you be here?"

She checked the clock. "Maybe eightish?"

"I'll have some sort of dinner waiting, even if I have to order in. We can stay in and you can tell us all about the progress you've made with Journey. I know you must be working hard."

She smiled. It seemed she wasn't the only one ready to work on things. She was really looking forward to it. "I'll call Mikey and see if he wants to stop by later." Maybe this could be a regular thing, family get-togethers. She could make a point of visiting more often. It was a step in the right direction at least.

Then her mind drifted to where it always seemed to. She wondered if she'd see Molly over the course of the weekend. She'd be lying if she said she didn't want to. The next day was Flour Child's last. Molly would be a wreck. She wanted to find a way to be there for her, but it just wasn't the best idea. It would be too difficult to be close to her and yet so far away at the same time.

Maybe Molly was right and over time it was something they could work up to. It was wishful thinking at its best.

❖

Molly checked her GPS. She was only twenty-two miles outside of Chicago and just thirty minutes from Jordan's apartment. When she'd explained her plans to the Tuscanas, they'd been helpful enough to provide her with the address. She could only hope now that Jordan would be home. It didn't matter though. She could wait if she had to. She'd waited this long.

So she sang to Janis Joplin and drove with the windows down, praying to God she'd be heard when she arrived. The buzzing from her back pocket snagged her attention. She checked the readout on her phone, and in strange news found it was coming from the clinic. "Hello?"

"Abort. Abort the mission."

"Joseph, is that you?"

"Yes. Turn around. The eagle is not in Chicago."

"Eagle? What eagle?"

"The target. The eagle means the target. Haven't you ever seen a spy movie?"

"I don't speak spy. You're telling me Jordan is not in Chicago?" She pulled her car off the road onto the shoulder. "What do you mean? Where is she?"

"Amalia just called. She's on her way to our house. She should be there any minute."

"In *Applewood*?"

"That's what I'm trying to tell you. How far away are you?"

"Far. It will take me a couple of hours. Are you sure she's there?"

"Dead sure. You better turn around. We can stall her."

She understood the implications of what he was saying to her, and her heart warmed. He was helping.

"Thank you, Joseph," she said. "For everything."

"You can thank me later. Just drive safe."

"I will."

With a flick of her wrist, she cranked the volume on the stereo even louder and turned that damn car around.

❖

"I'm stuffed." Mikey took in his plate, and in a nice touch, took Jordan's for her as well.

She grinned up at him as he passed. "Very chivalrous of you, Mikey. I'm impressed."

"Don't get used to it," he shot back. "I just happen to be in a good mood." He softened a little. "You see, I haven't seen my little sister in a few weeks. And here she is."

"Aww, I missed you too, Michael." She caught him on the return and pulled him into a hug he begrudged at first. Finally, he wrapped his arms around her snugly and placed a kiss on the side of her head.

"So there."

She grinned up at him and then turned to her parents. "Thank you for having me tonight and for dinner."

"Let's do this more often," Amalia said, cradling her chin in her hand. "It was fun to hear all you've been up to. I mean that."

"Thanks. Maybe we can. In fact, let's try. But for now, I better head over to Little Bobby's. I'm exhausted, and I hear he has the guest room all made up for me. I wouldn't want to stand the guy up."

"Why don't you stay here? With us?"

"It's just easier. There's a lot of work to be done over there. Plus, he kind of insisted."

"You can't leave yet," Joseph practically shouted.

"Oh. Okay. Is there something you—?"

"Pie! We haven't had pie. And we should." Joseph pointed at her.

"If it's okay, I think I'll pass. I'm just really full. The pizza was plenty."

Her father looked around furtively in a move that had her questioning his sanity. "You'll make your mother cry if you don't stay for one piece."

"I will," Amalia added. "I'll just cry. Tears. Is that what you want. Your own mother?"

She shot Mikey a questioning look, but he just shrugged, clearly as mystified as she was.

"Okay. No crying. Just a small piece though, and then I have to jet."

"Coming right up!" Joseph shouted. He was full of extra energy tonight. Geez.

Two bites into her coconut cream sliver, the kitchen door opened.

"Hey, Mol," Mikey said from the kitchen. "What's up?"

"Kind of a crazy, busy day, actually."

"Yeah?"

"You have no idea."

And then there she was. Molly. Standing in the entryway of her parents' living room. Her hair was a little windblown, which made it completely perfect. In fact, just the sight of her made everything else in the room pale.

❖

"Hey." Molly knew it wasn't the best opening line, but it's what came out of her mouth. Jordan looked completely surprised to see her there. That much she could tell.

"Hey." Jordan seemed to be clocking the exits, which wasn't a great sign. "It's good to see you."

"You too."

"I'd like to stay and catch up, but I'm supposed to meet Bobby and I'm already late." She picked up the bag next to her chair and slipped it over her shoulder, as Molly stood there paralyzed. Even though she'd had all these great things worked out to say, the minute she found herself face-to-face with Jordan, they were gone from her mind.

And this was too important for that.

"Don't go." That was step one. Stop her from leaving. Jordan turned to her in question. "I should have said all of this before, but I wasn't ready. I get that now. But just because I wasn't ready doesn't make what's happening in my heart any less true. God, I'm not making sense. How could you have possibly followed that?" She placed a hand on her forehead and commanded her mind to slow down.

"What's going on, Molly?" Jordan's eyes locked with hers, and the compassion there was unmistakable. That's when the world seemed to right itself, because just that look from Jordan was enough to set her back on track. Their connection was still very much intact.

"Do you want us to give you a minute?" Mikey asked.

"Shhh," Amalia said to him. "I'm trying to listen. I'm the mother."

Molly took a deep breath. "I know why you walked away."

The three other Tuscanas looked from Molly to Jordan and back again as if captivated by an unpredictable tennis match. But she didn't let it distract her. If anything, they *should* hear all of this.

She pressed on. "I was struggling and you saw that. You saw the doubt, the trepidation. And maybe you thought it was best for both of us if you gave me an easy way out."

Jordan listened, her expression guarded. God, what was she thinking?

"But it wasn't the easy way, because each day without you has been insufferable. The doubt, the trepidation was never about you. You've been the one true thing in my life through all of this, and my feelings never wavered."

Jordan's lips parted in surprise.

"I love you, Jordan. I'm *in* love with you. I'm sorry I didn't say it sooner. It took me some time to admit it to myself. But I'm sure now. You once talked about the grand gesture. And if I had a radio, I'd be holding it over my head right now. But, here I am in front of your whole family, putting it all out there. I wasn't ready before, and you were right to give me space. I'm ready now. No, excited is a better word. I'm excited for whatever life has in store for us. That is, if you are."

"Are you?" Joseph asked.

Mikey shot him a warning look. "Dad."

He covered his mouth. "Sorry."

All eyes were on Jordan, who wasn't saying a whole lot. The silence hung in the air between them.

"Am I too late?" Molly asked.

Finally, Jordan shook her head. "No. You could never be too late. I just—I want you to be happy, and I don't want to be the person who gets in the way of that. Because those are the kinds of things you think about when you love someone. And I do love you."

Molly moved to her then because those words were too powerful to keep her away any longer. She cradled Jordan's face in her hands delicately. "The thing is, I think you're kind of the key to my happiness."

Jordan seemed to take that in. "I am?"

"You are. Wait a sec. Did you hear all that?"

"What?"

"We're in love," she whispered.

A slow smile took shape on Jordan's face. "Best sentence ever." And she kissed Molly. Right there in the living room in front of everyone. Molly sank into the amazingness of that kiss. She marveled at how it felt so wonderfully perfect as Amalia sniffled into Mikey's sleeve.

"What?" she said when they all turned to her. "Am I not allowed to get emotional?"

Mikey eyed them, clearly in shock at this new development. Luckily, there was also a smile on his face. "You two have some big time explaining to do. And sometime soon. Way to keep a guy in the dark."

Molly slid her arms around Jordan's waist. "Sorry, Mikey. We kind of left you out of all this, didn't we?"

He held his thumb and index finger very close together and then turned his attention to Jordan. "Lucky for you, little sister, I'm a roll with the punches kind of guy."

"Yeah. Lucky me," Jordan looked at Molly purposefully.

It was time to get out of there. And Molly, for one, couldn't wait another minute.

She turned to the Tuscanas, who'd so graciously offered their house up in aid of her quest. "We should get out of your hair." She took a moment to hug each one of them. "Thank you," she said quietly. "For everything."

"Take care of each other," Amalia said. "That's the most important thing."

"You got it."

Once they were outside and alone. Jordan brushed a strand of hair from Molly's forehead. "So, hi."

"Hey," she whispered back. For a minute, she just stared. Marveling at how everything had turned out. That Jordan was here. In front of her.

Hers.

The night was balmy, and the moon three-fourths full. Jordan took her hand and threaded their fingers. Their lips were just an inch apart, and suddenly that became way too much. She leaned in and brushed Jordan's lips with hers ever so lightly, but that only made her crave more. It hadn't been her goal to make out with Jordan in the middle of her parents' driveway, but that's what happened. She just wanted to lose herself in Jordan and soon. She pulled back slightly and met her eyes. "Please tell me you're not going to Little Bobby's tonight."

Jordan's breathing was shallow as she stared back in all seriousness. "I think he'll understand."

"Praise baby Jesus."

❖

The thing about Molly was that it was very hard for Jordan to keep her hands off of her. And it had been a while since they'd been anywhere on her. She had been knocked off her feet in a really good way to hear Molly's words.

Molly was willing to fight for them. She'd told Jordan she loved her in front of her entire family. It meant *everything*.

And yes, it would have been simpler if they'd waited to ravish each other until they were safely ensconced in Molly's very comfortable bedroom. But unfortunately with them, it was never that simple. Their physical connection was not only still off the charts, it was hovering somewhere outside the time zone.

Their shirts and Jordan's bra had made it as far as the entryway. They'd bumped into doors and walls as they kicked their shoes off. Finally making it to the hallway off the living room, Jordan found herself pressed against the wall. Molly was kissing down her body and making quick work of her jeans. As Molly slid them down her legs, Jordan splayed her hands against the wall as an onslaught of arousal shot straight through her. Molly straightened and slid her body up against Jordan in the sexiest move this century. The physical ache she caused was almost painful. The town sweetheart was also a very skilled seductress.

Jordan eased her hand to the nape of Molly's neck and held her in place as she kissed her like she was drowning, which she was in the most welcome way. As Molly rocked into her, that hunger only grew.

Their mouths danced in rhythm, and Molly's hand dipped between her legs and brushed across her. Giving just the tiniest bit and then pulling back. God.

Then wordlessly, she led Jordan into her bedroom, where she eased her onto her back. Instead of following her down, Molly stood in front of her and slowly removed her remaining items of clothing.

And the temperature in the room shot up around them as Jordan looked on in captivation. "How are you so perfect?" she breathed. "Just look at you."

Molly held her gaze. Confident. Strong. "You make me feel that way."

She lowered herself onto Jordan and hitched in a breath as their bodies met.

And Jordan was home. She reached up and brushed the hair back from Molly's forehead "God, I've missed you."

"Never again," Molly assured her, and her lips descended onto Jordan's. She kissed her with skilled precision and began to move against her in a slow rhythm. The kind she knew drove Jordan wild. She then reached between them and began to stroke her as she sucked firmly on Jordan's nipple.

In surrender, Jordan threw her head back on the pillow, completely helpless to the rush of sensation. It was all she could do to just hold on. Molly continued her quest downward, leaving a trail of open-mouthed kisses on her breasts, her stomach, her abdomen. She parted Jordan's legs gently and her hands skimmed up her inner thighs, her thumbs meeting in the middle and brushing over her center. Jordan gasped. Molly leaned down and placed a gentle kiss on the inside of one thigh and then the other. But it was the first touch of Molly's tongue that caused her hips to jerk. The second and third swipe had her arching her back for more. But when Molly pulled her more firmly into her mouth, she tumbled over the edge, falling into a never-ending red-hot release. She dug her fingers into Molly's shoulders and rode out the shock waves.

Holy hell.

She collapsed limp and satisfied onto the pillow, her breathing shallow, but her heart full. Molly joined her there. She tipped Jordan's face up to hers. "I love you," she whispered and stroked her hair. Jordan nodded and stared into Molly's eyes. She savored the way Molly felt against her. The sound of her voice when she said her name. The ways her eyes lit when she looked at her.

She felt cared for. Safe.

Loved.

Jordan stroked Molly's cheek. "I didn't know it could be like this. Feel like this."

Molly kissed her. "We're lucky."

Jordan wrapped her arms around Molly's waist and pulled her in, sliding her thigh firmly against Molly, who closed her eyes and parted her lips in beautiful response. She was beyond ready. And Jordan was feeling impatient.

She wanted her hands on Molly. Her mouth.

Everything.

She was the sexiest thing she'd ever seen, and watching her climax had become her favorite drug of choice and she needed it now.

"Baby," she whispered as she rolled her over and lowered her head, running her tongue across her nipple, circling it slowly. Molly's hands were in her hair, softly encouraging her. As she pulled the nipple into her mouth and sucked, Molly began to make the most adorable tiny noises. She refocused her attention on Molly's neck, her collarbone. As she kissed the skin there, she massaged her breasts softly at first and then more firmly, squeezing her nipples until Molly was squirming wildly beneath her, looking for some kind of release.

"Oh God, I don't think I can—"

"Yes, you can," Jordan whispered in her ear. "Hold on for me." She stared into her eyes, and the vulnerability there staggered her. With nothing standing between them now, it was easily the most intimate experience of her life.

She rolled herself more fully on top and slid her hands down Molly's sides, cupping her hips and holding them in place as she pressed against her firmly. Molly whimpered quietly and closed her eyes. "More," was all she managed. But more she could do. She began to move her hips against Molly slowly in small circles. And though Molly attempted to increase their rhythm, Jordan held her in place, maintaining control. Finally, she reached a hand between them and slid into Molly, her hips picking up pace against her hand until Molly called out and shuddered against her in the most gorgeous display. Her lips parted, her hair fanned out across the pillow, Jordan made a point to memorize the image.

She kissed her neck softly and smoothed the hair from her forehead as her breathing slowed once again.

"Jordan?

"Yeah?"

Molly cradled her face in her hands and shook her head. "You undo me every time. You know that?"

"I think we undo each other." She kissed her cheek softly.

They made love again that night, waking up and finding each other. The touches were somehow softer with the understanding of what they meant, what they promised. It was a night Jordan would never forget. Because it wasn't about the moment at hand. It was about forever.

Chapter Twenty-nine

The sun was up early and streaming through the window, but Molly let herself sleep until seven.

Louise had opened up shop on what would be Flour Child's last day. Molly had scheduled herself for eight, knowing she'd have to stay late into the night to finish the last of the packing. She had to hand over the keys to the bank the next day.

"Are you going to be okay?" Jordan asked from the kitchen table where she nursed a cup of coffee in her jeans and T-shirt. She'd gotten up with Molly and seemed to be lingering close for moral support. It was sweet.

Molly attempted a smile, but it was weighted with sadness. "It'll be a rough day. The roughest. But if I have you waiting for me, I'm going to get through this. I feel like I have a lot to look forward to and I have to concentrate on that."

"You do." Jordan held out her hand, and Molly crossed the distance between them and allowed herself to be pulled into Jordan's lap. "So, there's a thing."

"A thing? You should probably elaborate."

"George is moving to Applewood." Molly raised an inquisitive eyebrow. "We'll get to why later. But the point is, he's now planning to commute to Chicago. To me. So we could work together. But if I were to move to Applewood, that wouldn't exactly be necessary. I mean we'd still have to go into the city for meetings, and of course on location for shooting. But if our office home base was here—"

She didn't get to finish because Molly's lips silenced her in a celebratory kiss. "Yes," she said to Jordan when they came up for air. "That sounds like the best idea I've ever heard. Did you hear me say yes? 'Cause I can say it louder. Yes!" she called out loudly to the room as Jordan laughed.

"I can get an apartment or…"

Molly took the leap. "Or you could move in with me."

A beat. "Really?" Jordan asked in a hopeful voice. She also looked especially adorable.

Molly looked down at her. "Uh-huh.. But if you're gonna move in, there'll have to be conditions."

Jordan grinned. "Conditions?"

"Oh yeah," Molly said quite seriously. "You'll need to pull your share of the handiwork around this place."

"Which would be?"

"Well, all of it. While wearing jeans and a tank top. That's also a condition by the way, because there will be lots of objectification."

"I love it when you objectify me."

"And I'll need to interview this cat of yours, Frankie, is it?"

"Francis Ford Coppola until you get to know him better."

"Pretentious."

"He totally can be, yeah."

Molly sighed happily. "So it's settled. You, me, a cat, and a fish in the blue house."

"How can you beat it?"

"Who would even try?" Molly murmured as she went in for another kiss.

That's when Jordan's phone buzzed. She checked the readout and took the call. "Hey, Bobby. I'll be over in just a bit."

She stared at Molly questioningly. "Yeah, she's right here. What's up?" Molly watched Jordan curiously, finally tilting her head to the side in question. Jordan took her hand in reassurance and smiled. "Okay, we can leave now."

"What?" Molly asked as she hung up. "Is everything okay?"

"I think so. But Bobby says we need to get over to Flour Child now."

Molly's mind raced with a million possible problems. "Is something wrong? What's going on?"

"Let's not wonder. Let's go find out." Jordan took her hand and they headed out.

❖

Molly heard them before she saw them.

As they rounded the corner to Main Street, the sight before them stopped her cold. There were people, throngs of them, hundreds in fact, gathered in front of the bakeshop. Some were carrying signs depicting the Starbucks logo with a line through it. Others wore homemade T-shirts. She didn't know what to make of it. She looked at Jordan, who shrugged in mystification.

The crowd started to cheer when they saw her. It was all very surreal. She moved among them, shocked at the sight. There was Mr. Mueller, the mailman; Deb from the diner; a whole grouping of her neighbors and former teachers. Hell, she could go on and on. It seemed like *everyone* was there. And that's when she saw him.

"Daddy? You're here too?" she said. "Do you know what's going on?"

He smiled and put his arm around her. "Turns out these folks don't want to see you close. In fact, they're here to show their support and vow to keep you in business."

"Gonna skip Starbucks from now on, Molly," Evan Thompson, from the auto body shop called out. "I don't care if they do have a drive-through. Your cinnamon rolls are fifty times better anyway. I'll be *here* from now on each morning. Promise ya."

"Thanks, Evan. But I don't think that's—"

Celia Foster pushed through the crowd. "None of us are going to that big chain store anymore. Flour Child is our bakeshop and we'd like it to stay that way. We're not willing to give it up."

"I'll be in at least twice a week. Three times if I get a raise," someone behind her called out.

Molly turned toward the voice. "That's so nice of you to say, Mrs. Abernathy, but I'm afraid there's not much choice. I have to close down today."

"Actually, you don't." It was Felix from the bank. Molly threw a questioning look to Jordan who squeezed her hand.

"I don't understand."

He handed her an envelope. "The mortgage has been paid, along with the secondary loan. You're free and clear."

She stared at him. "This doesn't make sense."

"A donor came forward. Paid it all off in your name." Felix looked to his right, and Molly followed his gaze.

There, standing at the edge of the crowd, feigning interest in the shop's awning and pretty much ignoring everyone was Mr. Jeffries.

He scoffed, catching Molly looking at him. "What?"

"Did you pay off my mortgage, Mr. Jeffries?"

He glared back at her like she was less than bright. "Well, I couldn't exactly have the shop close down, could I? A man's entitled to his routine, you know."

She didn't know what to say. "Thank you," was the start she went with. "I'll pay you back just as soon as I can." She couldn't quite process this turn of events.

"You will not," he grumbled. "You'll use the cushion to get ahead and the rest of the idiots will keep you afloat. Then everyone will be happy and shut up."

She scanned the scene, the faces of the people she loved most in the world. She turned around to face the shop. Eden stood in the doorway with her arm around Louise. Damon sat beneath them on the step.

The sight of them brought it all home.

They were wanted. The town was willing to stand up and say so. And that meant the shop was staying put. She'd get up the next morning and come in to work. And every morning after that. She'd hang the photo of herself and her dad back on the wall.

She walked to the corner of the group and threw her arms around Mr. Jeffries, who stood stock-still before softening and allowing her to hug him. "I can't believe you did this," she told him. "I won't let you down."

"Don't go getting all mushy on me. You got a business to run, girlie. Look alive."

She stared down at the envelope in her hands, and then looked to her father, who beamed at her proudly, his arm around Jordan. The Tuscanas stood a few feet away, holding a box of pastries purchased from inside.

They were all there.

She decided she better say something. "Thank you so much, everyone. Um…I guess as it turns out, we're not closing down after all." She lifted a shoulder and let it drop.

The announcement was met with applause and cheers from the more boisterous individuals. As she moved among the crowd, she was met even more with pledges of support and vows to patronize the shop every day. Wes Broll even offered his Web design services to get her set up for online orders for MollyDollys. She planned to take him up on it.

"Plenty of coffee and cinnamon rolls inside. Step right up!" Eden called out loudly from the steps. Needless to say, the line eventually worked its way down the block.

Molly found her way back to Jordan. "Can you believe this?"

"I can. I told you. You're the heart and soul of this town, Molly. These people aren't letting you get away that easily."

"I guess not." She surveyed the line happily, full of excitement. She could do cartwheels down Main Street she was on such a high. "I better get in there and get some trays in the oven. We're going to need more food."

Jordan gestured with a tilt of her head. "I guess I better get in line."

Molly tugged on her arm and pulled her into the shop. "Like I'd ever make you wait."

Epilogue

One Year Later

Jordan stole another glance down the aisle at the faces of her audience. It was absolute torture to sit in a theater while her friends and family watched her film for the first time.

The word nervous was too basic a term.

Sure, it had already done well at the festivals, even picking up a couple of awards here and there, but this was different. Crazy different. These were the people who mattered, and it was their stories she was telling up on that screen.

And, might she add, *sitting still* for eighty-eight minutes while the thing ran was virtually impossible. What she really wanted to do was pace, get out all of that extra energy coursing through her. Or better yet, get a drink and see them all once the whole thing was over.

Picking up on Jordan's restlessness, Molly placed a calming hand on her knee and offered her a smile. "Relax," she mouthed.

She nodded, already responding. Molly had a way of resetting her just when she needed it. She had to admit, it was beyond hospitable for the theater to offer a complimentary screening of the documentary for the citizens of Applewood.

A quick glance at the screen told her that the film had less than five minutes remaining. She could do this, she decided. In fact, the ending was her favorite part.

She settled back in her seat as the film cut to the final interview with George and Bobby. This was the denouement, the film's wrap-up section that tied everything up into a nice neat little bow. Not all films had the luxury of such an ending. She was glad this one did.

She'd shot the interview on their front porch, loving the texture the railing offered. Quaint. Very much in contrast to George's big city sophistication they'd established earlier in the film, which made it all the more perfect.

"You never know what life has in store for you," George told the camera before sneaking a look at Bobby, next to him. "Two years ago, if you told me I'd be living in a town like this one and enjoying every minute of it, I would have laughed in your face. But love has a way of changing things. I even wear less black now."

Bobby chimed in. "It's true. The love thing, I mean. He still wears a ton of black. When I think about my life just over a year ago, I'm amazed at the contrast. I was a closeted bartender who came home to the television and my Basset hound each night. I thought that was it for me. But my life was forever altered by a pretentious socialite from the big city."

George's mouth fell open. "Hey!"

"It's true, baby. Highly pretentious."

The audience laughed right on cue as the shot cross-faded to a largely pregnant Eden applying frosting to a batch of cupcakes at Flour Child. "I flat-out hated the guy. I'm not even going to lie about that. He got my fur up. Now, I'm having his baby and more excited than I've ever been in my tiny little life. We're decorating the nursery tonight. In pink."

The camera panned to Damon who stood across the prep table from Eden grinning at her like she'd hung the moon. He looked over at the camera, the tears visible in his eyes. "I still can't believe I'm about to have a family." He swiped at his face sheepishly as Eden came around the table and put her arms around him.

The screen went black and faded up on Molly's face. She looked past the camera as if lost in thought before finally settling her gaze just next to the lens. "You can't choose who you fall in love with. I used to think you could. But sometimes your heart overrules your head. And you know something? I think it knows what's best for you. Falling in love with Jordan was the most terrifying and worthwhile thing I've ever done. Trust me, I fought it. Our situation wasn't ideal, but then really whose is? Love takes work. But this"—she gestured with her head to the blue Beetle that pulled into the driveway—"this feeling I get when I see that she's home at the end of the day is pretty much the best thing ever. And while I'd love to talk to you about it some more, I'd much rather go kiss the woman in that car. So if you'll excuse me."

Soft guitar music strummed under the image of Molly pulling Jordan into her arms in the driveway, Eden and Damon hanging a mobile above a crib, and George and Bobby toasting over dinner. The film's title, *How Sweet It Is*, faded into the frame as the camera pulled back to slowly reveal Main Street, the center of Applewood.

The theater broke into massive applause, and a few folks even dabbed at their eyes. It was a more emotional response than a typical audience, and of course, Jordan understood why.

"They loved it," Molly whispered in her ear as the applause continued. "And you were right. Love in unexpected places was a better subject for your first project. It was absolute perfection."

"You should listen to me more often."

Molly grinned. "I will listen to you from here to eternity."

"Oh, good, 'cause I have a lot to say. Now kiss me so we can celebrate properly." And as the credits scrolled in beautiful white letters, they did just that. Finally, the words, *The End*, faded up languidly across the screen.

Jordan and Molly turned and looked, knowing that for them, it was anything but.

About the Author

Melissa Brayden is currently pursuing her MFA in directing in San Antonio, Texas. Recently, she's fallen down the rabbit hole and rediscovered her love of creative writing. She is a three-time Goldie Award winner for her books *Waiting in the Wings* and *Heart Block*.

Melissa is married and working really hard at remembering to do the dishes. For personal enjoyment, she spends time with her Jack Russell terriers and checks out the NYC theater scene several times a year. She considers herself a reluctant patron of the treadmill, but enjoys hitting a tennis ball around in nice weather. Coffee is her very best friend. www.melissabrayden.com

Books Available from Bold Strokes Books

Homestead by Radclyffe. R. Clayton Sutter figures getting NorthAm Fuel's newest refinery operational on a rolling tract of land in Upstate New York should take a month or two, but then, she hadn't counted on local resistance in the form of vandalism, petitions, and one furious farmer named Tess Rogers. (978-1-60282-956-5)

Battle of Forces: Sera Toujours by Ali Vali. Kendal and Piper return to New Orleans to start the rest of eternity together, but the return of an old enemy makes their peaceful reunion short-lived, especially when they join forces with the new queen of the vampires. (978-1-60282-957-2)

How Sweet It Is by Melissa Brayden. Some things are better than chocolate. Molly O'Brien enjoys her quiet life running the bakeshop in a small town. When the beautiful Jordan Tuscana returns home, Molly can't deny the attraction—or the stirrings of something more. (978-1-60282-958-9)

The Missing Juliet: A Fisher Key Adventure by Sam Cameron. A teenage detective and her friends search for a kidnapped Hollywood star in the Florida Keys. (978-1-60282-959-6)

Amor and More: Love Everafter edited by Radclyffe and Stacia Seaman. Rediscover favorite couples as Bold Strokes Books authors reveal glimpses of life and love beyond the honeymoon in short stories featuring main characters from favorite BSB novels. (978-1-60282-963-3)

First Love by CJ Harte. Finding true love is hard enough, but for Jordan Thompson, daughter of a conservative president, it's challenging, especially when that love is a female rodeo cowgirl. (978-1-60282-949-7)

Pale Wings Protecting by Lesley Davis. Posing as a couple to investigate the abduction of infants, Special Agent Blythe Kent and Detective Daryl Chandler find themselves drawn into a battle over the innocents, with demons on one side and the unlikeliest of protectors on the other. (978-1-60282-964-0)

Mounting Danger by Karis Walsh. Sergeant Rachel Bryce, an outcast on the police force, is put in charge of the department's newly formed mounted division. Can she and polo champion Callan Lanford resist their growing attraction as they struggle to safeguard the disaster-prone unit? (978-1-60282-951-0)

Meeting Chance by Jennifer Lavoie. When man's best friend turns on Aaron Cassidy, the teen keeps his distance until fate puts Chance in his hands. (978-1-60282-952-7)

At Her Feet by Rebekah Weatherspoon. Digital marketing producer Suzanne Kim knows she has found the perfect love in her new mistress Pilar, but before they can make the ultimate commitment, Suzanne's professional life threatens to disrupt their perfectly balanced bliss. (978-1-60282-948-0)

Show of Force by AJ Quinn. A chance meeting between navy pilot Evan Kane and correspondent Tate McKenna takes them on a roller-coaster ride where the stakes are high, but the reward is higher: a chance at love. (978-1-60282-942-8)

Clean Slate by Andrea Bramhall. Can Erin and Morgan work through their individual demons to rediscover their love for each other, or are the unexplainable wounds too deep to heal? (978-1-60282-943-5)

Hold Me Forever by D. Jackson Leigh. An investigation into illegal cloning in the quarter horse racing industry threatens to destroy the growing attraction between Georgia debutante Mae St. John and Louisiana horse trainer Whit Casey. (978-1-60282-944-2)

Trusting Tomorrow by PJ Trebelhorn. Funeral director Logan Swift thinks she's perfectly happy with her solitary life devoted to helping others cope with loss until Brooke Collier moves in next door to care for her elderly grandparents. (978-1-60282-891-9)

Forsaking All Others by Kathleen Knowles. What if what you think you want is the opposite of what makes you happy? (978-1-60282-892-6)

Exit Wounds by VK Powell. When Officer Loane Landry falls in love with ATF informant Abigail Mancuso, she realizes that nothing is as it seems—not the case, not her lover, not even the dead. (978-1-60282-893-3)

Dirty Power by Ashley Bartlett. Cooper's been through hell and back, and she's still broke and on the run. But at least she found the twins. They'll keep her alive. Right? (978-1-60282-896-4)

The Rarest Rose by I. Beacham. After a decade of living in her beloved house, Ele disturbs its past and finds her life being haunted by the presence of a ghost who will show her that true love never dies. (978-1-60282-884-1)

Code of Honor by Radclyffe. The face of terror is hard to recognize—especially when it's homegrown. The next book in the Honor series. (978-1-60282-885-8)

Does She Love You? by Rachel Spangler. When Annabelle and Davis find out they are both in a relationship with the same woman, it leaves them facing life-altering questions about trust, redemption, and the possibility of finding love in the wake of betrayal. (978-1-60282-886-5)

The Road to Her by KE Payne. Sparks fly when actress Holly Croft, star of UK soap Portobello Road, meets her new on-screen love interest, the enigmatic and sexy Elise Manford. (978-1-60282-887-2)

Shadows of Something Real by Sophia Kell Hagin. Trying to escape flashbacks and nightmares, ex-POW Jamie Gwynmorgan stumbles into the heart of former Red Cross worker Adele Sabellius and uncovers a deadly conspiracy against everything and everyone she loves. (978-1-60282-889-6)

Date with Destiny by Mason Dixon. When sophisticated bank executive Rashida Ivey meets unemployed blue collar worker Destiny Jackson, will her life ever be the same? (978-1-60282-878-0)

The Devil's Orchard by Ali Vali. Cain and Emma plan a wedding before the birth of their third child while Juan Luis is still lurking, and as Cain plans for his death, an unexpected visitor arrives and challenges her belief in her father, Dalton Casey. (978-1-60282-879-7)

Secrets and Shadows by L.T. Marie. A bodyguard and the woman she protects run from a madman and into each other's arms. (978-1-60282-880-3)

Change Horizons: Three Novellas by Gun Brooke. Three stories of courageous women who dare to love as they fight to claim a future in a hostile universe. (978-1-60282-881-0)

Scarlet Thirst by Crin Claxton. When hot, feisty Rani meets cool, vampire Rob, one lifetime isn't enough, and the road from human to vampire is shorter than you think… (978-1-60282-856-8)

Battle Axe by Carsen Taite. How close is too close? Bounty hunter Luca Bennett will soon find out. (978-1-60282-871-1)

Improvisation by Karis Walsh. High school geometry teacher Jan Carroll thinks she's figured out the shape of her life and her future, until graphic artist and fiddle player Tina Nelson comes along and teaches her to improvise. (978-1-60282-872-8)

For Want of a Fiend by Barbara Ann Wright. Without her Fiendish power, can Princess Katya and her consort Starbride stop a magic-wielding madman from sparking an uprising in the kingdom of Farraday? (978-1-60282-873-5)

Broken in Soft Places by Fiona Zedde. The instant Sara Chambers meets the seductive and sinful Merille Thompson, she falls hard, but knowing the difference between love and a dangerous, all-consuming desire is just one of the lessons Sara must learn before it's too late. (978-1-60282-876-6)

Healing Hearts by Donna K. Ford. Running from tragedy, the women of Willow Springs find that with friendship, there is hope, and with love, there is everything. (978-1-60282-877-3)

Desolation Point by Cari Hunter. When a storm strands Sarah Kent in the North Cascades, Alex Pascal is determined to find her. Neither imagines the dangers they will face when a ruthless criminal begins to hunt them down. (978-1-60282-865-0)

I Remember by Julie Cannon. What happens when you can never forget the first kiss, the first touch, the first taste of lips on skin? What happens when you know you will remember every single detail of a mysterious woman? (978-1-60282-866-7)

The Gemini Deception by Kim Baldwin and Xenia Alexiou. The truth, the whole truth, and nothing but lies. Book six in the Elite Operatives series. (978-1-60282-867-4)